PRAISE FOR *S.T.A.G.S.*

Shortlisted for the YA BOOK PRIZE 2018
Winner of the Warwickshire Secondary Book Award 2019,
the Great Reads 'Most Read' 2018 Senior Award and the
Sussex Coast Schools Amazing Book Award 2019

'*S.T.A.G.S.* is a pacey and well-plotted young adult story that
champions outsiders and questions out-dated viewpoints in
a constantly evolving world.'

CultureFly

'M. A. Bennett is brilliant at keeping the reader in suspense.'
Book Murmuration

'M. A. Bennett reinvigorates the boarding-school thriller ... This
is a darkly compelling examination of the allure of privilege,
and the unscrupulous means by which it preserves itself.'
Guardian

'*S.T.A.G.S.* is a thrilling and thoroughly enjoyable YA novel
with dark undertones. A fun mystery thriller that sheds light
on issues surrounding class and society. Highly recommend.'
Book Bag

'A gorgeous and compelling romp.'

ish Times

F.O.X.E.S.

Books by M. A. Bennett

S.T.A.G.S.
D.O.G.S.
F.O.X.E.S.

The Island

F.O.X.E.S.

M. A. BENNETT

HOT
KEY
BOOKS

First published in Great Britain in 2020 by
HOT KEY BOOKS
80–81 Wimpole St, London W1G 9RE
Owned by Bonnier Books
Sveavägen 56, Stockholm, Sweden
www.hotkeybooks.com

A CIP catalogue record for this book is available from the British Library.

ISBN: 978-1-4714-0859-5
Also available as an ebook and in audio

1

This book is typeset using Atomik ePublisher
Printed and bound in Great Britain by Clays Ltd, Elcograf S.p.A.

Hot Key Books is an imprint of Bonnier Books UK
www.bonnierbooks.co.uk

To the Fairhazel fox,
my midnight friend

The Fox may live,
When all the Hounds be dead . . .

Esmé Stuart, 3rd Duke of Lennox, 7th Duke of Aubigny
(Introduction to *Volpone* by Ben Jonson)

PART I
THE FOX

1

Last night I dreamed I went to Longcross again.

It seemed like I was watching myself, as if I were in a film, if that makes sense. There was a whole bunch of people on horses milling around in front of the grand entrance to Longcross Hall, all wearing their hunting stuff. And I was one of them. I was on this elegant grey horse, wearing boots and breeches and a midnight-black coat with a nipped-in waist and a black riding hat. I was holding the reins with one gloved hand, and in the other I held a little silver cup. I was drinking from it and smiling.

Shafeen and Nel were there with me too, both looking amazing in their riding gear; Shafeen, like all the gentlemen, wearing hunting red. Sorry: pink. The twins were there, immaculate on twin white – sorry: grey – horses, but when I looked for someone else, someone who also had blond cropped hair, he was nowhere to be seen. I couldn't see Ty either, and she definitely would've stood out in this company, as the only black person in the hunt.

We were all chatting and laughing, but there was an air of anticipation. The horses were shifting their hooves, the riders turning their heads with impatience. There was a bunch of hounds milling around, sniffing and yapping and weaving in between the horses' legs. We were all waiting for something.

And it came.

There was the sound of a horn, clear and sweet as death, and we began to move off. We all trotted down the drive and then began to gallop across the open fields. Then I saw everything from above, like that helicopter shot of the hunt at the beginning of *The Remains of the Day*. The hounds, who had picked up a scent, streaked ahead in a white-and-tan arrowhead. Beyond them a flash of fire – a fox, running easily and well ahead of us. He ducked into a covert and under the dark shadow of the trees of Longwood.

Once we followed it into the woods everything changed. This will sound weird, but the fox was now human, a figure dressed head to foot in red, a hood drawn over its head. It was running through the blackthorn of the undergrowth, the branches whipping at its face. I felt exhilaration and dread for the running figure. Jaws snapped behind it, and however fast it ran they nipped at its heels. It was no good. As we burst out into a clearing, the low sun in my eyes, the jaws closed on the red runner at last.

I crowded in with the rest of the hunt as the hounds tore at the red clothing. I watched in horror as the dogs ripped and wrenched, my whole body drenched in dread as riders jumped down to whip the hounds away and turn the motionless figure over. I was suddenly certain that when they did I would see my own face. But when the riders stood back, almost respectfully, the body was gone and there was just a fox, furry and forlorn, stretched dead on the winter grass.

Then my point of view spiralled up and up, over the hills and far away, until the fox, that little smear of red, could no longer be seen.

You see? Even my dreams have camera moves.

I didn't do that sit-bolt-upright-gasping-for-breath thing that they do in the movies though. I woke quite gradually, blinking myself into consciousness, and for a minute I didn't know where I was. It took me a good few seconds to click that I was in room K9 of Alnwick Cottage Hospital, and I was totally alone – just me and my throbbing thumb.

Slowly, as things do after a vivid dream, everything came back to me, resolving like a darkroom photograph. Only a few days ago I'd been onstage at the De Warlencourt Playhouse, the school theatre at STAGS. I'd been glorying in the triumph of my production of Ben Jonson's lost play, *The Isle of Dogs*. I'd been playing the character of Poetaster, the narrator of the play and a thinly veiled version of Ben Jonson himself, when everything had gone very, very wrong. While speaking the epilogue with my head in a noose (part of the play, don't ask), something had gone wrong and I'd been hauled upwards until I was hanging by the neck.

And that was when things had got really weird.

I'd found myself in the middle of a circle of figures wearing red hooded gowns and stag antlers, led by the Old Abbot – who was, oh yes, supposed to be *dead* – putting me on trial for the murder of Henry de Warlencourt.

Naturally, when I came round in this very hospital bed, I thought I'd hallucinated the whole thing, especially as I'd then had a cosy bedside chat with none other than my own

5

'murder victim', Henry de Warlencourt himself. And TBH, I would *still* think that I had been hallucinating if it wasn't for one little detail. The sentence that had been visited upon me by the Dark Order of the Grand Stag: the brand on my thumb. The same brand that had been burned into Ben Jonson's flesh 400 years ago.

M for Manslayer.

I squinted at my phone. It was actually quite a reasonable hour – but of course it was the dead of winter, so it was just getting light outside. In the weak winter dawn I held up my thumb to the light. It felt strange, as if I was doing a thumbs-up, as if everything was OK. But everything was most definitely *not* OK. I could see the newly healed scar tissue of my brand, that pink, slightly stretched look that scars have, making a perfect capital 'M' in the pad of my thumb.

As soon as my nurse, Nurse Annie, had unwrapped my thumb the night before and seen the brand, she'd kicked Shafeen and Nel out of my hospital room and called in my doctor, Doctor Kyd. He'd questioned me for about a decade about self-harm, and hazing, and online cutting challenges, and all this horseshit until I'd finally convinced him that *I* hadn't done it and I wasn't a danger to myself. This wasn't an easy task when you consider that I couldn't actually tell him who *had* done it. In the end Doctor Kyd formed the opinion that I just needed to go home for Christmas to have some R & R, but still I could only get him to leave on the condition that I agreed to come back to see him at the beginning of the Trinity Term (January to you).

SO . . .

By the time that was all over I was pretty tired but still nowhere near sleep, because then I was faced by the stone-cold realisation of what I couldn't tell the doctor: the only way that brand could have got onto my thumb was if it had been put there by the Dark Order of the Grand Stag. And that meant the whole trial in the De Warlencourt Playhouse at STAGS, far from being a figment of my oxygen-starved imagination, had actually happened In Real Life. And that realisation, let me tell you, was not exactly conducive to sleep. I must've slept eventually though, because I had the dream.

I lay there in the grey dawn trying to figure out what the hell it meant, but already it was starting to fade in that pesky way that dreams do. All I could remember, by the time Nurse Annie bustled in with a breakfast tray, was that it was about a fox.

2

'Your last gourmet meal, modom,' said Nurse Annie, in a terrible attempt at a posh accent. Her eyes twinkled. 'We're discharging you today.'

I scooched up a bit on the pillows and made a knee-hump for the tray. 'You are?'

'Yes, hinny. We need the beds and you need to get on with your Christmas holidays. A bit of fun and relaxation is what the doctor's ordered.'

Christmas. I'd almost forgotten. The big day was just over a week away, and I'd be seeing my dad. Back when life was normal (ya know, before my hanging, my trial by the Dark Order of the Grand Stag and my post-mortem chat with Henry), Shafeen and I had arranged to stay with Chanel in Chester for the week before Christmas. Somewhere in the middle of that week, unbelievably, was my Oxford interview, so I'd planned to train it there and back. Then, as Chester was pretty close to Manchester (by name and by nature), I was going to go home from Nel's on Christmas Eve. I guessed that, now I'd banned my dad from coming home early from his shoot in Madagascar, that arrangement still stood.

Sure enough, Nel turned up soon after breakfast with Shafeen in tow. They both looked quite different from their school selves. Shafeen wore a winter jacket over a wine-coloured hoodie and jeans, and Nel wore this fluffy peach jacket that looked like it was made out of Muppet skin.

They both hugged and kissed me, and Shafeen took my hand at once. 'Let me see.'

He and Nel bent over my thumb. He lifted his dark eyes to mine. 'So it *was* all real. The trial, I mean. Those *bastards*. We *have* to get them now.'

Nel said, 'Wait, what? What trial?'

'Not here,' I said, low-voiced. 'In the car.'

I thought Doctor Kyd and Nurse Annie were on the level, but I couldn't escape the fact that the Old Abbot had supposedly 'died' here, and the paramedics who had attended me at STAGS (and Henry at Longcross for that matter) were also from this hospital. My friends stepped outside while I got dressed – Nel, God bless her, had packed me some clothes in a wheelie case.

When I was done I examined myself in the mirror. Nel had chosen a kind of Victorian blouse to wear with jeans, and it had one of those high frilly necks so you couldn't see the fading rope mark at my throat. She was all thoughtfulness, that girl. But the white of the blouse only emphasised how pale I was. My black bob hung lankly to my shoulders and the fringe had done that annoying separating thing that it did when it needed a wash. Little wonder – I hadn't washed it since just before we'd performed *The Isle of Dogs*. But there was no real visible tell of my recent trauma, except perhaps a new and guarded look in my eyes. If it wasn't for the brand on my thumb, you'd never know. I pressed the print to my reflection, right where my nose was, and it left a smoky whorl with a perfect M in the middle. The thumbprint, and all it meant, terrified me. At that moment I wanted to smash the mirror, like Martin Sheen in *Apocalypse Now*. But surely there was nothing to be afraid of any more. I'd made it out of the heart of darkness.

Hadn't I?

I shrugged on a chunky cardigan and my coat, opened the door and smiled a smile I wasn't really feeling at Shafeen and Nel. 'Let's get the hell out of here.'

At reception I signed the discharge forms myself as I was over eighteen. I said my thank-yous to Doctor Kyd and Nurse Annie, and the reception doors whispered open as we left, letting in an icy northern blast. I felt a bit wobbly and I walked across the car park to Nel's gold Mini leaning on Shafeen's strong arm. Alnwick Castle cast a chill shadow over us, snow still on the battlements and the arrow slits watching us like eyes. It was nice to get into Nel's car and blast the heating. 'Shotgun!' I said out of habit, before I remembered that the word might have unfortunate connotations for Shafeen, since he was the one who had once been riddled with pellets from Henry's gun. But if it did, he said nothing. He just smiled and opened the passenger door for me in a courtly way, before folding his long legs into the back seat.

Needless to say, I did all the talking in the car. I had so much to tell, and I'd waited so long to tell it. I described my trial by the DOGS all over again, that circle of creepy, antlered figures in the theatre, led by the Old Abbot as judge. I went through it all in fine detail: what he had said; what I had said; what

10

I had felt. Then I filled them in about my two visitors from Longcross the night before, Cass briefly and then, at much greater length, Ty. I told them about Leon Morgan, Ty's tragic great-uncle who had been taken to Longcross when little more than a child and had never come home again. I told them about Ty being **mrs_de_warlencourt**, the mysterious Instagram messenger who had been my guide throughout the last crazy weeks, and that her last cryptic statement, 'There is another Place', had meant Cumberland Place, the de Warlencourt London home. And I told them about Ty's determination to return to Longcross to thwart whatever plan the twins might have and to end the cycle once and for all.

Of course, Shafeen and Nel had about a million questions and we were a long way down the motorway before a silence fell. There was this massive sign over the road saying THE SOUTH, with a huge white arrow beneath it, and as we followed the arrow my stomach flipped over. As we drove further and further south I thought about Ty. After a year of being three conspirators, I now felt that, without her, there was someone missing from our group. In that short intense conversation in my hospital room last night I felt that she had been a true friend to me, much more so than I'd been to her, and I felt incredibly invested in her welfare. I rubbed the pad of my branded thumb with the middle finger of the same hand, a new habit of mine that accompanied deep thought. I must have made some weird little sound because Shafeen leaned forward. 'Are you OK? Does it hurt?'

'No,' I said. 'It doesn't hurt. It's just . . .'

'Yes?' he prompted gently.

'It's Ty,' I said, letting out a long breath. 'I keep thinking of her, back at Longcross, without any of us. It just feels like we are ditching her.'

'We're not,' said Nel. 'Don't worry.'

But I did worry. It felt like she was up there, fighting the good fight against the Order of the Stag, and we were going to Nel's to swim in the pool, and watch movies in the cinema room, and go Christmas shopping in Chester. I wasn't sure I could enjoy all that while Ty was at the mercy of the de Warlencourts. I still wasn't certain in my own mind if the twins were goodies or baddies (to Cass I gave the benefit of the doubt; Louis, well – the jury was still out), but I was more worried about the creepy uber-Order who had tried and branded me. Moodily I stared out of the window, watching the road signs flash past. One of them said CHESTER.

I sat bolt upright. 'You missed it!'

'Missed what?' Nel didn't take her eyes off the road.

'The turn-off. To Chester.'

'I know.'

'Aren't we going to Chester?'

'No. I mean, yes, but not yet.'

'Where are we going then?'

I saw her eyes meet Shafeen's in the mirror, saw him give a tiny nod.

'We're going to another Place.'

I knew from the way she said it. She managed, just by some strange trick of speech, to put a capital on that last word.

We were going where Ty had told me to go.

We were going to de Warlencourt HQ.

We were going to Cumberland Place.

PART 2
THE ROVING

3

Cumberland Place just about knocked my eyes out of my head.

The house was *beautiful*, just beautiful and so . . . *grand*. It was quite different to Longcross, but in its own way just as imposing.

We took a collective deep breath. Since Nel had taken the road south, we'd had seven hours and two service-station McDonald's to come up with a plan. And we had, of sorts. Or rather, we hadn't. It wasn't so much a plan as the only option open to us. We were going to walk right up to the front door, say we were friends of Henry's and see what happened.

So, at four o'clock that afternoon, having negotiated the London roads with the grudging help of Nel's satnav and parked in a nearby mews, the three of us stood looking up at the house, mouths open.

It was set in its own gardens behind a wrought-iron fence, with neatly clipped hedges and stark winter trees. It was flanked on either side by impossibly grand houses, but Cumberland Place was the grandest of all. It was white, as white as the snow that iced it like a Christmas cake, and it had these grand pillars holding up a triangular portico. It had huge sash windows and two identical wings, giving the house an elegant symmetry.

It was set back from a quiet road winding through an immense snowy park, which looked so countrified that if it wasn't for the distinctive London skyscrapers in the distance, you could have been in the middle of nowhere. I'd only been to London twice, once on a school trip and once when my dad was getting a wildlife award, but Nel, who seemed to know it like the back of her handbag, reliably informed me this was Regent's Park. I guessed that Cumberland Place, although much smaller than Longcross, was probably worth just as much – a house standing slap in the middle of London and on the edge of Regent's Park must be worth squillions.

I felt a bit like my namesake, Greer Garson, in the *Pride and Prejudice* film, when she gets her gob well and truly smacked by the grandeur and elegance of Pemberley. And because Cumberland Place was a white house that looked just like, well, the White House, it was hard to believe that it could be, as Ty had suggested, the HQ of the Dark Order of the Grand Stag.

Nel was the first to pull it together. 'So,' she said, 'we knock. We say hi. We see who's home.'

'And what happens when they look at us like we are dog shit?' I asked.

'Then we go to Durrant's Hotel in Marylebone and check in. It's just round the corner and they know my dad.'

'What are we going to pay for that with?' I said. 'Magic beans?'

At that, Nel, without taking her eyes off the white facade, fished out her purse and put it in my hand. I opened it and it was like a gambler's deck – there were, like, fifty-two plastic cards in there. I swear I saw a black Amex – the Ace of Spades of credit cards.

'I'm on all of Dad's accounts,' Nel said.

'Of *course* you are.'

'So. We ready?'

'OK,' said Shafeen.

'OK . . . I *guess*,' I said, much more doubtfully. That doubt, that niggling misgiving in the pit of my stomach, had a name.

It was Henry.

The one thing I hadn't mentioned in the car, during all their questions about the trial, and the Abbot, and the brand, and Leon Morgan, was my strange meeting with Henry in the hospital. I had told Shafeen about it, in an unguarded moment, as he'd come to my room right after my spectral visitor. But I hadn't brought it up since, even to him.

Especially to him.

Firstly, I didn't want to piss him off by placing him in this weird Bella/Edward/Jacob love triangle, and secondly, seeing ghosts meant that I belonged in a cuckoo farm, didn't it? No. I had to face it: Henry was dead as a doornail.

But if that was the case, and Henry *was* dead as a doornail, then why, as we walked up to the doorway of Cumberland Place, was I wishing above all else that I looked a bit more put together, as if he was going to be there to fling open the door himself? Why was something, some visual cue just out of reach of mind and memory, nagging me that I *had* really seen him, that he *must* really be alive?

But, of course, the door was opened by . . . a butler.

He was dressed in the full rig: black tailcoat, white tie and

17

shoes so shiny you could see your face in them. His own face was long and stretched, with a domed forehead and slicked-back greying hair. He looked like Richard E. Grant in, well . . . anything.

He regarded us with absolutely no surprise, but to be fair he didn't seem like a dude who would ever show surprise. Or, in fact, any emotion. But in his first utterance that lack of surprise was explained.

'Her ladyship is expecting you.'

Really? We looked at each other, nonplussed, but before we could say anything else he turned to lead us into the house. There was nothing to do but follow.

The first thing we saw was a beautiful light atrium. A grand staircase curved away to the upper floors – a much more ornate affair than the great stone one at Longcross, which you could practically ride a horse up. High above was a domed frescoed ceiling and underfoot a vast Turkish rug. Curved double doors opened off the round space and the butler opened one set of them in a practised both-at-once way. We entered a grand drawing room, with pale gold walls and gilded furniture to match. Enormous windows gave out onto the park, and a fire burned in the elegant fireplace – there was a great garland of red-berried holly fixed along the mantelpiece. An enormous Christmas tree stood on one side of the fireplace, beautifully decorated with white candles and red rocking horses and golden bells – all the ornaments looked vintage, just like the ones at Longcross, and there was not a tacky coloured light or a gaudy strand of tinsel to be seen. I was so busy looking at the tree that it took me a second to see the woman sitting next to it.

She was perched on a rose velvet chaise longue, tall and well dressed, her long legs tucked neatly beneath her. I will never forget my first sighting of Caroline de Warlencourt, the Countess of Longcross. Although you could tell she used to be a stone-cold ten when she was younger, she looked ruined and utterly desolate. She was staring into the fire with unseeing blue eyes, pleating the material of her skirt with nervous fingers and mouthing something quietly to herself. She looked unhinged.

The butler led us right into the middle of the room and announced us, as if we were going to that ball in *My Fair Lady*. And I did feel a little bit Eliza Doolittle as I stood there in that fabulous room with my lank hair and faded jeans. But Lady de Warlencourt got up and actually clapped her hands. She expressed her joy in the most English way possible. 'Bates, more tea!' she cried. She was transformed, as if a light had been switched on within her.

Shafeen, the only one who was equal to this social situation, took her hand. Whatever his private feelings, etiquette prevailed. 'Countess,' he said stiffly, with a little bow of the head.

'Oh, my *dears*. Call me Caro.' She dropped his hand at once and came straight up to me, ignoring the other two as much as bone-bred good manners would allow.

'Now, don't tell me –' she placed one manicured fingertip under my chin – 'you must be Greer.'

She regarded me and I regarded her. The coiffured blonde hair. The pearls at ears and throat. The fine lines around blue eyes so like Henry's but paler, older and shadowed by unimaginable pain. It was good in a way that her finger was clamping my jaw shut because I wouldn't have known what to say to her.

How do you greet a woman whose son fell off a waterfall to his death right in front of you? Luckily she spoke first.

'He *said* you were beautiful.'

'He?'

'Henry. He told me you were coming.'

The lank hair crisped on my scalp. 'He's alive?'

'Dear me, yes!' she trilled. 'Why wouldn't he be?'

The glorious room spun around me and I sat down hard on the sofa, unbidden, before I fell down. *Before I fell down*. How could Henry have survived that fall? And how could I survive the fact that he had? My body was having this huge reaction – my skin felt like it was on fire, my pulse beat in my ears and my joyful, Judas heart just about burst out of my chest. I gripped my branded thumb with the other hand and looked fixedly at the pattern of the pale rug, pouring all my energy into controlling my emotions. I didn't dare look at the others, but I could hear Shafeen's sharp intake of breath.

'Why don't we *all* sit,' said Lady de Warlencourt graciously, as if she'd made nothing more than a bland comment about the weather. Nel was the first to recover from the shock and spoke for the first time.

'Where did you see him? Henry, I mean.'

Lady de Warlencourt picked up her teacup. 'At Longcross, of course. His ancestral home.'

'Where is he now?'

'Still there, I expect. We were all there for Louis's birthday. And Cassandra's, of course.' And even in the midst of that mental turmoil, I thought, *Poor Cass, always the afterthought*.

I found my voice at last. 'You *saw* him there?'

'Of course. He was keeping a low profile, but he was there.' She lifted her cup to her lips and her hand shook a little, but her voice was breezy.

'He'll be here by and by. He always turns up when you least expect him.'

You can say that again, I thought.

'He'll be delighted to see you. You simply must stay. Your rooms are all ready.'

We looked at each other, startled and horrified. 'Oh . . .' said Shafeen. 'I think . . . I mean to say . . . there must be some misunderstanding. We aren't *staying*. We just came to visit.'

Her smile didn't slip. 'Nonsense. You can't just have tea and drive north again now. Where else would you go? Some dreadful little hotel?'

'Well,' said Nel, 'the Durrant, actually . . .'

It was as if she hadn't spoken. 'But, my dears,' said Lady de Warlencourt, a tiny frown furrowing her brow, 'it's all settled. It's Henry, you see. Henry *said*.'

Before we could reply, the butler burst into the room, looking quite hurried and flustered – a complete contrast to the otter-smooth guy who'd opened the door to us. Then I'd thought he would never show any emotion. Now I revised that opinion. He just about skidded to a halt a foot from her ladyship and bent slightly in a bow, clearly trying to get his shit together. Lady de Warlencourt looked up from her teacup with mild surprise. 'What is it, Bates?'

The butler didn't seem sure. But then he said, as if he'd just thought of it, 'Just to say, your ladyship, that Lady Whitehaven is on the telephone.'

I exchanged a look with Nel and Shafeen. From the way the butler had looked when he'd come in, I'd expected the announcement of World War Three at *least*, not a phone call from some random friend. Even her ladyship raised her pale eyebrows. 'Thank you, Bates,' she said, sounding faintly astonished. 'Lady Whitehaven is my mother,' she said to us by way of explanation. 'She's over eighty now so one likes to keep in daily contact.'

Bates followed Lady de Warlencourt out of the room and for a moment we were alone. Needless to say, we didn't waste any time.

'Jesus,' Shafeen hissed. 'What do we do now?'

'Pretty awks,' agreed Nel.

But I had an answer. 'What if we just stay?'

'*What?*' Nel's volume turned right the way up. She toned it down again. 'She's clearly a bit loopy. And the Durrant's really nice. It's just round the corner and it doesn't have – oh, I don't know – *crazy* people in it.'

'Yes, but think about it,' I said, low-voiced and hurried. 'If we accept that Ty discovered that Cumberland Place *is* the HQ of the Dark Order of the Grand Stag, we need to take a good look around. We're not going to learn much from one half-hour afternoon tea. If we stay, we're exactly where we need to be.'

Footsteps approached. There wasn't much time.

Shafeen whispered, 'But why would we stay in the tiger's lair?'

I looked at them both in turn. 'Because Ty is doing it,' I said.

Lady de Warlencourt came back into the room looking a little flustered. 'The queerest thing. There was no one there.' Then her expression cleared and she smiled again. Bates came back into the room and started faffing around with the tea trays. I watched him through narrowed eyes. Something wasn't right. I met the butler's eyes as he handed me my cup and then I twigged. There wasn't any phone call. He'd come in at that point, and in that manner, expressly to stop Henry's mother talking about Henry. Lady de Warlencourt followed my gaze.

'Bates has been with us for thirty years,' she said fondly, 'both here and at Longcross.'

Bates was obviously a package deal who travelled with the elder de Warlencourts, because I'd never seen him at Longcross. 'Isn't that right, Bates?'

He nodded to his mistress, keeping his pale eyes on the floor, back to his former smooth demeanour. 'Thirty-one years in January, your ladyship.'

I couldn't imagine him as a child. I bet he never ran around or played or shouted or anything like that.

'So if there is anything you require during your stay, he's your man.'

This was the moment. We had to commit, one way or the other. We had to head to the hotel or accept her invitation. I spoke for us all. 'Thank you,' I said. 'You're very kind.' And that was it. We were staying.

Lady W neatly set down her teacup, but her hand was still shaking enough to make the bone china rattle in the saucer, with a sound eerily reminiscent of *that* scene in *Get Out*. 'I hope you'll be comfortable here, my dears. This part of the house was built in Georgian times, but the foundations are much older.'

I remembered then that Cass had said that Nazereth de Warlencourt had lived here. I was a bit sketchy about when exactly the Georgian period was, if I'm honest, but I knew if Nazereth had lived here, the house, or at least its foundations, must have been here at the end of the sixteenth century. It gave me a shiver to think of Nazereth occupying the same space we sat in now. And then another thought occurred – had Ben Jonson, his sometime friend and eventual assassin, been here too?

'So it's a little more modern than Longcross,' Lady de Warlencourt went on. 'And much less isolated. So much for you children to do in town, you know. Speaking of which, I'm sure you don't want to be chattering to me all afternoon. Let's have Bates show you your rooms, my dears. I am sure you'd like the opportunity to freshen up after such a long journey. We dress for dinner here, of course.'

Thanks to my Longcross weekends, I now knew what 'dressing for dinner' meant. It meant changing out of the clothes you had on and putting on much smarter clothes in order to eat dinner in them. I could see, now, a pattern emerging when you stayed at a fancy house. You got there, you got shown to your room, you 'freshened up' and then you ate dinner. And dinner, from my experience, was the theatre of war. That was when battle commenced. In posh houses the dinner gong was the bugle's call.

For the moment though, it was all pleasantries.

'You have a little time,' said Lady W graciously. 'Perhaps

you'd like to take a turn around Regent's Park. It's quite lovely in the snow. Rollo is at the House, so he won't be back until at least seven.'

No need to ask who Rollo was. We'd seen his name, etched unforgettably in funeral black, in the game book from 1969, along with the Grand Master and all the other guilty friars. Rollo was Henry's father. I wasn't sure what House his wife was referring to, but luckily Nel asked the question. 'I thought *this* was Lord de Warlencourt's house?'

'He's not Lord de Warlencourt, he's the Earl of Longcross, my dear. Until his death.' It was odd to hear her husband's demise spoken of so matter-of-factly. 'I know, the titles can be jolly confusing. Lord de Warlencourt is the title of –' she looked at Bates somewhat nervously – 'Rollo's heir.' *Rollo's heir*. We'd thought that, as of 17th December, Louis was the heir to Longcross. Now, if – incredibly – Henry *was* alive, I supposed it was still him. My tell-tale heart started to thud again.

'But the House I was referring to is the House of Lords. There's a sitting today. But he'll be back for dinner, never fear.'

That put a new perspective on everything. As we rose to follow the butler from the room I thought the following:

Rollo de Warlencourt was a hereditary earl of the realm.

As earl, Rollo de Warlencourt had the right to sit in the House of Lords.

Rollo de Warlencourt would be back late, because he was running the country.

4

As we followed Bates up the grand staircase to the first floor, I thought about this some more.

Rollo de Warlencourt, the master whom we'd not yet met. This was his vase, that was his portrait of one of the King Charleses – I or II, they both had long hair – on a horse. And that was his beautiful circular ceiling high above, where his fat cherubs blew his clouds across his heavenly sky.

Cumberland Place was so different to Longcross. There were no cracked windows or worn carpets; everything was pristine. The walls were painted in delicate shades of duck-egg blue or turquoise, and there was gilding everywhere – on mirrors, picture frames and the rims of priceless Chinese vases. Not footballer gold, but pale, delicate, expensive gold, just like in the drawing room. Here on the stair there was Christmas greenery too – great swags of holly and ivy above the pictures and mirrors. The carpets were deep and silent, the wallpaper hand-painted, the chandeliers dripping diamond brilliants. If Longcross Hall was dark wood, Cumberland Place was bright glass. If Longcross was medieval, Cumberland Place was Georgian. And it all brought home to me that throughout history, before, since and in between, the de Warlencourts had been at the top of the tree. At every step we'd passed maids and footmen and under-butlers who were scuttling about discreetly to do the family's bidding. Rollo had so much, and into the bargain he was running the whole show. He was the ruling class, and after him – could it be true? – his son would rule too.

If it bothered me, it bothered Shafeen a lot more.

Once Bates had shown us to three opulent rooms and then buggered off to have our cases collected from the car, we collected in the elegant chamber I'd been allocated and Shafeen went into full-on rant mode.

'It's shameful. Rollo de Warlencourt is an unelected representative, and he's making the laws of the land. All because he was born with a silver spoon in his mouth.'

Nel said, 'I thought members of the Houses of Parliament were elected.'

'The House of Commons, yes,' countered Shafeen. 'But the Lords are there either because they've been born with the privilege or they've been given a peerage by their cronies. No one's elected them. So it's full of the cream of society, as they are known.'

'Because cream rises to the top, right?'

He laughed bitterly. 'Samuel Beckett said it was because posh people are rich and thick. But you're right, of course.' He ran a hand over the silken curtains of the bed. 'Cream rises to the top. And you know what else rises?' He didn't wait for an answer. 'Scum. They are the scum of the earth, the Medievals, and the worst one is Rollo de Warlencourt, that arsehole who hunted my father at Longcross.'

27

I sat on the bed, which was nice and squashy. 'Oh give it a rest, Shaf. We've got bigger problems.'

'Like what?'

'Are you kidding? Like the small matter of Henry being alive.'

He didn't look at me or Nel, just shot back, 'That's *highly* unlikely.'

'Whaddya mean?' I replied. 'She *just* said it. His own mother saw him at Longcross and he told her to expect us.'

'And that's impossible,' he declared.

'Then how did she know we were coming? And who told her about the three of us?'

'The twins? *I* don't know.'

Nel said reasonably, 'I suppose, like she said, she *had* just seen them at Louis's – and Cass's – party.'

'Where she said she also saw *him*.'

There was one ace I wanted to keep up my sleeve – the unassailable argument that *I* had seen him. But I did have one other card I could play. 'Henry was not in the family tomb. How do you explain that?'

'Greer . . .'

'There was no one in the tomb,' I repeated stubbornly. 'You saw. You *both* saw.'

'But the priest –'

'Works for the family.'

'And the police report –'

'There were police reports both ways. One for alive, one for dead, remember. Each twin got one. And riddle me this: if Henry's dead, how did he know we'd come here?'

'If he's *alive*, how did he know we'd come here?' countered Shafeen. '*We* didn't even know we were going to come here.'

I got up and walked to the window and looked out at the snowy park. Everything was blunted with snow, like the furniture I'd seen waiting under the dustsheets at Longcross. But it was all still there, all underneath. 'When I went to Louis's room in Honorius he was playing chess,' I said. 'He said there's a human chessboard at Longcross and they all used to play on it when they were little: him, Cass and . . . Henry. And Henry had chessboard stockings, d'you remember, as part of his Medievals uniform at STAGS?' I turned to face them both. 'I think Henry's playing chess with us now. We are all sliding around the board and he's always one move ahead.'

'So you do honestly think he's alive?' asked Nel.

'Yes,' I said, just as Shafeen at the exact same moment said, 'No.'

'Then how do you explain what Lady de Warlencourt – Caro – said?'

He shrugged. 'There's something a little off.'

'About this place?'

'About her. About the Countess of Longcross.'

'How d'you mean?' I asked.

'She's so . . . twitchy and abstracted. She's like . . . Lady Macbeth in Act Five. All hollow and nervy and sort of not all *there*.'

I'd endured, rather than enjoyed, a movie of *Macbeth* recently. I remembered Marion Cotillard acting just like that as things started to unravel. Exactly as 'Caro' was behaving just before she realised we were in the room. *Lady Macbeth, Lady de Warlencourt.*

'And did you see how Bates shut her up at tea?' pressed Shafeen.

'I think we all saw that,' I said. 'It was pretty unsubtle.'

'I think he was trying to stop her saying something.'

'Exactly. That Henry was alive.'

It was all getting a bit fraught, Shafeen and I facing each other like a warring couple with Nel in the middle like the kid in *Kramer vs. Kramer*. I had to break the tension. I gave a little laugh. 'It's Mulder and Scully 101.'

'Not that again,' sighed Shafeen, sounding tired. 'Don't tell me – Mulder believed in aliens, Scully didn't.'

'Well . . .' said Nel slowly. She'd been fiddling with some monogrammed silver hairbrushes on the bedside table, trying to stay out of it. Now she spoke for the first time. 'It's not Mulder and Scully. But it is Louis and Cass. Cass wanted Henry to be alive. Louis didn't. You two are the same.'

This was awkward. I couldn't deny that I wanted Henry to be alive, but I didn't like to be so transparent.

Nel broke the silence she'd created. 'So are we actually going to stay here?'

'Where else can we go?'

'The Durrant Hotel. Like I said.'

'We can't exactly walk out now,' said Shafeen. 'Besides, we are here to do a job.'

'What job?' asked Nel.

'To find out what's going on,' he replied. 'To get to the bottom of all this conspiracy. I vote we stay.'

This, at least, we agreed on. 'Me too. If Ty's at Longcross, alone, we can cope here, the three of us. At least for one night. Dinner is always pretty illuminating at these places, don't you think?'

'And we get to meet the King of the World when he's back from a hard day of ruling,' said Shafeen scornfully.

I eyed him closely. I think whatever he said, he was dying to square up to the guy who had kicked sand in his father's face all those years ago. There were bound to be fireworks.

'Fine.' Nel headed for the door.

'Where are you going?'

She turned with a smile. 'To . . . what did she call it? Freshen up.'

Once the door had closed Shafeen drew me to him. 'I'm sorry, Greer,' he said. 'I lost my temper. There's no excuse, but there is an explanation.' He wound a strand of my gross hair between his fingers. 'Just when I think I can relax, someone else says that bastard is alive.'

This was so breathtakingly honest I couldn't help but react to it . . . In that moment I completely understood him. It was time to tell him what I'd decided in the hospital, that, whether Henry was alive or dead, it was Shafeen all the way, that I was ready to seal the deal. I hugged him tight, so tight. I kissed his lips tenderly and he kissed me back, not tenderly at all. My legs buckled and we ended up on the bed. Mostly my eyes were closed, but I opened them briefly and saw a flash of silver. What I saw made me shove Shafeen away from me and sit up.

'No,' I said. 'Not here. This is Henry's room.' I reached out

31

and picked up the silver-backed hairbrush from the bedside table. The one Nel had been fiddling with. I turned the back to Shafeen so he could clearly see the curlicued monogram engraved in the silver.

$$\mathcal{H}\ de\ \mathcal{W}$$

He sat up too. 'Jesus. They've put you in *Henry's* room?'

'Yes,' I said, sitting up. 'Look.' There was a hand mirror and a comb there too, all with the same monogram.

Shafeen jumped up, as if he couldn't bear to touch the covers that Henry had slept in.

'It's a double bed,' he said slowly.

'So?'

'Presumably they think their golden boy is going to come back from Longcross and share the bed with you. That's what all that "beautiful" stuff was about. *Droit de seigneur.* Jesus Christ!'

'I thought you said he was dead.'

'Oh, but it doesn't matter what *I* think, does it?' he said irrationally. 'It matters what *they* think.'

'Of *course* it matters what you think!'

I put my head in my hands, fingers raking through my greasy hair. 'Look. Can we not do this now? I need to –'

'Freshen up?' His voice had a dangerous edge.

I got up too. 'Well, wash my hair at least.'

'Why?' He'd gone suddenly still. 'Why, Greer? Why do you need to wash your hair? Who are you washing it for?' He looked me right in the eyes.

I couldn't reply, because the answer was loop-the-loop, round-the-twist, batshit crazy.

I hesitated a second too long.

'Got it,' he said.

And he left the room.

5

Defiantly, I *did* wash my hair, *and* I felt a whole lot better for it.

I tonged it straight and shiny, then turned my attention to what I was going to wear. Nel, bless her, had packed me a nice case but of course hadn't known she needed to pack for a full-on dinner, so I only had enough stuff for a week at hers. But I needn't have worried. Perhaps guessing that I wouldn't have the right gear for dinner, someone had obligingly put a blood-red midi-dress on the bed. It was made of that kind of material that has tons of tiny little knife-edge pleats. It was gorgeous but something about the colour gave me a funny qualm in my stomach. Red gowns would always mean my trial by the D.O.G.S. – but that dread memory did not quite chime with my feeling here. There was something else – something red – something I needed to remember . . .

I put it on regardless. It fitted me perfectly – as if it had been made for me. It had a full skirt and sleeves and a high neck to cover my rope burn. And it did make me look a better colour than the washed-out girl I'd seen in the hospital mirror that morning. I added a red lip and sat on the bed. I wasn't even sure what to do next – usually Shafeen or Nel would come for me, but Shafeen had seemed pretty mad and Nel might be tactfully staying away, as when she'd left us we'd been together.

Well. If my other Musketeers were busy, I'd check on my D'Artagnan. My Logan Lerman, if you will.

I checked my Instagram, which felt vaguely wrong in this house. I was sure they frowned on tech here as much as they did at STAGS and Longcross. I found **mrs_de_warlencourt**'s profile and messaged Ty.

    We're here

She replied almost at once and I felt a flood of relief. She was online.

    Where's here?

I typed:

    Cumberland Place

She came back:

    Yay

Then:

    That's my girl
        Are you OK? I asked.
    Yeah fine

35

```
    You're safe?
Yeah. All the guests gone for now. Just
chillin'
```

There was a pause.

```
See if you can find out about Foxes
```

I had to read that last word twice.

```
    Foxes?? How do you mean?
Dunno. Just something I overheard
```

Then:

```
Gotta go
```

It wasn't until I'd put down the phone and was just idly looking around, like you do when you're waiting for something, that I saw *him*.

There was a fox on the wall.

Not a whole fox, you understand – just a head, *à la* Jeffrey the stag. I was well used, by now, to the upper-class habit of nailing deceased creatures to the walls, like in that creepy room in *The Life and Death of Colonel Blimp*.

I got up and went closer to the fox. He looked pretty moth-eaten – he had a ragged, torn ear and his faded pelt was more marmalade orange than russet red. Jeffrey had been a peaceful soul, with his big, chocolatey eyes; this fellow had gone down fighting; his yellowing teeth were bared in death. The head was mounted on a mahogany shield, and there was a little brass plaque screwed into the wood below the snarling muzzle. I was just standing on tiptoes to read the wording engraved there when there was a knock on the door. I whirled around to find Shafeen.

He leaned on the doorpost and regarded me.

'Well,' he said, 'your hair looks lovely.'

As apologies went, it was pretty classy. I smiled.

'And the rest of you looks terrific too. I've never seen that dress before.'

'Neither have I.'

'Oh. Did the countess put it out for you?'

'Someone did. You look terrific too, by the way.' It was true. He had not gone full tux, but he was in a pewter-grey three-piece suit with a waistcoat, and he looked gorgeous. Shafeen was obviously better prepared than I had been, probably because he was due to go home to Rajasthan and I imagined he'd have some pretty formal dinners with his family, them being minor royalty and all. It occurred to me then that Shafeen's family were part of an unelected, hereditary ruling class too, but I didn't want to poke the bear when we were in the middle of making up. 'Oops, you missed a button though.' I came towards him and started to do up the bottom button he'd left undone on the waistcoat.

He laid has hands over mine, stopping me. 'It's meant to be like that.'

'What?' I laughed. 'Undone?'

'Yes.'

37

Now I was properly confused. 'Why?'

'It's a tradition supposedly started by Edward VII when he was Prince of Wales. He put on a bit of weight and couldn't do up the bottom button on his waistcoat any more, so everyone at court had to do the same.'

'When was this?'

'Eighteen-something, I think.'

'So people still do this because some prince, years ago, was a bit chubby?'

'Well, yes.' Shafeen half laughed himself as he confirmed it, as if it was ridiculous. And it was. But it was serious too.

'And everyone just *knows* this?'

'Well . . . some people.'

'The right people, huh?'

One of his hands took one of mine. 'Let's go get Nel.'

As I followed him I realised that, for the first time in our *Twilight* love triangle, now Shafeen and Henry were on one side and I was on the other. That gulf of generations of bred-in class felt like a divide I could never cross.

PART 3
SCENT

6

We went down the stairs all together like we were the stars of *Gentlemen Prefer Blondes*.

Our own blonde – Nel – looked the part in a baby-blue bodycon dress.

'Drawing room first, I think,' said Shafeen. 'There'll be a drinks tray.'

We went through the doors and a dude in white-tie was making up the fire. He sprung to attention when we came in and then melted away, leaving us alone with the drinks tray. Shafeen mixed us all gin and tonics and we sort of stood about by the fire, admiring the resplendent Christmas tree and classy swags of greenery hung about the mantel.

'What do we do?'

'We'll be shown to the dining room,' Shafeen replied calmly. 'You can relax – someone will come get us.' He seemed quite at ease in this world, and sipped his G&T with his back to the fire. Now the three of us were alone, I could tell my news. I filled them both in about Ty's Instagrams. They were relieved that she was OK, and both, predictably, picked up on the last message.

'*Foxes?*' queried Nel. 'That's all she said?'

'Yeah. *See if you can find out about Foxes.* Then she went offline.'

Shafeen looked thoughtful. 'Do you have any idea what she meant?'

'Well, funnily enough, there's one in my room.'

'What? How d'you mean?' Nel asked.

'You know in Longcross they have animals' heads on the wall. Jeff— I mean, the stag in Lowther, for example? Well, in my room here – Henry's room – there is a fox.'

'I've got one too,' said Shafeen. 'It's above the fireplace. How about you, Nel?'

'Not that I noticed,' she said. 'And I think I *would* have noticed. But then again,' she said bitterly, 'I've probably got the servant's room.' Then her eyes got all big and round. 'D'you think there's something behind them?'

'Like what?' queried Shafeen.

'Like tunnels. Like there was behind the portrait of Esmé Stuart in the library at Longcross?'

I was doubtful. 'I dunno . . . mine's pretty high up, and pretty small. You could basically hide a dinner plate behind him, if you wanted to. He has a little brass plaque though, if that helps.'

'Mine too,' said Shafeen, 'but I didn't get a chance to read it. I literally just spotted him before I came to get you.'

'OK – that's a job for later. Maybe we should –'

Then Bates came in, shutting us all up. He bent in a slight bow and greeted us all by name; all otter-smooth, emotionless demeanour once again. 'Good evening, Miss Ashton. Mr Jadeja. Miss MacDonald. Dinner is served. If you would follow me?'

42

He led us down a marble-floored passageway to another part of the house, and as we followed him past another bunch of priceless pictures and porcelain, I wondered why he'd named us in that order. Then I clicked: he'd done it by seniority of age. But that just raised another question – how the hell did he know our dates of birth? We followed his upright back through another grand set of double doors to what was obviously the dining room.

Lady de Warlencourt was already there, at one end of the table, wearing this bizarre Chinese-looking silk housecoat covered with writhing dragons, and she was dripping with diamonds like one of the chandeliers. Once again there was a moment – just a heartbeat – before she clocked us, when she was staring into space, mouthing something, turning the diamond rings nervously on her fingers. But then, once she noticed us, she clicked into action as if she'd just been switched to hostess mode. She didn't get up but smiled her charming smile and greeted us fondly as Bates pulled out the chairs to indicate where we were to sit. 'My dears! I hope your rooms are comfortable.'

I could hardly go on about how lovely her 'dead' son's room was, so I left the polite stuff to Shafeen. 'Perfectly, Lady Longcross.'

'Naughty!' She wagged a be-ringed forefinger at him good-naturedly. 'I said you must call me Caro. After all –' she beamed at me – 'we're almost family.'

I hardly dared look at Shafeen in particular, who had nothing to say to this bizarre statement but waited for his hostess to unfold her napkin before unfolding his. I'd already unfolded mine – whoops – and I eyed Shafeen closely. I knew he was going to be trouble tonight. He wasn't a big drinker, but he'd already downed his gin and was getting stuck into the wine the footman had poured. I swallowed a tiny sip of mine with a sense of misgiving. Shafeen could barely conceal his dislike of Call-Me-Caro; God only knew what he would be like once Rollo got here. After all, Lady de Warlencourt had not been named in the black hunting book of 1969; for all we knew, she'd never been involved in the whole huntin' shootin' fishin' thing. But Rollo? Earl of Longcross, sire of Henry, nemesis of a beloved father? Shafeen was clearly ready to go all *Gladiator* on him. Nel watched him warily, but I was watching the door, my heart leaping every time some footman came through with a silver dish or a decanter. Where was the earl?

As if she'd read my mind, Caro said, 'Rollo's been held up a little. The sitting ran long – I think it turned into rather a bunfight. He said we should begin.'

It was almost unbearable. We sat through the interminable process of being served a creamy white soup, the ladle clashing against the fine china, in a counterpoint to the agonising small talk. I did, fortunately, think of one thing to say. 'Thank you for the dress.'

'I beg your pardon, my dear?'

'The dress.' I touched the red silk at my throat. 'I love it. It was very kind of you to lend it to me.'

She turned her pale blue eyes on me and studied me closely. 'I? I'm afraid I cannot claim the credit. I've never laid eyes on it before.'

I looked at the others. 'Then who . . . ?'

'Haven't the faintest, child. One of the servants, doubtless.'

In the awkward silence that followed I had time to fantasise that the dress was, somehow, from Henry, before shooting a glance at the door again. When was his father coming? But eventually, just as we were all laying down our silver spoons, he arrived.

Rollo de Warlencourt was all Savile Row tailoring and high colour. He looked like Charles Dance, not the homicidal-maniac-Tywin-Lannister Charles Dance but the suave, tuxedoed-to-within-an-inch-of-his-life *White Mischief* Charles Dance. He was slim and tall and held himself straight as a poker. He had blond hair like Henry's, just whitening at the temples, and a noble Roman nose, and pale blue far-seeing eyes. He entered the room with the swagger and confidence of a man much younger, although if he was the same age as Shafeen's dad, he must be pushing seventy. I'd say Lady W was much younger, maybe even by as much as twenty years. As he walked towards us I caught a whiff of his aftershave. It was sweet and bitter at the same time – the heady smell of the sandalwood that Henry always wore. It sent me reeling back to the hospital room at Alnwick Cottage Hospital, where Henry, or a vision of him, sat by my bed. How could a dream have a scent?

The first words he uttered were 'Forgive me' in the confident, slightly too loud tones of someone who didn't think he needed to be forgiven for anything. He headed towards his wife, presumably to greet her, and then something caught his eye and he just stopped dead.

The something that caught his eye was Shafeen. Shafeen,

who always displayed immaculate manners even in the presence of someone he despised, had risen to his feet when Rollo de Warlencourt had entered the room. I stayed sitting, because I didn't know what to do in these situations. Nel stayed sitting too, as she probably didn't know the form either. But Lady de Warlencourt, who most definitely did know the etiquette, stayed seated too, so that was all right. So it was just the two men standing, exactly the same height as each other, on the same side of the table, as we ladies watched like an invited audience. I'd been quietly dreading this moment, as I knew that Shafeen would struggle to mask his utter hatred of Rollo de Warlencourt, even in the cause of finding out what the heck was going on up at Longcross. But the encounter didn't at all play out like I had imagined.

Rollo, statue still, just stared at Shafeen, his mulberry face draining of colour until it was as pale as the soup. Shafeen, totally taken aback, but taking refuge in good manners, put out his hand hesitantly as if for a handshake. Rollo's firm lips seemed to have lost all form and were mouthing something. Eventually the sound came out. '*Mowgli?*'

I took in a little gasp of breath. Could it be – was it possible that the Earl of Longcross had just called Shafeen by the name of the loincloth-wearing boy hero of *The Jungle Book*? If so, that might be one of the most casually racist things I'd ever heard.

I looked at Nel, eyes wide, and she mirrored my expression back at me. Then it was all eyes on Shafeen to see how he would take this. His face hardened, his eyes burning like black coals. I don't know what it cost him to keep his hand out in greeting, but he did, even though it shook a little. What happened next was almost unbelievable. Rollo slapped the hand away. Then he enfolded Shafeen in the biggest, tightest bear hug I've ever seen. If Shafeen was Mowgli, Rollo was playing Baloo the bear.

For a long moment Shafeen literally couldn't speak – I think he'd had the breath squeezed out of him. When Rollo released him, I swear there were tears in those blue eyes. Shafeen, quite huffily, twitched his jacket into place and touched his tie as if to straighten it.

'It's Shafeen actually.'

'Of course.' He looked at Shafeen almost as if he didn't believe him. 'Of course. But you are *his* son, aren't you? The son of Mowgli? Hardy, I mean?'

'My father's name is Aadhish Jadeja.'

'Yes, yes, of course. But when I knew him, he called himself Hardy. Used to insist on it. I used to say, "Kiss me, Hardy." But the others all called him Mowgli. Just as a little joke, don't you know.' I got the *Jungle Book* reference, because in 1969 the Disney animation must've just come out, but the Hardy thing went right over my head. I reminded myself to ask Shafeen later; right now, he was just coming to terms with his dad's two new nicknames.

Rollo took Shafeen by both shoulders and gave him a little shake. 'You have *such* a look of old Mowgli. I thought you *were* him for an instant. It's uncanny.'

Of *course*. Shafeen now was exactly the same age as his father had been at Longcross, when he'd spent that fateful 1969 Justitium weekend at the mercy of Rollo, the Old Abbot and the Friars. No wonder Rollo was spooked. I shot a look to Lady W to see how she was taking all this. She had her hands clasped over her chest and was smiling with her head on one side, in the way people do when they think something is really cute. I'm not at all sure she didn't have tears in her eyes too.

After this everyone sat down. Rollo kept chuckling and shaking his noble head, and patting Shafeen's forearm as if he didn't believe he was real. I noticed Rollo had a signet ring on the little finger of his right hand, a little nugget of gold with tiny black antlers etched on it. I knew then, if I hadn't before, that we were in the house of the enemy, of the Order of the Stag, and you may be sure I watched Rollo carefully. But he didn't return the compliment. Just as Caro had targeted me and didn't seem to see the other two, Rollo barely seemed to acknowledge me or Nel. He greeted us politely but abstractedly, and immediately turned back to Shafeen. He called for more wine – *'This is something to celebrate'* – which came in with the next course, and I can tell you, I took a big gulp of mine when it came around. This was like one of those bizarre interactive theatre experiences, but it was absolutely free of charge. As the footmen left the room I found myself wondering what the hell we would talk about next. Once again, I was surprised.

'I'll never forget the time your father came to Longcross,' said the earl.

Shafeen looked – and was – totally wrongfooted. If he'd expected Rollo to dance around the subject, he was wrong. 'I don't think he will either,' said Shafeen grimly.

'It was 1969. We all went down for Justitium weekend.' The far-seeing blue eyes gazed off into the distance. 'Yes, we were there for a spot of huntin' shootin' fishin'. Jolly good shot, your father, you know.'

'I do know,' said Shafeen, a touch of pride in his voice. That, I guess, was why Shafeen, too, was such a crack shot. It was in the blood.

'Not much of a man for fish, Mowgli. But a hunter? Lord! What a hunter. I never saw anything like it.'

Now Shafeen looked surprised. 'Really? My father?'

'Good God, yes. He seemed to have some sixth sense for game. He had a real instinct for the kill.'

'That I didn't know,' said Shafeen, sounding a bit bemused.

'He had this thing that he did. He would sort of meditate. Real holy-man stuff. You have to remember this was the Sixties, peace and love and all that. He used to sort of go into a trance, and he could tell you where the deer was at bay, or where the pheasants were roosting, or where the hares were hiding in the long grass. They couldn't hide from him. Nothing could hide from him.' The earl went off into a bit of a trance himself at that point, and then sort of snapped himself back. 'Jolly impressive it was. Turned our luck that weekend, I can tell you.'

I watched Shafeen trying to process this new picture of his dad. Not the craven victim, his rout recorded for all time in the game book, but a powerful predator.

'We went up to Oxford together, you know. Then Sandhurst. Then he went back to where he'd come from. Damned shame.'

'Yes,' Shafeen supplied. 'My grandfather died, and he had to leave the army and take over at home.'

'Of course, of course. Nothing more important than your son stepping up when it's his turn. Nothing more precious than an heir.' Rollo looked glassy-eyed again, but I didn't really get why. If Henry was alive, what was he sad about? 'A pity though. How is he?'

'He's, er, fine. He's fine. I'll be seeing him, as a matter of fact, over Christmas.'

'Capital!' said Rollo. 'Give him my fondest regards, would you? Will you remember? My fondest regards.'

Shafeen faintly agreed, but apparently this wasn't enough for Rollo. He grabbed Shafeen by the wrist. 'Promise? Promise you'll remember me to him?'

'I promise.' Shafeen freed his hand and Rollo took up his glass, satisfied. I watched Shafeen, and Shafeen watched Rollo, and I was pretty sure he was thinking the same as me. Were Rollo and Aadhish actually *friends*?

Rollo forked up his fish course with quite an appetite. 'For two pins I'd ask him back to the old place. D'ye think he'd come?'

Shafeen, who didn't seem to know anything with any certainty any more, had no reply to this frankly bizarre enquiry.

'As a matter of fact we've just been to Longcross, haven't we, Caro? For the twins' birthday. But you know the twins, of course, from STAGS. Growing into two very fine young people.'

This didn't seem to quite chime with what Cass had said about sending Henry's parents away. Then, it had seemed like there was beef between the two branches of the family. Now everyone was being nice as pie.

'Did you meet Ty when you were up there?' God bless Nel, bringing it all back to why we were actually here.

'The coloured girl?' asked Lady de Warlencourt.

All us guests flinched at the use of that word.

'The *black* girl, yes,' said Nel pointedly.

'She seemed jolly attached to Lulu,' said Lady W, looking to her husband for back-up. 'Didn't she, darling?'

'Yes, indeed,' said Rollo. 'Quite the romance of the century. She's still there, I think, even though everyone else has gone.'

I had to do it. I had to ask. 'Even Henry?'

The room suddenly went still. Then, I'll be damned if *Bates* didn't come rushing in again.

'Your ladyship, Lady Whitehaven is on the telephone.'

I watched Lady de Warlencourt dab her mouth with her napkin, rise hurriedly and swish out of the room in that long Chinese coat. It occurred to me then that Lady Whitehaven was Henry's grandmother, and if she was Henry's grandmother, she was the twins' grandmother too, and that set me wondering if she was the 'Grandmama' who had told Cass and Louis all about Nazereth de Warlencourt. But that wasn't a question I could possibly ask right now. And anyway, there wasn't time, because something properly weird happened. The minute, no, the *second* the door closed behind Lady W, the earl began to speak in a low and urgent voice.

'I say,' he began. 'I must explain something. My wife. She's . . . I'm afraid she's not well. She's had a few . . . funny turns.' I thought this was probably the Medieval way of saying she had mental-health issues. 'She's become, I'm afraid, a little delusional.'

I knew then what he was going to say.

'One of the forms it takes is, as you have already gathered, believing that our . . .' He hesitated and his voice cracked a little. 'That Henry is alive.'

51

No one spoke except the clock on the mantel, which gave tongue to a little silvery chime. Nel waited till it had finished, then said, 'So he isn't.'

The earl, suddenly looking very old, shook his head. 'I'm afraid not. It is all in her mind. She *wants* it so, you see.'

I did see. But at the same time my stomach felt like it was going down in a lift. Caro and I had a lot in common. I'd wanted to believe Henry was still around, so I'd never let him go either.

'I've been advised by Doctor Morand – he's our family GP, you know . . .'

I remembered Doctor Morand as the ancient physician who had patched up Shafeen after he'd literally had a shot in the arm.

'Morand says it is best not to contradict her. It's a fairly common symptom of grief, don't you know: denial. She finds it easier to cope if she can tell herself it is not true.'

I understood this very well.

'The old girl will come to it in her own time, he says. Realise eventually that he's gone. So while you are staying here, you should know that our strategy has been not to attempt to correct her, but to merely change the subject as soon as possible, take her mind away from it, so to speak.'

Which explained Bates's hasty entrances every time Henry's name was mentioned.

'I'd hoped to be here to greet you all – of course, as friends of Henry, you will always be welcome in our home . . .'

Shafeen leaned forward. 'Ought we to go, sir?'

He sounded all sympathetic and deferential, not at all the combative Shafeen I'd expected tonight.

Rollo briefly patted Shafeen's hand with his. 'Not a bit of it, dear chap. I wouldn't hear of it. I merely meant that I'd intended to be here, head you off at the pass, as it were, let you know the lie of the land, what. But that damned sitting at the House went on so long . . .'

I had so many questions, foremost among them: how did he even know we'd be coming here? Who had told him to expect us? And how could he possibly know what time we'd arrive? But Rollo wasn't finished.

'Forgive my haste, but I can't ask this in front of . . . in front of Caro.' He turned in my direction. 'You were the last to see him, Henry – correct?'

My heart started to thud. I pointed at my chest. 'Me?'

'All of you. And his other friends. You were all at the lake that day.'

'Yes. I suppose. I mean, yes.' I wondered, with a certain dread, what was coming next.

Rollo hesitated, as if he didn't quite trust himself to speak. 'Was he happy?'

God. I thought of that last sparkling morning in the boat on Longmere with Henry's arms wrapped around me as he helped me reel in the trout. His delight as I'd seemed, for that instant, to be a kindred spirit. *Was he happy?* 'Yes,' I said, with perfect truth.

Another pause. 'And did you . . . did you see him fall? Did you see how it happened?'

I was back at the top of the waterfall, watching Henry fall back into space, my hand grabbing for his, only to grasp air. But I had to keep to our story. 'No. No, I didn't.'

This was awful. I never expected to feel sorry for Henry's father. In this moment, seeing Rollo's grief, the truth of Henry's death seemed suddenly to become clear. And – underlying that feeling – I couldn't help feeling sorry for myself. Despite what I'd told myself in the hospital after hearing Leon Morgan's story – that Henry was evil and it was Shafeen all the way – the finality of his death was still hard to take. This past week had been a rollercoaster of *Flatliners* emotions – Henry was dead, then alive, then dead again. I rubbed my marked thumb with my forefinger. It turned out I'd deserved to be tried and branded; I *was* a manslayer after all. I had had enough. I couldn't do this any more. 'What does it matter how he fell?' I burst out. 'Either way, he's gone.'

Rollo looked straight at me with Henry's eyes. '*When the fall is all that's left, it matters a great deal.*'

He'd mangled the quote, but even so I recognised which film it was from. I was so conditioned to playing the movie game with my dad that I blurted '*The Lion in Winter*' before I could stop myself.

I felt as if he saw me properly for the first time. 'Yes,' he said, almost enthusiastically. And then, more soberly, 'Yes. *The Lion in Winter*.' He could have been talking about himself. Once golden and vital, now grey and grizzled, his heir gone, his kingdom passing to another.

And then the door opened, and so, thankfully, the English Inquisition could stop.

7

Lady de Warlencourt came back in with the meat course.

As the footmen placed these fancy-pants ribs (with little paper hats on the bones) in front of us, I was racking my brain to think of a topic of conversation that didn't make it so painfully obvious that we'd been talking about her. So I hurriedly asked the earl: 'What were you debating in the House of Lords? Can you tell us? Or would you have to kill us?'

Good, Greer. Once again, absolutely nailed it in terms of finding exactly the wrong thing to say in a given moment.

The earl didn't seem to mind my question. He even smiled. 'On the contrary. The proceedings of the House of Lords are a matter of public record.'

'Hansard,' said Nel. 'They make word-for-word transcripts of parliamentary debates.'

'Precisely,' said the earl, without looking at her.

'So what were you talking about today?'

He hesitated for just an instant.

'Foxes,' he said briefly.

Now I sat up. *See if you can find out about Foxes.*

'What about them?' He'd asked me some difficult questions;

it was time for him to answer some. You see what I mean about dinner with the upper classes being a battleground? 'I mean,' I said, emboldened by the wine, 'if we can read about it, you might as well tell us.'

Rollo cleared his throat. 'I'm introducing a bill for its first reading, early in the New Year. To reinstate fox hunting in England.'

'But it's banned now, right?'

'Since 2004. We used to ride to hounds at Longcross, until that damned bill outlawing it.'

'Ridiculous,' tutted the countess.

'They said it was *animal cruelty.*'

'A bunch of dogs tearing an animal apart,' said Nel drily. 'I can't imagine why.'

'Precisely, my dear,' said her ladyship, taking what Nel had said at face value. 'Such nonsense. Arrant nonsense.'

'It's valuable pest control,' chimed in Rollo. 'Damned liberals don't understand the countryside.'

'And the *hundreds* of jobs, darling,' broke in the countess.

'Hundreds of jobs,' her husband echoed. 'The hunt was a major employer in the countryside.' This was clearly a well-rehearsed double act. I wondered in how many great houses they'd performed this *Rain Man* back-and-forth they had going.

'Besides, it doesn't hurt them.'

Nel wasn't having that. 'Who says?' she asked bluntly.

'I *beg* your pardon?'

'Who says it doesn't hurt? The fox?' Nel was being pretty to the point – I wondered if she was a bit fed up of Caro sucking up to me and Rollo sucking up to Shafeen.

'Well,' said Rollo, blustering slightly, 'one can see. In fact, I think he enjoys it.'

Henry had said this too. Not just about the fox, but about me. He'd challenged me to tell him I hadn't enjoyed that first weekend at Longcross. Then I couldn't speak. Now I couldn't either.

'It's a jolly day out,' said Rollo. 'Fox bloody loves it. And it's a fair fight. Sometimes –' he pointed a long finger at the frescoed ceiling – 'he gets away.'

Not always, I thought, recalling the fox head in my room.

Shafeen said, quite loudly, 'That sounds like – what did you call it? Arrant nonsense.'

Even I thought that was a bit harsh. For a moment, the earl's face fell still and his eyes went small with anger. But then, just as his son had done when Shafeen had told his story about the tiger, he threw back his head and laughed.

Feeling braver, I prompted, 'But it didn't go well, did it? Today, I mean.'

Rollo looked puzzled. 'I don't quite follow you.'

'You had to sit late. So it can't have gone smoothly, can it?'

He smiled sadly. 'I can see why my son had such a penchant for you. Clever girl.'

The past tense was a hammer blow. As for the rest . . . I dared not look at Shafeen.

'No, it didn't go well,' continued Rollo in answer to my question. 'There was a bill ahead of it on the order paper. That one's on its third reading, and tomorrow it could pass into law.'

'What's the bill?' I asked.

'To ban hunting with hounds entirely.'

'I don't understand,' said Shafeen. 'You can't hunt foxes with hounds at the moment anyway, right?'

'Correct. But you can gather, in the traditional way, with a pack of hounds and have a trail hunt.' Rollo took a gulp of wine. 'One of the hunt servants drags a trail through the woodland for the hounds to follow.'

'With aniseed?' I looked at Nel then. She too was gulping her wine, clearly reliving the time when the hounds had followed her, followed the aniseeds in Henry's jacket pocket. My heart hardened against Henry then.

'Trail hunting usually uses fox urine . . .'

'Lovely,' I said.

'. . . but it's not the same as a real fox,' said Rollo crossly.

'It's not the same,' parroted Caro, a shrill echo.

'I say,' burst out Rollo, cutting across his wife, 'you all seem very much interested in the matter. Why don't you come to see the sitting tomorrow? All of you.'

Shafeen put down his glass. 'We can do that?'

'Naturally. After all, these are the people's laws we are ratifying, and it is your right to bear witness that everything is done with complete probity. It is a very transparent process.'

I looked at Shafeen to see how he was taking this. When the earl described the Lords like that, it sort of made sense. I knew Shafeen well enough to tell that he wasn't convinced, but he was intrigued.

'It's the final sitting of the year before the House rises for Christmas,' said the earl. 'Could be your only chance.' He was very persuasive.

'I'd like to very much,' said Shafeen.

The earl brought his hand down on the table with a crash, clearly delighted. It was as if that tragic little conversation when the countess was out of the room had never happened. The bombast and the slightly too loud voice were back. 'That's settled then,' he barked, smiling. He clearly didn't feel the need to check with the rest of us. 'Wear a jacket and tie and I'll get you in "below the bar" – that's the best bit of the public gallery. Ringside seats, don't you know.' He tossed down the rest of the wine in his glass. 'Come at the end of the session. That's when things should get dashed interesting, if I've got any say in the matter.'

After dessert, the 'ladies' rose to leave the room, presumably to leave the men to talk 'business' over the port. We went to drink coffee and manufacture some extremely awks small talk in the drawing room with the emotionally fragile Countess of Longcross. While smiling and nodding, I was wondering all the time what was happening in the other room. I no longer thought Shafeen would start a fistfight with Rollo though. There had been a sea change – I could smell it hanging in the air, like the lingering aroma of the earl's scent, even when he was in another room.

8

Just as we always used to at Longcross, we gathered in my room to chew things over.

We all sat on my bed – Henry's bed.

'Well,' said Nel, falsely breezy. 'Where to start?'

But we all knew where we would start.

'I suppose that settles it,' said Shafeen, arm about my shoulders. I could swear there was a tinge of relief in his voice. 'Henry's really gone.'

I had to say it out loud. I had to make myself. 'Yes,' I agreed. 'He's dead.' But I couldn't say more than that about Henry just now; I needed to get my own head clear, so I threw them off the scent. 'And how about Rollo taking you for your dad?' I said to Shafeen. 'That was so *weird*.'

'I guess I must look exactly like him. I mean, I know I do; I've seen the photos.'

'It wasn't just that,' I said. 'He thought you *were* him for a minute. It was like he'd seen a ghost.' It was obviously catching. I was glad I wasn't the only one.

'Well, he has lost a son,' said Nel. 'Maybe if Caro's cracking up, Rollo is too. Did you buy all that stuff about him being an ace hunter? Your dad, I mean?'

'I dunno,' said Shafeen. 'I mean, he did used to go tiger hunting at home. And he was pretty effective. But no, I don't really. It's just another form of racism. They see brown skin and think we are all shamans or some mystical bullshit.'

But still, his tone did not have the sting it had before dinner. I had a sudden jag of memory. 'He might be a good hunter though. *You* are.'

'How d'you mean?'

'You're a good hunter too. You tracked Chanel when we were at Longcross. You saw her hair extensions caught on the undergrowth, found her cap.'

Nel looked at Shafeen. Of course, she didn't know this bit. He looked embarrassed and shrugged. 'That's just tracking.'

I said nothing but I thought there might be something in it. Not innate or inherent or whatever the right word was, but just experience. If Aadhish had been brought up hunting tigers in Rajasthan, maybe he HAD developed an instinct. A Bruce Willis Sixth Sense; not for seeing dead things but for seeing live ones.

The recollection of that particular drag hunt brought me back to who we were really dealing with here. 'Whether or not the ability to hunt is inherited, we know that a murderous nature is. We can't forget that Henry was a murderer, and that only came from one place: Daddy.' It suited me to think badly of Henry at that point. It helped me bear the fact that he was gone.

'Well . . .' said Shafeen doubtfully.

'Well, what?' asked Nel.

'In the year we went to Longcross, no one died . . .'

'Not for want of trying,' I said.

'But still. And no one died at Longcross in 1969. My dad was injured. But that's it.'

'Leon Morgan died,' I said doggedly.

'Not at Rollo's hand. The dates don't add up. The good ship *Empire Windrush* docked in 1948, and Leon Morgan, from what you told me, went to Longcross the next year. Rollo is the same age as my dad, so he wouldn't even have been born then.'

'You're making *excuses* for him now?' I was incredulous.

'No,' said Shafeen very definitely. 'What they do at Longcross is abhorrent whether it results in death, or injury, or mental torture. But I think we need to be precise in our language. Neither Rollo nor Henry murdered anyone, as far as we know.'

'So you're letting them off the hook,' concluded Nel.

'On the contrary,' protested Shafeen. 'I want to find out what actually *happened* that weekend when my dad was there, as well as what they're planning for the future. Proof is what we need. Proof, proof, proof.'

'What do you call *this*?' I got up and showed him the pad of my thumb, the **M** brand in his face.

Shafeen drew my thumb to his lips and kissed it very gently. 'I call that circumstantial evidence. We need to catch them in the act. And we won't do that by being hostile. And besides . . .' he got off the bed and walked to the window. The snowy park was now luminous in the moonlight. 'I can't help feeling . . .'

'What?'

'This is going to sound really weird.'

'Go on,' prompted Nel gently.

He turned back to us. 'I feel like . . . like he *loved* my father.'

'That does sound weird,' I agreed. 'Speaking of which, what's all the "Kiss me, Hardy" stuff?'

'Nelson's deathbed. Admiral Lord Horatio Nelson.'

'The guy with the column in Trafalgar Square?'

'The very same – he had this best friend called Captain Hardy. They were devoted to each other, and Hardy was with Nelson when he died. Nelson's last words were "Kiss me, Hardy".

'And did he?'

'I guess.'

I studied him. 'What a lot you know.'

'Come to think of it, my father told me that.'

Nel said, 'But he never told you he called himself Hardy instead of Aadhish?'

'No. I guess he didn't want me to think he isn't proud to be Indian. He is, you know,' he said a little defensively.

Nel and I exchanged a look. 'We believe you,' I said, meaning it.

'It's just camouflage,' explained Shafeen. 'Back then, a lot of immigrants anglicised their names.' He loosened the knot of his tie. 'I can understand it, coming to a school like STAGS, the only brown kid.' I didn't know at that moment whether he was talking about his father or himself. 'He was being Aidan's stag, I guess,' he said sadly, 'making himself invisible.'

'That was my whole evening,' said Nel, lightening the mood. It was a joke, but you could tell she sort of meant it too. 'The earl targeting you, and the countess targeting Greer. I might as well not have been here. I was just the Uber driver.'

'It was kind of rude,' I said. I did think, then, that maybe it had to do with Nel being 'new money'. I remembered that bit in *Emma* when Emma (Gwyneth 'Goop' Paltrow) is talking about the Martin family and saying that she never has anything to do with the yeomanry, because the middle classes were as much above her notice as below it. I guessed what she meant – Emma, I mean – is that the rich only really take notice of people who are on their level (Shafeen) or properly poor (me). Middle-class folks with oodles of money just weren't on their radar.

I didn't say anything to Nel but put my arm around her reassuringly, although at that time I had little comfort to give. She shrugged under the arm. '*Some* people see me,' she said wistfully. But before I could ask who she meant, she changed the subject entirely. 'So. We're going to do this thing tomorrow? Check out the House of Lords?'

'*Hell* yes,' said Shafeen. He seemed keener than all of us. 'It's clearly no coincidence that Ty asks about foxes at the very moment that the earl is knee-deep in this foxhunting debate. I want to know what he's up to.' But there it was again, that change in his voice. He wasn't the Shafeen that had come raging up the stairs earlier, talking about unelected representatives. His hatred now seemed blunted – it was more like he was talking about a naughty child than a homicidal maniac.

'And what *about* all that House of Lords business?' I mused. 'What's going on there?'

'Well, he's obviously a man who doesn't like to be crossed,' said Shafeen, 'and he's going to try to block the legislation somehow.'

'But a lot of it was crap,' said Nel savagely.

'Do you mean the "fox doesn't feel pain" bit?' asked Shafeen, doing a passable Rollo impression.

'Yes, that, obviously,' I said, 'but also, are we really buying the story that they are only drag hunting?'

'No,' said Nel, who had been tapping away at her phone. 'It's totally a cover.' She held out the Saros.

I took the phone from her hand. She'd found an article in the *Independent* online. The headline shouted: DON'T BE FOOLED BY BOXING DAY TRAIL HUNTS – THEY'RE JUST AS CRUEL AS ILLEGAL ANIMAL HUNTING. The subheader below read: *When 'lethal' hunting was banned, trail hunting was invented, which still allows foxes to be slaughtered but claims it's an accident.*

I scanned the article, then passed it to Shafeen. Hunts were gathering legally for a trail hunt, and then the hounds would 'accidentally' follow the trail of a real fox instead, and, of course, once their blood was up, they couldn't be prevented from tearing the fox to pieces.

'That's the point of using fox urine for the trail, you see,' said Nel. 'It's the perfect cover. They can't expect the hounds to differentiate between the fox urine laid for the trail and the scent of a real, living, running fox. They can plead to protesters and the police that they are trail hunting, even if they're really hunting live foxes all along.'

'But if the law makes *all* hunting with hounds illegal, even trail hunting,' Shafeen finished, 'then they can't even gather a certain number of dogs together, and there's no opportunity to ride around in their fancy pink coats.'

I yawned hugely. 'OK, well, we'll learn more tomorrow. Let's hit the hay.' It had been a lot, this evening, a lot to process, and I was exhausted.

But when they got up to go I remembered the fox heads. 'Wait a sec,' I said, and led Shafeen and Nel over to the fireplace. This time, when I stood on tiptoe, I tried to read the little bronze plaque below the fox mask, but it was too high up. I grabbed my phone from the mantelpiece, zoomed in and took a picture.

We all peered at the phone and I pinched the photo to enlarge the plaque. It said:

Reynard
Michaelmas Justitium
2008

That date meant nothing to me. 'Funny that they named him,' I said. 'Poor Reynard.'

'That's a fairly recent kill – 2008,' said Shafeen.

'Well after the ban as well. I guess he must have been an "accidental kill",' said Nel with heavy irony.

'OK,' I said to Shafeen, 'let's do yours.'

Shafeen's room was as neat as ever, with the twin masculine smells of deodorant and aftershave. Above the mantel, in the same position as mine, was Shafeen's fox head. His was more grizzled and faded, seeming much older, and had a distinctive black snout. I took a pic in the same way and we examined it. This plaque said:

Reynard
Michaelmas Justitium
1969

'Reynard as well,' Nel observed.

It wasn't the name but the date that struck me though. I stared at it until the photo blurred. 'Justitium *1969*,' I breathed. I let Shafeen say it.

And he did. 'This fox was caught when my dad was at Longcross.'

'Do you think your father helped to catch him?' asked Nel. 'You know, all that mystical stuff about *nothing could hide from him* – d'you think he helped run this fox to ground?'

'I don't know,' said Shafeen, sounding troubled.

But I was caught in another memory – Henry on the rooftop, and a midnight vixen frozen in a photo moment on the lawn. *We don't foxhunt at Longcross*. But they had done in the past – 1969, 2008. And now the earl was trying to bring back the practice and was being thwarted. And I sensed that Rollo was not a man who liked being thwarted.

9

We all said goodnight, then Nel and I went back to our rooms.

There was no question, now, of Shafeen staying with me – it seemed disrespectful in so many ways. If we were going to take things to the next level, this was not the place. Henry's ghost had this one final power over us.

I felt Henry's presence keenly as I undressed. I kept bits of me covered as I changed, like you do in a communal changing room. I sat down on the bed in my PJs and updated Ty on the events of the night.

> The earl is into some debate on foxes in the
> House of Lords. Gonna go watch tomorrow

Then:

> Also there's this fox head on the wall in
> my room (H's old room), and another one in
> Shaf's room. Here's the pics.

I sent the two photos, then typed:

They're both called Reynard. Junior and
senior, LOL. D'you think these could be the
foxes you heard about??

I waited for a moment or two, staring at the two black stag antlers on a white ground in **mrs_de_warlencourt**'s Instagram profile, willing her to answer, but there was no reply.

I settled myself into bed and looked Reynard Junior in the face. Once again, I contrasted the fox's expression with that of the peaceful, cow-eyed Jeffrey, hanging placidly on my wall in Longcross. Jeffrey looked like he'd stuck his head casually through the wall, looking for snacks. Reynard was different. He looked like he'd run through the wall, escaping the hounds of hell. He wore the last – the very last – desperate expression of a dying fox being torn limb from limb. He must have made a peculiar and savage companion for a small boy. Henry had dropped some dark hints to me about a difficult childhood. Now I knew he was dead, I wasn't ready to forgive but I was beginning to understand.

And, just as little Henry de Warlencourt must have done, I watched that snarling, foxy face until I went to sleep.

PART 4
SOUND

10

I heard the sound in the dead of night.

A tiny shriek of metal on metal. It was enough to bring me swimming up from the depths of deep sleep to the shallows of wakefulness.

It stopped, and I turned on my pillow.

Then it started again.

I opened my eyes. I was facing the door and I saw the handle begin to turn, a tiny, tiny amount at a time, so slowly I wondered if I was seeing things. I sat up silently, heart thumping, feeling like the hapless heroine of *Rebecca* or something equally Gothic. I watched, wide-eyed with dread. It was definitely moving. Then the door opened slightly, creating a slice of light from the passageway, widening to a slab. A figure, silhouetted against the brightness, slid into my room.

It was Lady de Warlencourt.

I hunched back against my pillows, pulling the bedclothes up under my chin as if that would somehow protect me. What did she want with me? Did she want to talk about Henry, because I didn't think I could stand that. She closed the door nearly all the way behind her, just leaving enough light to illuminate the room.

I wasn't having that, so I clicked on the bedside light. Bad enough being trapped in a room with a woman you hardly knew, without also being trapped in a room with a woman you could hardly see. In the light of the lamp I could see she was wearing a white nightie and dressing gown, and her usually neatly dressed pale hair was everywhere. To add to her ghostly appearance, her skin had a grey sheen to it, and she was mouthing words that sounded like, and meant, nothing. I don't think I'll ever forget the sound of that speech. I couldn't understand a single syllable of it. She seemed to have constructed a whole new language. It sounded almost like an incantation, and I found myself thinking about *The Isle of Dogs* and the enchantress who could raise the dead. But Lady de Warlencourt's face was kind of benign and calm, and seemed to be at peace.

Then I understood.

She was asleep.

Emboldened, I sat up and waved my hand before her face. She didn't flinch and didn't stop mouthing the unintelligible words. She came over to the bedside table and put her hands on the silver-backed monogrammed brushes, rearranging them neatly since Nel and I had disturbed them. Once they were regular as soldiers, she left them alone and turned to the bed. I shrank back on the pillows, watching, waiting. Then something extraordinary happened. She bent and, before I could flinch out of the way, kissed me tenderly on the forehead, lifting my fringe so she could plant her lips there. This was plain weird, and certainly over and above what you'd expect from a hostess. Chocolate on the pillow, fine, but a kiss? Then, and only then, as if the kiss had given her the power of speech, or me the power of understanding, I got what she was saying.

'*I'll save you, darling,*' she said. '*I'll save you.*'

It was the creepiest thing ever. She was looking right at me, telling me that she would save me, like some weird negative of the Child Catcher in *Chitty Chitty Bang Bang*, but dressed in white, not black, and a woman instead of a man. Then I corrected myself. She was looking in my direction, but she wasn't looking at me, she was looking *through* me.

She was, very definitely, talking to Henry.

As she glided out of the room and noiselessly closed the door, I could hardly hear my thoughts over the thumping of my rabbit's heart. The goodnight kiss had been for *him*. The tiptoe visit, the door left open just a chink so the light wouldn't wake her sleeping child, the kiss on the forehead and the stroke of the hair – it must have been a nightly ritual when Henry was sleeping here.

I'll save you, darling. The terrible words meant, I knew, that she would catch Henry when he fell. Wasn't that what a mother should do? Always be there for her child, to pick them up when they fell down, to wipe away tears, to kiss grazed knees, to console and support and cheerlead? I wondered then, with a stab of longing, what it was to have a mother who loved you, who *truly* loved you, and always wanted to be there for you. I couldn't decide at that moment if I felt sorrier for Henry or myself. My mother had chosen to live her life away from me, but he'd had a mother who'd considered him the centre of the universe. But a love that intense had a flip-side now he was gone. What was left was a mother hollowed out by loss and regret. She hadn't been able to save him. She hadn't been there to catch him when he did fall. When it mattered, she'd failed him.

And that, in the moment, was the saddest thing in the world.

11

I was pretty knackered at breakfast the next morning.

You can imagine how hard it was to get back to sleep after a visitation from a sleeping countess.

I now felt properly sorry for her. In the bright morning room where we all met for breakfast, I greeted her ladyship more kindly than I'd spoken to her up to now. I still wasn't sure about Rollo, even though he'd been so nice about 'Hardy', but in this I seemed to have more reservations than Shafeen, who was showing every sign of being won over. He and Nel were down before me, and as I helped myself from the silver plates on the sideboard I watched Shafeen munching toast and talking respectfully to her ladyship about her husband's important duties as a sitting member of the House of Lords. I remembered him, just after Henry's death, saying that Henry's mum might be OK but that his dad was an arsehole. Shafeen might have changed his opinion, but I hadn't. I was definitely Team Caro.

To be fair, she didn't seem at all fazed by her midnight wanderings. True, there were faint violet shadows under those blue and beautiful eyes, but she was pretty chipper and talking away in a breezy fashion about the day ahead. 'I do hope you enjoy the House of Lords,' she said, delicately sipping tea from a china cup. 'It can be terribly tedious sometimes, but Rollo has something up his ermine sleeve, so to speak. He's already breakfasted and gone.'

I'd never heard 'breakfast' used like this before, like it was a verb, but I assumed if someone as posh as Lady de Warlencourt said it, it was legit. As I took my place between Nel and Shafeen, she busily organised us. 'You could have a little promenade around the park after breakfast. It's quite lovely in the snow. And there's lots to see in town. If you aren't going to the House until the afternoon session you could see something in the morning.' She reached for a neat triangle of toast, standing to attention with its identical fellows in a silver rack. 'Rollo's taken the car so I'm afraid you'll have to get a black cab or the Tube.' She gave a little laugh. 'So *long* since I've been on the Tube. Henry buzzes about on it all the time.' Her use of the present tense was as much of a jolt as her husband using the past tense was the night before. 'Jubilee Line, Bates, if memory serves?'

I hadn't even clocked that the butler was in the room, so smooth and silent was he.

'That's right, m'lady,' he said with a slight bow. Today he wore a black jacket with no tails and a black tie instead of a white one. I guessed this was casual dress for him. 'One simply takes the Jubilee Line from Baker Street directly to Westminster.'

'That's right. All the Christmas lights are up in the centre of town – quite jolly really.'

But I wanted to back the truck up. 'Did you say Baker Street?'

Lady de Warlencourt regarded me. 'Yes. It connects Regent's Park and Marylebone.'

I wasn't fussed about the geography. 'You mean, *Sherlock Holmes's* Baker Street?'

She looked amused. 'Well, yes. One can even see his house. Or rather, the house where Sir Arthur Conan Doyle based his novels – 221b.'

Oh, I knew the number all right. I turned to the other two. 'Can we go?'

They looked at each other and shrugged. 'Sure,' said Shafeen. 'Might as well if we're going past it anyway. I never picked you for a Sherlock fan.'

I wasn't. But I had a particular connection to the Great Detective. And the connection was through Henry. How could I forget that conversation about *Sherlock Holmes: A Game of Shadows* at the top of Conrad's Force? Not the best Sherlock Holmes film ever, not even the best Sherlock Holmes film by Guy Ritchie ever. But that had been the last thing we'd ever talked about – Sherlock and Moriarty tipping off the Reichenbach Falls, then Sherlock coming back to Baker Street to type a question mark after 'THE END' in Watson's account of his death.

No, I wasn't a superfan. I'd seen most of the films and read a few of the stories, but the adventure I knew best was *The Empty House*, the story I'd read in the library of Alnwick Cottage Hospital, because it was fresh in my mind. It was the story of Sherlock coming back from the dead. And it was the story Henry had referenced when I'd dreamed of him sitting at my bedside. *Where did Sherlock Holmes go after he fell? 221b Baker Street.* There was no way I was missing that house off today's tourist trek. I felt, in some weird way, that there would be a message for me there, some piece of the puzzle.

12

As we left the house after breakfast, all wrapped up against the cold, I told Shafeen and Nel about Lady de Warlencourt sleepwalking into my room speaking a word salad.

They listened soberly. 'I feel sorry for her,' said Nel.

'Me too,' agreed Shafeen.

'Me three,' I said.

We did have a wander through Regent's Park on the way to Baker Street. Maybe it was the power of suggestion – Lady de Warlencourt had mentioned it last night and this morning, and we felt sorry for her, so we went. It was really beautiful in the snow. We half-heartedly chucked a couple of snowballs, but since we were dressed semi-smartly because of the whole House of Lords thing, we didn't want to get too messed up. We did see a frozen lake with a bunch of very pissed-off geese shuffling about moodily on the ice, a little cafe among the trailing willows and bored yellow pedaloes stacked up until a warmer season. We also saw something else. In the midst of some naked trees, sitting there (literally) chilling, were two statues. One was of a crouching girl.

The other was of a fox.

We went right up close. They weren't actually statues as I'd first thought, but sculptures made of wood. They were in a rough, slightly childish style, with bold lines and chisel marks. The fox was sitting and the girl crouching, and the two figures regarded each other; just a girl and a fox sitting together as if it were the most natural thing in the world. I brushed the snow off the head of the girl.

'She looks like Ty,' said Nel.

'So she *does*,' I agreed. 'And it was Ty who said to find out about foxes.' I remembered with a pang that she still hadn't responded to my Instagram message from last night. 'Could this have something to do with that?'

'Well, if not,' said Shafeen, patting the fox on his snowy head in a friendly manner, 'that's one hell of a coincidence. She obviously meant us to see them.'

'Who? Ty?'

'No, you muppet,' he said fondly. 'Lady de Warlencourt. She seemed pretty keen that we come into the park. She mentioned it last night *and* this morning.'

'Hmm. It's a big place though. She couldn't know we'd necessarily find these guys. They are a bit out of the way.'

'Besides, why would *she* be trying to tell us something?' added Nel.

'Oh, I don't know,' I said. 'Trapped in a loveless marriage to a child-killing tyrant?'

'Again, he didn't *actually* –' began Shafeen.

'I know, I know,' I shut him down. 'Also, what could these two possibly tell us? They're just sculptures.'

'That we're on the right track?' mused Shafeen.

Nel said, 'The track of what?'

'The foxes. Whatever and wherever they are.'

I looked at the fox's pointy face, and the girl's blunt one. 'Come on, I'm freezing. Bye, Ty. Bye, Foxy.'

We left and wandered over two little blue bridges that looked like they'd come off a Chinese willow-pattern plate, then past a vast gold-domed mosque and a twin-towered white palace that would have looked more at home in Rajasthan. 'Bit eclectic this park, isn't it?'

'No,' said Shafeen. 'The theme is the British Empire. So it's utterly consistent. Steal from the best.'

We wound our way down to Baker Street, to find the famous address. When we got there, 221b – *chez* Sherlock – wasn't at all what I'd expected.

It was a modest townhouse with ivy growing up it, a discreet round blue plaque on the wall and a small queue of tourists outside speaking in a babel of languages. I thought it would be some horrible theme park, but it really wasn't. Sure, there was an element of tourist bait. There was the gift shop where you bought your tickets crammed with merch of Benedict Cumberbatch as Sherlock. There was a British Bobby on the door (who spoke with a Spanish accent) and lots of Victorian hats to try on while you were waiting. I brandished a deerstalker at Nel. 'Wanna selfie?'

Nel grabbed her extensions protectively. 'Free head lice?' she said. 'No, thanks.'

Perhaps because of the shop, I expected the house to be tacky, but it was actually really tasteful. Entering the hallway, it genuinely felt like you were going back in time – from Dr

Watson's little brass door plate with his medical credentials, to the friends' two distinctive hats hanging on a wall-mounted hook. Then I choked. Below the two hats hung a black-and-white illustration from *The Strand* magazine. It was of Holmes and Moriarty in hand-to-hand combat at the top of the Reichenbach Falls. I looked at the scratchy print of the two men teetering on the brink, just as Henry and I had done. I swallowed.

Nel pulled at my sleeve. 'Come *on*,' she said. 'There's a traffic jam.'

Conscious suddenly of the crush of Japanese students behind me, I followed Shafeen up the stairs.

On the first floor the study (*in Scarlet*) was pretty authentic too – someone had scoured the Sherlock Holmes books for every little detail of the friends' lives; every mention of the study and the bedrooms had been replicated. Hats, swords, medicines, medals from Afghanistan, the inevitable opium, the mandatory violin.

But I was just as interested in the view from the window. There was only a blank twentieth-century office block opposite, but it had great significance to me. I remembered reading *The Empty House* when I was recovering in hospital, especially the bit where Holmes had watched his own study from the empty house across the street, hour after hour, day after day, before deciding it was time to reveal himself as being still alive. I peered at the blank grey building. That was it – that was where the Empty House of the story would have stood. Today there were no twitching curtains, no twin flashes of binocular lenses, but I had an overwhelming feeling that I was being watched.

On the upper floors of 221b, taste left the building. There

were creepy waxworks which looked like they dated from the 1960s, recreating Holmes's greatest moments. But then, in 'Mrs Hudson's room', I got a shock. There were collected props from the best-known Sherlock stories, and one of them was the head of a huge black dog on the wall.

And underneath, the legend *The Hound of the Baskervilles*. Nel saw it first. 'My God, that looks like . . .'

'. . . Brutus,' I finished.

The face of the snarling black dog took me right back to that night in the subterranean tunnel to Longcross church, when Gamekeeper Perfect's scary hound had chased us down.

'Well, he can't hurt you now,' said Shafeen drily.

The joke helped me calm down. This was just a stupid prop. And *The Hound of the Baskervilles* was a story. It wasn't real. None of it was real. This was the house of someone who didn't exist.

Except.

Something nagged at my memory. I scanned the rest of the room silently, inviting the recollection to reveal itself. And while I read the synopsis of the story underneath that glowering hound's head, a name jumped out at me.

Henry

It was enough to make me read on.

Henry Baskerville, the duo finds out, has arrived in London to take up his post at Baskerville Hall, but he

has already been intimidated by an anonymous note
of warning and, strangely enough, the theft of a shoe.

And, just like that, the memory unlocked.

Something must have shown in my face or my posture,
because both Shafeen and Nel said, 'What?'

I pointed. They both read the label.

'Which bit?' said Shafeen. 'The anonymous note of warning?'

'No,' I breathed. 'The shoe,' I said. 'She lost a shoe.'

'Who did?' quipped Nel. 'Cinderella?'

'No, Ty. And he lost one too.'

'Who is *he*?'

'Henry.'

'De Warlencourt?'

'No,' I said again and pointed. 'Henry Baskerville.'

'I don't get it,' said Shafeen.

I didn't want to talk there, with all the tourists gawping.
I jerked my head at the door and we clattered downstairs,
much to the disgust of the Cumberbitches, who clearly
thought we weren't showing enough reverence for their
idol. We swept past the Spanish-cockney policeman and
out into the cold air.

'OK.' I pulled them both past the now-much-longer queue,
and stopped outside a deli called, inevitably, the Holmes Cafe.

'You remember that first night at Longcross?'

'Which time?' asked Shafeen.

'This year, not last. We were all wearing our fancy-pants
stuff, and Ty had this amazing white satin dress on, and she
teamed it with trainers?'

'Yes,' said Nel. Shafeen said nothing, probably because he wouldn't have noticed if she'd been wearing a bin bag. 'Well,' I said, 'I told her they looked great, and she said a weird thing. She said she hadn't planned to wear them, but that she'd lost one of her evening shoes. Not both. Just one.'

'With you so far.'

'OK, backstory: in the film of *The Hound of the Baskervilles* – got to admit, I've never read the book – Henry Baskerville, the American heir to Baskerville Hall, stays in London before going to the country to collect his inheritance. He stays in a hotel, and those were the days when you used to put your shoes outside the door at night to be cleaned. You know?'

They both nodded.

'So the shoe completely vanishes. Not both, but *one*. Anyway – spoiler alert – it turns out much later that the shoe has been given to the Hound of the Baskervilles to smell so the dog can hunt Sir Henry to his death. Same thing happened with Ty. They didn't use seeds in her pockets, like they did with you, Nel. She wasn't a drag hunt. She was a *human* hunt.'

'Who am I, RuPaul?' protested Nel saltily. 'I wasn't a drag race. I was a *human* hunt too.'

'You know what I mean. They stole her shoe, so that the hounds could smell it and learn *her actual scent*. The game is – literally – a foot.'

'So what are you saying?'

'I'm saying that Ty is in more danger than she thinks she is. I think this is all somehow about *her*.'

They both considered this in silence, as we watched the tourists filing in to the shop for their Holmes-pressos and

Watson-cinos. It was not until we'd started wandering towards the Tube that Shafeen spoke.

'Supposing you're right. And I'm not saying you're not – God knows I've learned that lesson by now. But that was at the beginning of the stay. Now she's with Louis. She might be pretending, but *he's* not. He likes her, and he's Lord de Warlencourt. I think he'll protect her.'

'She never struck me as someone who needs protecting anyway,' said Nel comfortingly.

I remembered Ty, when she'd visited me in hospital, saying: *I'm coming for them, Greer. I'm gonna let slip the dogs of war*. But then Shafeen said, 'Everybody needs protecting,' glancing at me.

'I'm going to call her,' I said decidedly.

'That *will* get her into trouble,' said Nel.

'Text then. Gimme your phone.'

After a year at STAGS I'd got out of the habit of bringing my phone out with me, but Nel, as ever, had hers. She handed it over. I signed in to Instagram and messaged **mrs_de_warlencourt**.

She still hadn't replied to my messages of the previous evening, about the Reynard fox heads. This made me even more uneasy, but I tapped in a new message anyway.

```
Hey - did you ever find your evening shoe?
The one that went missing before our first
dinner at Longcross?
```

I hoped against hope for an instant reply, but there was nothing. 'Check back later,' said Nel, and then we were at the Tube and Ty was forgotten in the palaver of tickets and trains.

PART 5
FOUND
(TALLY HO!)

13

When we emerged from the Tube, Parliament was right on top of us.

I vaguely remembered seeing it on that school trip from Bewley Park all those years ago. Usually things get smaller as you get larger – ever been back to your old primary school and tried sitting on one of the chairs? – but the Houses of Parliament obviously hadn't heard of this rule. It seemed even bigger than I remembered. It was massive and hugely impressive and made me feel weirdly proud. The building itself was mad – there were spires on top of spires, and gargoyles and buttresses like some giant Gothic OD. Iced with dollops of snow, it all looked amazing – cool, Christmassy and totally, totally British.

We wandered along for a bit, taking in the amazing architecture, the heavily armed gates and the statue of some random king on his horse. We looked up at his iron majesty, but his plinth was covered in snow. 'Wonder who he is.'

'Whoever he is,' said Shafeen, 'I bet he was injured in battle and died later from his wounds.'

Nel and I both turned to look at him. 'How on earth,' said Nel, 'do you know that?'

Shafeen grinned. 'There's this urban myth,' he said, 'about equestrian statues. Like a code. If one hoof is raised, the rider was injured in battle and died later. If two hooves are raised, so the horse is rearing, the rider died in battle. And if four hooves are planted on the floor, he lived to conquer.'

'Cool,' I said. We wandered along a bit more, and then back again. Even with our Baker Street detour we had a chunk of time before the parliamentary session. 'What shall we do?' I said. 'Get some lunch?'

'I'm still full of breakfast,' said Nel. 'While we're here, why don't we visit an old friend?'

'Whaddya mean?'

'Ben Jonson,' she said. 'He's buried over there in Westminster Abbey.' She pointed to a white stone church with twin bell towers, which in any other context would be massive but next to this huge citadel of a parliament looked a bit titchy.

'*Is* he?' said Shafeen.

Nel nodded. 'Yup.'

'Then let's go,' I said.

We joined this queue inside the abbey grounds – much, much longer than the one at Baker Street. We felt like proper tourists again as we shuffled in to buy our tickets and guidebook, our eyes adjusting from the bright snowy day outside to the incense-smelling twilight of a church. The smell took me back at once to the chapel at Longcross, but this was a different beast altogether. Beast was right, because being in the abbey felt a bit like being in the belly of some huge animal, with the white buttresses arching above us like a ribcage. There were candles in the gloomy

92

corners, and amazing stained glass splitting the daylight into all its colours.

'OK,' said Shafeen. 'Let's look for Ben.'

I looked doubtful. The place seemed bigger on the inside, and even at approaching-lunchtime the place was packed with tourists. 'Where shall we start?'

Fortunately, Nel seemed to be a bit more clued up. 'Poets' Corner, of course.'

Poets' Corner was easy to find as it was easily the most crowded bit of the crowded abbey. It was also mental. The name was quite misleading, as there were not just poets here but pretty much every famous writer you could think of. Everywhere I looked there were my favourite novelists. (OK, full disclosure: I hadn't exactly *read* all of them, I had at least *heard* of them.)

The Brontës, Dickens, Jane Austen, Lewis Carroll, C. S. Lewis, Rudyard Kipling, they were all here in the writers' Hall of Fame.

Nel turned around 360 degrees on her heels. '*God*, Nathaniel would love this.'

She meant, of course, her uber-crush Abbot Ridley. I hadn't heard her mention him this whole trip, but to be fair we hadn't had any girlie time alone just us two. I imagined that if our original plan had gone ahead – a cosy week in Chester, no horrifying end to the term – we'd have talked of little else. I remembered the kiss she'd given the Abbot in the wings of the De Warlencourt Playhouse, and remembered, too, the feeling of foreboding I'd had even then.

'I mean, all these writers, playwrights,' she qualified. 'It's right up his alley.'

I wondered if Nel was up his alley too. 'Did he say you could call him Nathaniel?' It came out a bit harsher than I meant.

Nel met my eyes. 'No,' she said softly, after a beat. 'But I do. In my head, that is.'

Sensing dangerous ground, I changed the subject. 'D'you think they all come out at night when everybody's gone?' I said, delighted with the idea. 'That would be one hell of a literary salon.'

'They're not *all* buried here, surely,' Nel said.

'I don't think so,' said Shafeen. 'I think these are memorials.'

'Well, Shakespeare's buried in Stratford-upon-Avon for a start,' said Nel, pointing at the bard's memorial, 'so he'd have a bit of a commute.'

'Doesn't seem to bother ghosts,' I said. I knew from experience that spirits could zip about the countryside with no effort at all.

After quite a bit of looking we found the memorial to Ben Jonson, in a gloomy corner perched above what looked like a medieval fire door. The monument was a massive disappointment. I'd identified with Ben all last term. Copying out his lines, I'd almost felt like I was channelling him, and when I'd played Poetaster in *The Isle of Dogs* I'd almost felt like I *was* him, but I felt no connection at all with this slightly pudgy stone effigy. That's probably why I said something so dumb. 'That doesn't look like him at *all*.'

Shafeen actually laughed. 'And how,' he said, 'do you know that?'

'Well, you know, like how I imagined him. And look – they even got his name wrong.'

94

It was true. They'd put an 'h' in Jonson, like the baby wipes I took my make-up off with.

'Like Shafeen said, that's just a memorial,' said Nel. 'That's not actually where he's buried.

'Well, that doesn't count then,' I declared. 'Let's find the actual grave.'

But that was easier said than done. The abbey was literally built on gravestones; they were set into the floor like the most Gothic paving stones ever. It was a vampire's castle, a necropolis. We saw memorials for everyone from Isaac Newton to Stephen Hawking in this giant mall of the dead, but no Ben Jonson. I felt like a crap version of Tom Hanks in *The Da Vinci Code*. His Robert Langdon had found what he wanted in Westminster Abbey right away. We, on the other hand, were not too good at this treasure-hunting lark.

'I'll just google it,' said Nel.

'You can't google in a *church*,' I said, shocked.

'Why not?' she asked.

'Because –' I couldn't actually think of a reason; my Medieval sensibilities just felt it was wrong. In the end I came out with a line from *When Harry Met Sally*. 'Because of *God*.' I looked for back-up. 'Shaf?'

Shafeen shrugged. 'Not my God,' he said to Nel. 'But I suppose Greer's right.'

Nel sighed and put the phone away. 'Fine. Why not ask the guys in red then?'

The guys in red were guides in red clerical gowns. Now, I had not been the biggest fan of red gowns ever since my trial by the Dark Order of the Grand Stag, but even I couldn't be afraid of

95

these characters. They were kind of churchwardens-slash-guides and were kind-looking, elderly, rosy, walking around with soft footsteps, helping dumb tourists like us with our dumb enquiries. The nearest chap was busy, so I looked about for someone else in red.

And that's when I saw it.

It was the figure from my dream.

Someone else in head-to-toe red, but this time a hooded onesie, standing in the middle of the transept, facing away from me. The figure was absolutely still as tourists milled around it, and something about the stance and the stillness gave me a thrill of fear. Wordlessly, as if I was back in the dream that had birthed it, I walked towards the figure.

But, as I started to walk, it did too. I broke into a trot, then a run, and it paced me, staying ahead. My feet pounded the paving slabs that separated me from the dead, and tombs, tapestries and shredded banners of battle flashed past on either side. I pushed past tourists, shoving and shoulder-barging, ignoring all the protests in different languages, and Shafeen and Nel calling *Greer!* as politely as they could from behind me. I followed the figure in red down the transept, round a corner and into the nave. I was pretty sure that running in a church was far more disrespectful than googling, but at that moment I didn't care. I had to see that face.

Suddenly the figure had to push through a guided tour and I was gaining. I shoved my way through the little knot of people listening to their guide in their shared language, reaching my hand out to grasp a handful of red cloth. I swear my fingertips grazed the fabric – the tough utility cloth of a pair of overalls. I had them now. I burst out of the other side of the group to find – nothing.

The figure in red had completely disappeared.

I spun through 360 degrees, just as Nel had done, but instead of wonder I felt only confusion. Where had they gone? The only figures in red that I could see now were the warden types. Mr Onesie had gone.

I looked down in despair, and there, right under my feet, was a black diamond of stone, worked with black lettering. Instantly I forgot the red runner. 'I found it!' I exclaimed – probably a bit too loudly for a church.

Shafeen and Nel caught up with me, breathing heavily. Nel leaned on a pillar and Shafeen doubled over. 'Greer,' he said when he could speak, 'what the *hell*? Why did you just take off like that?'

I didn't feel I could explain about the fox and the dream and the figure in red. So I just grinned cheekily. 'Ta-da!' I said, indicating, with magician hands, the stone beneath my feet. They both gathered around, forgetting to be pissed off.

The stone was a square with sides about the length of a school ruler, hewn out of dark slate and set on its point like a diamond. In the dim transept it would have been easy to miss. We could have walked around that abbey all day and never found it. It occurred to me then that, were it not for the red runner, I might have missed it completely. Was this what they had wanted to show me?

We knelt on the cold stone reverently and took a closer look at the grave. The writing was not that easy to read, seeing as it was carved into black stone, but in the gloom we could just make it out.

O RARE
BEN JOHNSON

'Spelled wrong again, poor fella,' I said sadly. 'And what is that line? *O rare Ben Jonson?* It doesn't make sense. He wasn't rare, he was unique.'

Shafeen said, 'It doesn't look like the right spacing either.' He was right, the O and the RARE were too close together. It looked like they'd just not bothered to get anything right – the spelling, the lettering and certainly not the content.

'You'd think they could have written something better than that,' I said, 'for the grave of someone who was so good with words. You know, used one of his best lines, his greatest hits.' I was getting angrier than I had any right to be, but I felt that it was pretty pathetic for a playwright of Ben's stature. 'It's really small too,' I said. 'Why didn't he get a huge tomb?'

'Well, I won't suggest *googling*,' said Nel testily as we all got to our feet. 'Although, at the end of the day, it's just *reading*. Why it's any different from reading a guidebook, which *everyone* is doing, I don't know.'

Then I realised what I'd been holding in my hand the whole time. The Poets' Corner guidebook they'd given me with the tickets. I waved it. 'Good call, Ms Ashton. It probably says right here.'

I leafed through the glossy book and found the right section. I felt it dissed Ben a bit as he was shoved in with *Shakespeare and Other Elizabethans*. 'Here we go. Oh, this is really *sad*.'

'Go on,' prompted Nel.

'It says here that the Dean of Westminster promised Ben Jonson that he could be buried in the abbey,' I said, 'but Jonson said he was too poor for a normal grave and that two foot square would do for him. That's why he was buried upright.'

I remembered Abbot Ridley saying something about that, when we'd discussed Ben Jonson last term. *Buried standing up.* Suddenly I found that small black diamond of stone incredibly moving. It seemed so tragic that, when other, richer poets could rest in peace on their fat backs, poor Ben had to stand up for all eternity. It was then that I realised I really felt a kinship with the playwright. I had shared more than his work. I had shared his trial. I knelt again and put my thumb on the stone just under his name, the thumb that had been branded just like his. It left no mark, but that didn't matter. I felt that the ghostly Ben Jonson, from that other plane, was reaching up to touch my thumb with his own. Like I was high-fiving the dead.

I stood up to find the other two looking at me with wary concern.

'What now?' asked Shafeen.

The tension needed breaking. I made an attempt at a smile. 'I could really use a burger.'

14

I needed the daylight, and the cold, and that sparkling walk over Westminster Bridge, to bring me back to myself and the realm of the living.

We ate burgers and drank milkshakes on the South Bank, looking at the shimmering winter Thames, and there the talk was all of my interview at Oxford the very next day. It had really crept up on me, what with the play, the hospital stay and the resurrection – or not – of Henry de Warlencourt taking up all the RAM in my brain. The interview was with Professor Nashe, Abbot Ridley's old Oxford tutor, a distinguished scholar who had last seen me hanging from a noose at the close of our performance of *The Isle of Dogs*.

'You'll be *fine*,' said Shafeen.

'Totally,' agreed Nel.

'All very well for you to say,' I grumbled, peeling, as I always did, the sad and soggy lettuce leaf out of my burger. 'Neither of you have had yours yet.'

It was true. Classics and medicine were in January, and personally I thought it was pretty barbaric that English with drama was before Christmas. Nel was comforting. 'She as good as said you'd got in. Professor Nashe, I mean. She said to Nath—Abbot Ridley that she couldn't wait until you went there.' She still couldn't say the Abbot's name without turning pink.

I gave her a stern look. 'Hmm. Getting the grades *might* be OK, unless I completely screw up, but I definitely have to nail the interview.'

'It might help that you saw *him* though.' Nel jerked her head in an across-the-river direction.

'Who?' For a moment I thought she meant Henry.

'Benny-boy. It might help that you, you know, popped in to say hey.'

'She's right, you know,' said Shafeen. 'If nothing else, it's certainly a good opening gambit, especially if Nashe is a world expert on Ben Jonson.'

'Don't you mean "O rare Ben Jonson"?' I finished my milkshake with a slurp of the straw. 'That really was a *shit* line.'

Then Ben Jonson and his standing-up grave and his rubbish epitaph were forgotten, because it was time to walk back over the bridge for the most surreal part of the day – our visit to the House of Lords.

15

It felt pretty special just swanning in to the Houses of Parliament.

After getting past security – Rollo's name was obviously enough to snowplough through any obstacles – we'd passed through a vast room decorated with giant paintings. One of them depicted the Battle of Trafalgar and – whaddya know? – there was old Captain Hardy at the centre of it all, cradling a dying Lord Nelson in his arms and giving him that farewell kiss. Funny how someone tells you something and then that's *all* you see.

Just past the painting were these huge doors into the chamber itself. We were settled in a gallery under an impossibly high gilded ceiling, painted with Tudor roses and Scottish thistles like some sort of expensive inverted garden. Below us were long benches of oxblood leather, crowded with England's nobility talking to each other in a polite murmur. I half expected the Lords to be dressed in robes and ermine like you see on the TV.

They weren't, of course. They were in suits and ties and the women were in sort of smart ladies-who-lunch gear.

The chamber, though, was stunning. At the far end of the room sat a carved golden chair, empty, under an ornate gilded canopy.

There were quite a few other people in the public gallery. Some, I think, were Muggles like us, but others – well, I got a very strong feeling they were journalists. They didn't exactly have notebooks out or PRESS signs stuck into the brims of their hats like in *Bugsy Malone*, but they sort of had an *air* of being journalists, if that makes sense. There was a buzz about the place, like something was about to happen.

I looked down at the chamber. It too was packed, like when two teams everyone cares about are playing a football match. I was on one side of Shafeen, and Nel was on the other, so I could only really talk to him. 'So who *are* all that lot?' I asked out the side of my mouth.

'The Lords? Oh, you know, earls, dukes and the odd viscount.'

I didn't know the difference but it sounded like Shafeen did. So while we were waiting for something to happen I whispered, 'I'm still not totally down with this whole titles thing.'

'What's messing you up?'

'So, Caro is the Countess of Longcross.'

'Yes.'

'So why is Rollo not a count?'

'Because he's an earl.'

'Aaargh. So an earl is married to a countess?'

'Yes.'

'Not a count?'

'No.'

'But there are counts.'

'Only abroad. We have viscounts here.'

'And where do they come in?'

'Above barons.'

'Is Rollo a baron?'

'No. He's an earl.'

'And you call him Earl to his face?'

'No. You call him Lord Longcross. And Caro's Lady Longcross.'

'I've been calling her Lady de Warlencourt.'

'I know.'

'Thanks for the heads-up.'

'Consider *this* the heads-up.'

I thought for a moment. 'Why *isn't* Rollo Lord de Warlencourt?'

'Because that's Louis. As the heir apparent, he takes the subsidiary title of the earl.'

'I give up.'

I went back to watching the proceedings below. Something was happening at last. A man dressed in black came into the chamber carrying a long golden sceptre thingy. Then a grey-haired bloke who resembled a heron processed into the room, wearing a long black robe. You could just tell by his bearing that he was the boss, so I expected him to sit in the golden carved chair, but he bypassed that and sat on a huge overstuffed red cushiony thing. The golden sceptre was laid there too. I bent to Shafeen's ear. 'Why's he on the sofa?'

'The Woolsack,' he corrected. 'That's the Lord Speaker's ceremonial seat.'

'Doesn't he sit in the fancy chair?'

He looked amused. 'That's not a chair. That's a throne.'

I gulped. 'The queen's coming?'

He smiled. 'Not today, sorry. Only on ceremonial occasions.'

I stared at the throne. I was in a room where the queen had sat. Me, Greer MacDonald. This definitely wasn't Kansas any more.

Even *sans* Queenie there was plenty of pomp and ceremony and arcane language going on, and something about the gathering, the grown-up-ness and tradition and ceremony of it, recalled my trial to me in a sweaty, damp-palmed panic. I clasped my branded thumb in my other hand as a horrid thought jolted me. Had Rollo, sitting calmly in his place somewhere far below, been in that ghastly circle of red-cowled Grand Stags? If he had invited the Abbot and the Friars to Longcross in 1969, along with 'Hardy', and if the Old Abbot had been the one to try me, had Rollo de Warlencourt been there too? And even if he hadn't been there, as part of the Dark Order he would know that I was guilty, and if that was so, why was he treating his son's manslayer as an honoured guest and why was his wife treating me as 'practically part of the family'?

But I couldn't say anything to the others right then. The Lord Speaker was getting to his feet, and everyone shut up to listen.

His elderly but carrying voice floated up to us. 'My Lords. The proposition to put to the House to vote, in this, our last session before the Christmas recess, is as follows: that any gathering of hounds with the intent to hunt a living animal *or* follow an artificially laid trail shall be absolutely prohibited.'

He consulted the notes in his hand over his half-moon specs. 'This proposition, entitled the Hunting with Hounds Bill, is on its third reading, and if carried this day will duly pass into law, and be written into the statute books, to be followed on the pain of prosecution.' He looked out at the gathered peers. 'Before we put the proposition to the vote, we will hear the Honourable Members debate the bill for the final time. First, the Honourable Lord Longcross, Rollo de Warlencourt.'

Rollo got to his feet and I looked down at him objectively, as others must see him. He cut an impressive figure – tall and slim, in his impeccably cut navy suit, the silver-blond hair brushed back from the noble brow. He had a slim book in his hands, and as all eyes turned to him I wondered what on earth was coming. The whole chamber fell quiet, and there was a huge air of expectation among that little group I'd already identified as 'press'.

But if I'd thought pretty hard with every brain cell I had for a million years, I could never have accurately guessed what Rollo de Warlencourt was going to say.

The meet was at 'The Cock and Pye
By Charles and Martha Enderby,'
The grey, three-hundred-year-old inn
Long since the haunt of Benjamin
The highwayman, who rode the bay.
The tavern fronts the coaching way,
The mail changed horses there of old.
It has a strip of grassy mould
In front of it, a broad green strip.

A trough, where horses' muzzles dip,
Stands opposite the tavern front,
And there that morning came the hunt,
To fill that quiet width of road
As full of men as Framilode
Is full of sea when tide is in.

There was a murmur around the chamber, and Shafeen, Nel and I exchanged a look. What the *hell*?

Rollo was clearly reciting some sort of poem from the book that he held, but why? Was he trying to make some comment about hunting, and his right to continue? I waited for him to stop quoting and explain his point. But the earl didn't stop.

Of horses' stables and the savour
Of saddle-paste and polish spirit
Which put the gleam on flap and tirrit.
The grooms in shirts with rolled-up sleeves,
Belted by girths of coloured weaves,
Groomed the clipped hunters in their stalls.

He just went on. And on. Not hurrying; in fact, quite the opposite – he was, if anything, talking deliberately slowly. Five minutes, ten minutes. The poem was naming every kind of person that had ever been on a hunt – a soldier, a doctor, a parson, a farmer on his big-boned shire – everyone was described in minute detail. Fifteen minutes, and some distant parliamentary clock chimed the quarter. Twenty minutes. I started to think that he wasn't just reading a poem from the book; he was reading out the whole *thing*. People started shuffling in their seats. My mind wandering, I let my eyes wander too, from the church-like stained-glass windows, with the night falling outside of them, to the incredible lit interior of the golden ceiling. Thirty minutes, and the earl was still going. I had never been so bored in my life. I turned to Shafeen and mimed a discreet yawn, and he gave a little nod. Looking at the age of some of the Members of the House, I thought there was a very real risk that some of them would go to sleep. I reckoned that even the queen, had she been there, would have dropped off too, on her gilded throne.

Wind-bitten beech with badger barrows,
Where brocks eat wasp-grubs with their marrows,
And foxes lie on short-grassed turf . . .

Suddenly I sat up. Had I imagined it or had Rollo just said *foxes*? I started paying closer attention.

Nose between paws, to hear the surf
Of wind in the beeches drowsily.
There was our fox bred lustily
Three years before, and there he berthed
Under the beech-roots snugly earthed.

Still the earl talked. But now I was spellbound. I couldn't have slept if someone had knocked me out with a frying pan. I wanted to know what happened to the fox. Just as in my dream, I kept pace with the creature's every footstep, as Rollo narrated how the horses and hounds chased him relentlessly across the English countryside.

The taint of fox was rank on the air,
He knew, as he ran, there were foxes there.
His strength was broken, his heart was bursting,
His bones were rotten, his throat was thirsting,
His feet were reeling, his brush was thick
From dragging the mud, and his brain was sick.

Go on, I willed the fox, as I had once tried to will a stag to safety. *Run. Get Away.*

He thought as he ran of his old delight
In the wood in the moon in an April night,
His happy hunting, his winter loving,
The smells of things in the midnight roving;
The look of his dainty-nosing, red
Clean-felled dam with her footpad's tread,
Of his sire, so swift, so game, so cunning
With craft in his brain and power of running,
Their fights of old when his teeth drew blood.
Now he was sick, with his coat all mud.

I felt the sickness too, the sick dread of the fox's inevitable end. And when it came, Rollo had everyone's attention. The dozing peers woke, the press leaned forward, the speaker turned his heron's head.

The beech wood grey rose dim in the night
With moonlight fallen in pools of light,
The long-dead leaves on the ground were rimed.
A clock struck twelve and the church bells chimed.

And, incredibly, it was over. Rollo stopped speaking for the first time in God knew how long, and into the silence, the clock, nestled somewhere in those stone spires and pinnacles above, chimed the hour. As in *Cinderella*, the slipper fell and the world was changed. The winter meadows disappeared and I was back in the gold-and-scarlet chamber. The two peers either side of Rollo leaned forward, looked at each other and gave a very definite nod. I was just wondering what they were signalling about when the Lord Speaker rose, and the Earl of Longcross, clearly exhausted, almost fell back into his seat.

'My Lords,' said the Speaker, with this strange tone to his voice, half amused, half exasperated, 'I thank the noble lord for his –' he raised one grey eyebrow – 'remarks. Sadly, our time has run out and our session is at an end. The Hunting with Hounds Bill will be suspended until we may take a vote at our first session in the New Year. We now recess for Christmas, and I wish you all the compliments of the season. All rise.'

16

We waited for Rollo outside the ornate door to the chamber, watching the peers stream out into the lobby.

Some looked furious, but some were laughing. Many of them looked pretty relieved, and more than that – triumphant. If they weren't, well, Lords and Ladies and stuff, I got the feeling they'd be high-fiving each other. But I guessed the nobility didn't high-five.

The earl was all swagger when he bounced out of the chamber. He shook Shafeen warmly by the hand and kissed me on the cheeks, and then even kissed Nel. He rubbed his hands together until the knuckles cracked. 'Well,' he chuckled, '*that's* shot their fox for them. Jolly good day's work.'

'What was good about it? You stopped any work being done.' Nel sounded pretty pointed, but you couldn't deny the truth of what she'd said. The earl didn't seem to mind though – he was so buoyant that nothing could prick the balloon of his self-confidence. 'We don't sit again until 20th January. It will be too late for them to stop it by then.'

'Stop what?' I asked.

'The Boxing Day meet at Longcross of course. What the devil d'ye think this was all about?'

Of *course*. The earl had wanted to block the bill so that he could have his big Boxing Day hunt – the one that Cass had spoken of. He'd talked and talked until the time to debate the bill had run out, forcing a delay until after Christmas.

'But you still can't hunt *foxes*, can you?' I said.

'Not yet. But as I told you at dinner, alternative arrangements can be made. The main thing is, it is still legal to gather with a pack of hounds. We'll have a trail hunt on Boxing Day and next year . . . well, we'll see. Now – come with me. Let me show you the Members' Bar.' He practically skipped up the stairs, and we followed him. I felt pretty conspicuous being in his team – all eyes were on us as we entered this fancy upstairs dining room. Huge portraits hung on walls papered with gold filigree, and even their subjects seemed to look down on the earl with approval. I wasn't at all sure I wanted to share in his reflected glory, but Rollo was unstoppable. 'Just one G&T to celebrate,' he declared, 'and then we must get home to the old gal for our nosebag.'

As the hero of the hour, Rollo was given the best table, and as we all settled in overstuffed chairs overlooking a wintry River Thames, Shafeen said, 'This isn't just about being allowed to gather with hounds, is it, sir?'

'Of course not, my boy. It's about getting our rights back. Our God-given right to hunt our own foxes on our own land.'

After two years of STAGS I knew the Bible pretty well, but I must have skipped the part where it said that it was OK to hunt foxes.

'Tradition, my boy. Tradition!' Rollo knocked on the table to emphasise his point, making the waiter who was putting down our drinks jump a little. 'One can't put a price on it. One has to stand up to these bleeding-heart liberals and animal-rights crackpots. With enough support, we'll repeal the fox-hunting ban entirely. I've entered a bill for a first reading early next year. And then we're home and dry.'

'How can you be sure you'll get the support?' I asked curiously.

'Oh, we'll get the support,' he said confidently.

He was right. Everyone he greeted said, *See you on Boxing Day, old chap*, or, *See you at the meet, old boy*. Most of them asked to be remembered to Caro. It was just one big club. One old dude even said, 'Haven't heard that poem for *years*. Used to recite it at school, d'you remember?' Which meant that the old dude in question clearly went to STAGS.

'What *was* that poem?' I asked, curious. 'It must be the longest one in the world to take that long to read aloud.'

'Oh, it is. Well, you saw. It's the length of a novella. The Friars used to make us learn great swathes of it by heart. And if you got a word wrong, they'd wallop you with the cane.'

I swallowed. The Friars were obviously a lot more hardcore in Rollo's day.

'I loved it though. Still my favourite poem, in fact. By John Masefield, you know.'

I didn't. 'What's it called?'

'*Reynard the Fox.*'

Then he turned to talk to the next sprig of English nobility to drop by, and I was left to appreciate the irony that the fox heads in mine and Shafeen's rooms were clearly named after

113

the very poem that Rollo had just used as a device to bring back fox hunting.

I badly wanted to talk to the others, but there was no opportunity for any privacy. I had no choice but to sort through my own thoughts. They were pretty muddled, but one thing was clear. Rollo's plan was to bring all his noble buddies to Longcross to be wined and dined and treated like the royalty some of them undoubtedly were. The ones who didn't love hunting yet were sure as hell going to love it by New Year. And then, you could bet all the gold in the House of Lords that fox hunting would be making a comeback.

I wasn't sure if it was the gin or that thought that was making me feel a bit sick.

17

At dinner the Earl of Longcross was cock of the walk, boss of the town, king of the hill.

Caro fluttered and flattered around him, and he positively lapped up the attention – they were behaving like newlyweds. The food, of course, was amazing and the talk was all of hunting – having stopped the total ban, Rollo was excitedly gearing up for his big Boxing Day meet.

'Full regalia, old thing, full regalia,' he kept saying to his wife, as he forked up the fancy tartlet we'd been served as a starter.

I thought he meant at the House of Lords. 'But you weren't in the furry robes. Today, I mean.'

'No, not in the *House*. Full regalia at the *meet*. Proper field dress. No tweeds, no ratcatchers. In the pink, my dear. In the pink!'

I twigged. He meant everyone at the Boxing Day meet had to be in those red coats. When I'd first gone to STAGS I thought those red coats people wore out hunting were called . . . well, red. Since then, I'd learned that they were known as hunting pink. Now was the time to ask. 'Why *are* those coats called pink?'

'There was an eighteenth-century London tailor called Mr Pink,' said Rollo. 'He made the classic hunting coat. So nothing to do with the colour at all, really.'

'Henry looks wonderful in his hunting togs,' said Caro dreamily, out of nowhere. 'He'll look magnificent on Boxing Day.'

Of course there was nothing anyone could say to that. Rollo and Bates exchanged a look, and we all stared down at our plates. 'Your father too,' said the earl to Shafeen. 'Mowgli looked top-hole in the coat.'

'My dear,' chided Caro gently.

'Quite right. Mustn't keep calling him that. Not quite the ticket in this day and age, eh?'

Or any day and age, I would have thought.

'Hardy, I mean.' It was almost laughable that he still hadn't got the name right, preferring to give Shafeen's father yet another name of Rollo's own choosing. But we didn't laugh. 'Looked dashed handsome in that colour. In the pink, one might say.' Rollo chuckled at his own joke.

Shafeen lined up his already dead-straight cutlery. 'So you *did* ride to hounds when he was at Longcross?'

'Of course,' said Rollo. 'Different times then. None of this animal-rights rubbish. That's when we nabbed that fierce little bugger on your wall.'

'Reynard,' I said. 'Like the one in the poem.'

'Clever girl,' Rollo said approvingly. 'That's right. We were doing it at school, I remember. Our English Friar made us damn near recite it by heart. We all moaned at the time, as one does, but I'm jolly glad now. Ripping poem, that.' I couldn't disagree with him there. I remembered the excitement of hearing him recount it in the ancient chamber, willing Reynard on, wanting to know what happened next.

'Meet after meet we had him on the run. But he always got away.'

'What changed?' asked Shafeen.

Rollo gave a little bark of laughter, foxlike himself. 'Your father, that's what.' He took a mouthful of blood-red port. 'In '69, we had Mowgli with us. He was the secret weapon, what?'

Shafeen leaned forward, an oddly intent look on his face. 'Could you tell us, sir, a little of what happened?'

Rollo wiped his mouth on his napkin, leaving a red-wine stain as if his lips bled. In answer, he addressed not Shafeen but the butler. 'Bates,' he barked. 'A bottle of the Veuve Clicquot '84. We're celebrating.'

The butler bent slightly in a bow. 'The '84, my lord. Very good,' and he melted away. I wasn't sure Rollo had even heard Shafeen's entreaty, but as soon as the door closed, he put his elbows on the table and clasped his hands together like he was telling a story. We all leaned in – it seemed the right thing to do.

'We'd been after this fox for a few seasons. Five years old, we reckoned, by his teeth when we finally nabbed him. Always the same little bugger with a black snout. Fast as you like. Led the hounds a merry dance. Sometimes we'd see him stop on the hill, let them catch up – freeze for a second like he was posing for a bloody photo. Then he'd vanish like a ghost.'

'We?'

'The other Medievals of my year. Miranda, Charlie, Serena, Francesca. All of them ended up teaching at the school. And

Gideon, of course, became the Abbot.' He checked himself, as if he'd remembered something. 'May he rest in peace.'

That blessing came a bit late, I thought. Was the Abbot really dead or not? If he was, how could he have tried and branded me? By habit I rubbed my middle finger on my thumb. I wished people would decide if they were one thing or the other.

'So of course it became a thing. By that Justitium weekend we were champing at the bit to catch him. And that's when we brought old Mow— Hardy along.'

Everyone was silent, rapt, listening to the story like kids at bedtime. For the second time that day the Earl of Longcross had a room in his thrall, hanging on his every word.

'Well, Hardy was a game-changer. He said he wanted to look at the fox. Look him in the eyes. He said we should give him a name, and that's how we'd get him. So we decided on Reynard, because we'd been doing the Masefield poem at school, and took Hardy out cubbing. Let the dog see the rabbit, you know?'

Now I was really lost. Rabbits? I needed some exposition. First things first. 'What's cubbing?'

'It's something you do before the hunt proper. You take the hounds to the covert where you'll be hoping to hunt.' Rollo began to rearrange the place setting in front of him. He pushed his plate away and put a small silver salt cellar before him – presumably to represent the fox. Then he encircled it with six crystal glasses (all empty – Bates was sure taking his time with that champagne). 'You let the hounds get used to the smell of the foxes, teach them not to get distracted by the smell of hares or ferrets or the like. And if you see any grown foxes –' he moved the salt cellar to the edge of the circle – 'you turn 'em back so they'll give you a good run on the meet day.' He nudged the salt cellar with the nearest glass, making a clinking sound. The salt fell over, bleeding whitely onto the tablecloth. I remembered, fleetingly, that to spill salt was unlucky. 'We thought we'd have to teach Hardy to ride, but no.' Rollo glanced at Shafeen. 'Wonderful seat your father had.'

For a surreal moment I actually wondered if Rollo was complimenting Aadhish's bum.

'It means he can ride,' murmured Shafeen in a whispered aside. 'Yes,' he said louder to Rollo, 'he's been riding since the day he could cling onto a mane.'

'One could tell. Anyway, we went into Longwood to turn the foxes back. I knew Reynard would show his pointy little face. So we surrounded the covert and waited. I remember it was a foul day, rain dripping from the trees, collars up, all waiting. Well, we all started complaining, moaning about the cold and wet. Not your father. He was silent as the grave.'

We were silent too, even Caro, entranced, listening.

'We'd put him on a horse called Satan. He was a devil by name and by nature, jittery bugger, big as a house, would take off if you so much as snapped a twig. But even old Satan was still, four feet to the ground. They looked like one of those old statues – you know?'

We did. I remembered our conversation from that morning. Four feet to the floor meant the rider lived to conquer.

'Seemed like hours we waited. We saw a few young cubs and let the hounds chase them away, but there was no sign of Reynard. I was about to call the whole thing off – couldn't feel my fingers on the reins – when damn me if he wasn't there. Little triangle face, black snout.

'He saw us at once and was about to slide away when he sort of checked himself. He just stopped, like he used to do on the hill, one foot up. And he was looking at your father.'

'What do you mean?' asked Shafeen softly.

'He was looking at Hardy, and Hardy was looking at him. I'll go to my grave swearing they were . . . well . . . *communicating* with each other. It went on for quite a few heartbeats. None of us could move, even the hounds.'

'And?' prompted Shafeen.

'Then your father gave a sort of tiny nod – without breaking eye contact, you know – and Reynard just . . . *went*. He buggered off – slid past us in the undergrowth like a shadow. It was like he'd been given permission to go.' Rollo shook his head, as if dislodging the memory. 'It was a dashed queer thing.'

For a moment no one spoke. Then it was Nel who said, 'What happened next?'

'Well, not to put too fine a point on it, I was bloody furious. We'd been after Reynard for years, and we wanted to make a run for him the next day at the meet. Hardy should've turned him back, but he just let him go.' Rollo, to this day, still sounded angry, but then seemed to relent. 'He didn't know the form, to be fair on him. Got confused by the name "cubbing". He thought it meant one had to turn back the tiny ones, the little balls of fluff, you know. But, by God, he knew his error after that.' Rollo twirled his glass in his hand – the champagne still hadn't come. 'We were a tiny bit beastly to him that night if I'm honest. I don't think he had a very jolly time of it.'

Shafeen put down his own glass sharply. 'What did you do to him?' he asked, in a dangerously quiet voice.

'Nothing, nothing,' laughed Rollo dismissively. 'Just joshing. Only sport. Boys will be boys, you know. Anyway, it all came good because you should've seen him the next day at the hunt. Like a different chap, he was.'

'What happened?' I asked.

'Well, come morning we took the hounds out and went after Reynard. Hardy was at the front, leading the field. Like the bloody Charge of the Light Brigade, it was. Never seen such a thruster. Popped over every five-bar gate like it was nothing. And we were always one step ahead of Reynard. Cut him off at every covert, every spinney, every ditch. It was like they were playing chess and Hardy was always one move ahead. We cornered Reynard in a valley on the far side of Longwood.'

Into the Valley of the Shadow of Death, I thought.

'That's when we got him. One last check, where he looked at us all. He knew he was finished. Brave little sod – he snarled at us right at the end.'

I knew the expression well – Reynard had snarled at me like that from the wall.

'Then the hounds took him limb from limb. They were in such a riot Perfect had to whip them off.'

It was an oddly brutal thing to be discussing at dinner, especially as at that moment we were tucking into some pretty pink-looking roast beef. I pushed mine away.

'Then we blooded Hardy, of course. After all, it was him who'd caught the fellow really.'

121

Now I sat up. Here it was. We were getting, at last, to the meat of what had happened in 1969. Why Aadhish had appeared in that black morocco leather-game book.

'*Bloodied* him?' I asked.

'No, my dear. Blood-ED. Somebody – usually the Master of Foxhounds, but that day there were only a few of us – takes a little of the fox's blood and dabs it on the new hunter's forehead. Right between the eyes.' He turned to Shafeen. 'Your lot do that anyway, don't you? Sikhs and whatnot? You know, the little red dot? He must've been used to it.'

Shafeen's face went still. 'I think you're referring to the Hindus, sir,' he said tightly.

Rollo didn't even acknowledge the reproach. 'We offered him the mask, of course.'

'The mask?' queried Nel.

'The fox's head. Perfect clipped it off for Hardy.' That repellant phrase conjured up the incident horribly – young Perfect, no doubt tall as a sapling already, shearing off brave Reynard's head where he lay stretched out, a smear of red on the winter grass. Where had I imagined that before?

'But he didn't want the mask. Hardy, I mean. Seemed dashed sorry for Reynard in the end. So I had it mounted and put it in my room.'

I sat back in my chair and considered what we'd been told. None of this explained why Aadhish was in the game book. Huntin' shootin' fishin' was how it went on Justitium weekend. Aadhish had been listed on the pheasant page, so he must have been shot, just like Shafeen. When? And why?

But I couldn't think about that just then. It was getting

late, and I was conscious of the drive to Oxford the next day. Suddenly exhausted, I couldn't face the thought of dessert, then coffee, then port, standing like five-bar gates between me and bed. I put my stiff linen napkin on the table and tried to think of the right words. 'Might I be excused?' I asked, channelling *Downton Abbey*. 'I have my Oxford interview tomorrow.'

Rollo looked up. 'Ah. I'm afraid I'll be needing the car – day at my club, you know. But one can easily train it from Marylebone.'

Nel, the Uber driver, said drily, 'I'm taking her.'

Rollo turned to Shafeen. 'And what about you, old chap? You could come along to the club with me.'

I'd sort of taken it for granted that Shafeen would be coming with me to Oxford, but I didn't protest. I didn't want to be *that* sort of girlfriend.

'What club?' Shafeen asked curiously.

'Why, the STAGS Club of course.'

'There's a *club*?' I exclaimed before I could stop myself.

'Of course. The alumni of the school, and any other decent chaps who've been nominated by a STAG. Fellows from the city, politics, the media. That sort of thing.' Rollo looked back at Shafeen. 'Ideal opportunity to come along if the ladies are in Oxford.'

'Why?' asked Shafeen.

'It's Stags only, don't you know. No Does. No women allowed.'

'Wow,' said Nel to no one in particular.

But Rollo didn't notice. He got all misty-eyed. 'I never got to take Mowgli. Hardy, I mean. Sad thing, really. He would've loved it.'

Shafeen looked at me, and to my surprise he said, 'If you don't mind?'

I shrugged. 'Sure, why not?' I was fine with it. I really was. No one was going to make me feel less nervous about the interview, and if Shafeen could get closer to Rollo and find out what went on inside the STAGS Club, that could only be a good thing. Besides, I could see he wanted to go. This was something his father had never done, an inner sanctum to which Aadhish had never been admitted. I was not about to stop him going.

Rollo watched us both. 'Here's a compromise. Women *are* allowed in the dining rooms, so why don't you ladies join us for dinner when you get back from Oxford? It's in St James's. You can drop off that jolly little Mini here and get on the Tube to Green Park, what?'

I looked at Nel and she nodded. 'Sounds like a plan.'

Still in *Downton* mode, I felt vaguely that we ought to express our gratitude for all this hospitality. 'Thanks very much, by the way,' I said clumsily as I got to my feet. 'For, you know, everything.' I sort of tailed off.

Rollo, who'd sprung to his feet as soon as my butt had left the chair, bowed his head gallantly. Then he studied me, his eyes curiously bright. 'Any friend of Henry's,' he said, 'is a friend of ours.'

It was uttered with great chivalry. But as I mounted the carpeted stairs I turned the phrase over in my mind. I wasn't thinking about the gallantry then, but the implied threat.

How welcome would we be if we were no longer friends of Henry's?

18

Back in Henry's room, I went up to Reynard Junior before I'd even kicked off my shoes.

I looked at the fox mask in a new way that night. I was no longer afraid of him. *He* was afraid of *me*. A word of Rollo's came to mind. 'You poor bastard,' I said.

I took off my make-up and just before I got into Henry's bed I hesitated in front of the closed door.

I couldn't decide whether to lock it and risk Lady Longcross trying to get in (do sleepwalkers get angry? I didn't want her doing a Jack Torrance in *The Shining* and taking an axe to the door), or whether I should just lock it and hope that if she found it closed she'd drift peacefully away.

I turned the key in the lock.

In the end I couldn't tell you whether or not she visited, or rattled the door like a restless spirit, because that night, thank God, my sleep was deep and dreamless.

PART 6
AWAY

19

Oxford was a Wonderland.

It had snowed again overnight, so the city looked stunning in the low sunshine – half Gormenghast, half Winterfell.

It was lucky we couldn't park, because we got to see *everything*. Nel nosed the gold Mini around the narrow streets and I swear we actually followed one of those open-top tourist buses for a good twenty minutes. We glimpsed the quiet quads of the colleges, the mad, bike-crammed stone bridges and the snow-kissed spires reaching into the bluest of skies. 'Good job we left early,' said Nel ruefully, negotiating a cobbled street.

Actually it gave me time to think. Somewhere beyond the anxious, pattering thoughts about the interview, it occurred to me that I had never really thought too much about my application to Oxford – intellectually, as it were – what with all that had been going on at STAGS. In fact, I'd pretty much applied here because at STAGS that was just what you *did* – here or Cambridge. I'd plumped for Oxford basically because my friends had applied here; that thing your teachers say you must never, *ever* do. I realised, on that little Magical Mystery Tour in search of a parking spot, that I'd never really considered actually *living* here, studying in all the buildings we were passing – that huge square library and that big round reading room and that fancy theatre with the big Greek heads outside it. It occurred to me, too, that if I had the smallest ghost of a chance of getting into this place, I'd been helped, in the weirdest and murkiest of ways, by the Dark Order of the Grand Stag itself. If I hadn't been manipulated into putting on *The Isle of Dogs*, and Professor Nashe hadn't come to see it, I would probably not be here now, having an interview with the world's foremost Jonsonian expert. Did that go some way to compensating me for the trial, the hanging, the branding? I sucked my branded thumb like I was a child, and then pressed it to the chilly window. It left a silvery thumbprint, with a clear little M missed out of the middle.

We finally parked right by Christ Church, the college I had applied to, and as I unfolded myself from the little car I saw, with rising panic, that this was the biggest and grandest college we'd yet seen. At the gatehouse Nel said goodbye.

'Where will you be?' I asked nervously, like she was my mum.

'Starbucks,' she said. Nel was a globalisation girl to her acrylic fingertips. 'I saw one when we were driving round. Actually I saw it about ten times.'

Her tiny joke relaxed me a bit. 'Call me when you're through,' she said. 'Go get 'em.' And then she gave me this massive hug. I was properly touched. As she walked high-street-wards I gave my name to the porter guy who was actually wearing – I'm not kidding – a bowler hat. Then we passed through the arch into the main quadrangle, and that small sliver of hope I'd felt in the car disappeared. My own cheek almost made me

130

laugh. What? Greer MacDonald actually dared to think she could come *here*, to this golden palace of a college? Lewis Carroll himself had studied here, had walked this quad. Had found a low door in the wall of the college gardens which had inspired him to write *Alice-in-fricking-Wonderland*. I'd recently seen that crazy cheese-dream of a film version by Tim Burton, and I felt like I was living it now. I was truly Through the Looking Glass. My nerves, my lack of preparation because I'd had my head in this STAGS/DOGS thing – how could I not be found out?

I followed the porter up a winding stone stair to a solid oak door. He knocked on it for me before touching his bowler and leaving, so I couldn't even chicken out. I had no choice, when a faint voice said 'Enter', but to go in.

At the desk, Professor Nashe was writing without looking up, her iron-grey hair escaping from her messy bun. 'One moment,' she murmured, so I waited, looking round the room as I did so. There were three walls of books crammed onto dark-wood shelves, and the fourth wall was taken up with a huge leaded Tudor window, opening out onto a snowy quad and a frozen fountain. A grandfather clock stood tall in the corner, ticking ominously, and a rogue sunbeam struck through one of the diamond panes straight into my eye. The scratching of the pen and the ticking of the clock and the sunbeam were hard to bear. I felt the weight of no one speaking pressing down on me. I don't know if this was part of the test, but if it was, I failed it. I blurted out: 'I saw Ben Jonson.'

She looked up. Despite the grey hair, she had a young face, and she was much sterner than I remembered. Of course, I'd never actually met her – I'd been otherwise engaged hanging from the rafters of the De Warlencourt Playhouse – but I did recall her smiling at some gag of Abbot Ridley's during his introductory speech to *The Isle of Dogs*. But she didn't smile at me. In fact, she looked a bit startled.

'When?'

'Yesterday. I went to Westminster Abbey. I saw the standing-up grave and the . . . questionable epitaph: O *rare Ben Jonson.*'

She looked *almost* like she might smile, but then said, 'Oh – it's not such a bad epitaph when you come to think about it.'

Wow. What a great start – I'd pissed her off. I backtracked. 'Well, he was rare, I suppose. Or even a one-off.'

She didn't reply. Instead, she indicated a chair with her pen, and I sat in it. 'You know Ben Jonson lived here, I expect?'

'Yes.' It was one of the things Friar Waterlow, the STAGS librarian, had told me.

'Only for a short time. But that's why the Ben Jonson Institute, of which I am the principal, is based here.'

I looked out of the window, and could almost see Ben crossing the snowy quad, in a black Tudor coat like the ones we wore at STAGS. Professor Nashe spoke again, pulling my attention back into the room.

'So. Greer. I very much enjoyed your production of *The Isle of Dogs*. Quite a coup.'

'Thank you.'

'I have, of course, since your performance, read the play in some detail, and it has now been registered and catalogued with the British Library.'

I swallowed. This was big stuff.

'And you've applied here to read English with Renaissance drama, so today we are going to have a conversation about some of the aspects of your chosen subject, in the historical context of the times. There are no right or wrong answers. I just want to hear your ideas.' She shuffled her notes and looked at me with a direct gaze. 'So, tell me, Greer: what is the purpose of a play?'

I thought back to my conversation with Nel earlier that term. 'To be performed.'

She nodded. 'Why?'

'To entertain?'

'Yes. Anything else?'

'I guess . . . to change the way people think.'

'Yes,' she said, very definitely this time. 'Have you read Jonson's play *Volpone*?

Great. I'd fallen at the first fence. 'No. I mean, not really.'

She folded her hands together and fixed me with green eyes that reminded me of her past pupil Abbot Ridley. 'Expand.'

'I mean, I had a look at it when I was doing *The Isle of Dogs*. I read the argument at the beginning.' In fact, I'd copied it out for Nel when I'd discovered the Longcross acrostic in the *Lorem Ipsum* text. 'You know, the bit at the beginning that spells out VOLPONE.'

She nodded. 'You know what the word "Volpone" means, I suppose?'

'Yes. It means . . .' I stopped, thunderstruck. Then I recovered myself. 'It means "The Fox". *See if you can find out about Foxes*. But what Ty had messaged couldn't have anything to do with this, could it? Surely she'd meant what we'd found out yesterday, about the law Rollo had blocked and the Boxing Day foxhunt at Longcross? 'I'm sensing that Jonson liked the fox metaphor,' I went on. 'You know, because of the character of Volpone in *The Isle of Dogs*.' The one that Cass had played.

'Well, he certainly liked foxes. The creature, that is. He even had one of his own.'

'What, you mean like a *pet*?'

'Yes. It lived in his house at Blackfriars. It was tame as a dog. He even named it.' She fixed me with her green gaze. 'He called it Reynard.'

I think I stopped breathing for a second. In my mind Ben Jonson crossed the quad again, black as a crow, and this time a fox trotted after him, a red smear against the snow. This was too much of a coincidence. Ben Jonson had named his fox *Reynard*, the same name as the fox in the Masefield poem Rollo had used to frustrate the law in the House of Lords, the same name as the fox heads that adorned the walls of Cumberland Place.

'Why'd he call it that?' I asked breathlessly.

'Because of the medieval literary convention. There were a number of twelfth-century folk tales from all over western Europe featuring a red fox who was a trickster figure, always called Reynard. *Renard* is French for "fox" of course.'

'Oh. Yes, of course,' I said, trying to sound intelligent.

'Ben Jonson added to this convention, the notion of the wily fox, in his own beast fables. Volpone as a character in *The Isle of Dogs*, then his play *Volpone*, subtitled *The Fox*.'

A thought occurred. 'Wait, so is it the same guy from *The Isle of Dogs*? The *Volpone* character, I mean. Is *Volpone* a spin-off? Like the *Han Solo* movie was a spin-off of *Star Wars*?'

For the first time she gave a tiny smile. 'Well, you could say that. I mean, I wouldn't make the *Thor* comparison, but recent scholarship suggests that *Volpone* in the eponymous play represents Robert Cecil, the same courtier who was represented by the character of Volpone in your *Isle of Dogs*.'

I liked the way she called it mine.

'By the time *Volpone* was written, Robert Cecil was King James's chief advisor. He was the most powerful man in England, after the monarch. He was also an extremely dangerous man and concerned himself with the interrogation and torture of those he considered a danger to the state. For many, Cecil's face was the last one they saw.'

I shivered a little, and not from the cold.

'So what do you think that says about Ben Jonson, that he wrote a play satirising Cecil?'

I didn't even have to think about this one. 'That he liked taking shots at authority. I mean, the whole of *The Isle of Dogs* was a critique of Elizabeth I and her courtiers, and that got him thrown in jail. And *then*, if he *was* poking fun at Cecil in *Volpone*, now that he was Top Dog – no pun intended – well . . . I think he must have been a bit of a rebel.'

She looked at me, considering. 'He was a *lot* of a rebel.'

'How big? Extinction Rebellion big?

'Try the Anonymous movement. Hacktivists. Occupy. The *gilets jaunes*.'

I didn't know much about those guys, so I just said, 'Cool.'

'Yes. Jonson went to prison on several occasions, not just for the murder of Gabriel Spenser. Although that was the worst time of course. His nearest squeak.'

She didn't have to tell me. I'd lived it. 'Did he get in trouble for *Volpone*?'

'No. He was in an interesting position by then.'

'Interesting how?'

'Cecil thought Jonson was on his side.'

'Why?'

'Because Jonson was a double agent. A spy.'

I whistled. 'James Bond,' I breathed.

'Indeed. What do you think about that?'

'I think he is even cooler than I did before, if that's possible.'

I could see she liked that. Encouraged, I asked, 'But who did he spy for?'

'Other rebels. Catholics.'

'Like who?'

She raised an eyebrow. 'I thought *I* was conducting the interview.'

I wound my neck in. This was an interview about my future. I needed to focus on that. 'Of course.' I tried to answer intelligently her questions about my Probitiones syllabus, and other Renaissance dramatists, but I was really thinking about Ben Jonson being a spy.

'And have you given any thought to the dissertation that you will have to complete if your application is successful? No matter if not – it is not required until your third year.'

'Well, I mean, and this is just off the top of my head as I've literally just heard about it, but I'd like to do something about sedition in drama. I mean, using words to communicate stuff.' *Jeez, Greer, get it together.* There was something about Professor Nashe's penetrating green gaze that reduced my vocabulary to that of a Valley Girl. 'I mean, using dramatic ideas and tropes to communicate radical or even revolutionary ideas, possibly leading to political insurrection.'

She gave a tiny nod. 'Ha,' she said. 'Just like Nathaniel.'

'Nath— you mean Abbot Ridley?'

'Yes. He wrote something along those lines himself. His conclusions were very interesting *indeed*.' I didn't mind at all that I'd said something unoriginal. As far as I was concerned, if I'd hit on something Abbot Ridley had done, and he was her star student, then I was doing something right. 'You must be very proud of him. Nathaniel, I mean.' It felt weird using his first name.

'In what way?' she said guardedly.

Stuttering a little, feeling as if I was suddenly on shaky ground, I said, 'Well, he's the head of a major private school and he can't be more than, what . . . thirty?'

Professor Nashe was silent – she seemed reluctant to confirm or deny her former student's age.

Nervous, I blew more smoke. 'I mean, he's a credit to you. To have got that far, that young. It's pretty . . . unusual.' I meant it as a compliment, but it was something I'd wondered about before. Abbot Ridley had been parachuted in when the Old Abbot 'died' – fair enough, they'd needed someone quickly. But an emergency temporary position was one thing – how had someone so young been given the abbot gig for keeps?

Professor Nashe breathed in through her nose, the fine nostrils flaring a little. 'Nathaniel Ridley's credentials are impeccable, and for that I can only take partial credit. He was the head of Ampleforth College, you know, before he came to your own establishment.' Ridley had told me this before, so Professor Nashe was only backing him up, but somehow her saying it made it sound even less likely. That meant Ridley was a headmaster of a major private school in his late twenties? It just didn't add up. But I was *definitely* being warned off. 'If you're good, you're good, no matter how youthful you may be,' the professor went on. 'Ben Jonson wrote *The Isle of Dogs* aged twenty-five, you know. Now –' she shifted slightly in her chair – 'let's leave aside the achievements of others, and return to yours.' She looked at me closely. 'In conclusion, I'll ask you again: what is the purpose of a play?'

This was clearly the last question, so I had to make it count and show I had learned from our conversation. I was determined to give a definite answer and not do that Australian rising-at-the-end-of-a-sentence thing that made all my previous answers sound like questions. I said clearly, 'To start a fire.'

She nodded slowly, over and over again, like those toy dogs you see in the back of cars. But it was impossible to tell, just from that, whether she was thinking that *I* was right, or whether *she* was thinking that *she* was right in thinking that I was a moron. So I just rose when she rose and politely shook her proffered hand. 'Have you any other plans, while you are in Oxford?'

We hadn't really. 'Just to look around. I haven't been to Oxford before. It all seems so beautiful.'

This seemed to please her. 'The Ashmolean Museum is really wonderful. Not to be missed.'

She held onto my hand as she said this, and it seemed less like a Tripadvisor recommendation than a direct order.

'Oh, OK,' I said faintly.

As she showed me to the door she said, in the same make-sure-you-do-this tone, 'Don't forget to read *Volpone*.'

'I won't.'

She fixed me with that green gaze once more. 'Remember, Remember,' she said.

'I will.'

And then she smiled properly for the first time.

20

I found Nel inside the Starbucks on the high street. On her phone, of course.

'How'd it go?' she asked immediately.

I considered the question as I slid into the seat opposite her. 'I *genuinely* don't know. I bullshitted my way through most of it. But I got this really uncomfortable feeling.'

'What kind of feeling?'

'That she was kind of . . . steering me to see something. Or to say something.'

'And did you?'

'I don't know. She did ask me to read this Jonson play. Twice actually; *Remember, Remember,* she said. And she really seemed to like my dissertation idea.' I left out the part when she said it was similar to what the Abbot had done. I didn't want to set Nel off – good to let sleeping dogs lie.

'Well,' she said, 'no point trying to second guess what will happen. They must know what they are looking for. I bet you did better than you think.'

'Hmm.' Then, 'We don't have to rush back, do we? I mean, we can't see Shafeen till tonight because of the STAGS Club's very enlightened no-women policy.'

Nel checked her phone – the Gen. Z version of a watch. 'I guess we could hang out for a bit.'

'OK, great, because the Ashmolean is just round the corner. The Prof said it wasn't to be missed.'

'What's that?'

'Really cool museum apparently.' I fiddled with the little corrugated cardboard jacket they'd given Nel for her takeaway cup. I still felt oddly unsettled, like I hadn't given the best of myself in the interview, like I'd missed something out, or missed something I had been told. I shook it off. Professor Nashe wouldn't be recommending museums, and plays, to someone she thought was a drop-kick, would she?

'Yeah,' said Nel to the museum idea. 'Why not?'

It started to snow as we walked up the high street, not loads, and certainly not enough for me to fear that we'd get stuck getting home. Just pretty, Christmassy snow, which went with the pretty, Christmassy lights. Time and again since that day I've asked myself if the snow was enough to fool our eyesight or to conjure up what we saw, but I don't think so.

It was just as we turned the corner and first caught sight of the museum. It had a beautiful frontage with marble steps and lofty pillars, and these two modern metal dog sculptures kind of guarding the entrance. But they weren't the startling thing. The startling thing was coming down the steps.

It was a man, tall and slim, with brown curls blowing in the bitter wind. His stubbly cheeks were flushed and his green eyes bright with cold. He wore a leather jacket and a chunky charcoal scarf wound round his neck. He could have been a movie star, but he wasn't.

He was Abbot Ridley.

It took me a split second to recognise him because he wasn't wearing his abbot's robes. But Nel was way ahead of me. She screamed out, '*Nathaniel!*'

I'm ninety-nine per cent sure he saw us because I am sure there was the briefest of pauses before he jogged down the steps and away down the street, shrugging himself down into his scarf as he went. Of course we followed him. But he'd vanished into this Dickensian-looking street in a swirl of snow – almost as if he was the Ghost of Christmas Present. Nel and I stopped, breathing hard, and looked at each other. The snowflakes had settled on her lashes and lips, her blue eyes blazed. *Oh God*, I thought. *She really loves him.* 'Now what?'

'He must not have seen me,' she wailed. 'I *know* he'd have stopped if he had.'

'Nel,' I warned, 'you've got to admit that thinking you guys have a future together is pretty crazy.'

'Crazier than thinking that Henry is alive somewhere, hanging out with Elvis and Tupac?'

She had me there.

'I just wish I had his number is all,' she lamented.

'If he's a proper Medieval, he won't have one,' I said. 'I wonder what the hell he's doing here.'

'It's not *that* weird, is it? I mean, he used to be at Christ Church. Maybe he's still got buddies living here. Or maybe he came to visit her, you know, Whatsherface.'

'Professor Nashe. Yes. Yes, I suppose teachers have to go *somewhere* in the holidays.' I remember, when I was little, seeing one of my primary-school teachers in Sainsbury's and being

142

properly freaked out and hiding behind my dad. Back then I still thought on some level that teachers just got packed away in a box outside of school hours. It was certainly strange seeing the Abbot out of context like that. 'I suppose it *was* him, wasn't it?'

'Definitely,' she said. 'I'd know him anywhere. I just wish we knew where he was going.'

She sounded very downcast, and I was sorry – she'd done me a real solid driving me here for my interview, and I'd wanted her to enjoy our day in Oxford. 'Look,' I said, 'we don't know where he's going, but we do know where he's been.'

She looked up.

'The museum, remember? We might as well have a look.' I suddenly had a burning desire to know what the Abbot had been looking at, and I knew how to sell it to Nel. 'Then you guys can chat about it when we get back to school.'

That seemed to lift her spirits. 'True.'

We drifted back to the museum, past the metal dogs and into the atrium. Swerving, as I always did, the 'Suggested Donation of £5' boxes, we found a floor map. 'Where would the Abbot have gone?' I asked, trying to cheer her up. 'You know him best.'

She looked at the dates on the floorplan. 'Easy,' she said. 'Got to be Tudor and Stuart. Downstairs.'

'And look,' I said, 'there's even a guy pointing the way.' It was true. In the atrium stood a marble statue, holding his arm out as if indicating the right direction, urging us with the blank gaze of his white eyes. We followed the arm into a basement gallery.

And that's when it got weird.

There was this little gallery off to the right, full of the usual standard-issue museum glass cases. But over the entrance of the gallery itself, in a case of its own, was a huge set of stag's antlers.

I suddenly went cold. Somewhere in this gallery, the one marked by the antlers just like our school, was something we were meant to see.

We walked under the antlers, and for the second time that day I was reminded of first walking into STAGS. My flesh tingled. The room was reasonably quiet, with only a few knots of tourists milling around, using those muted library voices that also seem to double up for museums. We glanced at the cases – there was one called 'Rarities of the University', collected by one Elias Ashmole, who I supposed had given his name to the museum. There was the usual collection of swords and pots and jewellery and little explanatory signs.

'Yes,' said Nel fondly. I don't think she'd noticed the antlers. 'This looks like his kind of thing.'

My skin was still prickling. I was convinced the Abbot had been here for a reason. Something was here, some clue. But how could we possibly know what?

And that's when I saw it.

A thumbprint, planted squarely on the glass, so clear that the *CSI* whorls were clearly visible. A thumbprint on a glass case was not so unusual, but this one had something particular about it that turned my blood to ice.

A letter **M** was missed out neatly from the middle.

I held onto Nel and pointed, because I couldn't actually speak.

'What?' she asked, then clocked the print. 'Well, it's yours obviously.' She peered in close. 'The little M shows up perfectly, doesn't it? Presumably your thumbprint will be different forever now. I guess that rules out a life of crime, unless you –'

'No,' I interrupted. 'It's not mine.'

'Are you sure?'

Just for a nanosecond, my brain spun into a mess of time-slice conspiracies. *Had* I been here before, touched the glass and left my unique mark, just like I had done in the frosty car this morning? Had we come round this way once already and walked back on ourselves? Or had another version of me from another moment in time visited this place, *Avengers: Endgame*-style, and rested her thumb on the glass? But in the next moment my thoughts ordered themselves. That was all impossible. We'd just come down the stairs and this was the first gallery we'd visited. 'I haven't been near that case. I swear it.'

And that meant only one thing.

I bent and breathed on the glass so we could see the print even more clearly. Then I planted my own thumbprint right next to the other one. The Ms were the same but that was it. Even Dr Watson would have seen that the whorls were entirely different, and even if they weren't, this was a much bigger print.

A man's print.

'It's not mine,' I said. 'It's his. The Abbot's.'

Nel flushed, as she pretty much always did when anyone mentioned him. 'I would have noticed if he had a brand.'

'*Would* you?'

'I know him pretty well, Greer. And we acted together a lot.'

'Yes, but would you notice a brand on someone's *thumb*? *I* never did. And when I first met him I looked at his hands a *lot*, believe me.'

'Why were you looking at his hands?' She sounded almost jealous.

145

'C'mon, Nel, why d'you think? Because I was looking for a ring. Either a signet ring like the STAGS wear – Rollo's got one, did you see? – or a kiss-my-hand ring like the Old Abbot had. But just because I didn't notice a brand, doesn't mean he doesn't have one.'

Nel screwed up her eyes at all those negatives in one sentence.

I clarified. 'I definitely think it's his.'

We both stared at the print. 'But why? Why would he have a brand like yours?'

'There can only be one reason,' I said. 'He must have been tried like me. He must have caused the death of one of the STAGS. Why else would he be branded M for Manslayer?'

'All right, then explain this. Why put a thumbprint *here*? It can't be accidental. You don't lean on the glass with your thumb. If you lean on glass, you use your whole hand.' She demonstrated.

'Unless you're sending a message.'

'Who to?'

'Maybe to us.'

'How could he possibly know we'd come here?' she scoffed.

Then it dawned on me. '*She* told me to,' I said slowly. 'Professor Nashe. His old tutor.' I looked around at the innocent-seeming tourists and drew Nel closer to me. 'We're being played. They want us to see something.'

'See what, though?'

'This, I guess.' The dark shape of a single exhibit, squatting in the corner of the glass case as a silent witness to our conversation, aligned itself exactly behind the thumbprint.

We both shifted focus and stared, not at the glass now, but

through it to the object it contained. It was about a foot high, dark, leathery and slightly forbidding.

'Is it a helmet?' asked Nel uncertainly.

'Too narrow,' I said. 'You'd have to be a real pencil-head to fit that. What's the number? There must be a card.'

Nel peered into the case. 'Two.'

'Two, two, two . . .' I scanned the labels beneath the objects. 'Here we go: *Guy Fawkes's Lantern. Presented by Robert Heywood to the University of Oxford in 1641. Around 1600.*'

'Really?' said Nel in surprise. 'Guy Fawkes? As in the Bonfire Night dude?'

Yes. I read aloud the museum text on the little card.

Guy Fawkes was reportedly carrying this lantern when he was captured on the night of 4–5th November 1605 in the cellar of the Palace of Westminster. The Gunpowder Plot aimed to blow up James I and the Members of Parliament and the House of Lords at the State Opening of Parliament the next day. Robert Heywood's brother, Peter Heywood, was a magistrate in Westminster and one of the men who discovered the plotters in the cellar. Peter reportedly took the lantern from Guy Fawkes, and so prevented him from lighting the fuse.

'Wow.' We both stared at the lantern. It looked different now. It was no longer a rather sad-looking leather cylinder. It was an instrument of terrorism, as surely as a suicide vest. I pictured Guy Fawkes, his fingers slippery with sweat, opening the little lantern door to expose the flame to the gunpowder. Then

Peter Heywood snatching the thing from his hand. The flame kindling, instead of the gunpowder, the faces of the guards; their expressions telling Guy Fawkes that the game was up, and he was a dead man. 'Imagine how many people would have died if he'd succeeded,' I breathed. 'Both houses of Parliament, and King James I.' Suddenly I felt all goosebumpy. 'Quite spooky to think that Guy Fawkes was trying to blow up the very institution we were sitting in yesterday.'

Nel shivered prettily. 'Don't.'

'I mean,' I said of the lantern, 'it's pretty cool once you know what it is. But I don't know why the Abbot would have been looking at this exhibit particularly. Much less why he would have wanted *us* to see it.'

'Maybe it's less to do with who owned it and more about what it represents.'

'How d'you mean?'

'Well . . .' she said, piecing the thought together. 'Maybe the Abbot was trying to shed light on something? Like a lantern.'

'Then why not just tell us?'

'Got me.'

I looked back at the black lantern, squatting on its little white plinth. Suddenly it seemed malign, evil. I wanted to be away from it. 'Let's go.'

'Don't you want to see anything else?'

'No, no.' The thumbprint had thoroughly spooked me. 'I think we should go.'

And when we returned to the car, I could see that my own **M** thumbprint, on the passenger-side window, was still there, a ghost of a smear on the cold glass.

21

Of course, on the way back to London the talk was all of Abbot Ridley and the thumbprint at Guy Fawkes's lantern.

Some strange part of me felt almost comforted that there was someone else with the brand. I'd high-fived (or high-thumbed) the ghost of Ben Jonson in Westminster Abbey, because 400 years ago he'd got the Manslayer brand too.

But this was different.

This was someone *alive*.

I'd had my doubts about the Abbot in the past, especially when he'd been gaslighting me about that Esmé Stuart thing – I still swore he'd said he was a she – but I now thought that he might be a valuable ally. He'd cut me down from the noose, covered up for me with Professor Nashe and sent me flowers in hospital. If he *had* left that thumbprint, and he *did* have a brand, then he was a kindred spirit. Only he, possibly in all the world, knew what I'd been through. I really, badly wanted to talk to him, but unless I went through Professor Nashe, which I couldn't picture myself doing, I would have to wait until the beginning of term.

So as Nel began to negotiate the roads into central London

I mentally shelved the Abbot and my thoughts turned instead to the STAGS Club and what awaited us there. By the time we'd parked the car at Cumberland Place to head for the Tube it was nearly six o'clock, and Shafeen, so far as we knew, had been at the club all day. I wondered what he'd found out. We had so much to tell him; maybe he had something to tell us.

PART 7
THE FIELD

22

The STAGS Club, in London's St James's, was the second place that day where I felt I really didn't belong.

Walking though unmarked grand doors, in an exclusive backstreet of Westminster, I felt even more awkward than I had that morning treading the hallowed quad of Christ Church. Of course, the first thing I saw was a massive pair of antlers over the inner door, and beyond that, a passageway bristling with ancient-looking guns hanging on the walls. The metaphor wasn't lost on me. I was a huntin' shootin' fish out of water.

Luckily Nel had a bit more natural courage than me – presumably she'd grown up going through fancy doorways and being made just as welcome as her father's wallet. She greeted the mountain of a man who was standing, hands clasped, in front of the door like a high-class bouncer. He didn't speak (rude, I thought) but indicated down the passageway with one massive paw. We walked in the direction of the hand and the passageway turned into a grand, open space. If I'd expected a cosy couple of rooms with leather armchairs and a fireplace like in *Around the World in Eighty Days*, I was mistaken. This place was like a hidden palace.

The atrium of the STAGS Club was hushed and dim, with marble pillars rising to the ceiling and a grand stairway curving out of sight. Underfoot was a black-and-white marble floor in the shape of a compass rose, as if indicating that the STAGS' power reached to all points of the compass and to the ends of the earth. In the dead centre of the design was a mahogany writing desk, with a little man in white-tie and tails sitting at it.

Nel marched over to him and gave our names. This guy, unlike the bouncer, was uber-polite. 'Ah, Miss Ashton, Miss MacDonald, guests of the Earl of Longcross. His lordship is expecting you.' He wrote in a ledger with a fountain pen, then turned the book round to face us. 'If you wouldn't mind?'

We signed our names at the foot of a page entitled 'Does' (as in, a deer; a female deer), under some very grand female names. Like the guns on the walls, they were all double-barrelled. These were obviously the other honoured ladies who'd been admitted to the club for dinner. I made quite a mess with the ink pen, but the guy was far too well bred to burn me for it.

'Lord Longcross is in the Crusader's Library with Mr Jadeja. Jack will show you.' He beckoned the giant from the door, who led us up the grand stair in absolute silence. I was getting some serious Perfect vibes – Jack obviously went to the same charm school as everybody's favourite gamekeeper. It was a bit awks because you couldn't even hear our footsteps. Just as in Cumberland Place, our feet made absolutely no sound on the thick carpets, which were the red of arterial blood. As we climbed I could hear a hubbub of talk – no raucous laughter or shouting, nothing so coarse; just the murmur of perhaps a hundred people chatting at low level in a big room. It made me nervous.

When we walked through the grand doors of the Crusader's Library I spotted Shafeen at once. It was easy. He was the only person of colour in the room. He was standing talking happily to someone in a bow tie, as if he too was a member of the club and he'd been coming here all his life. Just for a moment, in that removed way I'd viewed Rollo the day before in the House of Lords, I saw Shafeen as other people must see him. Tall, handsome, urbane, wearing a grey suit over a white shirt open at his brown throat. I felt a jag of pride, of love – and of pity. If it weren't for the colour of his skin, he'd fit right in in this room.

And the room itself was quite something. Above rows and rows of dark-wood bookshelves stuffed with ancient volumes, there were huge frescoes on the walls depicting various battles of the Crusades. There was no blood and guts, just these stagey, polite-looking scenes of Christian victory. I thought they were paintings, but as we advanced into the room I could see they were mosaics, artfully made up of a thousand tiny glass tiles. I imagined that each nugget of glass was less than worthless, but crafted together like this those panels would be priceless. From what (very little) I know of decorative art stuff, I would have said it was Victorian – all maidens with flowing hair and knights on white horses. The infidels, of course, had mean faces, swarthy skin and stylised turbans. Their mouths, like their swords, had a cruel downward curve to them. I was wrong; there were other people of colour in the room besides Shafeen. It's just that they were on the walls, crudely represented and trapped in a perpetual losing battle.

I turned my attention to the victors in the room. I'm not kidding, but I recognised some of them from the TV. I'm not massively into politics but even I knew some of the characters that were huddled into the oak-panelled corners, parcelling up the world. There was that chubby blond one with the messy hair. There was that skinny dark one with the glasses. Finding Rollo in this room was a bit like *Where's Wally?* However different their physical attributes, somehow everyone in the room looked like him. Eventually I saw him, accepting a glass of something from a tray. He had just taken a sip when he spotted us, and he did that gulp-and-beckon thing that people do when their mouth is full and they can't speak.

We all converged by Shafeen and his new bow-tied buddy. The earl kissed me and Nel, with practised ease, on each cheek. Bow tie excused himself to Rollo in that bluff and friendly way that meant they were old pals. Because it seemed the right thing to do, Shafeen kissed us both too. But his lips lingered on my skin and his dark eye winked. He was *happy*. 'Who was that bloke?' I murmured as our cheeks met.

'Head of the General Medical Council. He is being incredibly helpful.' His whisper was warm in my ear.

'Are you kidding?'

'I'm really not.' Then, out loud, he asked me exactly the same question that Nel had outside Starbucks, in exactly the same way. 'How'd it go?' Beneath his positivity and confidence, I could detect a little anxiety about my performance at that morning's interview. He badly wanted us both – all – to get into Oxford so we could be together.

'Ah yes, the interview,' chimed in Rollo. 'I went up to Oxford myself. They asked some dashed difficult questions, I seem to recall, but I scraped in somehow.'

I just about passed out with the effort of not rolling my eyes. Of *course* he'd got in – his pathway smoothed by money and privilege and the old-school tie. 'I remember reading once that Prince Charles got in with two Es at A level, so I can't help thinking that a little detail like being heir to the throne might have helped him out.'

'Ah,' said Rollo, waving his already empty glass. 'But nowadays one's just as likely to be discriminated against because one *has* a privileged white background. Times are changing. *Quotas. Diversity*.' He spoke the words as if they were curses. 'Iconoclasts breaking statues of great men because they had some tenuous connection to the slave trade. The decolonisation of the curriculum. They are even talking about taking the word "Empire" out of the honours system and replacing it with "Excellence". *Order of British Excellence*, for God's sake!' Rollo was getting puce in the face as he warmed to his theme. 'Empire has become a dirty word, blackened with the stain of slavery. No mention of the manifold good the Empire did. Oh no.'

'Like what?' asked Shafeen.

'Railways, roads, education, government – to name but a few. No. The achievements of the Empire are trodden into dust. Everyone's forgotten that Britannia ruled the waves.' He sounded truly sorry that the world was changing, just as his son had been one autumn night, sitting on the moonlit roof of Longcross with me, a million de Warlencourt bricks under his arse.

I glanced at Shafeen to see how he'd taken Rollo's extraordinary speech. Normally he'd have about a million scornful things to say in response, but today he was listening quite placidly. Still, I thought I'd better get Rollo off the dangerous subject of Empire and back to the safer ground of privilege. 'I suppose private-school kids could always go to the local state school if they feel discriminated against,' I said. 'I bet they wouldn't though.'

'No,' Rollo agreed, 'but you must concede there is now mobility the other way. That nice coloured girl my nephew Louis was wrapped around at Longcross, I believe she is attending STAGS in a bursary in Henry's name.'

'Yes,' I admitted. 'And I got a scholarship too. From my Manchester slum.'

He ignored my jibe. 'But you went to the Oxford interview with exactly the same advantage I did, namely that you went to STAGS.'

He had me there. I supposed I was now one of the privileged.

'So by your logic,' he continued, 'you've got a jolly good chance of getting in.'

I shrugged. 'Unless I screwed up the interview with my low ways.'

'And did you?' asked Shafeen tensely.

'I don't *think* so. The Prof recommended some holiday reading, so it might not have been a total bust.' Professor Nashe's other recommendation to visit the Ashmolean, and the chance meeting it led to, would have to wait for later, when we were alone.

'Well, that deserves a drink,' said Rollo, who seemed fired up. I sensed that he liked a fight – especially one that he could win. 'Jack!' he called above the hubbub. I expected to see the huge door giant scuttling over, but this was a different guy. He wore white-tie and black tails, just like the desk jockey downstairs, and bore a silver tray on his white glove. Rollo put his empty glass on the tray smartly, unbalancing the waiter guy a bit. 'I think champagne, don't you?' he said to all of us at large, but it wasn't really a question. I expected him to ask for his favourite vintage, the Veuve Clicquot 1984, but he didn't specify. Obviously whatever vintage the STAGS Club had going was eminently drinkable.

'Very good, my lord.'

Once the waiter was out of earshot I remarked, 'Same name as the door guy.'

'What's that, my dear?'

'The guy on the door is called Jack. So's this one. Quite a coincidence.'

Rollo threw back his head and laughed so much that he showed all his teeth, white and sharp and animal, with no fillings to be seen. 'They all are.'

'Huh?'

'It's a STAGS Club tradition,' he replied, still smiling. 'All the staff are called Jack.'

'But what are their real names?'

'Lord knows,' he said dismissively.

I looked about me. At other points in the room I saw a few girls in black-and-white maids' outfits. Nel, as she often did, read my mind.

159

'What about the women?' she asked. 'What are they called?'

'Why, Jill of course,' Rollo replied.

Shafeen widened his eyes at me so that you could see the whites all around the dark pupils, but he was amused where yesterday he'd been outraged that his own father had been misnamed Mowgli. He *must* have had a good day.

Rollo looked round impatiently for our waiter. 'Jack downstairs is known as Jack-door. Like the bird, you know. Jackdaw. Rather good, that. The rest of 'em are just plain Jack.'

'Plain Jack' was back with the champagne – four tall glasses on a tray. Rollo doled them out without a thank-you. I smiled at Jack and this time I studied him as a person. Stubby blond eyelashes, ears red at the tips, young enough to have acne scars. I found myself wondering about his mum or his partner, where he lived, what kind of music he liked. Did he like working here? Did he mind not having a name of his own until he got home to the people who loved him? He didn't smile back.

'Let's drink to your Oxford admissions. Thanks to our shared alma mater – STAGS – it's in the bag.'

I supposed this was a hunting term. I raised my glass half-heartedly and the bubbles went straight up my nose.

I was dying to ask what Rollo and Shafeen had been up to today, and luckily Rollo spotted someone he knew and said, 'Ah, the Attorney General. Excuse me. I must invite him to the meet.'

And we three were alone, a little island in the middle of that breathtaking room.

'How's dear Rollo been?' asked Nel, with a twist of a smile.

160

'Good as gold,' said Shafeen. 'He couldn't have been nicer or more helpful. He's introduced me to pretty much the most powerful men in the British medical profession. As well as the Medical Council chap, I met the Secretary of State for Health, and the Surgeon General. Then the editor of *The Lancet*, only Britain's foremost medical journal. Rollo seems to really want to help me get on. I think it's something to do with my father.'

'But do *you* really want to get on in that way?'

Shafeen looked into his champagne glass, as if he might find the answer in there. 'I don't know, Greer. I really don't know. It's a means to an end. I *could* take a stand, right up there on the moral high ground.' He pointed to the frescoed ceiling, to the cherubs parting the clouds. 'But who would I be hurting but myself? If I end up where I want to be, and spend my life helping people, including people who look like me, would that be so bad?'

I supposed it made sense. But it was strange to hear Shafeen talking like that. He'd been so bullish about unelected privilege only the day before. This was quite the turnaround. But was it any different to me taking a place at STAGS, and all the privileges that came with it? I wondered what had won him over, and I thought I knew the answer. 'What did you do all day?'

'We had lunch, then we had coffee and brandy in the Smoking Room. That's when he introduced me to the medical types. Then we played billiards in the Billiard Room.'

'What's billiards?'

'Posh pool,' said Nel.

'How do you know that?'

161

'Cluedo,' she said briefly.

'Then we went upstairs to this amazing place on the first floor called the Fencing Gallery,' Shafeen went on. 'It's this really long room – the length of the whole club – so it's apparently three townhouses. There were black-and-white tiles on the floor, like a chessboard. I'm not describing it very well.'

'No, I think I know what you mean,' I said. 'There's something similar in *Die Another Day* – sidebar: my least favourite Bond film – when Toby Stephens fights Pierce Brosnan.'

'I'll take your word for it,' Shafeen said drily. 'Anyway, there were two guys there fencing, and we watched for a bit. They were all done up in the white suits and the face guards, really going at it. They were attached to the wall by a rope to pull them back if they got too feisty.'

'God,' said Nel. 'Sounds serious.'

'Well, yes, but they then stopped at the end of the bout and shook hands. Rollo told me they used to have duels up there. Proper ones with swords. On some of the white tiles you can see bloodstains that they couldn't wash out. And they even fought with pistols there too. There are musket balls buried in the wall.'

'Wow,' I said. 'Way to settle a dispute.'

'Quite. Then he took me down to the cellars. They're amazing – they must go right down under the street, they're so huge. There are just racks and racks of the most incredible wine.'

'Probably where Rollo got his expensive tastes,' said Nel, sounding more admiring than critical. 'I'll bet they're full of – what's his favourite? – Veuve Clicquot 1984.'

'Probably. He showed me this one bottle which was worth 40k.'

I could feel my lip curling. 'That could almost pay two nurses for a year.'

'Well, that's what I thought. But then he took me upstairs again and said he had a meeting and would I like to sit in. They were talking about all the charities they support, and all the fundraising they do, and allocating the money. That was really interesting because they do work in a lot of Commonwealth countries, former colonies. Places like India. It was as if they were –' he searched for the words – 'trying to make amends.'

I said nothing.

'Then we came up here, and he introduced me to Lord Fenton – the one in the bow tie. We were talking about vaccinations and herd immunity. I suggested that the STAGS club members support this vaccination project that I know of back home in Jaipur. And he's going to bring it up at the next meeting.'

His eyes were shining.

'Wow,' I said, not wanting to rain on his parade. 'That's quite a day.'

'Yes. And there's something else.'

Here it came.

'Greer, Nel –' he bit his lip with something like joy – 'Rollo invited me to join the STAGS Club.' He lifted his chin an inch, defiantly. 'And I'm thinking about it.'

Just then, into our stunned silence, Nel's phone rang.

It was a shrill, shocking sound – she had it on that classic, jaunty, tinny little tune. Everyone shut the hell up and their noble heads swung round to look right at Nel. I'm pretty sure that sound had never been heard in this hallowed place before. The metallic robot song sliced through the dusty silence as Nel scrabbled, scarlet-faced, in her bag. Of course, when you want to find your phone you never can, and it took what seemed like an eternity of her fishing beneath gum and gloves and Tube tickets before she could shut it up. The Christians and infidels on the walls suspended hostilities to glare down at us, united in their disapproval. By now the assembled gentlemen in the room were muttering, magenta-faced, and a few of them began to approach. But before they reached us, Jack from the door – Jackdaw – had appeared at Nel's elbow, and Plain Jack the waiter, almost as puce in the face as Nel and clearly hating this, stood before her.

'Excuse me, miss. Regrettably, I will have to ask you to leave the premises.' His voice, high and nervy, broke unimpressively in the middle of the sentence, but Jackdaw still stood over Nel, impassive, his bulk underwriting the threat.

None of us moved, our tableau as still as the mosaics on the wall, until Rollo sailed over and broke the deadlock.

'That's all right, Jack. The young lady is with me. We're going in to dinner now. There will be no further . . . disturbance.'

This was a definite *These-aren't-the-droids-you're-looking-for moment*. Plain Jack stood for a moment, torn between the power of the STAGS Club and the power of Rollo. Rollo won easily.

'Very good, my lord. But . . .'

Rollo turned and fixed the unfortunate Jack with his steely blue de Warlencourt gaze. To give him credit, the waiter just

164

about stood his ground. 'The Secretary's compliments, but I must ask the young lady to hand over her mobile telephone. It can be collected from reception on her departure.'

For a moment I thought Rollo would rip his head off, but he just nodded. 'That seems fair. My dear?'

As ever, he didn't look at Nel. But those last two words were a direct order.

I saw Nel clock the little 'missed call' banner before reluctantly placing her treasured phone in Jack's sweaty palm.

'Your ticket, miss,' said Jack, sounding visibly relieved and handing over a ticket bearing two little black antlers and the number seventeen.

At that, both Jacks pissed off with Nel's phone, and we had to follow Rollo all the way through the library, this time enduring the stares of all the STAGS members and their shocked tuttings and mutterings.

Once we were on the stairs and Rollo and Shafeen were well ahead, I murmured to Nel, 'Well, that was great timing by someone. Are you OK?'

She was still absolutely scarlet in the face. I could tell Nel didn't like what had just happened. The beautiful confidence she'd shown downstairs, while I'd cowered behind her, had evaporated. Now she looked near to tears. Suddenly I was angry. Screw those guys and their rules, making Nel feel like shit.

'It was Ty,' she said in a small voice.

'What?'

'The phone call. It was *Ty*.'

Dammit.

'Did she leave a message?'

165

'Gee, Greer,' she said snippily, 'I don't know. Maybe I could check when the phone Nazis *aren't* breathing down my neck.'

She had a point. We followed the two gentlemen in silence and were in time to hear Rollo say to Shafeen, 'I say, old boy – about what we were saying earlier . . . I think there's something you'd like to see.'

He stopped on a corner of the stairs and pushed at a picture, a large hunting scene (of course) featuring a red stag. A door opened from nowhere, like the bit in *The Remains of the Day* when Anthony Hopkins appears on the stairs as if by magic. Not knowing if we were invited or not, Nel and I followed Rollo and Shafeen into a darkened room.

Right away I felt afraid, but at first I didn't know why. It was just a long room with seats either side of it, almost like the choir of a great church. In between the seats was an ornamental scarlet carpet, woven with – yet again – a hunting scene. And at the far end of the carpet was a chair.

I knew then that it was the chair that made me afraid. It was as if the evil in the room was emanating from it, as if it had some power of its own. You know in the summer when the council doesn't take the bins away for a couple of weeks, and you might see a maggot or two on the bin lid, then you open it to put the bag in and there are millions of maggots squirming around the bottom? The chair was like that – it was the source of something rotten. I could swear it was humming with some strange energy, humming very, very faintly like a dormant generator. It was a big thing, more like a throne, made along medieval lines with a tall, triangular back. The arms were ornamented with carvings and worn smooth with use.

Horribly, the four legs of the chair all terminated in the cloven hooves of a deer, a design that reminded me uncomfortably of the Longcross portrait of Elizabeth I, with those greasy, hairy feet and glossy cloven hooves.

We must've been at the top of the building because there was one window in the place and it was above that chair. A shaft of light cut through the dark like a knife-strike and illuminated the great wooden throne, highlighting the oddest thing of all. The chair had wooden antlers rising out of the headrest, all of a piece with it, as if it was all carved out of one huge block of wood. The antlers reached, branch-like, up to the light, as if it were a tree craving the sun.

'There,' said Rollo, with reverence, laying his hand on the horns. 'This is the chair of the STAG. New members sit here to be invested.'

'What happens at the ceremony?' I asked, half in dread. 'Is there an oath and stuff? Do you roll up your trouser legs?' It seemed very necessary, suddenly, to make a joke.

'I can't say, I'm afraid,' said Rollo enigmatically. 'Only STAGS members find out, and they *never* tell.' He turned to Shafeen. 'Try it,' he prompted.

I thought Shafeen would refuse, but he only hesitated for a moment before sinking down onto the scarlet cushion.

The antlers were clearly designed to line up perfectly with the sitter, because they looked like they were sprouting from Shafeen's head. And they changed him. He looked like a king on that throne, but a bad king, a murderous Mughal, a rajah of darkness. With those antlers sprouting from his forehead, he looked like the Grand Stag. And suddenly, under his evil eye,

I was back in the De Warlencourt Playhouse and once again on trial. My heart began to race, and my breath seemed to stick in my throat. I'd never revisited the subject of the trial, not since we'd gone over it all in the car. Of course, so much had happened, but truly? I found it too frightening. Of all the strange things I'd been through since I first went to STAGS, I'd found that trial the most terrifying. I think my mind, even with the daily reminder of the brand on my thumb, had blocked it out. But now I could feel the panic rising. I didn't know Shafeen any more, or what he might do.

I would have turned and run, but at that moment he got up from the chair and was himself again. He lingered for a moment, patting one of the arms affectionately, even longingly. But I couldn't get out of there fast enough. As Rollo held the door I pushed past him, back onto the staircase where I could breathe again. I grabbed Shafeen's arm to hold him back as we followed Rollo along yet another grand passageway.

'You're not serious about joining, are you?' I whispered.

'If I did, it would be to change things from within.'

'And Rollo's told you that you can? He's told you there's a place for you?'

'Well, he would nominate me. And then you need a second, but he said Lord Bow-tie would do that. But as to the place, they come up very rarely. It's literally dead men's shoes. They have an opening.' He didn't quite look at me. The penny dropped horribly.

'Because of Henry?'

He said nothing but looked straight ahead as he walked.

'It is, isn't it? You're literally taking Henry's place.'

'He didn't say it in so many words. But I guess so, yes.' Shafeen still couldn't quite look at me.

'Jeez . . .' This was a whole new creepy dimension to the whole creepy business.

23

Rollo led us into the dining room, and I began to feel a little more comfortable.

The room was light and airy, and it looked a bit like the Raffles Hotel from *Crazy Rich Asians*, all rattan furniture and leafy green plants, very Empire. (There was that word again.)

Expensive-looking couples talked in hushed tones over the candles and silver cutlery, and groups of important-looking men huddled together in important-looking clothes having important-sounding conversations.

'Four of us today, Jack,' Rollo announced in the doorway to the tailcoated maître d'. You obviously didn't have to book if you were Rollo de Warlencourt.

'Very good, my lord.'

We started to walk, but this new Jack got in Shafeen's face before he could fully enter the room. 'Begging your pardon, sir, but might I assist you with a tie?'

Rollo turned back. 'Ah yes. *Mea culpa*. Should have told you. Neckties for dinner, old boy. Club rules, you know. Jack will give you a club tie.'

The smooth maître d' guy had already produced one, magician-like, from his sleeve. It was a bottle-green colour, bearing a discreet gold imprint of a stag's head. It looked refined, classy and very, very expensive.

Shafeen looked at the thing dangling from the maître d's hand as if it were a snake. I saw that his cheeks had a high colour, as Nel's had over the phone incident, and that this was *his* particular humiliation. Rollo had neglected to tell us about either the phone or the tie rules. Was it deliberate or genuine forgetfulness? Either way, I wondered what my humiliation would be.

To begin with, I didn't think that Shafeen would put the tie on – yesterday's Shafeen wouldn't have. But after a long moment, never breaking eye contact with the maître d', he turned up his collar. He took the thing from Jack's hand and expertly tied the tie, flipping it and tucking it rapidly, turning his back to the dining room as he did so, as if he did not want to be seen, as if he was doing something shameful. When he turned back I could see at once how much the green tie suited him. The newest Jack of the evening clearly agreed with me. 'Very nice, sir,' he said, and got out of Shafeen's way, holding out a white gloved hand to usher him into the room.

We followed Rollo to the best table in the room, right next to a series of tall windows, looking out onto the festive darkness of St James's, with a constellation of Christmas lights piercing the night. I noticed that between all the tables, including our own, were glass cases full of odd-looking animals, peeping out of this strange jungle of hothouse greenery and rattan chairs. They weren't quite recognisable, but all looked a bit like something. You know that card game where the top half is one animal, and the bottom half is another? They were all like that. The one nearest to our table was a bird with a hooked beak, half puffin, half pelican, and I thought I had seen this one before, in Disney's *Alice in Wonderland*. As I sat in the chair Jack pulled out for me, I asked, 'Is that a dodo?'

'Yes. That's the very last chap,' Rollo said with something like relish. 'He died in 1700 and he's been here ever since. They are all extinct if you look . . .' He waved an expansive hand around the room, indicating all the glass cases. That was obviously why all the creatures looked so weird – they had kicked the Darwinian bucket; they were aberrations, too strange to live. I didn't feel that it would be the moment to ask if the STAGS members had actually made them all extinct by killing the last specimen of each, but I wouldn't have been at all surprised.

Shafeen, leaning back to lay a snowy napkin in his lap, asked: 'How long has the club been here, sir?'

'Since 1690,' said Rollo. 'My ancestor Edwin de Warlencourt was one of the founder members. And then George de Warlencourt, the one who put the new frontage on Longcross, he used to sit at this very window table with Lord Longleat. He once bet Longleat 30,000 sovereigns on which raindrop was going to get to the bottom of this windowpane first.' He tapped on the glass next to him with his signet ring. The sound made me uncomfortable – and the ring made me think of Henry.

'Did he win?' asked Nel.

Rollo smiled a wolf's grin. 'What d'ye think paid for the frontage?' He smoothed his own napkin over his thighs. 'And

of course, the *duelling* in those days. My *goodness*. Hardy –
beg pardon, *Shafeen* will have told you ladies about the
fencing board. That's what they call it. It's a like an elongated
chessboard upstairs, where the chaps used to fight. Quite a
few wingings and woundings back in the day, and a couple of
deaths.' He spoke of the combatants like they were hunting
fowl. 'Of course,' he said with a smile, 'the duelling has tailed
off somewhat nowadays.'

I didn't think so. I thought the duelling was still very much
going on. I hadn't missed Rollo calling Shafeen Hardy. As
careless with names as ever.

'Jill.' Rollo raised his hand to a passing waitress. 'A bottle
of the Sancerre, please.'

Jill brought the wine and also some small starters, which,
like the things in the glass cases, all looked a bit like something
but were not totally familiar.

'Can I pass you ladies anything?' asked the earl. 'Looks like
Patum Peperium and Welsh rarebit.'

I didn't know what any of that was, but I was pretty hungry,
having not eaten since the Oxford Starbucks, so I fixed on a
word I recognised. 'Well, I don't want to eat rabbit. Even Welsh
ones. So I'll have the other one.'

He looked slightly surprised. 'It's not rabbit. It's rarebit.'

I was no wiser.

'Sort of cheese on toast, with milk and mustard,' whispered
Shafeen.

Well, that sounded disgusting. So I took the other choice off
the proffered silver platter: a neat little triangle of toast spread
with something brown. I took a tiny bite. It was mega-fishy.

I made one of those polite faces people make when they are tasting food on cooking shows.

'What is it?' I murmured to Shafeen out of the side of my mouth.

'Gentleman's Relish,' said Shafeen.

I gave him a look.

'Anchovy paste,' he expanded hurriedly.

Since I'd spent a lifetime picking anchovies off my pizzas, I left the little toast discreetly on the side of my plate.

The next issue was that I couldn't see a menu. I made the charades sign for a book opening to Nel, and she shrugged; clearly she wasn't going to ask, after the phone disaster. I wasn't about to prod Shafeen either, after the tie thing. 'Is there a menu?' I asked eventually.

Rollo shook his handsome head. 'Jack or Jill will tell us the bill of fare. All seasonal, you know. All seasonal. Sinful to eat out of season, eh?'

Sure enough, a different Jill came over to the table and told us the specials. 'This evening we have grey partridge with roasted vegetables and a red-wine jus, chicken curry with jasmine rice and Scotch woodcock with Cheddar-and-chive mash.'

OK. After the rabbit thing I was determined to get this right. The other three chose the partridge, then it was my turn.

'Hmm, two game birds,' I said, showing off a bit. 'Which one to choose? I think I'll get the Scotch woodcock.' I could see Shafeen shaking his head, trying to stop my flow. I couldn't interpret the signal, so I ploughed on. 'I suppose I'll have to pick out the shot. That's right, isn't it?' I turned to Rollo, who was looking a bit amused. 'When I was at Longcross – the first

174

time – I had a pheasant with all the little bullets in it.' I always babbled when I was nervous, and I was babbling now. 'So I'll have the woodcock, please, but leave the shot on the side.'

Jill looked at Rollo, then back at me. 'Erm, that won't be necessary, miss. Scotch Woodcock is scrambled eggs, capers and anchovies on toast.'

'Ah. OK. I mean, yes, I know,' I said faintly. 'I'll have that.'

I hid my scarlet face in my wine glass. It had been a long time coming, but I'd been taken down too. *Dumb club*. Nothing here was what it seemed. People had names that weren't their own, fowl were eggs and rabbits were cheese. Once again, I felt I was Through the Looking Glass.

When the food came, it was, as you might expect, absolutely delicious – like a really top restaurant, which, I suppose, it was. The only gross bit was the anchovies, which I ended up having to pick out as usual. It might as well have been a Domino's.

Rollo waved his fork in Shafeen's direction. 'Thought you'd've had the curry. It's jolly good here.'

Nel and I froze at this and looked at Shafeen. If there was one thing I knew about him, it was that he wouldn't ever order the curry. He'd once told me that he never ordered it outside of Rajasthan because it didn't compare to the cuisine at home, but I thought today he'd had a different reason. I thought he wanted to fit in.

Rollo ploughed on. 'Reminds me of the time your father made us have it at Longcross. Gave us quite a shock.'

It was a surprise to hear that Aadhish had made a point of having curry at Longcross. He must have been one brave kid.

Shafeen put down his knife and fork and looked Rollo straight in the eye. Maybe it was his father's courage that made him brave enough to ask then what he did. 'Was my father afraid of you?'

'Of *me*?' Rollo sounded genuinely surprised, rather than shocked or angry. 'No, old chap. Never in this world.'

Shafeen said carefully, 'I thought he was bullied.'

'Is that what he told you?' asked Rollo gently.

'No.' Shafeen took a sip of wine. 'He never said a word about STAGS.'

'And yet he sent you there. Doesn't that say something? A chap doesn't send his only son into danger.'

Rollo could have been talking about Henry, but there was no tell-tale sign of grief – no tear in the eye, no catch in the voice, nothing.

'So he *wasn't* bullied?' I asked.

'Well –' Rollo drummed his fingers uncomfortably on his chair arm – 'one does always beast the new chap rather. But no, he wasn't afraid of me.' And then he said something entirely unexpected. 'I admired him greatly. I would have liked him to be a member here. I would like *you* to be a member here.' He leaned forward, persuasive. 'Think about it, Hardy. That –' he tapped the knot of his tie – 'could be yours for real.' I don't know if Shafeen noticed the name slip again or not – but I did. I'd been wrong. Shafeen wasn't taking Henry's place at all. He was taking the place Rollo had intended for Aadhish all those years ago. Was the earl trying to make amends for something?

Rollo was super-charming for the rest of the meal; part, I was sure, of the hard sell on Shafeen. But we all benefited. He couldn't have been more hospitable. He pressed us all to have the pudding of the day – spookily called 'Morgan's pudding'. It was autumn pears and blackberries, and every mouthful reminded me of Ty. Why had she called Nel? Had she left a message? I was suddenly impatient to go, to be reunited with Nel's phone, but there was the compulsory coffee and brandy still to come. After that there was another wait – Shafeen excused himself to go to the toilet. He'd been drinking more than he usually did – a sure sign that he was enjoying himself. With a sinking heart, I knew that him joining the STAGS Club was as good as a done deal.

I thought it would be a bit awks making conversation while Shafeen was gone, but Rollo sprang up too, excusing himself to talk to some other powerful person he'd spotted. He was working the room, pressing backs and elbows, patting shoulders, clearly persuading everyone in sight to come to Longcross. Nel and I talked softly, about nothing much, both united in the feeling that anything private would have to wait. We were interrupted by the return of Shafeen, looking pretty peculiar.

'What's the matter?' I said, alarmed. 'Did someone steal your lunch money?'

He looked sick, and was taking off the club tie as if it burned him.

'What happened?' asked Nel.

'I wouldn't join this place in a million years.' He said it so forcefully that the people nearest to us turned to look.

I pulled him down into his chair. 'What are you talking about?' I hissed. 'What happened?'

'The urinals in the toilets. They're Pygmies. Actual Pygmies.'

'What? Real people?' My mind couldn't grasp what Shafeen was saying.

He snorted. 'No, they stopped short of that. Some colonial booty from somewhere or other in the Empire of the STAG. If I was to guess, I would say they were made of ebony.' He looked straight at me, quite his old self again. 'You piss into their *mouth*, Greer.'

'No *way*!'

'I swear to God. Go and have a look.'

I shook my head. 'That's definitely *not* something I'm going to do. It's the men's toilet. What if the Foreign Secretary or somebody is having a pee?'

'Just hang around,' he said. 'Someone will come out at some point. Then just look in the door. I'll say you've both gone to the toilet.'

'Oh, come *on*,' said Nel, dragging me up. 'Rollo'll be back in a minute.'

We found the gents, which had, of course, a stag's head with antlers on it. The ladies – indicated by a deer with no antlers – was next door, so we hung about, pretending we were waiting for a friend. Then someone came out of the gents and just for a second we had a glimpse of the inside. I saw rows of little black men, ebony-dark and shining, cruelly caricatured with pot bellies, Afro hair and rings in their ears. Their heads were thrown back and their giant mouths wide, utterly humiliated, baby birds waiting gladly and humbly for the bounty that was coming.

Then the door closed on the nightmarish scene. Sickened, Nel and I looked at each other. She said what we were both thinking. 'Let's get the hell out of here.'

When we returned to the table Shafeen and Rollo were

ready to go. Subdued, we filed down the stairs after our host to the cloakroom, where Nel exchanged her numbered ticket for her phone. Jackdaw – for it was he – handed the Saros back without a word.

'Did Ty leave a message?' I asked as the gentlemen shrugged on their coats.

'No,' whispered Nel. Then she said slowly, 'Or if she did, it's not there now.'

'Huh?'

She looked at me, blue eyes very direct. 'They had the phone for at least an hour.'

I understood. The phone, that savage little Trojan horse we'd brought into the STAGS Club, had given us away. We'd been found out, and we were no longer welcome. I suddenly felt that we were very exposed in that grand marble atrium, that there were eyes and ears everywhere. I couldn't wait to be gone. Jackdaw walked to the door and held it open for us, and the icy blast from the chill street seemed as welcoming as a hug. Jack did not look at us but acknowledged Rollo with a polite nod. That farewell summed up the evening.

'Doesn't say much, does he?' I grumbled, once the giant had gone back inside.

'That's because he can't,' said Rollo, waving to his driver.

'What, he's not allowed to?' I thought this was going a bit far, even for the STAGS Club.

'No, he *physically* can't,' said the earl, stamping his feet a little against the cold. 'He's mute.'

Rollo was looking impatiently left and right for the car, so he probably missed our astonished faces. 'Jackdaw was a boxer in the East End,' he explained. 'He lost the power of speech from a boxing injury. We helped him out, that's all. The STAGS like to do our bit for the community – employ the disabled, all that.'

That *so* didn't sound like something that the STAGS cared about. As we waited for Rollo's chauffeur-driven vintage Rolls-Royce to creak to a halt in front of us, I thought it was more likely that Jackdaw had been hired for a less charitable reason. I remembered in the Sherlock Holmes stories that the doorman of the Great Detective's own club – the Diogenes – was a mute, so he couldn't share the members' secrets. I looked back at the smart but shuttered frontage of the club and thought about the Pygmy toilets and the STAGS chair squatting evilly in that secret room.

If Jackdaw couldn't speak, he couldn't tell.

24

Back at Cumberland Place, Bates greeted us with the news that coffee and sandwiches were in the library.

Caro had already retired to bed, and Rollo, probably exhausted by his Ancient Marinading, went straight up to join her.

We, of course, went to the library, because there was so much to say. If I'm honest I wondered why anyone would need coffee and sandwiches after a slap-up dinner, but there they were, all laid out. We ignored them, and as soon as the door closed we settled around the fire in leather chairs the colour of dark chocolate, with only the walls of books to overhear us. Shafeen spoke first. 'I can't *believe* I was actually thinking of becoming a part of that club.'

I leaned back in my chair, suddenly exhausted.

'You're not going to join and change the toilets from within?' I was teasing slightly, but only out of relief.

Shafeen didn't smile back but got up and walked to the mantelpiece to fiddle with a (probably priceless) china shepherdess. 'I think this whole thing has gone up a notch. I think it's about race as well as class.

'I genuinely think that Rollo and his kind are afraid for the white patriarchy. They think *they* are under threat. It's pure Replacement Theory.'

Nel had taken the chair on the other side of the fire, mirroring me. 'That's quite a leap from a toilet.'

Shafeen put the shepherdess down, probably not with as much respect as she deserved. 'Why did this whole thing start? Conrad de Warlencourt coming back from the Crusades. You saw the mosaics on the walls in the STAGS Club. That room was even called the Crusader's Library. And the urinals were absolutely symbolic of that.'

I didn't quite know how to frame my question. 'Aren't they just a joke? A terrible one, yes. But a joke all the same?'

'No,' he said hotly. 'It's not a joke. A whole bunch of white guys pissing in the faces of people of colour. Not just people, but really badly caricatured racist stereotypes. You can't possibly know how it feels as a person of colour to see something like that. You ask Ty.'

'I wish I could,' I said.

'God, I wish we knew what she wanted when she called me,' said Nel.

'Try her now,' I urged.

'Well, OK, but remember she has a normal BTEC smartphone. Not a Saros.' Nel wasn't boasting about her father's tech, just stating a fact. 'She doesn't have the coverage of the Saros Orbit. Signal's pretty crap up there.'

'But she managed to call earlier. And message yesterday. She was still at Longcross then.'

'So far as we know,' said Shafeen. 'Haven't you heard what

I've been saying? She's obviously in danger. On Boxing Day, I'll bet you everything I have that they'll be chasing *her*. I think the foxes are quite safe.'

It was the first time anyone had said it out loud. But of course we'd all been thinking it, since we'd piled into the car to leave Ty to her fate. It all made sense – her shoe had been stolen to give the hounds her scent. That night when the dogs had come for us in Longwood was just a rehearsal. But it was still, despite all our experiences of the de Warlencourts, hard to believe.

'But Louis *likes* her,' I said. 'I'm convinced of it. So won't he keep her safe?'

'You thought Henry liked *you*. But he was planning to kill you all along.'

I thought of dream-Henry's denials in the hospital. He'd said, then, he would never harm me. But I couldn't say that without sounding cuckoo.

Instead I hit back: 'And you think Rollo likes *you*.'

'I thought so,' he said, almost sadly. 'Now I'm not so sure. Supposing it's all a plot to put us down?'

'Us?' I pointed to the three of us in turn.

'No, not *us* us,' he said impatiently. '*Me and Ty* us.'

He paced before the fire, trying to explain. 'I'm here, the guest of the earl. Ty is at the manor house, by the side of his heir. But there's something wrong about it. It feels like . . . like a trap.'

I felt a shiver, even in front of that roaring fire.

'The writing was literally on the walls of the Crusader's Library,' Shafeen went on, on a roll now. 'Here they still are – the white knights putting down the infidels. I think they see us almost as . . .'

'As what?' prompted Nel.

'As *rebels*,' he finished.

The word nudged my memory. Who else had been talking about rebels? Then it came to me. 'Professor Nashe was talking about rebellion. Today. In my interview.'

Shafeen turned. 'In what context?'

'We were talking about Ben Jonson, and the purpose of his plays. Right at the end of the interview I said that he meant to start a fire, and she agreed. It was the first time I got the feeling that I'd said something right. She said *The Isle of Dogs* was an act of rebellion.'

Shafeen stopped pacing. He sat down in one of the big winged leather armchairs and faced me, long fingers steepled together. 'What else did she say?'

His tone freaked me out a bit. '*She's* not mixed up in this, is she?'

'Why not?' said Shafeen. 'She's at an ancient college.'

'The one that Nath— the Abbot just happened to go to and you're applying to as well,' put in Nel. She sat up suddenly. '*And* she was actually *there* on the night of your hanging. She was in the audience; why not in the circle of DOGS who tried you too?'

Shafeen held up both hands, pale palms outwards. 'Hang on, hang on. We're floundering a bit here. What exactly did she say?'

I thought back. So much had happened that it was hard to believe that my interview had been only that morning. 'Oh, she said that Ben Jonson had a pet fox. Called – wait for it – Reynard.'

'As in, actually living in his house?' Shafeen sounded disbelieving. 'Probably a bit dangerous.'

'Oh, I don't know,' I said. 'They probably get domesticated, right? Just like dogs. That's what Nashe said.'

'Hmm,' said Shafeen doubtfully. 'I think they're pretty vicious when cornered. What else?'

'Lots of stuff about Extinction Rebellion, and the Occupy movement, and . . .' I stopped.

'What?' said Nel.

'The only thing that she was really insistent about,' I said slowly, 'was that I read *Volpone*. Another play by Ben Jonson.' This last bit was to Shafeen by way of explanation – he hadn't been there by the Paulinus well at STAGS when I'd talked to Nel about *Volpone*. 'In fact, Nashe was so insistent she said it twice as I was going out the door. She said, *Remember, Remember.*'

'Well,' he said, 'let's do it. Maybe that will give us a clue.'

'Do what?' I was one step behind.

'Read it,' he said simply.

'How?' asked Nel.

Shafeen flung out his arms. 'Look where we are.'

He was right. Every wall was crammed with books, from floor to ceiling.

We all got up, and for the third time in our relatively short acquaintance, began to peruse the shelves of a de Warlencourt library. Shafeen took the right side, I took the left, and Nel went up to the mezzanine. This time it was relatively easy – no dark and hidden shelves, no secret doors behind paintings. I found the play almost at once, and that was because I was almost sure someone had just been reading it. It was sticking out from the shelf, just a tiny bit, a little to the left of the mantelpiece. The gold letters imprinted on the spine were almost glowing in the light of the fire. I slid the book out. It was a slim volume, a rusty red colour – the colour of a fox.

'Found it!' I called, and Nel clattered down from the mezzanine so fast she was almost at my side at the same time as Shafeen, who only had to cross a room.

We all crowded around the play as I opened the cover gently – it was pretty old – to find the usual publisher's deets and printed engravings. This edition was not original – it was dated 1870 – but it still might tell us what we wanted to know.

'What's it about?' asked Shafeen.

'Well, why don't we let Ben Jonson tell us?' I turned to the Argument at the front of the play, the acrostic that described the plot of the play in a few lines. It was the very acrostic I'd written out for Nel only a few weeks ago. I read it out:

V olpone, childless, rich, feigns sick, despairs,
O ffers his state to hopes of several heirs,
L ies languishing: his parasite receives
P resents of all, assures, deludes; then weaves
O ther cross plots, which ope themselves, are told.
N ew tricks for safety are sought; they thrive: when bold,
E ach tempts the other again, and all are sold.

Shafeen shook his head. 'Nope. I'm no wiser.'

'Here,' said Nel, and she shoved her phone in his face. It was a funny scenario, and it totally encompassed the Medieval and the Savage. Me with a book on one side of Shafeen, Nel with the phone on the other. It was like that bit in *Animal House* where there's an angel and a devil on some guy's shoulders, both tempting him. But which of us was which?

'Look,' said Nel, 'good old SparkNotes. Here we go: plot summary.' She handed the phone to me and I scanned the synopsis. The play was apparently about an uber-rich old Venetian guy (Volpone) who had three friends squabbling over who would inherit his money. In order to screw with them, he cooked up a plan with his deputy, Mosca. According to SparkNotes:

> Volpone spreads a rumour that he has died and then tells Mosca to pretend that he has been made his master's heir. The plan goes off perfectly, and all three legacy hunters are fooled. Volpone then disguises himself as a Venetian guard, so that he can gloat in each legacy hunter's face over their humiliation, without being recognised. But Mosca lets the audience know that Volpone is dead in the eyes of the world and that Mosca will not let him 'return to the world of the living' unless Volpone pays up, giving Mosca a share of his wealth.

I looked up. 'It's about Henry and Louis.'

'Uh, OK, Greer,' said Nel, mock-agreeing with me. 'Ben Jonson, who was born in the sixteenth century, wrote a play about who was going to inherit Longcross?'

'No, not *that* way round. What if we're being directed to this because it's what happened at Longcross? What if Henry faked his own death, handed over the estate to Louis, and now Louis won't give it back?'

'Give it here,' Nel nabbed the phone back off me. 'Look.' She scrolled furiously. 'It's not about Henry. This Google Books page says that *Volpone* was a thinly veiled attack on Robert Cecil.' She turned to Shafeen, probably conscious that he was the only one out of the three of us who hadn't lived and breathed *The Isle of Dogs* all term. 'You remember in *The Isle of Dogs*, the characters of Lupo and Volpone represented William and Robert Cecil, the father-and-son team who were Elizabeth I's chief courtiers?'

'Yes, of course,' said Shafeen.

'Well, according to this –' the Saros lit up Nel's face – 'by this point in history, daddy was dead and gone and Robert Cecil was *James I's* chief advisor. And he was a bit of a badass by all accounts – the most feared and hated man in England.'

'That's exactly what Professor Nashe told me,' I broke in.

'So if *Volpone* was about Robert Cecil,' said Shafeen, seizing on the idea gladly, it seemed, to get us off the subject of Henry, 'then this play is a sort of spin-off of *The Isle of Dogs*. But this time Ben Jonson made Robert Cecil his central character.'

'So it *is* like the *Han Solo* movie,' I burst out.

'*What?*' they chorused.

'Nothing,' I said hurriedly. 'How about this. I'll take the play up to bed and see if I can make any sense of it. There's no point guessing until at least one of us has read the whole thing.'

'Looks like someone got there before you,' said Shafeen. 'There's a bookmark. See?'

He gently took the volume from my hand and showed us the gilt-edged pages. Sure enough, they didn't entirely close. There was something in the book, parting it a little. Shafeen flipped the play open at the marked page.

Some sort of business card had been used as a bookmark.

You may be sure we looked very closely at the page that had been marked. As I scanned the text I fully expected this bit to be about Volpone's faked death, but it was just some piece of 'comedy' about a foolish knight called Sir Politick Would-Be, and didn't seem to have any relevance at all. 'Hmm,' I said. 'Well, I don't think there's a shortcut to this. I'll just have to read the whole thing, and –'

'Maybe there is a shortcut,' Shafeen interrupted. He was looking at the little card in his hand. He turned it round between his fingertips and showed it to us.

I took it from him. It was a beautiful thing – firm creamy card with a lovely rough texture. It was the kind of card they use for very posh invitations – one, I remembered, in particular. On the front it said:

L. Cornellisen & Son
Artists' Colourmen
Est. 1855

And underneath the printed text, in handwriting, were the words:

De Warlencourt. Order date 01/12
Ready for collection 21/12

'What's a colourman?' Nel asked.

'I suppose,' teased Shafeen, 'someone who makes colours?'

'It must be a posh paint shop,' I said. 'I wonder what they ordered. Something to do with art? Do you think Caro dabbles in watercolours? It's a very upper-class thing to do.'

'Hard to know from this,' said Shafeen, taking the card back and studying it. 'All it tells us is that whatever it is took three weeks to make.'

I took the card in my turn. 'I wish it told us more.'

'It does,' said Nel. 'It tells us that whoever ordered whatever it is was reading this play very recently. In the last three weeks in fact. Perhaps the order is connected to the play.'

'Well, let's find out, shall we?' suggested Shafeen. 'It says ready for collection on the twenty-first of the twelfth. That's tomorrow.'

Nel looked doubtful. 'You mean we sort of lurk around the shop and see what they collect?'

'No,' said Shafeen. 'I mean we just go and get it.'

'What?' I said. 'Just walk in there and hand over the card? No offence, Shaf, but none of us exactly looks like a de Warlencourt. Least of all you.'

'Doesn't matter. We can just say we're picking it up for them.'

We looked at each other and started to smile. 'OK.'

Nel, the Queen of Google, had been tapping her Saros. She said, 'Cornellisen's is right by the British Museum.'

'Huh,' I snorted unattractively. 'Maybe we'll see Abbot Ridley again. He seems to like hanging around museums.'

'Wait, what?' asked Shafeen.

'Of *course*,' I exclaimed, 'you don't know this. We saw the Abbot. This morning. In Oxford.'

We told him about our sighting of Abbot Ridley outside the Ashmolean Museum, and Shafeen's conclusion was much the same as ours. 'I guess he was just visiting his old uni. Or his old tutor.'

'But there's more to it than that,' said Nel. 'We *do* know why he was there.'

I explained how we had gone into the museum and found the branded thumbprint in front of Guy Fawkes's lantern. Shafeen blew right past the lantern bit and focused in on the thumbprint, as well he might.

'Wait, so you're saying Ridley is branded too?'

'Yes,' I said very definitely. 'If the print was his. And I don't see who else's it could have been.'

'You definitely didn't touch the glass yourself before you saw the print?' asked Shafeen.

'That's what *I* said!' Nel broke in.

'No,' I said. 'I swear.'

Shafeen looked at me for a long moment. 'All right. Then we have to assume he too has been tried by the Dark Order of the Grand Stag and branded a Manslayer.'

We let this sink in for a moment. 'My question would be, who did he kill?' My voice was a whisper.

'I'm sure he didn't –' began Nel.

'Never mind that,' Shafeen cut in. 'Why would he be working at the *school*? Right in the tiger's den? I mean, it's run by the Order who tried him, no?'

'At least that means he isn't one of them,' said Nel defensively.

'Well . . .' I whined.

She turned on me. '*Really*, Greer? After he cut you down and everything?'

'It's just the Esmé Stuart thing, remember? He said she was a woman and then changed his mind and said he was a man. Then he totally gaslit my ass about it afterwards.'

'All right,' Shafeen stepped in. 'Supposing he *is* one of the good guys. And supposing he did want you to see – what was it?'

'Guy Fawkes's lantern,' Nel and I chorused.

'Then why didn't he stop and say, *Hi, girls, fancy running into you – while you're here you should really go and look at Guy Fawkes's lantern.*'

'Maybe he *didn't* see us,' I said.

'He did,' said Nel vehemently.

Now Shafeen looked at her for a second, pressing his lips together, and I wondered what he wasn't saying. Then he spoke. 'All right,' he said again, with sudden authority. 'Let's get to bed. We've got a mission in the morning.'

We all said goodnight at the top of the stairs. There was no chance that Shafeen would stay with me in Henry's room, but as Nel went ahead I did linger behind for a second to kiss him goodnight. The kiss was so good I had to break away. I breathed in his ear, 'What weren't you saying just now? That you didn't want to say in front of Nel? Do you think Abbot Ridley *didn't* see us? Do you think he *is* one of the bad guys?'

'No,' he said. 'Look, I know Nel has a thumping great crush on Ridley, so I didn't want to spook her.' He sighed. 'He saw you all right. But I think he was being followed.'

192

25

Once I'd locked the bedroom door I texted Ty straight away.

```
Are you ok? PLEASE txt me
```

I kept checking, but there was no reply. I was pretty tired, as it had been such a long day, but I still sat down with *Volpone*. *Remember, Remember.* There must have been some reason why Professor Nashe had been so keen for me to read it.

It was quite different to *The Isle of Dogs* – for a start, all the action took place in one day. For another, it was set in Venice, a place I didn't know at all. It was quite a cool story, about a nobleman obsessed with money and status, who was amused by his three so-called friends squabbling over who would become his heir. I couldn't particularly see how it could be interpreted as an attack on Robert Cecil though. To be honest, I couldn't see past what I'd mentally called the De Warlencourt Gambit: Volpone faking his own death just so he could screw with everybody, and the squabbling of his heirs over his fortune, and his eventual heir, Mosca, refusing to give up his inheritance. After all, if you'd convinced everyone you were dead, and all your friends and family were mourning you, it would be pretty hard to come out and say, *Only kidding!*

Wouldn't it?

I don't know how long I slept, but I do know that I was wakened, in the dead of night, by a weight on the end of the bed. The mattress sagged, as if someone was sitting on it.

And someone was.

Shafeen, I thought. I'd half expected him. That kiss had been an invitation, as surely as a card pushed beneath a door. Even Henry couldn't keep us apart for long.

But then I saw the bone-white curve of a naked back, and the blond hair like silver in the moonlight. 'What are you doing here?'

'It's my room.' There it was, that cut-glass upper-class English voice. 'Can I get in? It's jolly cold.'

'I guess if it's your room, it's your bed. Just . . . just keep your distance.'

He got under the covers and we faced each other, my head on one pillow, his head on the other.

I looked at him, he looked at me. Here was Greer MacDonald, there was Henry de Warlencourt. We didn't touch. We didn't do anything, we just looked, each drinking the other in. In the near dark this Henry didn't look like himself – the gold hair silver, the blue eyes black. This was the Henry from the other side of the Looking Glass, the Henry from the ether. Did everyone look like this in the Valley of the Shadow of Death?

He took my hand. He was warm for a ghost. Then he did something odd. He raised it to his face, found my branded thumb and kissed it. Then it came to me.

I'd done this to him.

I'd let him fall Through the Looking Glass.

I was a Manslayer.

I looked at our hands together, clasped tightly. I remembered then the top of the waterfall – his fingertips grazing mine as he fell back into space.

And then I said something I'd been thinking about a lot, something I'd wanted to say for a year. 'I'm sorry I didn't save you. Even though you were a monster.'

He smiled. 'If I was a monster, why did you try?'

I thought about this. 'Because if I didn't, that would have made *me* a monster.'

'Then what's this?' He waggled my thumb.

I didn't pull it away, but I said, 'I'm not a killer.'

'I'm not a killer either.'

'Then why did you want to kill *me*?'

Before he could answer there was a sound at the door – that familiar little grate of metal on metal as an unseen hand turned the handle. Henry sat up with a start, backing away in terror. I'd never seen him afraid before, even when he met his end. The blond hair was ruffled, and there was a sheen of sweat on his moonlit skin.

'Calm down,' I said. 'It's only your mum. She still comes in to kiss you goodnight, you know.'

The handle turned back on itself and footsteps trod away. He lay back down, smiling, and put his hands behind his head. I could see the dark shadow of hair under his arm. 'Dear mater.'

'Your father misses you too.'

The smile disappeared. 'I doubt that.' He turned once again

to face me. 'Ask him about my childhood. Ask him about his "parenting" style. See what he says to *that*.' Henry's voice was heavy with scorn.

'Are you saying it was somewhat . . . Medieval?'

'You said it.'

I remembered then what he'd said before, that other dream-Henry by my hospital bed, hinting at the horror of his childhood, by way of some explanation as to how he'd become what he had become. I remembered, too, the poor baby elephants tied to obedience by a puny rope. By the time they were old enough to break free, they no longer wanted to.

I tried to recall how Rollo had been when he'd spoken of Henry. 'But he seemed quite tearful when he was talking to Shafeen. About a man and his heir.'

'Well, he has one now, doesn't he? Louis, Lord Longcross. Sounds rather well, doesn't it? A good bit of alliteration.' The scorn was back.

Then I remembered. 'In the hospital you said it suited you to let Louis be the heir for a little while longer. What if he enjoys being the lord? What if he doesn't let you back in? Like Mosca?'

'He will.'

'Henry?'

'Greer?' It always shook me when he spoke my name.

'Do foxes mean anything to you?'

'What a funny question.'

'If it's funny,' I said, 'then humour me.'

'They are reddish dog-like creatures that one chases across the countryside,' he said, smiling slightly. 'Why?'

196

'Ty said: *See if you can find out anything about Foxes.*'

'Who is *Ty*?'

'Louis's . . . girlfriend.' Then I remembered something else. 'She's actually got a scholarship to STAGS in your name.' In all the madness, that suddenly struck me as funny.

'Ah yes.'

'Did you meet Ty at Longcross?'

'Meet? No. I was keeping somewhat of a . . . low profile.'

Then I twigged. I rose up on my elbow and studied him. 'Why didn't you ask me who Mosca is?'

'What?'

'You asked me who Ty is, even though if you *were* at Longcross you've actually seen her. I imagine she stood out quite a bit at the twins' party. But you didn't ask me who Mosca is.'

'All right. Who is Mosca?' he drawled, amused.

'A character in Ben Jonson's *Volpone*, as if you didn't know.' I was perfectly sure he *did* know. 'Someone's been reading the play. Downstairs in the library. Was it you? Were you getting ideas?'

He looked amused. 'I don't know what you mean.'

'Yes, you do.'

'Shh.' He put a thumb to the lips he'd once kissed. Not a finger, but a thumb. It was all a bit *Cape Fear*, but hot. Officially, of course, I should have been outraged. *Man shuts up woman by putting his thumb over her lips.* But it just felt tender and fond.

'Go to sleep now.'

And I must have done, because I don't remember anything else.

When I woke up, of course he was gone. Dreams don't hang around in the daytime. There was no impression of a Henry head on the opposite pillow, no golden hairs in the bed. Groggily and, if I'm honest, a bit regretfully, I got up and dressed for breakfast.

PART 8
THE RUN

26

Cornellisen's was the most Diagon Alley shop I'd ever seen outside of the Harry Potter movies.

We'd had a polite breakfast with the countess, at which I'd found it really hard to look at Shafeen. I hadn't actually done anything with Henry (and, duh, it was all in my own subconscious), but the dream did feel kind of . . . cheaty. So I was extra affectionate as we took the Tube to Central London, almost to the point where I probably pissed Nel off a bit.

We'd got off at Tottenham Court Road, straight into the mental Christmas shopping mayhem that seems to grip everyone the week before Christmas. We then walked for a bit, and just as we got to a pretty part, the snow – as if on cue – started to fall. That gave the shop when we found it even more of a movie-set feel. The outside was painted a lovely aqua colour, with square Dickens-type shop windows, like in *The Muppet Christmas Carol*. When we went in the door, a little bell chimed above us, bobbing on a curl of bright brass.

Entering Cornellisen's was like stepping into a rainbow. The walls were stacked high with every colour of paint in the spectrum, in tubes and pots and blocks and palettes. Not just paint, but pencils, crayons, pastels and every size of paintbrush from huge hairy ones down to the thinnest little whisker. There were also reams of multicoloured paper and shelves of sketch books from ring-bound to leather-bound. The smell was a weird hybrid; partly chemical, partly animal. Paint and bristle, ancient and modern, Medieval and Savage. It was all very cool, but my heart sank a little. We weren't going to learn anything from picking up art supplies for the countess's boredom-busting hobby.

The shop was empty except for this chilled-looking hipster behind the counter. Not for him the manic Christmas crowds. He wore a check shirt, had long hair twisted into a man-bun and this amazing waxed moustache, which looked not unlike two paintbrushes repurposed as face furniture. He looked oddly appropriate as a staff member for that place – like he'd just stepped out of Victorian times. Behind him, floor to ceiling, were rows of square black drawers set into the wall and numbered in gold like an advent calendar. It gave the place an even more Christmassy look.

'Greetings,' said the hipster, getting out of the chair reeaaally slowly. 'Can I help you?'

'We hope so,' said Shafeen. As this had been his idea, we'd agreed he would do the talking. He handed over the little card we'd found in *Volpone. De Warlencourt 21/12.*

'Ah yes,' said the chilled-out fellow. He opened one of the drawers behind him – number seventeen, it was – pulled a volume out of it and brought it back to the counter.

As soon as he laid it down, I recognised it.

Although it was brand new it looked really old, with one of

those aged greenish-black leather covers that on books they call 'morocco'. The hipster stood the book on its end and showed us the spine. The black leather was inscribed with a decade tooled in gilt numbers.

Our decade.

Then he laid the book tenderly on its back and opened it at random. The dark volume was as creamy white inside as the wound of an axe. He riffled through the pages, and the paper was as thick as quality, smelling freshly milled and slightly chemical. That was the modern tang lying within the antique leather aroma of the shop. The pages were blank and unlined, ready to be inscribed with death.

It was a game book.

None of us looked at the others. We all just looked at the book. We all knew what it meant.

It was the hipster who broke the silence. 'Is it OK?'

'Yes,' said Shafeen softly. 'Yes, I imagine that's *exactly* what's required.'

'Cool,' said the hipster.

We all smiled politely as the guy started getting bits and pieces together to wrap the thing up. It suddenly occurred to me, with a lurch of panic, that we might be required to pay for this prince among books, but the hipster wrapped it obligingly in this lovely paisley paper, securing it with a golden sticker saying *L. Cornellisen*, without asking for any of our cash. I guessed it was all pre-paid. 'Need a bag?'

I was about to say yes, as a book as precious as this could easily get trashed in the snow, but Shafeen said *no* so abruptly that I fired him a glance. I'd never picked him for a massive eco-warrior, but he turned down the plastic bag like he was Greta Thunberg. He took the package in his hands, just as it was, and made as if to head for the door. Nel and I were still standing there like fools when he turned back.

'Actually, you know what? I think we might pop to the British Museum, since we're in the area and all that. So can we come back and pick it up after?'

'Sure,' said the hipster calmly. 'We're open until five.'

'Great,' said Shafeen, placing the package tenderly back on the counter. 'But in case we miss you – you know, if the exhibition is really amazing or something – can my . . . uncle pick it up another day? We'll tell him it's ready.'

'No worries,' said the hipster, sinking back in his chair again and opening his book. 'Catch you later. Or not. Whatever.'

Nel and I shared a WTF look, but there was nothing else to do but follow Shafeen out of the shop.

'Shafeen, what the actual?'

'Shh,' he said. 'Let's go towards the British Museum in case he's watching.'

'You mean he's *not* nailed to that chair?'

We walked the short distance down the road to the great grey frontage of the British Museum. It looked not unlike the Ashmolean – pillared portico, grand sweeping steps – but this was way bigger: epic and impressive, the daddy of all museums. We sat on the steps, among the sea of selfie-takers, and when we were settled on the chill stone Nel said, 'What was all that about?'

Shafeen turned up his collar against the cold. 'It occurred to me that if we pick up the book, and then they go to get it and it's not there, there might be some awkward questions.'

I saw. And he'd been quite clever with that little fake-out that he was going to take the book, but then turning back to leave it. 'There still might be anyway. What if Rollo goes in and the hipster says, *I met your Indian nephew the other day?*'

Shafeen shrugged. 'He might. But he didn't strike me as a massively chatty type.'

'And,' added Nel, 'unless they get it soon, we'll be long gone.'

'Well . . .' I said.

They turned to me, both with wary expressions. I saw that they knew what I was about to say.

'We *have* to go back there. You *know* we have to go back there.' I didn't have to say where *there* was. They both got it.

'They've got the book. They've got the victim. They've got the meet all arranged. Rollo even bent the law so they can have a jolly good Boxing Day hunt. We can't leave Ty to her fate.'

Shafeen exhaled, his breath winter white. He spoke to the air. 'She's right, you know.'

'We'll just ask them tonight if we can go,' I said, reminding myself of the night I'd begged Louis to let us go to Longcross.

'Well.' Shafeen slapped his hands decisively on his knees. 'That's settled then.' He hauled me to my feet, and I helped Nel up in turn. We didn't even go in the British Museum but turned our back on the building and everything in it – a big colonial toy box we didn't have the heart to play with today.

We all walked sombrely down the steps, walking away from history, walking towards it, a little funeral procession.

For me, every step was a sigh.

I'd known all along, really, that I wasn't done with Longcross.

27

At dinner that night we asked if we could go to the Boxing Day meet.

We all agreed that Shafeen – the golden boy – should do it, because it honestly didn't feel like Rollo would refuse him anything. And indeed he didn't.

'Capital!' Rollo exclaimed, and from my short acquaintance with him I knew this was his highest expression of joy. 'This calls for a bottle of fizz. Bates –' he summoned the butler – 'the Veuve Clicquot '84.' As Bates left the room, Rollo rubbed his hands until the knuckles cracked. 'This is really wonderful. This could be the making of you, Hardy. I mean, Shafeen.' He leaned forward and tapped his nose. 'And I'll tell you why. I just had word that one of the royal princes will be there, and quite a few of the cabinet too.'

He was all smiles, as was his wife. It was odd, I reflected, sitting there in my red dress, having dinner with psychopaths – and not, of course, my first time. Odd that they were perfectly good company, just as their son had been. Odd that we knew they were planning a manhunt, or woman-hunt, and we could all just sit here, shooting the breeze, waiting for Bates to bring up the special bottle of champagne, instead of running from the room screaming. I was reminded of my day fishing with Henry. It was one of the most fun days of my life – right up until the bit when he pushed me in the lake.

Henry's father eyed us all fondly. 'I suppose you can ride, all of you?'

We'd discussed this on the way back from town. Nel, of course, had her own pony (called Gary, which I thought was just the best thing in the world). Shafeen had been riding, bareback and saddled, since he was old enough to hold his head up. And I'd learned in a most peculiar way, but entirely in keeping with my strange itinerant life with my dad. One summer holiday, when I was in Year 7, my dad had been filming in Austria, a documentary about those Lipizzaner stallions. You know the ones? They are these really amazing horses which are born black, then turn completely white when they are grown, then they get taught how to dance. It sounds really circus-y, but it's not – it's sort of grand and noble. Those little black foals end up as white stallions in golden ballrooms in Vienna, rearing and revolving in a ghostly kind of ballet. Anyway, the point of all that is that I had to stay at the Lipizzaner stud farm for the whole summer, so my dad got me riding lessons while I was there. I got pretty good – I mean, I can ride, and jump, and basically stay on a horse, but whether or not the Austrian style I was taught would pass the test at the hoity-toity Longcross meet was another matter.

'We stable some horses in Hyde Park,' said Rollo. 'Why don't you ride out tomorrow? Unfortunately I have some business in town.' We looked at each other nervously, all hoping that the 'business' wasn't picking up the game book from Cornellisen's. 'But Caro'll take you. Won't you, old girl?'

The countess didn't look old at that moment at all, but about twenty-five. She had that shining Christmas-tree look about her, just as she had the day we'd met. 'Of *course*,' she said keenly. 'I need to get my eye in before the meet, just like the rest of you.'

Bates came back in – without the champagne, I noticed. I guessed they'd run out of Rollo's fave. But Rollo didn't seem to mind. 'Bates – could you call the livery stables and have the horses ready for tomorrow? Four mounts.'

'Very good, my lord.'

Caro turned to us. 'We'll go directly after breakfast. The weather should be perfect for it. It will be *such* fun.' She looked entirely happy and sounded entirely sane.

For the rest of the meal Henry's parents were utterly charming. They were the consummate hosts, and they had this positive air about them that I struggled to define. After thinking about it really hard, I could only describe their air as *triumphant*. And I came away from that dinner feeling that our asking to go to Longcross wasn't really a surprise to them at all.

28

When I got back to my room I texted Ty again. This time I was more specific.

```
We think the Boxing Day meet is a Ty hunt
```

And then,

```
Hold on
We're coming to get you
```

I waited for a moment, staring at the bright little screen. There was no reply, as I knew there wouldn't be. I lay flat out on the bed, fully dressed, as Reynard the fox watched from the wall. I was so tired that it took me some time to realise there was something on my pillow. There, in the golden circle of light from the bedside lamp, lay a dog rose.

I picked it up and studied the velvet curling petals, and clutched it to my heart, the thorns piercing the material of my frock. I caught sight of a movement in the mirror, turned in a panic and saw only myself.

There was too much red. Now I knew why I hadn't liked the colour of the dress. Yes, it was the colour of the ghostly judges at my trial. Yes, it was the red of a fox stretched on the winter turf. But it was also the red of the dog roses winding over the stable-yard at Longcross, and standing proud in a vase beside my hospital bed, and now on my pillow at Cumberland Place. *That's* when I knew what had been bothering me. That colour, the colour of the red, red rose, was the key to the mystery. Who had brought the very same dog roses, the roses that grew at Longcross, to my hospital room – half a day before Cass had even got to me – if it wasn't Henry?

Then I was sure.

Henry's mother was still coming in to see him because he still from time to time slept here. He had slept here last night, really slept here. He hadn't been a dream. He had left before I woke up.

His mother wasn't crazy, and neither was I.

Henry was alive.

PART 9
FULL CRY

29

After breakfast the next morning, there were strange clothes laid out on my bed.

I hadn't told the other two about Henry at breakfast. Shafeen for obvious reasons. Nel I didn't tell because I was afraid. I was afraid she'd tell me I was crazy. And now I was so sure I wasn't. I had evidence. I'd put the dog rose in my water glass by the side of my bed – Henry's bed. It stood out stark and dark against the white lace doily on the table, blossoming like a bruise.

I had a proper Longcross flashback as I picked up the unfamiliar garments from my bed, felt the fine cloth between my hands and read the smart labels from St James's. But these clothes were nothing like the ones I'd worn at Longcross, that trio of easy, tweedy outfits for huntin' shootin' fishin'.

There was a pair of buff jodhpurs, supple as suede, a well-cut midnight-blue jacket and a velvety black riding hat. There were leather boots too, not new but soft as butter and buffed to a dull shine. I put everything on, right down to the riding gloves, and regarded myself in the mirror. I certainly looked the part, but I was pretty sure that riding the upper-class way was one of those skills you couldn't really bullshit.

Before I left the room I took one look at the dog rose. The velvety red petals were fully open.

30

I met the others downstairs – Nel in a fetching mulberry jacket, Shafeen in night black.

The countess – in a jacket as green as poison – led us out of the door, and the de Warlencourts' silent chauffeur drove us to the stables, which were not far at all. The huge car nosed its way over Oxford Street and past Marble Arch to another huge expanse of green, this time apparently Hyde Park. The driver dropped us all off at a lovely little mews, where four seemingly massive horses waited for us, their shifting feet clopping on the cobbles. Four cheery grooms greeted the countess respectfully, and she nodded at them in return. Here she seemed to have more authority and I was reminded of Cass at Longcross – she was in her domain here. I only had to watch Caro mounting her horse, unaided, to understand that she was a brilliant horsewoman. Shafeen vaulted onto his glossy black beast like the princeling he was, and Nel, too, seemed to be as comfortable on her horse as if she was sitting on a sofa. As for me, after what seemed like an eternity of bouncing around with one foot in the stirrup, trying to get some purchase on the saddle, while my awkward bastard of a horse moved around, swishing its tail in my face, one of the grooms had to shove me up like a sack of potatoes. I felt like everyone was watching me by that point so I tried desperately to remember what I'd learned all that time ago in Austria, about straightening my back and gripping with my knees, but despite my efforts, when my horse – who was apparently called Snowflake – moved off with a lurch I nearly fell to the cobbles. The mare seemed impossibly high. If I didn't improve fast, *I* would be the one who wouldn't survive the hunt.

I had to admit that riding in Hyde Park was pretty magical. There was obviously a fair bit of muscle memory involved in riding a horse, and once my body had remembered how to walk, trot and canter, and I'd got used to the quite scary distance between me and the friendly floor, I began to enjoy myself. There was snow on the ground, but even with just a velvet jacket I quickly started to warm up with the exercise. The park looked beautiful – hard to believe really, looking at the trees and the vast glassy lake, that we were in London.

'This is Rotten Row,' said the countess, waving her crop at the broad sandy track running through the green park. 'Laid down in the reign of William III as a direct route between Kensington Palace and St James's Palace.'

'What's rotten about it?' I asked. 'It looks lovely.'

'Nothing,' she smiled. 'The name is a corruption of *route de roi*, the way of the king. It became a place for the quality to ride in their finest clothes – to see and be seen.'

Just as we were doing today. We all looked perfectly dressed for riding and undeniably posh – all in hats and boots, with our jackets in varying dark hues of velvet. Shafeen, ramrod straight, looked amazing on horseback, like he'd been born in the saddle. Nel was more relaxed, holding the reins with one hand in a chilled fashion, and I tried subtly, and unsuccessfully, to somehow combine both their styles of riding. I didn't have to worry though; help was at hand. The countess seemed happy to correct any bad habits I'd picked up in Austria.

'Sit square, Greer,' she said. 'Back straight. Head *up*. Imagine a string pulling you up from the top of your head. And heels down, that's right. Hold the reins like you're holding two china teacups – they should be in a straight line from the bit to your hands – no sagging. Don't yank them though. Tell the mare where you want to go with your knees.'

There was a lot to remember but I tried my best, and she seemed pleased with me.

'Very good. We'll make a proper rider of you yet. Are you ready to gallop?'

She made a little clicking noise with her mouth, and her horse began to go faster. I remembered this from my early lessons, the rush as your mount took off at speed. For an instant I lurched in the saddle until I found my seat – and suddenly the world became smooth. I had a real moment out there in the snowy park, galloping shoulder to shoulder with Shafeen, our eyes sparkling, laughing, gulping the cold air. At last we jogged to a halt, and turned the horses to wait for the others. Caro, following behind us with Nel, eyed me in a pleased fashion. 'There!' she cried. '*Now* you remember. *Now* you understand.'

I was reminded, once again, of Henry; of that last day fishing in Longmere. He'd looked at me just like that when I'd killed the brown trout. Like I was one of *them*.

She didn't say a word to the other two. Maybe she could see, with one eye, that they were streets ahead of me (literally) on the riding front. But it felt like there was something else there too – some other purpose. It felt like she was grooming me. Not in a fifty-year-old-man-on-the-Internet way. A Julie-Andrews-in-*The-Princess-Diaries* way. She was training me – preparing me for something. But for what?

When it was my turn to ride alongside the countess we spoke, inevitably, of Henry. Oddly, on that ride down the sandy track of the park, we were now on a different footing. For the first time I felt a kinship with Lady Longcross. She and I, alone in that company, knew what we knew – that her son was alive. Now, when I spoke to her, she hadn't changed, I had. But *because* I had changed, she was now transformed to me. She wasn't some mad old bat. She was a loving mother. Once again, I wondered what it would be like to have one of those.

As we rode side by side, I wondered how Henry fitted into the foxhunting plan. Was he a part of it? Or was this Rollo's gig? Or even Louis's, the temporary heir to the throne? Did Henry even know about the meet? And why was he in hiding? How could he bear to let Louis strut around as Lord de Warlencourt, even for a single second? But I could ask none of these things of Henry's mother. Instead, I asked the question that had been bothering me ever since her son had shared my bed. What he'd said then, about her, about Rollo, had piqued my interest. 'What was Henry like as a little boy?'

She smiled. 'Adorable. Just like an angel. Such an affectionate child. We were so close – still are.' It was still a jolt to hear him spoken of in the present tense. 'I think I spoiled him because Rollo was very hard on him, you know. Fathers have to be.'

I wasn't sure about this. I imagined it was possible for a dad to raise a boy successfully without being a dick.

'He was our only one, you see, our son and heir. We never had any more.' She said this very matter-of-factly, with a stiff upper lip. I didn't feel I knew her well enough to ask if they'd wanted more kids. But she carried on. 'We married late, you know – well, Rollo did. He was quite the stud – busy playing the field – until he met the right girl of course,' she said archly. Caro didn't seem at all bothered by her husband's womanising past; if anything, she sounded kind of *proud*. 'He was over fifty when we had Henry. And once he had his heir, well . . .' She paused delicately. 'He thought he was a little too old to have the spare.' It was hard to tell from her voice whether or not she minded. 'Henry was at home with us until he was eight, with his nanny, you see. Then he went to STAGS prep.'

'At *eight?*'

'Yes, of course.' She said it as if it was the most natural thing in the world. 'So Rollo's notion was that he only had until eight to discipline him – you know, to really whip him into shape.'

The phrase sat uncomfortably with me. I wondered just what shape that discipline took. But then something else claimed my attention. There was a crowd gathering under a little knot of trees at the corner of the park. They caught my eye for a particular reason – they were all wearing red hooded onesies, just like the mysterious figure I'd chased through Westminster Abbey. I reined Snowflake in. 'What's going on?'

'Speaker's Corner,' said the countess with disdain in her voice. 'A designated space where any crackpot can say anything at all to any other crackpot who will listen.'

There was indeed a person in red standing on a kind of stepladder making some sort of shouty speech, and another, taller person – also in red – at the front, seemingly firing up the scarlet crowd. They were not passive spectators, not a quiet assembly, but an edgy, noisy mob, buzzing like a hive of bees. That wasn't the strange thing about them though. The strangest thing was that, as well as having the same clothes, they all had the same face.

It was vaguely nightmarish. They were all wearing the same distinctive mask. It was white, and oval, and had a smiling face on it, with holes cut out for the eyes. Above the eyeholes were quizzical raised eyebrows, and over the smiling mouth was an old-fashioned, Errol-Flynn-in-*Robin-Hood*-style black moustache. The grin was broad, there were hectic pink highlights on each cheek, and the expression as a whole spelled mischief. Something about it struck a chord in my memory. The mask was vaguely familiar.

As we passed, the crowd's general hubbub began to crystallise into a chant. I couldn't quite hear it at first, then I figured it out. They were chanting: '*Beat the Elite. Beat the Elite.*'

I began to feel uneasy. We couldn't have been in a worse place at a worse time in all our pristine riding gear. The horses started dancing around a bit. Shafeen gathered his reins. 'Let's go back.'

But it was too late. We'd been seen and the shouting began to be directed towards us. It was creepy, all those red-hooded figures, all those white faces with smiling mouths, and the angry, incoherent shouts coming from behind the masks. Then something detached itself from the crowd and came flying – directly towards me. It was a balled-up piece of paper, probably a leaflet or something, and it didn't hurt at all. But it was enough to spook Snowflake and she reared like a statue.

I very nearly toppled off, and my panicky brain dredged up the thought, *Two hooves up – died in battle*. I wasn't about to die in this one. I gripped with my knees, hauling on the reins, and Snowflake, amazingly, dropped down to all fours.

Shafeen and Nel were still reaching out to me, shouting to see if I was all right, when Caro reacted completely differently. She gathered her reins and rode directly at the red-clad protesters, crop raised high. The imagery was uncomfortable. I was reminded of those YouTubes I'd seen of Masters of Foxhounds thrashing hunt saboteurs with their whips. In that moment the countess looked scary – transformed from the gentle, slightly spacey aristocrat to an angry harpy. I thought of little Henry being 'whipped into shape'. A masked figure cowered beneath her, then Shafeen blocked her with his stallion. He caught her wrist in one gloved hand. '*No*,' he said. Then, more gently, 'Let's go back to the stables.'

It was the upper-class equivalent of those people in British gangster movies who stop fights with the immortal line: *Leave it, ee's not wurf it*. For a moment Caro held Shafeen's eye and he held hers. I was back at Longcross, with Henry and Shafeen having their stare-out contest after Shafeen had told his tiger story. Now, as then, the de Warlencourt broke first. Caro freed her hand and turned her mount away. The tall man who seemed to be the ringleader of the protesters grabbed his paper-chucking friend and pulled him away.

As we rode off, I looked back nervously. The crowd had

turned back to their speaker, all except the tallest guy in the gathering, the ringleader. He stood slightly apart from the other scarlet figures and watched us go. Then he did this odd thing. Looking at me the whole time, he tilted his head slightly to one side like a dog. It was truly creepy. I kept my eyes on him until they streamed in the cold. As we turned onto the sandy path, just before they were lost to view, was I imagining it or did the tall figure in red raise his hand to give me a thumbs-up?

I didn't really have time to process this because the countess was raging. '*Dreadful* people. How *dare* they? I've got half a mind to call the police.' She gathered her reins tighter in disgust. 'But they'll do nothing. It's not like the old days. They used to hang people here, you know,' she said, with obvious approval.

'Good times,' said Shafeen wryly, disapproving just as obviously.

Nel seemed shocked. '*Did* they?' she exclaimed, looking about her. And in this lovely corner of London it did seem unbelievable.

But I *could* believe it. Suddenly it all came back to me: the trial, the beeswax of the candle in my nose, the fear that that would be the last scent I ever smelled. 'Ben Jonson,' I said, with a sudden chill that had nothing to do with the weather. 'It was here.' Here, in this green and pleasant land, on this very spot, he'd had a noose placed around his neck, and here he'd spoken the neck verse, just as I had, to set himself free. *Miserere mei, Deus, secundum magnam misericordiam tuam.*

'Yes,' said Caro. 'The gallows of Tyburn were on this spot. This is where they hanged the criminals. And if you ask me,' she sniffed, 'they still should.'

31

No one said much in the car on the way back.

Caro, still fuming, went to change for lunch, and the smooth and silent Bates showed us to the drawing room, where a bright fire burned and the sherry tray was waiting. For once I gratefully accepted the heady little amber drink. In fact, I practically grabbed it out of Shafeen's proffering hand and downed it in one.

'Well,' I said, the fire in my throat, 'that was quite a morning. I wonder what they wanted. The mask posse, I mean.'

'I thought they made it perfectly plain,' said Shafeen, sipping his sherry more calmly. 'They want an end to all this,' he waved his little glass around the room, encompassing the gilt and crystal and original paintings – the whole pricey pile of Cumberland Place. 'Elites. The patriarchy. Old money running the country.'

'So we're sort of on the same side,' I said.

'Well, their grievances are more general,' he replied. 'We're going to war on one family.' I thought, guiltily, of Henry.

'Speaking of which, did you *Remember, Remember* to read *Volpone?*' asked Nel.

'Yes,' I said, determinedly turning my mind away from the weirdness in Hyde Park. 'It was good and all that, but there was nothing that really jumped out from the plot that seemed relevant to all the STAGS stuff. Not like in *The Isle of Dogs*, I mean, which was clearly a satire on the practice of the death hunts. I don't think this play has any significance besides pointing us to the card for Cornellisen's and the game book. It's a *piece* of the puzzle, not the whole jigsaw. Maybe . . .'

I stopped.

'What?' said Nel.

'*Remember, Remember,*' I breathed. That did it. Suddenly I remembered where I'd seen that mask before. The quizzical eyebrows, the mischievous smile, the curling moustaches and neat goatee beard. 'It was *Guy Fawkes*.'

'What was?' asked Shafeen.

'In Hyde Park. It was Guy Fawkes.'

Nel said, 'Which one? The one that chucked the paper?'

'*All* of them. They were *all* Guy Fawkes.'

Nel set down her glass and leaned forward in her chair. 'OK, *walk* us through it, Greer.'

'That mask is from a film called *V for Vendetta*,' I explained. 'At least, it became a film. It's actually originally from a DC comic. After the film's release, that mask of Guy Fawkes's face became the symbol for every anti-Establishment anarchist and freedom fighter there is. It's a massive movement.'

'Well, we could see that today,' said Nel. 'That was a lot of Fawkeses.'

'Yep. I knew I'd seen that mask before somewhere, and

when you said *Remember, Remember*, I clicked.' I pointed at Nel. 'Why *did* you say that?'

'You told me Professor Nashe said it.'

'Exactly. She said it *just* like that. She repeated the word remember.' I was piecing it together as I went. 'I thought it was odd at the time, a verbal tic. I thought she just really wanted me to read *Volpone* and was telling me twice. Now I don't. It's from that rhyme, isn't it? The one you learn in primary school. About Bonfire Night.'

Shafeen looked lost. 'What rhyme?'

'It goes, *Remember, Remember the Fifth of November . . .*'

'Oh yes!' said Nel, joining in. '*Gunpowder treason and plot.*'

'*We see no reason why gunpowder treason should ever be forgot,*' we chorused, finishing the rhyme together.

Shafeen was looking at us like we were both crazy. 'I've *literally* never heard that before.'

'That's because you were at school in Jaipur before STAGS. If you're in a primary over here, they teach it to you. It's a British schoolkid's first real encounter with revolution. Terrorism 101. Civil Disobedience for Dummies.'

'OK,' said Shafeen. 'So you're saying Nashe gave you a coded message about Guy Fawkes.'

Was I? 'I guess I am, yes. Then Abbot Ridley led us to Guy Fawkes's lantern in the Ashmolean Museum. Containing the very flame Fawkes was going to use to light the fuse and blow up both Houses of Parliament – Guy Fawkes's suicide vest. Then we go riding in Hyde Park, and who is at Speaker's Corner? A bunch of anti-Establishment protesters, all wearing Guy Fawkes masks.'

I spread out both my hands, waiting for them both to catch up.

'Think about it.' I took a breath. 'There's some connection between *Volpone* and Guy Fawkes. And Ty found out about it. Ty said, *See if you can find out about Foxes*. Volpone literally means "fox".'

'When was *Volpone* written?' asked Shafeen suddenly.

Nel flipped out her Saros and tapped away. 'Late 1605 to 1606.'

'And when was the Gunpowder Plot? November, obvs, but what year?'

Tap, tap. Nel looked up, and we knew from her face what the answer was before she even said it. 'It was 1605.'

'OK,' said Shafeen. 'That's suggestive. Let's have the facts about the Gunpowder Plot. I know a bit but not enough. A gang of young nobles, wasn't it?'

'Hello, Wikipedia,' said Nel, typing rapidly with her thumbs. 'Here goes:

The Gunpowder Plot of 1605 was a failed assassination attempt against King James I by a group of provincial English Catholics led by Robert Catesby. The plan was to blow up the House of Lords during the State Opening of Parliament on 5th November 1605. Guy Fawkes, who had ten years of military experience fighting in the Spanish Netherlands in the failed suppression of the Dutch Revolt, was given charge of the explosives.

'Why didn't they like James I?' I wondered aloud.

'Other way round,' said Nel. 'According to this, the king had renounced the Catholic church and ordered all Catholic priests to leave the country. But I'm not sure the plot was personal against James – it says here the plan was to get rid of senior judges, aristocracy and bishops, who'd all be attending the State Opening of Parliament on 5th November. In other words –' she looked up –'the whole of the elite Establishment.'

'Beat the Elite,' said Shafeen. 'And why didn't the plot *work*?'

'Hang on.' She swiped up the screen with her forefinger. 'Ah, OK: *The plot was revealed to the authorities in an anonymous letter sent to William Parker, 4th Baron Monteagle, on 26th October 1605. During a search of the House of Lords at about midnight on 4th November 1605, Fawkes was discovered guarding thirty-six barrels of gunpowder – enough to reduce the House of Lords to rubble – and arrested.*'

'Presumably holding the lantern you saw,' put in Shafeen.

'Yes – there's a picture of it here,' said Nel. 'It even says *Ashmolean Museum.*'

'There we go,' I said.

'Ooh, also there's a section on the actual Monteagle Letter. They've reproduced the text here.'

'Read it,' urged Shafeen.

Nel did. And as she read, she didn't sound like everyday Nel. This was Chanel the actor, the player who had spoken Ben Jonson's lines so beautifully in *The Isle of Dogs*.

My Lord, out of the love I bear to some of your friends, I have a care of your preservation. Therefore I would advise you, as you tender your life, to devise some

227

excuse to shift your attendance at this parliament; for God and man hath concurred to punish the wickedness of this time. And think not slightly of this advertisement, but retire yourself into your country where you may expect the event in safety. For though there be no appearance of any stir, yet I say they shall receive a terrible blow this Parliament; and yet they shall not see who hurts them. This counsel is not to be condemned because it may do you good and can do you no harm; for the danger is passed as soon as you have burnt the letter. And I hope God will give you the grace to make good use of it, to whose holy protection I commend you.

'So whoever sent the Monteagle Letter,' said Shafeen slowly, 'just wanted to warn one bloke – Lord Monteagle. They didn't necessarily want to stop the plot. It was just a warning to a friend to stay away. But Monteagle told the authorities.'

I was caught up in the drama of it all, just as I had been in the Ashmolean. Fawkes, in a dark and cavernous Westminster cellar, crouching over his fuse with his lantern. And, above ground, Lord Monteagle's fastrider galloping through the streets of London, hooves sparking on the cobblestones, riding, riding, to warn the king. I could almost see it playing out like a movie, and it was an effort to wrench myself back into the real world. 'This is all very cool,' I said, 'but what does it have to do with *Volpone*?'

'Dunno,' said Nel, scrolling up and down. 'No mention of the play here.'

I grabbed the phone. 'Let's put both search terms in.' In the search bar, I typed *Volpone/Gunpowder Plot*.

The long list of answers came back in less than a second. 'There *is* a connection besides the date,' I said. 'The results are mostly about one book by a writer called Richard Dutton.'

'A novel?'

'No, more like a textbook. It's called,' I looked up, '*Ben Jonson, Volpone and the Gunpowder Plot.*'

'Well, that's pretty clear,' said Shafeen. 'What's his argument?'

'Let's see.' I tapped one of the results, which seemed to be giving some sort of summary. 'Listen: *Dutton's basic argument is that Jonson's play reflects directly (if obliquely) on the events of the 1605 Gunpowder Plot, and that in particular the playwright seems to have taken subtle but satiric aim at the role of Robert Cecil, Earl of Salisbury and James I's chief minister, in that nearly explosive affair.*'

'All right,' said Nel. 'So this play, as well as taking a shot at Robert Cecil, was a reflection of the Gunpowder Plot, which makes sense as it was written just after.' She turned to me. 'Did you clock that when you read it?'

I skimmed my hand over my hair in a whooshing motion. 'Nope. Went right over my head.'

'But if that *is* the case, what does that mean for us, and for Ty,' asked Shafeen, 'in the here and now?'

I handed the phone back. 'It's clearly directing us to some sort of plot. Has to be, doesn't it?'

Nel pocketed her phone. 'But what kind of plot?

'Well, we're pretty certain they're going after Ty on Boxing Day,' I said. 'But there's something bigger here. What about a medieval plot by the Dark Order of the Grand Stag to remove the non-white threat to the white Establishment, one kid at a time? Starting with Ty?'

'Well, that would certainly fit with what we saw at the STAGS Club, and with the new game book. They're up to *something*, that's for sure.'

'This is making my head hurt,' I complained. 'But we have to figure it out. Tomorrow is our last day here. Then it's Christmas Eve and we go home before meeting back at Longcross.'

'Actually, that reminds me –' Shafeen checked his watch – 'I'd better call India.'

Shafeen left the drawing room to make the phone call he'd been dreading. He had to tell his parents that he wouldn't now be coming home for the holiday. If he was determined to come to Longcross on Boxing Day, which he was, it wouldn't be worth flying to Jaipur and back before school started, as he'd only have a few days. Nel and I chatted idly about the logistics of our journey back to the North – she was going to drop me and Shafeen in Manchester on the way to Chester – but really we were waiting for Shafeen to come back.

When he did, he had an unreadable look on his face.

'Was it OK?'

'–ish.' He flopped down in an armchair and blew his hair out of his eyes. 'Mother was OK. Father was . . . well, he was really upset actually.'

'Had he made loads of plans for you?' asked Nel.

'Yes, but it wasn't that. He doesn't want me to go to Longcross.' He looked thoughtful. 'It was the first time I've heard my father call the house by name. And it was the first time he's given me anything approaching a warning.'

'What did he say?' I asked gently.

'Nothing explicit. He just told me to be careful. The only thing that shut him up was telling him we were going to help a girl in trouble. That, for some reason, he got.'

'Did you tell him everything would be OK?' said Nel.

'Sort of.'

'You didn't, did you?' I said.

'Well –' he shrugged – 'I thought it would be tempting Kismat.'

'What are you talking about?' I asked.

'You know,' he said, '*fate*.'

Before he could explain further, Bates entered the room, opening both doors at once with that silent flourish only he could pull off. 'Her ladyship's compliments, but if you would like to change for lunch, it will be served shortly.'

It was obviously more of an order than a suggestion, so we all trotted upstairs to get out of our horsey clothes.

After lunch, which the countess spent complaining angrily about the 'vermin' at Speaker's Corner, we went to the library. Soundproofed by all those books, we tried, once again, to contact Ty – and once again there was no reply.

'That's been two days now,' I said. 'Nothing since the STAGS Club night when we missed her call.'

We sort of sat about, at a bit of a loose end, until Shafeen said, 'Fancy seeing how the other half lives?'

'How d'you mean?'

'Well, before we go haring off to Longcross, there might just be some other people in London that Ty *has* been in touch with.'

'Who?' asked Nel.

Shafeen said, 'Her family.'

'God!' I exclaimed. 'I'd completely forgotten she was from here.'

'Well, she's not from *here*, is she?' he said pointedly. 'She's from somewhere quite different.'

'You know what I mean,' I said. 'That she lives in London.'

'We should at least check with them, shouldn't we?' asked Shafeen. 'See if they've heard from her.'

'Have we even got her address?' queried Nel.

'I have,' I said. We'd exchanged addresses the very first time she was invited to Longcross. She'd promised to send me a postcard. 'It's in my phone somewhere.'

'Let's go then,' said Nel. 'We've got time before dinner.'

And that's how, on a snowy December afternoon, we found ourselves heading to a place we'd all heard of a thousand times but never seen. A place that had enormous significance to all of us, but where we'd never set foot.

We were going to the Isle of Dogs.

PART 10
VIEW HALLOO

32

From the minute we got off the train we knew we were in a different world.

We'd taken the Docklands Light Railway from the space-age silver city that was Canary Wharf, and got off at a stop called, unpromisingly, Mudchute. Mudchute was surprisingly green and open, but as we followed Google Maps to the Limehouse Estate, our expectations lowered all the time. Ty's 'manor' was even more grim than we'd anticipated. There was an old sofa in the middle of the scruffy courtyard, like it was *The Wire* or something. Everywhere we looked there was graffiti – huge bubble letters saying SLUG. I don't know who Slug was, or is, but he got through a lot of spray paint in his time. There was a helpful map, also graffitied, with a faded schematic of which block was which. We identified Topcliffe House and headed in what we hoped was the right direction. Even the snow, which had looked so beautiful in Regent's Park, looked quite different here. It was slushy and brown, punctuated with broken scooters and old bike wheels, and personified by a threatening-looking snowman with a backwards baseball cap.

I have to admit, and I'm not proud of this, I felt really uneasy.

It was way too quiet, with the snow muffling everything and the blank windows on four sides of the flats watching us like eyes. I was glad, then, that we'd dressed down. Only that morning we'd been in velvet jackets riding in Hyde Park. This afternoon, without even discussing it, we'd all put on the most casual clothes we had with us – Puffas, hoodies and jeans. Even then I felt like we stood out way too much as we made our way up a pee-smelling stairwell, where the ubiquitous Slug had also sprayed his tag.

Along a balcony littered with pushchairs and kids' bikes, we found Number 2, Topcliffe House. We tried the doorbell, then knocked, but there was no answer. After a moment we peered through the window. There was a plastic windmill stuck in a plant pot on the windowsill, revolving sadly in the bitter wind. Beyond its sails and through the glass we could see a little black kid looking at us with round eyes. At the sight of us he turned and scrambled under a table as if he'd had the four-minute warning.

Somebody came up behind us, jingling housekeys belligerently. 'Oi!' said the somebody, and it seemed like such a London syllable. 'What you lot want?'

I turned to see a girl no taller than me but with enough aggression to scare all of us. She had on a silver Puffa jacket, and her snaky dreadlocks were tied up in a red do-rag. I couldn't blame her for looking annoyed. We were, at that moment, engaged in looking through the window at what was presumably her brother. This girl had such a resemblance to Ty that I realized she must be her sister. And she got right up in our faces.

'Sorry,' I said instinctively, backing away. She was so threatening, even though we outnumbered her, that we were very much on the back foot. 'We're friends of Ty Morgan's – schoolfriends – and we just came to – we wanted to . . . say hi?' I finished weakly.

At that the girl completely transformed. She smiled a welcoming smile and clasped my arm so tightly it almost hurt. 'Come in, come in! Don't just stand there. I'll put the kettle on.' She unlocked the door and we filed in after her. She threw the keys on a little side table with a clash. The front door opened right into the living room. In the corner there was a tiny Christmas tree standing sentinel over a bunch of wrapped presents, which were so large they seemed to take up most of the room. As we crammed into the tiny space she called, 'DeAngelo! You can come out, baby. Mama's home.'

Shafeen turned to her, wide-eyed. 'Are you . . . Mrs Morgan?'

'That's me. But I don't need no title. Missy's my name, so you might as well use that.' She laughed loudly. She was lovely: ballsy, warm and much, much younger than I'd expected.

The kid we'd seen came out from under the table. I'm crap at guessing little kids' ages but he looked maybe six or seven. His expression explained her aggression. She was being a tiger mother. He half hid behind his mum and looked out at us with enormous eyes.

'Where's your book, DeAngelo? You do your reading while I talk to these nice people. I'll be testing you later. These are Tyeesha's friends, baby.'

She crossed over to the kitchen, which was just behind this kind of breakfast bar, so really also in the living room. She clicked the kettle on and got out a bunch of mugs with a clatter and started chucking tea bags into them. She did everything in a hurry, as if time was precious to her. She talked loudly over the rising kettle. 'So who we got here? How d'you know my Ty?'

'I'm Greer,' I said. 'I directed the play she was just in.'

'And I'm Nel,' said Nel. 'I was in it too.'

'Oh, I know all about you girls,' she said, delighted. She pointed a long fingernail at me. Her nails were amazing – long acrylics, and the one she was pointing had a crystal set in it. 'You were Poetaster, and you –' she moved the fingernail to Nel – 'was Canis. Right?'

She mashed the teabags vigorously and then lobbed them accurately, Kobe-style, at the bin. She jerked her head at Shafeen. 'And who's this one?'

'I'm Shafeen. Let me help you.' He sprang up to help distribute the teas. None of the cups matched. The mug he put in front of me was enormous and said SPORTS DIRECT on the side. The tea was nothing like the anaemic Earl Grey that we'd been offered at Cumberland Place in wafer-thin bone-china teacups, but it tasted about a million times better.

Missy watched Shafeen as he passed her a cup, looking him up and down in a comic way. 'Charmed, I'm sure. Right young gent, ain't he?' She sat down at the table with the heaviness of the bone-tired. Now she pointed at Shafeen, eyes narrowed. 'You wasn't in the play though, hun, else I would've heard about it.'

Shafeen smiled shyly and shook his head. 'No. I saw it though. Ty was tremendous as the queen.'

Missy put those amazing fingertips up to her mouth, then moved them to her heart, her breath a catch of regret.

'I *so* wanted to go to that play. *Isle of Dogs*, hey? Like it was meant. And my girl getting the main part in her first term! But I had two shifts, and DeAngelo's Nativity play. Playing the star, weren't you, D? Cos you are a star, right?'

DeAngelo had nothing to say to this.

'Then I had Dwight's football trials. And Rose had her dance exam the next day.'

It took me a while to realise that she was making *excuses*. She was actually apologetic that she hadn't made it to Ty's play, this multitasking machine with three other kids. It seemed so unfair that this . . . this *superwoman* should feel anything approaching guilt. Suddenly she seemed much older. The lines around her eyes, and from nose to mouth, were more pronounced. She did look, at that moment, as if she could have a seventeen-year-old daughter.

'Don't worry,' I said soothingly. 'None of ours made it either.'

She looked like she'd been given a present. 'Really?'

'Yup. My dad was working too.'

Then she looked sadder again. 'There's Ty's dad,' she said, motioning to a framed picture on the wall. It was a lovely picture – Ty looking about thirteen, with train-track braces, smiling an enormous tin grin with her dad's hands on her shoulders.

'Where does he live?' asked Nel gently.

Missy smiled at Nel sadly. 'You think he left. Bad Babyfather, that's it, isn't it? Probably got another family.'

'I never –'

'It's all right, girl. That's what white folks think. But that ain't it. He was the best man, my Desmond, but he died. A man can't help that. Can he?'

'No,' said Shafeen soberly. 'A man can't.'

'So now there's just me.' I wanted to say that was more than enough but couldn't think of a way to say it that wouldn't sound incredibly patronising.

But she changed the subject. 'Where you guys staying?' she asked brightly.

'Regent's Park,' Nel replied.

'Ah. I bet that's nice,' she said. 'I never been, 'cept to the zoo once.'

'It's a bit fancy,' I said, trying to downplay just how palatial it was.

She wagged her finger in my face. 'Never mind that, girl. It's safe. That's what you want. *That's* the real treasure.'

She pulled DeAngelo to her and kissed the top of his head. 'Safety. That's what you want for your family. It ain't about just money, or nice clothes or food. You want *safe*. I want DeAngelo and Dwight to be able to walk the streets without being shanked by some little toerag.' DeAngelo squirmed away and his mother took a gulp of tea. 'I've told him how to get off the Isle of Dogs. I told all of 'em. Book learning.' She nodded her head decidedly. 'Book learning did it for his sister. My girl Ty studied *up* and look where it got her. Scholarship girl.'

I thought of Ben Jonson, literally saved by the book.

'Books are a fire exit,' she said. 'They're a door to somewhere else.'

'Like Narnia!' I said. Then I explained, 'It's a magical land that you reach through a wardrobe door.'

240

She put her head on one side. 'Girl,' she said, 'I know about Narnia. Who you think book-learned all these kids?'

I could feel myself going red and shut my stupid mouth. Who was I to school this woman?

In the awkward silence that followed, Shafeen and Nel stared into the depths of their tea. Registering the sudden quiet, DeAngelo peeped over his book with his enormous eyes. That kid was as cute as a button. I made a funny face at him, and the eyes disappeared behind the book again. We all laughed and it broke the tension.

'Have you heard from Ty?' asked Shafeen as casually as he could.

'Bless you, darlin', not a word since she went up to that big house. She text me to say she got there OK, then *nada*.' Missy smiled wistfully. 'But I don't expect it. If she's livin' her best life, that's enough for me.'

I looked at the presents, wrapped with such love, and Mrs Morgan followed my gaze.

'We miss her. Of course we miss her. But she did so *good*, that girl. Look where she is! Great school, fancy house, nice young feller! Of *course* I'd love her here for Christmas Day. But that's being a mother, ain't it? You gotta let them go. You can't stand in your kids' way.'

I compared her love and dedication to my own mother's. The hours Missy had worked, the sacrifices she'd made. My mum had pretty much given birth to me and then pissed off.

We didn't have to worry about outstaying our welcome. Missy, in the nicest possible way, threw us out, as she had to get to her second job. But she piled us up with a box of

Quality Street from under the tiny tree and all good wishes for Christmas. Her generosity nearly made me blub. She gave DeAngelo firm instructions about not answering the door, telling him that his sister Rose had keys and would give him his tea when she came home from her dance club.

As I got up from the table and headed for the door, I spotted something. DeAngelo had his book upside down. His mum had gone ahead to see us out so I discreetly turned it the right way up for him. As I did so, I realised he had his phone hidden behind the pages.

He looked at me with his huge eyes.

Busted.

I'm pretty sure he thought he was in trouble. But I was just thinking what a perfect Medieval/Savage thing it was to do. As he stared at me, I closed one of my own eyes in a conspiratorial wink.

And, for the first time, he smiled.

33

When we left the house we sort of wandered for a bit, strangely unsettled by the meeting.

On the corner of the road I noticed a pub and idly read the sign. It said THE FERRY HOUSE. This was the pub Ty'd told me about, where her uncles used to drink. I remembered what she said about being able to hear the ghosts of Elizabeth's hunting dogs barking at twilight, so I looked over the silvery winter Thames, straining my ears to hear the baying across the centuries. But there was nothing to be heard other than the sounds of traffic and a plane high above, heading to City Airport – Savage sounds crowding out the Medieval past. 'Let's go in here,' I said.

Inside the pub was welcoming. It was one of those old-fashioned ones – no dove-grey paint and blackboard menus, but crap carpet, a telly on and a dartboard. We all ordered Cokes. It was a beverage I'd never seen on offer at Cumberland Place. At a sticky corner table, we discussed our encounter.

'So I guess Missy doesn't know what Ty is up to,' said Shafeen.

I said, 'But she *must* know about Leon Morgan, no?'

'Not necessarily,' said Nel. 'He was the dad's uncle.'

'How do you know?' I demanded.

'Because he was called Morgan, dummy.'

She had a point. I thought then of the game books at Longcross. One of them, way back in the stacks, would have held Leon Morgan's name. Then I thought of the new game book, squat and malign, lying on the counter at Cornellisen's. That book, like all the others, would soon be written with death. But then I looked at Nel and Shafeen and was sure of two things.

One, there was no way that we could tell Missy Morgan that Ty was in danger.

And two, there was no way we were going to let any harm come to Ty on Boxing Day.

34

When we got off the Tube and walked through the snowy twilight of Regent's Park to Cumberland Place, it felt as though it was us who had pushed our way through the wardrobe door and got into Narnia.

It was hard to believe the difference between where we'd just been and where we were staying. I had to admit to myself that I felt completely safe walking across Regent's Park in the near dark, and had none of that prickly, edgy feeling I'd had walking through the Limehouse Estate in broad daylight. It was then that I truly understood what Missy Morgan had been saying. The things you wanted for your family were not only material. You wanted safety too. How could two boroughs of the same city be so different? How could one family have so little, and another have so much? This afternoon I'd been drinking tea from a Sports Direct mug. Tonight I'd be drinking Veuve Clicquot 1984 from a crystal glass. Not for the first time that day, I began to believe that all those anti-Establishment protesters we'd seen at Speaker's Corner, wearing the face of Guy Fawkes, had a point.

PART II
LAST HOPE

35

After another one of those politely charged dinners at Cumberland Place, Shafeen, Nel and I collected in the library – something that had become a habit.

That booklined room, with the eternal fire, was the nearest thing to cosy that the grand house could provide. We could, of course, have retired to one of our bedrooms to conspire, but that would have felt too obvious. Besides, as I was beginning to understand, there were certain rules in this world. The privileged elites of the Order of the Stag might be cavalier about the sanctity of human life (so long as you were poor, common or a person of colour), but they would freak out if a young man was in a bedroom with two unmarried girls. In the library we knew we would be alone and could say what we pleased, with the early-warning system of the double library doors to protect our privacy. We could be safe and secret unless someone came through those doors. And that night, someone did.

It was Bates. He looked as he'd looked that first day, not smooth and composed, but grey and sweaty. He kept looking over his shoulder, as if he was more worried about being overheard than we were. He spotted us with something like relief, and then crossed the room to where we were. High in his hand he held a silver tray, like he was a cocktail waiter. There appeared to be nothing on it, certainly no glasses or coffee cups or anything like that, but when he lowered it we could see that there *was* something there, something so flat that it did not even protrude above the lip of the tray. Bates bowed his head slightly and addressed Shafeen.

'I'm glad I caught you, sir. A letter just arrived for you.'

Shafeen took the letter from the proffered tray. 'Thank you, Bates.' He had authority, did Shafeen, but he didn't quite have the haughty entitlement that allowed the Medievals to totally wipe the phrase *thank you* from their vocabulary. Shafeen looked at the writing on the front of the letter and raised one dark eyebrow. '*Just* arrived? A bit late for the post, isn't it?'

'This was hand-delivered to the house, sir.'

'By whom?'

I was impressed that even under duress Shafeen didn't forget his grammar.

Bates looked shifty under Shafeen's glance – in fact, he looked positively ill. 'That I can't tell you, sir.'

'Can't?' queried Shafeen somewhat sharply.

Bates looked a bit panicky. 'Merely a figure of speech, I assure you, sir. I meant only that I am unable to satisfy your curiosity, because unhappily I did not see the messenger.'

'Very good, Bates. Thank you.'

'Thank *you*, sir. Goodnight.'

As soon as Bates had pissed off, us girls crowded round the letter in Shafeen's hand. 'Who's it from?'

'Dunno,' said Shafeen, much less formally. 'I don't recognise the writing. And who even knows I'm here?'

'Enough speculation,' said Nel. 'Just open it.'

He turned it over and instead of a normal envelope flap, there was a fold secured by a seal.

I went cold. It reminded me strongly of The Invitation, the missive that had set all of these events in train.

'Wait,' I said, just as he was about to crack the seal with his long fingers. 'Look at the device first.'

It was hard to see what was stamped into the wax in this low light, so we took the letter to the fire and crouched on the hearthrug. The wax was not the blood red of the seal I remembered from The Invitation, the red of the STAGS stockings and the Longcross dog rose. It was a more orangey, rusty red. And the imprint on the wax was not a pair of antlers but a face.

A pointy animal face.

Nel was the first to say it. 'It's a fox.'

'May I?' said Shafeen elaborately, and we both nodded vigorously. He broke the seal. 'What the . . . ?'

We craned over his shoulder. There, printed in neat calligraphy, were the following words.

My Lord, out of the love I bear to some of your friends, I have a care of your preservation. Therefore I would advise you, as you tender your life, to devise some excuse to shift your attendance at Longcross; for God and man hath concurred to punish the wickedness of this time. And think not slightly of this advertisement, but retire yourself into your country where you may expect the event in safety. For though there be no appearance of any stir, yet I say they shall receive a terrible blow this Boxing Day; and yet they shall not see who hurts them. This counsel is not to be condemned because it may do you good and can do you no harm; for the danger is passed as soon as you have burnt the letter. And I hope God will give you the grace to make good use of it, to whose holy protection I commend you.

We all looked at each other, the firelight kindling our faces.

'It's the Monteagle Letter,' whispered Shafeen. 'Someone sent us a Monteagle Letter.'

'Sent it to *you*, you mean.' I had a revelation. 'Do you think it's from your dad?'

'Don't be a dumb bunny,' he said fondly. 'How could it be, possibly, when I only talked to him about Longcross this afternoon?'

'Then who could be trying to warn you?' asked Nel. 'Who else do you know here?'

'It says for the love they bear *my friends*,' he said. 'Monteagle passed on his warning to King James. Maybe I'm just the messenger. Perhaps whoever it is is really trying to save you two.'

'Probably Greer,' said Nel, without malice. 'No one's really noticed I'm here. Who would try to save you, G?'

Henry, I thought, but I said nothing and just shrugged.

'OK, let's leave aside *who* gave us the warning for a moment,' said Shafeen. 'Next question: are we going to listen? And act on it?'

'Of course not,' I said at once. 'If we are being warned off, that gives us even *more* reason to go. There's something

252

happening that has to be stopped. We can't leave Ty to her fate.' Especially not now we had met her mother and little DeAngelo.

Shafeen folded the paper decisively, and Nel said, 'And are you going to burn it like they asked?'

He looked at the fire and the flames burned in his eyes. 'I think I'd better.'

'Really? To protect us?'

'No,' he said seriously. 'To protect whoever sent it.'

He tossed the thing on the fire and we waited until the letter glowed, flamed and fell into ash before we felt it was safe to go to bed.

36

I waited up for Henry until my eyes were closing.

I was pretty sure he of all people would know exactly what was going to happen at Longcross, and why it was so important that we stay away. But that night I didn't feel his weight on my bed or hear his mother at the door. There was just me, and Reynard on the wall. Under the terrified eye of the dying fox, a question occurred to me: if Henry was real and alive, how had he entered the room if a locked door kept his sleepwalking mother out? I didn't think it was 'all a dream', like some story you write in Year 6 English, because I had the dog rose from Longcross. But there were only two explanations, and as I drifted to sleep I turned them over in my mind.

1) Henry was a dream after all.
2) Cumberland Place had its secrets, and somewhere, somehow, there was another door.

PART 12
CHECKED

37

I knew that the de Warlencourts were Catholics, and had been for centuries, so I suppose I shouldn't have been at all surprised that on our last evening at Cumberland Place, 23rd December, we should be invited to a Christmas Mass at their church.

Their church was in Kensington – where else? – right by the Victoria and Albert Museum. It was called the London Oratory, and it was properly posh. That evening we put on our smartest stuff, our going-to-the-House-of-Lords outfits, and we were decanted from the car with the earl and countess outside what seemed like a mini white cathedral. The night was cold and clear, and about a million Christmas stars shone above the dome of the church. As we filed in with all the smart churchgoers, the inside was a jewel box of gilt and marble. By the light of a thousand candles I looked at the mosaic of Jesus Christ above the golden altar, and he looked back at me.

As we walked down the aisle with the de Warlencourts – who were obviously important enough to sit right down the front – they both seemed to stumble. I put out an arm to save Caro, like a mum crossing the road with her kid, but it was fine – they were both just bobbing a little curtsy to the altar, after which they crossed themselves. As we shuffled into the front pew, I suddenly found it unbelievable that these God-fearing pillars of society were planning to celebrate the Saviour's birth, and then hold a death hunt for a young black schoolgirl before Jesus had even blown out his candles.

I was sitting between Shafeen and Nel. Shafeen had the honour of sitting between me and the earl, with Caro sitting beyond him, and Nel was between me and a pillar. Someone unseen rang a bell, and the carol service began.

I say carol service – actually, this was not like any carol service I had ever known. This was not a jolly romp through the Nativity story interspersed with popular Christmas hits. This was much more serious, and quite beautiful.

For a start, it was all in Latin. I was not too bothered by the Latin-ness. It was actually nice to tune out and just listen to the music of the words. Of course I'd taken a Latin class at STAGS, everyone had to, but I wouldn't say I was brilliant. I only caught the odd word here and there. I recognised the paternoster – Lord's Prayer to you – but that was about it. Shafeen was probably the same level as me. Nel was the real expert, as she was taking Latin for her Probitiones, so I could see she was really listening.

And the carols were amazing. The Oratory had a really excellent choir, who, like the choir at STAGS, gave you that cold-water-down-your-back feeling. The carols weren't all the well-known Victorian ones – although they did sing 'O Come All Ye Faithful' in Latin – but medieval ones, properly medieval, with those lovely crunchy discords and monkish chants. Then came the confession, and everybody knelt at the sound of the overworked bell. Apparently the priest confessed and we forgave him, then the people confessed and he forgave us. At least, that's what I thought was going on. Of course, I didn't have a clue what I was saying, but the bits we were supposed to speak were helpfully typed in bold on the service sheet, so I did my best, mumbling along with the rest of the congregation.

Confiteor Deo omnipotenti, beatae Mariae semper Virgini, beato Michaeli Archangelo, beato Ioanni Baptistae, sanctis Apostolis Petro et Paulo, omnibus Sanctis, et tibi Pater: quia peccavi nimis cogitatione verbo, et opere: mea culpa, mea culpa, mea maxima culpa. Ideo precor beatam Mariam semper Virginem, beatum Michaelem Archangelum, beatum Ioannem Baptistam, sanctos Apostolos Petrum et Paulum, omnes Sanctos, et te Pater, orare pro me ad Dominum Deum nostrum.

I would have managed it OK except right at the end of the prayer Nel clutched at my arm and whispered something at me, putting me right off my stride. It sounded like, *Where are we?*

I thought she had actually nodded off for a minute.

'In church,' I said. 'Are you OK?'

'Yes. Where are we?'

'At the carol service.'

She rolled her eyes with frustration. 'I'll tell you later,' she hissed.

38

It wasn't long until the end of the service, but of course we had to drive back in the car through a Christmassy London and say our polite goodnights to the de Warlencourts before we could retire to the library and I could ask Nel what the hell she meant.

'OK, what? What did you mean in the church?'

'When?' asked Shafeen.

'In the confession,' I told him. 'She nearly nipped my arm off, and then said: *Where are we?*'

'I didn't,' she said. 'I said, *Orare.*'

She pronounced it *Or-are-ee*.

'What's an *Orare?*' asked Shafeen.

'You've heard it before,' said Nel. 'That is, you've seen it. Maybe it would make more sense if I wrote it down.' She went to the blotter on the desk and took up a pencil. She slid a piece of Cumberland Place headed notepaper from its stack and scribbled a word. Shafeen and I craned to look.

ORARE

'Still no clue,' I said.

Nel said, 'Maybe you'd recognise it if I wrote it like this.'

O RARE

Then she added two words:

O RARE BEN JONSON

'His epitaph,' I said. 'Ben Jonson's epitaph.'

'Yes,' she said. 'It's not in English. It's in Latin. You see? We all said the spacing was funny, and the epitaph was weird. O *rare Ben Jonson* – it didn't make sense. But in Latin it does.' She looked at us both, her eyes very blue. '*Orare* means pray. His gravestone says, "Pray for Ben Jonson".'

This gave me a shiver.

'He arranged his own burial, remember?' said Nel quietly. 'With the Dean of Westminster. He wrote instructions and paid for it himself. That's when it was decided he didn't have enough cash to be buried lying down. And it was then that he must have chosen for his epitaph to be in Latin.'

'So?' I said. 'Churchy things always are.'

'Not then,' broke in Shafeen suddenly. 'Only if you were a Catholic.'

A silence fell and all we could hear was the crackling of the fire and the ticking of the grandfather clock.

'So at some point,' I said slowly, 'Ben Jonson became a Catholic. Even though it was a *really* dangerous thing to be. I wonder when.'

'Don't wonder,' said Nel, getting out her phone. I was struck, as I had been before in this house, that it was pretty weird to be sitting in the middle of a room full of books and searching for information on a phone. But that was the way of the Savage world – Google was the world's library now, an infinite digital bookshelf of noughts and ones.

'You're not going to believe this,' said Nel, her face backlit by the Saros. 'Ben Jonson converted to Catholicism when he was in prison for – wait for it –'

'– putting on *The Isle of Dogs*,' I finished.

'Yup.'

'Makes sense, I guess,' said Shafeen. 'Queen Elizabeth threw him in jail, so he embraced the religion she hated.'

'Betcha he'd been leaning that way before that,' said Nel. 'Remember, in *The Isle of Dogs* it was the Catholic rebels who got munched by the hounds. Jonson was pretty critical about that.'

'True. I wonder if . . .' Then I stopped and head-palmed myself so hard it hurt.

'What?' said Shafeen.

'We were looking for a connection between *Volpone* and Guy Fawkes. It was there in front of us all the time. The connection isn't the play. It's the play*wright* – Ben Jonson himself.'

'Explain,' said Shafeen.

'Well,' I said, 'we've got two historical figures here: Guy Fawkes and Ben Jonson. They both lived at the same time, right?'

'Yes,' said Nel. 'The Gunpowder Plot was an attempt to kill James I. Ben Jonson was James's court poet.'

'And,' I went on, 'Professor Nashe told me that Ben Jonson was a spy. He worked for King James and Robert Cecil, but he was playing a double game. I asked Nashe who he spied for, and she said other rebels. She meant Catholics. So what if Jonson and Fawkes are – ya know –' I said, going all *Fargo*, 'connected? What if Ben spied for Guy Fawkes?' I grabbed Nel's phone. 'I bet you any money they knew each other.' I typed frantically into the search bar.

It took me all of two seconds to find an article on *Prospect* magazine online entitled '*Gunpowder, Treason and Jonson.*' I scanned it quickly and could feel my eyes getting wider and wider.

'Well?' prompted Shafeen.

'Did they know each other?' This from Nel.

'*Know* each other?' And then I told them.

That Ben Jonson and Guy Fawkes had served together in the army in the Netherlands. That as a convicted killer and Catholic, fresh out of jail, Jonson had been an obvious choice to be drawn into the Gunpowder Plot. That he had been to one of the thirteen conspirators' earliest meetings at a house on the Strand, at the invitation of chief conspirator Robert Catesby. 'And here's the best bit,' I said. 'When Guy Fawkes rented the cellar under Parliament where he stored the gunpowder, he used the name John Jonson. Fawkes took the surname of his co-conspirator and brother-in-arms. He gave the name Jonson again when he was arrested. And then, of course, Ben was arrested as a suspect too – almost certainly because Fawkes had used his name.' I imagined another scene in my mental Gunpowder Plot Film – Ben Jonson's moment of panic when he got *that* knock at the door; the constables' torchlight in his face; his pupils contracting; his panicked mind fluttering like a caged bird trying to find an escape. 'For Ben that would have been his third strike with the law, after *The Isle of Dogs* and the murder of Gabriel Spenser. He was in deep shit.'

'So that's presumably where the spying comes in?' asked Shafeen. 'Jonson changed sides and started working for the Crown?'

'Not quite as scumbag as that,' I said defensively. 'He was a double agent.' I read off the little screen, my eyes one step ahead of my mouth. 'After Guy Fawkes was caught in the act, with his lantern in Parliament's cellars, there was no saving him. But Robert Cecil still needed to find the rest of the plotters. He wanted to find a connected Catholic priest to flush out all the other conspirators. But it was a capital offence to be a priest at that time, so Cecil needed a known Catholic to access the secret networks. He called on Ben Jonson, known Catholic, ex-criminal, but court poet.'

'And did Jonson find anyone?'

'You'll be amazed to learn,' I said drily, 'that after trying *really hard*, he couldn't find a single priest. I guess as an insider, he was able to protect his Catholic friends. But then, of course, Cecil went another way – he tortured Guy Fawkes so mercilessly that he gave up all the other plotters. Oh Jeez,' I said, for the search had thrown up something else, something I would rather have not seen. There was a little picture of two signatures, both saying *Guido Fawkes*. One was written by Fawkes before his torture. The other signature was from his confession, after his muscle and sinew had been stretched on the rack.

It was so apparent that he'd been broken by that dreadful machine of torture – that second, terrible signature was shaky and fragmented and barely legible. Clearly, he could barely put pen to paper.

'Does it say if Guy Fawkes named Ben as one of the conspirators?'

I scanned the page. 'No, but I don't think he can have done. Everyone he did name was executed. Maybe his "brother" was the one person he couldn't give up.'

Nel said thoughtfully, 'But Ben Jonson's involvement in the Gunpowder Plot doesn't explain what Guy Fawkes has to do with the Order of the Stag, and with Longcross, and the Boxing Day meet. Ty said to see if you can find out about *Foxes*.'

Then my brain, in that funny stained-glass habit it had of slotting different-coloured thoughts together to make a whole, put everything into place.

The lantern at the Ashmolean with the tell-tale thumbprint.

Nel saying *Orare* and me mishearing.

The mask the protesters were wearing at Speaker's Corner.

All those Jacks and Jills at the STAGS Club.

Shafeen saying, *They can't even be bothered to get their names right.*

Right there in the middle of all those books, with the firelight on one side of me and the phonelight on the other, I said, 'What if it wasn't *Fox*?' It was almost a whisper. 'What if it was *Fawkes*?'

'Are you saying,' asked Shafeen slowly, 'that Ty overheard something about Guy Fawkes?'

'Why not?' I asked. 'She thought she heard the word fox, and she asked us to find out about it.'

'And yet,' said Nel, 'this whole thing *is* also connected to foxes. What about that session in the House of Lords? What about the Boxing Day meet? What about the plan to reinstate the foxhunting?'

'I know,' I said, staring into the fire as if I might find the answer there. 'That I can't explain. But all I'm saying is, it's possible that whatever the Longcross plot is, it's somehow connected to that *other* plot 400 years ago.'

'Well,' said Shafeen, 'there's only one way to find out what Ty heard. And that's to ask her. We'll be seeing her in three days. Only two more sleeps until Christmas.'

It seemed incredible that the next day was Christmas Eve, and I'd be going home. Suddenly I wanted my dad very much. The world of dark cellars and plots was suddenly genuinely frightening. Like a kid, I thought tomorrow would come more quickly if I went to bed.

So I did.

PART 13
'ON'

39

And, of course, that was the night I saw Henry again.

I don't remember sleeping or waking; I just had a consciousness that he was there, once again, sitting on the end of his own bed. This time he was clothed, in some sort of dressing gown.

I hauled myself up on my elbows. 'Where have you been?'

'In the ether.' I couldn't see his face, but he sounded like he was smiling.

'Bullshit,' I said, sitting up. 'I got the dog rose. You're no more dead than I am. So: where have you been?'

He turned a little so I could see his profile, luminous in the half dark. 'You mean all this week?'

'Try all this year.'

He seemed to think for a moment. 'In hiding.'

'Does your mum know? And your dad?'

'Of course.'

'So your dad was lying to us. And your mum was telling the truth.'

'No change there,' he said drily.

'Does Cass know?'

'Yes.'

'And Louis?'

He hesitated for a microsecond. 'No. Not yet.'

'So you *are* letting him think he's the heir. You *are* doing a Volpone.'

'If you like.'

'And where have you been?'

'I told you in the hospital. I went home.'

'To 221b Baker Street. Very clever. Only it wasn't quite true, was it?'

'How d'you mean?'

'Well, you didn't just "go home".'

'I did,' he said. 'It just so happens that, unlike Sherlock, I have three Holmes, if you'll pardon the pun.'

'Three?'

He counted them off on pale fingers. 'Here, Longcross and Castle Macleod in Scotland, another ancestral home. And there's always the STAGS Club – one can always get a room there with the utmost discretion.'

My lip curled a little. 'The Establishment closes ranks to protect one of its own. Is that it?'

He shrugged elegantly. 'As you say. It's relatively easy to keep out of most people's way.'

'And how do you get about?' I asked. 'You were in the hospital, then at Longcross, now here. Got your own Uber, have you?'

'In a sense.'

'Oh.' I remembered. 'In your case, Perfect. Your tame goon.'

'Correct.'

'So the staff know too? Bates, and the rest?'

'Of course.'

I clicked. 'So Bates *was* trying to get your mum to stop talking about you. All those funny times when he burst into the room?'

'Yes. He was only obeying orders, as they say.'

'How can you trust him?'

He shrugged again. 'One just does. If you have faithful old retainers, they're not going to betray the family. They know which side their bread's buttered.'

'So, why turn up now?'

Henry patted the hump of covers that was my feet. 'I thought you might want some company.'

I retracted the feet and clasped my hands around my knees in a defensive position. 'I've got Reynard.'

Henry looked up at the fox mask with a strange combination of hatred and . . . fear? 'You talk to . . . *him*?'

It didn't seem like the moment to tell him that I had form when it came to talking to his family's taxidermy – I was pretty tight with old Jeffrey the stag head back at Longcross. I just said, 'Sometimes. I feel sorry for him.'

His face hardened. 'I don't. He deserved to die.'

Somehow it was this, more than anything else, that made me finally realise what Henry was. It wasn't what he'd done to Nel, or Shafeen, or me last year, not even what he was planning to do to Ty this Christmas. But *this*. That he could look at that fierce little face, that red fox who had run across the green field, gloriously alive, and say that he deserved to die. Something snapped in me. I sat up straight and looked

271

witheringly at him where he sat, on his bedclothes, on his bed, in his house. 'You don't change, do you?' I threw back the covers. 'Alive or dead, I'm done with you.' I had to get up. This was all kinds of wrong. How could I share a bed with him? What about Shafeen?

He grabbed my arm as I made to leave. 'Wait. Let me explain.'

'Explain what?' I spat.

'*Why* he deserved to die. Just give me that. Just that.' He was pleading, and even in my disillusioned state, he was hard to resist. 'And then I'll let you go. Forever. I won't stop you. I won't come to Longcross. You won't see me again.'

That, the finality of it, stopped me. But still, I sat on the other side of the bed, like those couples in Thirties movies who had to keep their feet on the floor for public decency. I wasn't going to lie in his arms. 'This better be good.'

'Oh, it is. Or rather, it isn't. It's bad. In fact, it's the worst. It's all to do with him.' He pointed an accusing finger at the wall. 'I was out cubbing when I first met Reynard. That's when you get the hounds used to the scent of the fox and sort out the ones that will give you a good run.'

'I know what cubbing is,' I stated coldly, even though I'd only learned about it two days ago, when Rollo had told us about Aadhish.

'I saw a fox in the covert, trying to slide past me. He practically weaved through my pony's legs. I let him go. I thought he was cute, with his bright eyes and red fur. The pater saw what I'd done and dragged me home. I've never seen him so angry.'

This was so reminiscent of Aadhish's story that I wondered if the whole tale was a lie. Inexperienced hunter goes cubbing, lets a fox go and invites the fury of Rollo de Warlencourt. But I didn't interrupt Henry's flow.

'There's a cupboard in the boot room where we keep old wellingtons and shooting sticks and things. The pater slung me in there and locked the door. It was the middle of the day, but it was still pretty dark. I waited for him to cool down and let me out, but he didn't.'

I swallowed. That was pretty cruel, to 'Harry Potter' Henry in a cupboard like that, but I wasn't going to soften up.

'To start with I wasn't worried. I tried on every boot, sat on the shooting stools, played with the fishing flies. You know, kids' stuff. At that point I was more bored than scared.'

'How old were you?'

'I must have been eight, because it was just before I was sent away to school.'

God. *Eight.* This was different to Aadhish. This wasn't even a teenager, this was a child. 'What happened?' I said, more gently.

'The door opened and I thought I was free. But the pater wasn't letting me out. He was locking someone else in. It was the fox. The pater had caught him in a net and brought him into the house. He threw him in with me and said if I liked him so much, we should get to know one another.'

Now I just listened, mouth open.

'For a bit it was all right. The fox was young, he hadn't really learned to be afraid of man. I gave him a name – Reynard. It was one that I'd always heard associated with foxes. There was this poem the pater liked . . .'

'I know it,' I said quietly.

'Reynard even let me stroke him. When I touched his fur

I knew I'd done the right thing in saving him. He was lovely. He didn't deserve to die.'

I was captivated by the story – it was so . . . touching. But it couldn't all be this cute. 'Then what?' I said with a certain dread.

He turned a desolate face to me. 'He didn't let me out, Greer. He didn't let me out.'

I thought I'd misheard. '*What?*'

'He didn't let me out.'

'How many hours were you in there for?'

'Hours? Try days.'

'Days?' I was turning into an echo, but I was just so shocked.

'Yes. I lost track of time, but it must have been three days. Perhaps more.'

I couldn't think of anything to say to this. Three *days*, in a cupboard, with no windows. And not just alone, but with a wild animal. It was worse than cruel, it was perverse.

'And in that time,' Henry went on, 'Reynard changed. The first night, he curled up in the small of my back. I was quite happy – I thought they'd let me out in the morning. I could measure the time of day by the slice of light coming from under the door. When dawn came I thought it was nearly over. I had a nanny, who always ran my bath and gave me breakfast in the nursery; a tutor, who would teach me lessons in the schoolroom. But nobody came. I was so hungry, Greer, so thirsty. And I knew Reynard felt the same.' He shot a nervy glance at the fox's mask on the wall. 'For a time we were in it together – just two hungry and thirsty friends in a tight spot. I found a water bottle with a dribble of water in it, and I even gave him some. There were old biscuits in

274

a jacket pocket and I shared some of them too. But as time went on he started to suffer. His eyes were dull, there was a white paste around his mouth. His black lips were cracked, his breath was ragged. And on the second day, he started to attack me.' He turned back to me. 'Then I knew that we weren't friends. We were animals, he and I. And it was all about who was the top predator.' He lay down on the bed as though he had a pain inside. I didn't – couldn't – stop him. 'For hours, he kept coming for me and biting me. It was in his nature, you see.'

I remembered Shafeen saying, *I think they're pretty vicious when cornered*. I'd thought a pet fox would be just like a lap dog, but of course they would always be wild. *Furry on the inside*, I thought. *The Company of Wolves*.

'He was just hungry and thirsty,' Henry went on, 'but it felt like he *hated* me and was trying to kill me. I was in short trousers at that time, and my legs were running with blood. I was screaming and screaming, but nobody came. Not the mater, not nanny, not anyone.'

I shifted closer to sit by him, hand on his hunched shoulder, but couldn't speak.

'I couldn't stand it any more. Just cowering in a corner, watching for those amber eyes burning out of the dark, waiting for the next attack. My nerves were in shreds. I thought he would eat me alive. So the next time he came for me, I fought back.'

'What did you do?' It was a whisper.

'I bit him.'

'You *what*?'

275

'I don't even know how it happened,' he said. 'He leaped for my throat and I sort of grabbed him.'

He was shaking now. 'He was trying to bite my neck and I was wrestling with him. Suddenly I found there was fur in my mouth and I bit down, hard. I tore his ear. I tasted his blood.' He sounded as if he could still taste it now. 'Then he screamed, Greer. You never heard anything like it. It was strangely human, and utterly horrible. And so piercing. I knew they would hear it all over the house. And the second it happened, the *second* it was the fox who screamed, not me, the pater let me out. He knew the tables had turned, you see, that I'd bested the fox somehow, and the natural order had been restored. Freedom was my reward.'

'*Either a hunter or the hunted be*,' I murmured.

'That's it,' said Henry. 'That's it in a nutshell. And if that fox hadn't screamed, I don't know if he would *ever* have let me out.'

I wanted to say this was ridiculous. I wanted to say that there was no way Rollo would let his son and heir starve if he couldn't stand up to a fox. But I couldn't say it. I just wasn't sure. 'What then?'

'They put me to bed and called Doctor Morand. He patched me up as if I'd just fallen over in the playground. He didn't ask any questions. He never does.'

I remembered that this was the elderly doctor who had treated Shafeen after he'd been shot. Then I'd thought it barbaric that he should be fine with a guest being shot in the arm on the estate. Now I realised he'd seen much worse in the course of his medical career.

276

'So what happened to Reynard? They put him down, right?'
'No. They let him go.'

My mouth dropped open. 'They *didn't*.'

'They did, you know. And a few days later, at the Boxing Day meet, we chased him with the hounds. My legs were still in bandages, but the pater expected me to get up and ride. I remember to this day putting tight riding boots over those dressings. The blood started seeping through the bandages, but I was determined to pull them on. I wasn't about to let the pater down.' Henry clasped his hands around his knees, as if his legs still hurt him. 'And Reynard gave us the run of his life – everyone said that meet was legendary. Even grizzled old colonels who'd been hunting for years said that was the best hunt they'd ever been on. I was only eight, it was my first hunt, but I rode like a maniac. And eventually we caught him. Reynard.'

Now it was me who looked at the fox on the wall, as if the creature was eavesdropping.

'I knew it was him, because of the ragged ear where I'd bitten him. When the hounds ripped him apart, I was right at the front of the pack. I loved every *second* of it, Greer. They "blooded" me with his blood and I felt it warm on my forehead, and I was glad. I was so exhausted I nearly went to sleep in the saddle on the way back to the house. The pater kept laughing and patting me on the shoulder, saying things like, *Young puppy's ridden himself into the ground*. For the first time in my life I felt like he was proud of me.'

His voice wavered dangerously, but he carried on.

'The next day they mounted the fox mask on the wall in my

room, and he's been with me ever since, to remind me of our battle. *Reynard 2008*. A week after that Boxing Day meet, at the beginning of January, the pater sent me to STAGS prep. He said – and I remember this quite particularly – he said: *You're ready now.*'

Somehow, in the course of this terrible tale, he'd curled into a foetal position and I'd reclined on the bed and was lying next to him again, like we were a couple. We faced each other as we'd done that first night when he'd put his thumb on my mouth, mirror images. Then I'd thought him a dream, a wraith from the other side of the Looking Glass; then the dividing line between life and death ran down the middle of the bed between us. Now we were both living in the here and now, and the playful banter of that night was gone like a dream itself. This was the most real Henry had ever been with me, the most raw.

'Since then I've hated the pater. And the mater too.'

The crack in his voice told me that he didn't hate either one of them. But I wasn't about to argue with him right then.

'I get *him*,' I said softly. 'But why her?'

'Well . . .' he reached out and lifted a lock of my hair out of my eye, tucking it behind my ear. His hands were cold. 'Let me ask you a moral question. What's worse: to be a monster, and to torture someone, or *not* to be a monster, and to stand by and watch that someone suffer, without having the courage to do something about it?'

I understood. It was why we were going to Longcross. If we didn't help Ty, that would make us worse than the Order. 'Is there . . . is there a chance she didn't know?'

'No,' he said stiffly. 'She used to come every day and knock on the door, try the handle and talk to me gently through the wood.'

Then I understood why he'd looked so terrified the other night. When he heard the creak of the doorknob. It had taken him back there, to that dreadful cupboard in the boot room.

'But she never let me out, however much I begged and pleaded. Because she feared *him* more than she loved *me*.'

'She *does* love you,' I said gently. 'I'm certain of it. She never stops talking about you. And she comes in this room every night, or tries to.' Then I realised the meaning of what the sleepwalking countess had been saying that night. When she'd murmured, *I'll save you*, she hadn't meant she would save Henry from falling from the waterfall. She'd always known he was alive. She'd meant she would save him from Reynard, all those years ago; but she hadn't had the courage.

'She's like she is because those few days broke her,' he said coldly. 'She's been . . . struggling, mentally, ever since. She tried to compensate; she smothered me with love. But I could never forget that she'd left me in that cupboard.'

I imagined him trying to deal with the trauma, an eight-year-old, on his own. He should have had counselling, therapy, but these were relatively new sciences. The Medievals didn't do that. They were all about the stiff upper lip. And this was the consequence. They'd taken an innocent little boy and created a monster. 'Who else knows this?'

'Just Cass,' he said. 'I had to tell someone. That's why she hates the pater so much. And the mater too.'

That explained a *lot*, not least why Cass herself had so many issues of her own following Henry's 'death'. But this didn't have to go on for ever. There didn't have to be endless generations of messed-up privileged kids. The cycle, surely, could be broken. 'Why don't you change? Why don't you help *us*? There's some dark plot going on and you must know all about it. We're pretty sure something's going to happen to Ty at the Boxing Day meet, but it's more than that, isn't it?'

For the first time that night, he was silent and wouldn't meet my eyes. But I wasn't about to give up on him.

'You've *literally* been given a second chance at life. Why not live this life differently?'

He looked at me for a long, long time, then seemed to make up his mind. He got up off the bed and held out his hand. 'Come with me.'

For the second time in my life, Henry de Warlencourt took my hand and led me through a secret door. But this time we went down, not up – not to heaven, but to hell.

40

The secret door was – Narnia of Narnias – in the back of the mahogany wardrobe.

It clicked open mutedly to reveal a little spiral staircase, with that ancient but familiar smell of old stone, which led us down and down to the bottom of the house and below.

I kept one hand in Henry's with the other trailing down the gritty wall, the stone rough under my fingertips, wondering all the time where we were going. As we corkscrewed down into the blackness, I started to see a glow of light. It might have been comforting if it wasn't for what I heard.

Chanting.

This spooky, monkish chanting, of a lot of people in an echoing chamber. We rounded the last turn of the stair, and the world opened out again, into a vast, cavernous space.

We were in some sort of underground chapel. I remembered then what Caro had said – *the house was built in Georgian times, but the foundations are much older*. This must have been part of the original house – the one where Nazereth de Warlencourt lived. I looked about me in the candlelit dimness. There were no windows, but a forest of pillars around the perimeter of the room reaching up to arch and meet at the top in these monastic-looking cross-ribs. The place was lit by about a thousand candles set into little niches. We were in a stone gallery high up in the eaves of the vaulting, and Henry ushered me along it, a finger to his lips. We had an ideal vantage point, completely hidden from below but with the scene set out beneath us, complete and perfect, as if we were sitting in the stalls of a theatre. We stood, leaning together on the stone balustrade and looking down.

And I could hardly believe what I saw.

Far below, on a paved floor of a complicated design, stood probably about fifty figures. They were all in floor-length red gowns with deep cowls that entirely hid their faces. Set upon their heads were black antlers.

For the second time in my life, I came face to face with the Dark Order of the Grand Stag.

It was then, after all this time, that it hit me. I'd buried my trial so deep that I wouldn't have to think about it. The horror of facing a circle just like this one, of being questioned with my neck in a noose, of being branded on the thumb, the searing and sudden pain, all came back to me. I think on some level I'd been able to convince myself it had all been some sort of nightmare, despite the brand that was with me every second of my life as a permanent reminder.

For a horrible moment I thought Henry had brought me here to serve me up like a Christmas turkey, as some sort of sick STAGS sacrifice. I started shaking until he put an arm about my shoulders and pressed his lips to my hair. 'Steady,' he breathed. 'Steady. They're not here for you.'

'Jesus,' I breathed, 'what *is* this?' I turned to him. 'Henry. What is this?'

I could see him struggling with himself. I honestly think that until that moment he hadn't fully committed to betraying them.

'It's the Red Mass,' he murmured. 'The Order's ritual.'

I looked down upon the scarlet circle, blood racing. I had to grip the balustrade in front of me to stay upright, and my suddenly sweaty fingertips began to slip on the cold stone. The circle stopped chanting – I'm sure it was Latin, but I was so scared I could be wrong; they could have been talking backwards. It was a dreadful inversion of the innocent Christmas Mass we'd been to earlier that same night. If the London Oratory had been God's House, this – with the horns and all the red – seemed like the dwelling of the Devil.

One of the number turned from the circle, mounted a dais and sat in a chair exactly like the one in the STAGS Club – maybe it *was* the one from the STAGS Club – with antlers growing from it like twin saplings. Another two figures approached, holding a book between them. Once their leader had taken his seat, the others sat too, on these ornamental stools set into niches around the walls. The seated figure read from the page his assistants held open. You know how, when you're just about to faint, your blood kind of roars in your ears? Well, mine was roaring so hard it took me some moments before I could register what the Grand Stag was saying.

And Samson said concerning them, 'Now shall I be more blameless than the Philistines, though I do them a displeasure.'

I got that churchy flashback again. He was reading some sort of Bible lesson.

And Samson went and caught 300 foxes, and took firebrands, and turned tail to tail, and put a firebrand in the midst between two tails. And when he had set the brands on fire, he let them go into the standing corn of the Philistines, and burnt up both the shocks, and also the standing corn, with the vineyards and olives.

I imagined the foxes with tails aflame, running in terror from their own brushes, spreading fire throughout the Philistine corn.

I registered the image a second before I recognised the voice. It was one I would never forget. I'd heard it interviewing me for STAGS, I'd heard it telling the story of St Aidan's stag at Justitium Mass and I'd heard it trying me for the murder of the young man I was sitting with now. 'Is that the Old Abbot?'

'Yes,' said Henry.

'Not dead then?'

'Not so much.'

'Did they get him away from STAGS because I'd figured out who he was?'

'It was safer that way.'

Another thought struck me. 'And is Abbot Ridley here? He's in this too, right?'

'Who's Abbot Ridley?'

'The new Abbot. He runs your Order's school.'

'Never heard of him.'

284

This was striking. I thought I could tell when Henry was telling the truth by this point, and I thought he was telling it now. Maybe Abbot Ridley *was* innocent, despite him gaslighting me about Esmé Stuart and skulking around Oxford in the snow like a modern-day Harry Lime. But I couldn't question Henry further because the Old Abbot was speaking again.

'Brother Longcross? How many foxes for our Boxing Day meet?'

'One. Tyeesha Morgan.' I recognised Rollo's voice and shivered despite myself. So there it was: what we'd suspected, confirmed. Despite her courage, and despite Louis's regard, Ty was indeed to be the prey for this sickest of hunts.

'One?' the Abbot sounded surprised, and not in a good way. 'Not two?'

'One only.'

'Are you sure?'

'Quite.' Rollo did sound sure, to be fair.

'You know to whom I am referring,' said the Abbot in steely tones. 'What of the boy? What of Shafeen Jadeja?'

Shafeen. It was a shock to hear his name like that, in this company. I waited, heart thudding.

'No.' In that moment Rollo sounded even more of a boss than the Old Abbot. 'The boy will not be touched.'

Warm relief washed over me, but Henry's reaction was quite different. His face hardened and his grip tightened on my arm. At that moment I understood. He was *jealous* of Shafeen. And not just because of me. Because his *father* liked him – a father who had locked his own son in a cupboard with a fox, a son who was never good enough for him.

'And the recent threat?' The Old Abbot sounded a bit huffy but had definitely climbed back in his box a bit. I wondered if there was a bit of a power struggle going on between these two – contemporaries, STAGS old boys and . . . rivals?

'The Manslayer was tried and branded, as you know, and brought within this house.'

Another jolt. Now they were talking about *me*.

'And?'

'She is being handled,' said Rollo calmly. 'No further action will be needed.'

'Meaning?' The menace had returned to the Old Abbot's voice.

'We have brought her into the fold.'

I looked sideways at Henry, and his eyes flickered to mine sheepishly. 'They're talking about you, aren't they?' I whispered. 'Is that your job? To *handle* me? Is that what you're doing now?'

'No, of *course* not. Why would I bring you here if it was?'

I saw his point. If he'd wanted to woo me onto Team de Warlencourt, he would never have brought me to the Red Mass. Roses on the pillow were one thing, midnight conspiracies to murder quite another. The Grand Stag was speaking again.

'Very well. And now, back to our Yuletide endeavours. What of the meet at Longcross? How many brothers and sisters of the House of Lords have you managed to shepherd into the herd?'

'Many,' said Rollo. 'Most. Our gatherings will have little interference in the new year, once our bill goes through the House.'

'And the prince?'

'Will attend.' I took my breath in a little gasp. Rollo didn't specify which royal family this 'prince' was from, but if it was the British one, then this thing went right to the top, just as it had in Elizabeth I's day.

'Very well,' said the Old Abbot, sounding a little less pissed off. 'We all meet at Longcross on Boxing Day, and at our next Mass, with the will of the Stag, we will rejoice at the success of our endeavours. Now we sing.'

I totally knew what their hymn would be. I knew every word of it. *As the running deer seeks the flowing brook, even so my soul longs for you, O God.*

As they sang, Henry leaned in to my ear once more.

'It's coming to an end. You should go back.'

Moments ago, I would have given anything to run from this place. Now I couldn't leave him. 'What about you?'

'I'm safe here,' whispered Henry. 'I'm one of them.'

His words chilled me. And then I realised. The cold silk, the flowing gown. He wasn't wearing a dressing gown. He was wearing a red robe.

Under the cover of the singing, I fled back up the winding stairs. At the top I turned and shoved the door closed, and you couldn't even see the join. I knew it was futile, but I pulled the heavy chest of drawers in front of the wardrobe. Then a chair, then a footstool on top of the chair.

By the time I'd finished my makeshift barricade the grey of dawn was bleeding through the curtains. As I fell into bed, the last thing I noticed was that the dog rose by my bedside had shrivelled into a little organ, pink as flesh, the vivid red quite gone.

41

Next morning, we left Cumberland Place early with no breakfast, on the (perfectly true) pretext that we had a very long drive up north.

I couldn't wait to get into the small and safe space of the Mini. I had so much to tell Shafeen and Nel, and I couldn't bear to sit through another meal with Lord and Lady Death and be polite through my teeth. It was hard enough to go and thank them in the drawing room where they were having their morning coffee, the countess behind *Country Life* and the earl behind *Horse & Hound*.

Rollo got to his feet when we entered the room and I marvelled at what a dreadful contradiction he was – he would happily brand my thumb and chase Ty with a pack of hounds, but God forbid his arse cheeks should remain in a chair while a 'lady' was standing.

Manners still uppermost, he warmly shook Shafeen's hand. 'Goodbye, Hardy,' he said. 'Beg pardon – Shafeen. We'll await you at Longcross.' He waved his arm to encompass us girls too. 'It will be ripping to see you all again.'

Ripping, I thought as we went out to the car.

Ripping, I thought as I remembered Henry telling me of Reynard tearing his flesh.

Ripping – I thought of my dream and the fox torn apart by the hounds.

I had to hand it to Rollo. He could hardly have landed on a more fitting word.

PART 14

THE LIFTING HORN

42

The hardest thing of all, on that long car journey north, was dealing with my own feelings about Henry.

I recalled that little boy shut in the cupboard with Reynard – the sick fear as their predator/prey dominance swapped over, then swapped back again. No wonder Henry had become what he had become. Then I would remember the red robe and his words: *I'll be all right. I'm one of them*. I was more confused about Henry than ever. He was, undoubtedly, one of the DOGS. I had been tried and branded for his murder, they had named him as one of their number and his name was on the family tomb with the other DOGS.

But.

He'd taken me to see the Red Mass and allowed me to overhear their terrible plans. Was he turning good? Could a baddie also be a goodie? Was Henry like *Leon*, a cold-blooded assassin, but a good guy inside?

Then there was the guilt and the grief – even now. If Henry was alive, then I shouldn't be feeling either, right? But I'd been carrying those twin burdens for a year, and it turned out they were hard to set down. You couldn't just switch feelings off, any more than you can stop loving someone if they die. Anger was also added to this perplexing mix. If Henry had swan-dived off Conrad's Force and secretly been living the high life quite happily for a year at one of his many houses, how dare he put me through all that bereavement and regret? Then at other times I would feel the creeping certainty that I *had* killed him, and that I had somehow, through the performance of *The Isle of Dogs*, brought him back. Because if I *hadn't* killed him, why had I been tried as a Manslayer by the DOGS? And if I believed *that*, then that made me, surely, crazy.

I felt like I needed some time to myself, like Tom Hanks in *Cast Away*, just to work out what I felt about it all. But that wasn't to be. I had to come to terms with everything in a brand-new Mini Cooper with my best friend and my boyfriend. I had to face it all through talking, and there was plenty of time for that.

Shafeen's reaction to the story of what had happened the night before was, perhaps predictably, disbelief. Shafeen the pragmatic, the practical, the prospective med student, just could not bring himself to accept the return of Henry de Warlencourt.

'I'll believe in him when I see him.'

'Then what's your explanation?' I demanded.

'That you were having a dream. A very vivid dream.' He half turned from the passenger seat so that he could talk to me where I was sharing the backseat with our bags. 'Think about it in filmic terms. The setting for the scene came from earlier in the evening when you'd been to the Christmas Mass at the London Oratory. The throne was the chair from the

STAGS Club. The actors – the only people who spoke in this scene – were what we might call "established characters"; Rollo, the Old Abbot. And the only people they mentioned – Ty, me – were also known to you.'

'There were two guys with a book,' I protested. 'And about fifty guys in robes.'

'Did they speak?' he asked.

'No,' I admitted.

'So they were, effectively, extras. And you have been harbouring, self-evidently, buried trauma from your trial,' he finished.

'I suppose you think that was a dream too, Dr Jadeja.' I muttered resentfully.

'No, of *course* not,' he said. 'You have the brand. That's empirical evidence. But there's no empirical evidence to prove that Henry is alive, so I happen to think that he's gone.'

'Think? Or *hope*?' I said, rather unfairly.

'Let me ask you something else,' he said, ignoring my jibe. 'What did you find out? Something we already know. Aren't we sure there's a bigger conspiracy to do with a fox or a Fawkes or whatever? But what did you learn from this "Mass"? That Ty was going to be hunted on Boxing Day, and we'd figured that out for ourselves. That can't be the whole plot. It's going to take a while to get rid of all of us non-whites if they do it one at a time.'

'What is this, Groundhog Car?' I grumbled. 'I'm getting used to not being believed in this Mini. OK, so what about the "fox in a box" incident? The story of Henry and Reynard in the cupboard?' I'd had to give it a trivial name because I found the notion of

Henry locked in the box room with Reynard completely horrific.

'You dreamed that too,' said Shafeen simply. 'Foxes are all we've been thinking about for the last few days. Your mind has constructed a way to explain away Henry's horrible character, and a reason for Cass's dislike of the earl and countess.'

'And the flower by my bed?'

'Rollo and Caro had just been to Longcross,' he said. 'They could easily have brought one back. There were flowers in my room too. Yours, Nel?'

'Yep,' Nel, eyes on the road, confirmed.

'Dog roses?' I asked.

'Well, no, but –'

'It's not about who put the flower in my *room*. It's about who brought them to the *hospital*.'

'Cass,' said Shafeen.

'Who hadn't arrived by then. Henry was my first visitor.'

For the first time, Shafeen's assurance slipped a little. 'Well, that I can't explain. But I'll bet the Longcross Estate isn't the only place you can get those particular roses in Northumberland.'

Everything he said made a certain sense – that was what was so irritating about it. I appealed to Nel. 'Nel? What do you think?'

She *almost* met my eyes in the rear-view mirror. 'Well . . . Shafeen does have a point.'

I didn't reply but looked out of the window at the speeding motorway. I *knew* I was right about this. But I knew I was right about something else too. I was certain that Henry would make an appearance at Longcross. Then Shafeen and Nel would *have* to believe me.

43

Whatever the other two said, by the time we'd reached Chester, all half-timbered and Christmassy under starry skies, I'd reached my own conclusions.

A) Henry was alive.
B) Somehow he'd survived the waterfall and had been hiding out for a year. (Or the play had actually brought him back, but even I couldn't make a logical argument for that.)
C) Louis didn't know he was alive, and Henry, for the moment, was letting his cousin think *he* was the heir of Longcross.
D) Henry may now be 'Kylo Ren', i.e. turning away from the Dark Side to the Light.

But I kept my opinions to myself as we drove through the electric gates of Nel's house. It was a huge and floodlit mock-Tudor mansion outside of Chester called Alderley Nook. In a way it was as palatial as Cumberland Place, but here everything was brand new – there was no peeling paint or speckled mirrors, but a cinema room, a pool and lots of gold taps. Her dad wore lots of jewellery and her mum wore lots of make-up, they both called me 'luv' and they were the nicest people in the world. Nothing was too much trouble for them. They had no problems welcoming their daughter's schoolfriends to spend Christmas with them, and actually on Christmas morning Shafeen and I both got a new phone, the Saros 9S. Best of all, Nel's parents weren't members of a death cult.

After a lavish Christmas breakfast Nel drove us the short distance into Manchester, and I fell into one of my dad's legendary bear hugs. Dad's hair was longer, and his beard was shorter, but otherwise he was just the same. After cups of tea, and a shower of hugs and kisses and thank-yous, Nel left and Dad did us an amazing Christmas lunch, which turned into Christmas dinner. He'd done turkey, crackers, paper hats, the lot. Happily, he'd always got on well with Shafeen, and they talked a lot about India, as my dad had filmed there loads. As twilight fell, and the candles were lit, and we sat in our paper crowns, the conversation got more in depth. We talked about everything, including, quite surprisingly, my mum.

'What was Greer's mum like?' Shafeen asked, when we'd all had enough wine to loosen our tongues.

'Ambitious,' said my dad, leaning back in his chair. 'Driven. Funny. She had a great sense of humour. Has. I don't know why I'm talking in the past tense. She's not *dead*.'

'Are you . . . still in touch?' asked Shafeen.

'Of course.'

Shafeen glanced at me, seeing if I minded all this interrogation about my mum. I didn't. I was listening. 'Where is she now?'

'Prague,' said Dad. 'She's costume designer on a feature film. One of those interminable Marvel ones. Presumably making spandex onesies, as that's all they ever seem to wear.'

I took a swallow of wine and asked the question that had been bothering me a lot recently. 'Does she ever ask about me?'

'Constantly. I send her all your news, and school reports.'

Suddenly my paper hat was annoying me so I took it off, laying it among the cracker debris. I'd successfully shut my mum out of my mind for so many years, but I'd been thinking about her much more lately. Maybe it was meeting two other mothers from their respective places on the good mum/shit mum spectrum; Missy Morgan and Caro de Warlencourt. 'Why doesn't she ever get in touch with *me*? I mean, today's Christmas Day. Would a present have killed her? Or a card?'

He shrugged. 'I know. She was never very practical. Even when we were together, I would do all that stuff. She *wants* to get in touch, badly. But she thinks she's given up the right to interfere in your life.'

'I'll say.'

'She thinks any contact ought to come from you. She's just waiting until you're ready.'

He looked at me, his paper hat at a crazy angle.

'*Are* you ready?'

There was a lot going on in my life right then. I had to make sure Ty was all right first – at the moment I felt more like a mother than a daughter. 'Maybe in a bit.'

'You could drop her a line. I've got her email address.'

'No,' I said, looking at Shafeen. 'That seems a bit too Savage. I think I'll write her a letter. But not yet. Soon.'

44

Dad's flat in Salford Quays only had two bedrooms, but the sofa in the living room was a fold-out futon for guests, and my dad had very pointedly rolled it out and made it up for Shafeen.

My dad was cool about us, but not *that* cool. When Shafeen was in the toilet I stood in the doorway with my dad, his arm round my shoulder, looking at the arrangement of pillows and duvet. As ever with my dad, I fell into playing our movie game. This time I was looking for a film where a dad was trying to frustrate his daughter and her boyfriend sharing a room. '*Meet the Parents?*'

He did a terrible Robert De Niro impression. 'You talkin' to me?'

'Your house, your rules, huh?'

'Yup,' he said, smiling.

'Dad,' I said, 'I'm an eighteen-year-old.'

'Oh, I know,' he said. 'But you're *my* eighteen-year-old. So if there's going to be any funny business, you can at least have the decency to sneak around behind your old dad's back, like we did in my day.'

I hugged him and kissed the side of his beardy face. He was pretty cool after all.

Shafeen did, indeed, pay me a midnight visit in my bedroom. We kissed for a bit, and things were getting pretty hot and heavy when I saw my old soft toy Tigger. I'd got him for my fourth birthday, when I'd decided, with the certainty of a toddler, that he was the only character in the Hundred Acre Wood worth knowing. He looked pretty sad now, the black and orange of his stripes more grey and marmalade, but I'd loved him for fourteen years – longer than I'd loved anyone, except my dad.

As well as Tigger, there was a picture of my mum and my jewellery box with the ballerina inside it, waiting to revolve to ice-cream-van music when you lifted the lid. I might've been eighteen, but this was a child's bedroom. I gently pushed Shafeen away. 'Not here,' I said, through the hot jumble of lips and hair and teeth.

He rolled off me, lay on his back and sighed heavily. 'Not here,' he sing-songed. 'Not at Longcross. Not at Cumberland Place. Someday, somewhere, Greer, we'll find the right bed.'

I hoiked myself up on my elbow and put my chin in my hand, looking down at him. 'Wow, Shafeen, I really didn't think you were that kind of guy.'

'What kind of guy?

'The sort to pressure a girl into something she's not ready for. Not very *gentlemanly*, is it?'

That struck home. He backed off straight away, actually getting up off the bed as if it had burned him and apologising profusely, and then of course I felt terrible. I tried to explain. 'I mean, of course I'm *ready*, but I don't know why it doesn't ever seem to be the right place.'

'I'm just not sure it's geography that's stopping you.'

'What else would it be?'

'*Who* else, you mean?'

He sat on the edge of the bed, continents away from me now. 'It was hard enough to battle him when he was dead. If you really think he's alive, that's another matter.'

'Why? Last time he was alive I still chose you.' I didn't stop to think about the lunacy of this sentence.

'*Did* you, Greer? We only started going out once we thought he was dead.'

There was really no arguing with that piece of chronology.

'And even then,' Shafeen went on sadly, 'he was still getting between us.'

And I understood, then, just how much he'd had to put up with. Really, he did deserve some sort of an explanation. We were both eighteen. We'd been going out for a year. It was fair enough for him to expect that we would take things to the next level. But he was perfectly right. There was something holding me back. And it was time to give it a name.

'You're right,' I said. 'I have been holding out on you. And it is because of Henry.' I took Shafeen's hand in mine as I tried to explain. 'We started going out in the wake of his death. And I felt guilty, and sad, and a whole mess of emotions. I think that did stop me getting . . . close . . . to you. I was grieving, yes, but I was also dealing with the fact that I'd effectively ended someone's life.' He looked so forlorn I put my hand to his cheek. 'But it wasn't because I had *feelings* for him. I mean, I had feelings *about* him, but I hated him.' If I said it, it had to be true, right?

Shafeen looked at me intently. It was hard to hide from those dark searching eyes. 'That may have been true . . . then,' he said, echoing my own word. 'But it's different now. You are more . . . *sympathetic* towards him.'

He was right again. It was all because of the 'fox in a box' story. 'Look,' I said, 'even if you think Henry in the cupboard with Reynard was a dream, I still think Henry had a pretty difficult childhood.'

Shafeen's answer was surprising. 'Oprah Winfrey,' he said.

I thought I'd misheard him. 'What?'

'Oprah Winfrey,' he repeated. 'She had a terrible childhood and suffered dreadful abuse. Now she's one of the richest and most successful women in the world, and, more importantly, she's a noted humanitarian, doing tons of charitable work and loads of good deeds.' He shifted his weight a little on my duvet. 'What I am saying is, even if Hitler was smacked as a child, it was still his fault he turned out to be Hitler. He was solely responsible for all the horrors he perpetrated. There's such a thing as personal responsibility, Greer. It *is* possible to escape your upbringing.'

I sat up against the pillows and thought about what Shafeen had just said. He was right, but I realised it was only fair to tell him what I'd been thinking ever since the Red Mass. No – before that. Since *The Isle of Dogs*, and the incantation of the Grand Stag – the same incantation which, *maybe*, had brought Henry back to life, *Practical Magic* style. It was time. I took his hand again. 'In the play – *The Isle of Dogs*, I mean – the enchantress warned Queen Cynthia that if she brought a loved one back from the dead, it might not be in a form she recognised – or even desired. That the Earl of Greenwich might be horribly changed. And in fact, he was.'

'OK,' said Shafeen. 'So?'

'So,' I said slowly, piecing together my thoughts as I went, 'that was what happened when a *good* man was raised up. He became this evil entity, the Grand Stag.'

'With you so far.'

'All right, but what if a *bad* man was raised up? What if this Henry is *good*? He is the one who took me to the Red Mass. He revealed the whole plot to me. What if Henry has changed for the better?'

Shafeen's expression was unreadable. Disbelief, disappointment, concern – none of those seemed to cover it. He got up and straightened the duvet in the spot he'd vacated as carefully as a chambermaid. 'I'll see you in the morning.' And he vanished, as cleanly and quietly as a ghost.

45

Of course there was no way I could sleep after that, what with the conversation just gone and the day to come.

I padded into the kitchen to raid the fridge, and saw, to my surprise, Dad working on his laptop, an apple stuck in his mouth like one of those pigs at Christmas.

His eyes twinkled at me over the apple. Had he seen Shafeen?

'You on the night watch?' I said lightly.

He took the apple out of his mouth and balanced it carefully on the table. With the bite out of it, the apple resembled exactly the glowing logo on his Mac. 'No. I'm not spying on you. I'm doing prep for this Mexico shoot. What cameras we need. Lenses. Blah, blah, blah.'

I took a chair and we talked about his work for a bit, and I found it – as I always did – oddly comforting. He talked about the animals they were hoping to film in Mexico. Coatis, ocelots, axolotls.

'Dad,' I said, 'have you ever filmed foxes?'

'Yes, of course.'

'Somewhere glamorous, I'll bet.'

'Very.' He smiled. 'Northamptonshire. It was a documentary

about farmers controlling the fox population. Beautiful creatures, they were. But the farmers insisted they needed to be culled so we tried to show both sides.' He winked. 'BBC balance.'

I remembered Henry saying the same thing as the farmers. That if a population got too robust, it needed to be controlled by a higher predator. That was back when I still thought he was talking about foxes. Then, abruptly, I remembered the Bible lesson that the Abbot had spoken at the Red Mass. Just another reason that the Mass had to be real – I couldn't have dreamed up a whole Bible verse, could I? 'Do they ever set fire to them? The foxes, I mean.'

'Set *fire* to them? God, no. Why would they do that?'

'In the Bible. The fiery foxes in the Philistine corn. Samson sets fire to their tails. Of course the foxes die.'

'I should think they do.' He shook his head. 'Blimey. My fault for giving you a religious education, I suppose. What *do* they teach you at that school?'

I wasn't going to open *that* particular can of worms. Instead, I asked another question. 'If you see something bad happening to an animal – when you're filming, I mean – do you step in?'

'Well, it depends,' said my dad. 'If it is just nature taking its course, then no. I've had to stand back before.'

'Backstory, please.'

'OK.' He pushed his Mac away. 'Well, for example, we were filming flamingoes in Ghana. They stand in this salt lake to fish, but if they stand in one place too long they get salt deposits on their legs, which grow like shackles. Eventually the shackles drag them down into the water and they drown.'

306

I thought about that. 'How very sad.'

'Yes. And the temptation is, of course, to catch one, take out your penknife and hack off the salt. But you can't.'

'Why not?'

'Well, because it's natural selection. The ones that move around so much that they don't get salt deposits are the better hunters. This way the sedentary ones die out and the species becomes more successful – *all* of them become better hunters. It's the survival of the fittest, Darwinism in action. In those cases, you just have to let nature take its course.'

At that moment I thought of the bliss of staying here, safe in that warm kitchen with my lovely dad, and letting everyone at Longcross just get on with their own warped version of Darwinism.

'But if someone was *deliberately* harming an innocent creature,' I persisted, 'in a way that *wasn't* just . . . nature, you'd stop it, no? I mean, if a farmer *was* setting fire to a fox's tail, the film crew would step in, right?'

He looked at me steadily for a moment. I could see the exact second that he clicked that we weren't talking about foxes. 'Yes,' he said seriously. 'Of course I would.' He leaned in and gave me a massive hug, the kind that only my dad could give. He spoke into my hair. 'Greer. Is there anything you want to tell me? Anything I need to do?'

'Like what?'

'Step in. Stand between you and harm. Like dads do.'

Like some dads do, I thought. *Not Rollo*. 'No,' I said aloud. What could Dad do? Go up against the de Warlencourts? Tell the police, who were in the family's pockets? Maybe make himself a target? 'It's all under control.' And I wondered if that was true.

Then Dad held me away from him. He grasped both of my shoulders and looked me full in the face. 'You'd better go to bed then. If you're going to put out some fires tomorrow.'

He knew. Of course he knew. Not the details, but that we were going back to Longcross to save someone's skin. He hugged me again and this time he wouldn't let me leave the hug for a long, long time. 'Greer,' he said, 'be careful. You're all I've got.'

PART 15
MOURNE
END WOOD

46

As we drove down the great sweep of drive to Longcross Hall, I could see at once that our Christmastide visit was destined to be very different to the times we'd stayed before.

There were people everywhere, buzzing about, carrying things, wheeling things, cleaning things, busy as bees. It was like the *Downton Abbey* movie when the king and queen were about to arrive. When we'd been before, it had been just us – a strange little teenage island like *Lord of the Flies*, no adults to rule over us. When the cat's away, the mice will play. But this time the cats, or in this case the DOGS, were most definitely at home.

Nel drove carefully on the approach to the house, Frogger-dodging all the other traffic in the drive – guests arriving in boxy estate cars or sleek black government Jaguars. Trading vans bearing royal crests delivered not people but pâté, or caviar, or fine wine. When we drew up at the entrance Betty was there, directing operations.

Betty was dressed in the full rig of black dress and white apron, with a lace hat on her iron-grey hair. Unsmiling, she bobbed a little curtsy at us. 'Welcome back, sir and miss. And miss.' She nodded grudgingly at me. 'It's wonderful to see you back at Longcross. I'll show you to your rooms.' Already on the move, Betty was clearly in a hurry. I imagined she had a lot to do that day, with the house at full capacity. She took us through the tradesmen's entrance and along the kitchen passageway – I like to think it's because we were regular guests and considered family, but more likely it was because there were far more important people going through the front door.

'Lord de Warlencourt asks that you change immediately – the meet will be gathering for the stirrup cup at eleven sharp.'

Lord de Warlencourt – was she talking about Henry? Or was he still in hiding and letting Louis wear the title for a few more days? There was no way we could ask – we'd just have to wait and see.

Dodging Longcross's collection of excitable and flabby Labradors, Betty led us into the flagged passageway leading to the back stairs, and there we saw a familiar face. A figure in a black tailcoat was unloading a crate of wine so large it almost blocked our way. 'Bates!' I exclaimed, as if greeting an old friend.

The butler jumped about a mile in the air, almost falling into the dark doorway that was open at his back. I glanced past him and down a stone stairway I'd never seen before – this must be the wine cellar. Bates was obviously stocking it up for the evening – I imagined at a Hunt Ball the booze would be flowing. I glanced at the glass bottles in the crate. They looked dusty, expensive and they all had the same label – Veuve Clicquot 1984. I picked one up out of its straw bedding. It was surprisingly heavy. 'Ah, I teased. The famous Veuve Clicquot '84.

Perhaps we'll get to taste it tonight. You seem to have plenty.' Bates looked a bit doubtful and I got that. It was probably about a thousand pounds a bottle, and too good to waste on us kids. In fact, the butler looked positively ill as he took the bottle from me, cradling it like a baby. 'Oh, Miss MacDonald, you have to be careful.' He darted a look at the others and attempted a smile. 'I mean . . . the bubbles, of course. You must be very careful with a champagne of this vintage. If you were to shake it – disaster.' He looked all grey and sweaty – that must be some booze to get so worked up about it.

'Sorry,' I said cheerily.

Shafeen nodded behind the butler. 'Those the cellars?'

'Yes, sir,' Bates replied. 'They go all the way under the house. Longcross has some of the finest wine cellars in England.'

'Cool,' said Nel. 'Maybe we can take a tour sometime.'

'Of course, Miss Ashton,' he said, recovering a little now he'd laid the dark green glass down in its straw. 'But, if you'll forgive me, miss, not today.'

We got the hint. 'Yes, yes, you do your thing,' I said. 'We've got to get changed anyway.' This was too much information, but I did feel genuinely glad to see someone we knew there – a beacon of familiarity in a sea of scary strangers.

The kitchen clock struck ten just as we were walking through – not much time to change and get our horses. We cantered up the stairs after Betty to be shown to our rooms. I couldn't quite believe that we'd all have our usual rooms, as we passed about fifty guests just on our short route, bounding up and down the stairs in varying stages of readiness, all talking loudly and excitedly, all greeting us cordially as we passed. They

313

were all much older than us, and I felt sure that we would have been moved to some tiny little windowless bedrooms somewhere in the attic, to make room for the all the government ministers and the royalty. But no – I was in Lowther, and there was Jeffrey on the wall and a bunch of impeccable riding stuff laid out on the bed. I was dropped off first, and in parting Betty said, 'Lord Longcross's compliments, but would you all go down to the stable-yard as soon as you are dressed to collect your mounts?'

This was scary enough, but I couldn't worry about my horse just yet. I had a more pressing concern. Before Betty could close the door I asked, 'Which room is Miss Morgan in?'

'Miss Morgan resides in Fenwick, miss – the room she had before Christmas.'

I gave the others a look that meant *Meet me there*, and as soon as the door had closed and Betty's footsteps had receded I was out of my room again, padding down the passage to Fenwick.

47

The three of us practically met at Ty's door, and I lifted my fist to knock.

I couldn't quite believe we were about to see Ty again after a week of waiting and worry. We'd repeatedly tried to get hold of her before Christmas with no success, so it was hard to believe the moment of contact was actually here. I tapped, then rapped on the door. And, of course, there was no answer.

Now wasn't the time for privacy. Nel turned the handle and we all piled in.

Ty's room, like Henry's just a few weeks before, looked as if it had just been left. A little fire burned in the grate, the remains of a cup of tea stood on the bedside table and there was a bathrobe slung over the desk chair. ('Damp,' said Nel.) The dressing table was a whole mess of make-up and hair products, some with the tops left off. 'Yup,' I said fondly, 'that's Ty.' In the bed, half hidden by the rumpled covers, was the sleep mask she wore, with a self-referential design featuring a pair of closed eyes, and the wardrobe drawer was pulled open to reveal a colourful tangle of underwear. Ty, it seemed, had dressed in a hurry.

'Well, she *has* been here . . .' I said.

'. . . but she ain't here now,' finished Nel.

'I guess she's already down at the stables,' said Shafeen, walking to the window.

'Or she's tied up in the cellars,' I said darkly.

'Your imagination really *is* working overtime these days,' said Shafeen. 'In the *cellars*? Why would she be in the cellars?'

I couldn't really explain, but I'd had a funny feeling when we'd been talking to Bates at the top of that dark stair. 'Well,' I said, making it up as I went along, 'if she is the prey for today, they're going to have to make sure she doesn't make a run for it before the right moment, aren't they?'

'I suppose,' said Shafeen, 'but the cellars would be a bit Gothic, even for them. Besides, they were packed full of all that Veuve Clicquot '84. Did you see how much they had?'

'Man, all that wine must be worth something,' said Nel, who was always interested in wealth-related stuff. 'Let's find out.'

'I don't know that we really have time . . .' I began. But Nel had already flipped out her Saros and was tapping and typing as expertly as ever. I was pretty much out the door when she said, 'Hmm. That's weird.'

I closed the door again. 'What's weird?' I asked.

She scrolled and scrolled, her acrylic nail tapping smartly on the screen. 'It doesn't seem to exist.'

'Huh?'

'That champagne,' she repeated patiently. 'It doesn't exist.'

'Do you mean that it's not available?' asked Shafeen. 'Maybe the de Warlencourts bought the whole lot.'

'No, it's more than that.' She flashed a picture at us. It seemed to be some sort of golden staircase; magical fairy-tale stairs, framed in an archway, leading to nowhere. It was the gilded version of the dark stair we'd glimpsed earlier at Bates's back.

'This is the staircase of the champagne cellars at Veuve Clicquot at Reims in France,' Nel explained. 'Each step is carved with a date, for every year the cellars produced a vintage.' She pinched and expanded. 'Look closer.'

We did. The steps went from 1983 straight to 1985.

'See?' said Nel. 'Veuve Clicquot 1984 *literally* doesn't exist. According to this, they never made a 1984 vintage. There just isn't one.'

'But – they ask Bates for it all the time.'

'Yes,' she said. 'But have you ever seen him *bring* it? Have we ever tasted it?'

I thought hard. Nel was absolutely right. 'I guess . . . well, no.'

'Maybe,' said Shafeen, twitching Ty's robe into place over the chair, 'the vineyard made some in secret especially for the de Warlencourts, and consequently it's so rare it's massively expensive. That sounds quite Medieval, doesn't it?'

'I suppose,' said Nel doubtfully.

'Anyway, this is all very interesting,' I said, anxious to get everyone back on track, 'but it doesn't help us find Ty. Let's get changed and get down to the stables. She's got to be our priority.'

48

So, once again, I underwent one of those strange Longcross transformations.

Back in Lowther, under Jeffrey's interested eye, I put on the clothes that were laid out on the bed. These were grander even than the riding clothes we'd worn in Hyde Park. There were creamy-white breeches, shiny black boots of supple leather and a button-up shirt. A black velvet coat, a waistcoat and a snow-white tie knotted at the throat completed the look. There was no hat, which was a bit of a worry, but Betty came in holding a hatbox just as I'd finished pulling on the boots. It was lucky I'd come back to my room in time.

'Your hat, miss. I've just given it a brush.' I expected her to take out one of those velvet riding helmets but out of the box she lifted a bowler hat, just like the ones in *The Thomas Crown Affair*. 'What, no top hat?' I joked.

Betty looked surprised. 'Not when the meet is in the morning, miss. You only wear a top hat in the afternoon.'

That told me. 'Of course. I knew that,' I murmured faintly and sat obediently before the dressing-table mirror. I've said this before and I'll say it again: Betty might be a sour-faced Mrs

Danvers character, but she sure could dress hair. She secured my bob in a neat little bun at the nape of my neck, swept my fringe to one side and placed the bowler firmly on my head, slightly down over one eye at a dashing angle. Then she stuck a silver tie pin in the shape of a fox into the knot of the white tie at my throat. 'There,' she said, meeting my eyes in the mirror. 'You look splendid, miss.' It was the kindest thing she'd ever said to me.

I felt entirely different going down the grand staircase to how I'd felt coming up. Then, in jeans and a hoodie, I hadn't fitted in at all. Now, in a riding habit and a bowler, I did.

Despite me trying to hurry the others up, I did feel I had to make one stop on the way to the stables. In the boot room, as I breathed in the familiar smell of leather and polish, I couldn't help but look below the sporting prints for the outline of the box-room door. If there wasn't a cupboard, then there wasn't a Henry.

But there *was* a cupboard.

The door wasn't even concealed, like the one that had led to the ceremonial chamber of the STAGS Club, or the chapel staircase in Cumberland Place. It was a sturdy wooden door, obvious as anything. I laid a hand on the latch. Inside, the cupboard was just as Henry'd described, a mess of fishing rods and shooting sticks and welly boots. There was even – my stomach gave a lurch – the wetsuit I'd worn the day I'd been 'fished' out of Longmere, in a little rubbery pile like a shed skin. It wasn't a large space at all, not even for a boy and a fox. I crouched to the floor, making myself small, making myself an eight-year-old. Here, I thought, here Henry had been locked with Reynard in their formative battle. Here he'd became what he was. No. What he *is*.

I felt a watching presence and spun to find Bates standing over me.

Man, that guy could move quietly. I sprang to my feet. 'Bates,' I exclaimed breezily, breathing hard. 'You gave me a shock.'

'My apologies, miss.' He didn't sound apologetic.

'I was just looking for . . .' My sluggish mind panicked. 'A riding crop.'

'They will be located in the stables, miss,' he said rather sternly. 'The head groom will be able to assist you.'

'The *stables*,' I babbled. 'Yes, of course.'

He stood aside for me to get by, and then closed the door firmly as only he knew how. The gesture gave me a thought. 'Bates,' I said, 'you've been here, what . . . thirty years?'

'More.' He spoke to the door, making sure it was secured.

'So you'd have been at this house when Mr Henry was a boy?'

He turned. 'I had that honour.'

As I met his guarded grey eyes, I knew. I knew he'd been here when Henry had been in this cupboard. I could see, too, that he had not approved. For the first time I got the feeling that he was not entirely on Rollo's side. Had Bates been the Alfred Pennyworth to Henry's Bruce Wayne? Had he wanted to help Henry? Had he not dared? 'Bates?'

'Yes, miss.'

'Thirty years. It's a long time.'

'Indeed, miss.'

'Can I ask you a question?'

'Of course, miss.' But the grey eyes flickered with something like fear.

'Have you never wanted to . . . to do something else?'

He looked a little relieved, as if he'd been expecting something different, but at the same time a bit taken aback.

'Should I not have asked?'

'Not at all, miss. It's just . . .' He hesitated.

'Just . . . ?' I prompted.

He let out a long breath. 'In all my years of service I've never been asked that question.'

'So?' I persisted. 'What else would you have done?'

He got this faraway look in his eyes and answered me in quite a different tone, the deference gone, like we were, just for that instant, friends. 'I've always thought I should like to fly.'

'Planes?'

'Planes, helicopters, gliders. Anything airborne.'

Now I was surprised. It seemed like such a Savage ambition to be uttered in this place. 'My father was in the Royal Air Force, you see, but was killed in action. I think I should have liked to be up in the clouds. Looking down on everybody.' He forgot to call me *miss*.

'Thank you, Bates,' I said gently.

He remembered himself. 'Will that be all, miss?'

'That will be all.'

He bowed slightly, smiled slightly, and left me alone with the boots.

PART 16
'DONE'

49

We were a glamorous little party who met outside the stable-yard.

Nel looked the same as me except she was holding her bowler between her knees as she attempted to tie up her hair. Evidently she hadn't benefited from Betty's attentions, and once again I wondered why I'd been singled out for special treatment. Even in that slightly awkward position, though, Nel still looked gorgeous. But it was Shafeen who won the Who Wore it Best? prize. As a man (of course) he had the scarlet – sorry, pink – coat, and he looked amazing in it. And there was some other strange transformation. He looked born to wear it. He looked lofty, a little bit scary and super-handsome. I felt almost shy of him, but there was no time to be the simpering secondary female character. We had to crack on and collect our horses.

Passing under the stable arch I was jolted by the sight of the dog roses, shrivelled by winter, their blooms deflated and faded, like the one at my bedside in Cumberland Place. The stable-yard was as busy as the rest of the house. It was positively swarming with grooms, most of whom I'd never seen before, sporting smart tweed jackets and flat caps instead of their usual Barbours. We were standing, wondering what to do with ourselves, when someone blonde cannoned into me and hugged me hard, holding me back from the others. For a split second I thought it was Henry.

'You came!' It was Cass. Of course she suited the hell out of the hunting gear, and typically she'd chosen to flout convention by wearing, not the ladies' black, but the gentlemen's hunting pink. She absolutely rocked it.

I hugged her back as the others walked ahead. 'Yes, your uncle invited us. He is very hospitable.'

'He always is,' she said grimly, and I remembered then that she knew what Henry had been through in that box room with Reynard, because her cousin had told her.

'Good Christmas?' I asked.

'The best!' Cass's eyes were shining, her skin flushed – she'd never looked prettier, or rather, more handsome. She clutched my arm. 'I saw him, Greer. On my birthday. And again on Christmas Day yesterday. It was the best present ever.'

She nodded to Nel and Shafeen, who had gone ahead to pet the horses. 'Don't tell them. They wouldn't understand. They don't love him as we do.'

As we do. The present tense. Cass saying that made it all real.

'Does Louis know?'

'Not yet. Henry wasn't at the party, or Christmas lunch. He just came to me in my room at night.' I wondered then if Henry was the only secret Cass had ever kept from Louis. 'I thought he was a ghost at first – but he wasn't, he *wasn't.*'

I knew the feeling.

'I think Louis'll find out tonight,' Cass went on, 'at the Hunt Ball. I think everybody will. There's going to be an announcement.'

Jesus. This was just what I'd feared (or hoped?), that there was going to be some sort of *Peter's Friends* revelation, probably at the stroke of midnight or something significant. But I couldn't think about that now. There was more pressing business. 'Where's Ty? Is she OK?'

Cass looked faintly surprised. 'Ty? Why wouldn't she be?'

That was a relief. 'Where is she?'

She actually looked around. 'She's here somewhere. They've been inseparable, her and Louis.' I wondered where that left Cass, but she didn't seem to care. It was as if Louis didn't matter now she had Henry back.

The others, realising that I wasn't with them, had turned back and came over to greet Cass, and she hugged them enthusiastically, shooting me a conspiratorial wink over Nel's shoulder. She was happier than I'd ever seen her. You know when people say someone is glowing? She looked like that – lit up like a light bulb. 'Come on,' she said. 'Let's get you mounted. Can't keep the fox waiting.'

She strode up to the grooms, tapping her thigh with the riding crop she held, as if impatient for the day's sport. 'Fowler,' she called, and the head groom came running over. He was a friendly-looking fellow with that weather-beaten, apple-cheeked country look that comes from being outside a lot. He was a distinct improvement on the fiendish Perfect, whom we hadn't yet seen.

'Ah yes,' said Fowler, consulting a crumpled list from his

pocket. 'Her ladyship has already sent word. Took you all out riding in London, didn't she?'

We nodded mutely.

'She said Charlie and Snap for these two more experienced riders –' he indicated Shafeen and Nel – 'and Sweetbriar for this young lady.' He waved the list at me.

When the horses were led out of the stables by the undergrooms, their hooves clopping on the cobbles, I was relieved to see that although Shafeen's and Nel's horses seemed stupidly large and apt to dance about, mine was a smaller placid grey who regarded me with a kind eye. I patted her neck gingerly. 'Be nice to me, please, Sweetbriar.'

'Bless you, miss,' said Fowler. 'She's such a good mare, that one, you could let off a gun in her ear and she still wouldn't shift.'

Now that *was* good to hear.

'And she'll follow the Master because of Harkaway.'

'What's Harkaway?'

'The Master's horse. They're stablemates, and the best of friends.'

It was a bit weird to me that horses had BFFs like humans. But I wasn't going to question it. As Fowler helped me into the saddle and I gathered the reins, I saw Cass expertly vault onto her own grey. Someone handed her a black bowler and she put it on. 'That's everyone now, Fowler,' she called down to the groom. And then, to us, 'Follow me, chaps, I'll take you round.'

As we moved off, Cass called over her shoulder, 'Has someone explained hunting to you?'

'Sort of,' I replied, remembering Rollo's diatribe at dinner.

'It's pretty straightforward. The riders follow the hounds once they've picked up the scent. The hunting horn tells you when to ride. You mustn't crowd another rider or get in his "line" and the cardinal rule is that you must never, *ever* get ahead of the MFH – the Master of Foxhounds.'

'Ooooh.' I clicked. 'So when Fowler said the *Master*, he meant the Master of Foxhounds, not the Master as in the *earl*.'

'He meant both in this case,' said Cass. 'Dear Uncle Rollo *is* the Master of Foxhounds. Who else?'

She had a point.

That tiny ride with just me, Shafeen, Nel and Cass was the nicest part of the day. I look back on it now, that moment when all of us could have time-slipped back hundreds of years, riding sedately to the front of this amazing country house, as the highlight – before things all got very, very dark.

Because as soon as we rode around the corner to the splendid frontage of the house, I rode straight into my dream.

The Longcross hunt gathered in front of the great house, with the ladies in black and the gentlemen in hunting pink. As a servant came up to us in full white-tie and passed us each a little cup on a silver tray, I realised with a chill that every detail was just as I'd foretold. That last night in Room K9 in my dream in the hospital, I'd seen *exactly* this. I was watching myself, as if I were in a film. There I was, on my elegant grey horse, holding the reins in one gloved hand and a little silver cup in the other. Just as in my dream we were all chatting and smiling and there was this air of anticipation. The horses were shifting their hooves, the riders turning their heads with impatience. There were tons of white-and-tan hounds milling around in a rippling fluid wave, sniffing and yapping and weaving in between the horses' legs. We were all waiting for something.

'I still can't see Ty,' I said fretfully as Cass rode off to find her brother.

'Don't worry too much,' Nel said. 'Remember, she's been investigating this for years. She's probably way ahead of us. We're coming in and doing the classic White Saviour thing and she's probably got this whole thing figured out by now.'

'I hope so,' I said uneasily. 'But certain things *we* figured out, in London. Why they wanted to steal her shoe, to imprint her scent. And the game book.'

'Actually, what we *should* be worrying about,' said Nel, 'is whether the earl or countess picked up the game book from Cornellisen's and that hipster guy mentioned that we'd already been in. *Then* they'll know we are onto them.'

We couldn't get into this shattering statement right then, because Louis rode over, looking genuinely pleased to see us. He certainly looked very lordly, even in that company, immaculately turned out in his hunting gear. As it was impossible to hug him we all shook hands, and even that was a feat since I was still holding my little silver cup. Fortunately, it had a handle, like a teacup, but I still spilled a bit while trying to hold it and the reins at the same time.

We exchanged the usual small talk about Christmas, then I was straight in there.

'Where's Ty?' I asked.

He looked around, just as his twin had. 'Isn't she here? She's around somewhere. She came down with me. Don't worry, we

330

can't exactly start without her.' Although this was a slightly ominous statement, for the moment I was steeped with relief. I just wanted to see her with my own eyes. 'There are some other familiar faces though,' Louis went on, waving his cup towards the grounds.

I followed the gesture with my eyes, looking, despite myself, for Henry. Of course, everyone looked pretty similar, either in black or red like the dark chess pieces, but as I looked under the riding caps I did indeed recognise some faces. Some from the STAGS Club, some from the House of Lords, some, even, from the telly. We were really playing in the big league now. At that moment I really thought it would be all right. It was inconceivable that they would all – these fancy Establishment types – be complicit in a death hunt. They had too much to lose. I was sure, now, that whatever had happened at the Red Mass, *this* particular day was all about foxhunting. All about the de Warlencourts. Maybe, *maybe*, some of them were involved in the darker stuff, but not on this scale, not today. And there, at the centre of this, the smartest crowd in England, I saw who Louis must've been talking about. Rollo and Caro, their horses standing placidly side by side, were talking to a small knot of people who were also on horseback.

I turned back. 'Oh yes, your aunt and uncle. We've just been staying with them in Cumberland Place.'

'I know,' he said enigmatically, 'but not them. Look further.'

Then I looked at the faces of the people they were talking to.

And I nearly fell off my horse.

Piers Holland.

Henry Cookson.

Charlotte Lachlan-Young.

Esme Dawson.

Lara Petrova.

All the Medievals. All the entitled, elite little group of prefects who had plagued our lives at STAGS, then threatened our lives at Longcross.

They all looked exactly the same as ever. Piers was tossing back the stirrup cups, one after another, so rapidly that the servant by his saddle didn't even bother to move away but just stayed there with his silver tray. Esme was tucking her golden hair under her hat. Cookson was looking around as if wishing this were all his, while Lara was looking bored. And Charlotte was chatting away and gesturing with her free hand. As if bidden by my stare, Charlotte looked over and started waving like a windmill. '*Greer!*' she called in her piercing upper-class voice. 'How *delightful* to *see* you!'

Then, as one, they all turned and looked at me. And that's when I knew.

That all we'd feared was about to come true.

That Ty was in mortal danger – she *was* the prey, and we had to find her, *now*.

I turned to Louis and grabbed his scarlet sleeve.

'Seriously. Where. Is. Ty?'

'Keep your voice down,' he hissed.

'I won't.' I was talking loudly now and didn't care who heard. 'I swear to *God*, Louis, you show me Ty right now or I'll make *such* a scene . . .'

Shafeen and Nel brought their horses to flank me. They'd seen the Medievals too. 'Better tell her, old boy,' said Shafeen with a threat in his voice. People were starting to look, and Louis actually dropped his reins to hold out his hands to placate us, blue eyes wide. 'You'll see her in a minute. I *promise*.'

We all looked at each other. He seemed genuine.

'You have my word as a *gentleman*.'

This, we knew, was Louis's equivalent of swearing on his own life. But before we could reply, Rollo tapped two of the silver cups together to gather everyone's attention. He cleared his throat and it sounded like the bark of a dog. 'Before the fun starts, I'm obliged to remind you of the Hunting Act of 2004, part one, section one: *A person commits an offence if he hunts a wild mammal with a dog*.' He smiled a wolfish smile. 'And for those of you who are a little hard of hearing, I repeat: it is *absolutely forbidden* to hunt a wild mammal.' He gave the word special emphasis and winked and there was laughter. I got it; we all did. We weren't allowed to hunt a wild mammal. But that was OK, because we wouldn't be hunting a wild mammal. We'd be hunting a girl instead.

Hearing them all chortling about a potential murder did it for me. I'd had enough of this bullshit. 'Let's get out of here,' I murmured to Nel and Shafeen. 'Nel's phone's in her room – let's call the police.' They barely had time to nod when, as promised, we saw Ty.

By the time I realised it was her she was already well away, running across the grounds and into the open fields. She wasn't dressed like us but in a scarlet onesie, as red as the fox of my dream. I realised with a jolt that she was dressed in exactly the same way as the red figure in Westminster Abbey who had led me to Ben Jonson's grave, and in exactly the same way as the crowd of Fawkeses at Speaker's Corner.

My first thought was vast relief that she was alive and well, in one piece. But how long would that last if she was, as it seemed, the fox? I made an instinctive movement forward, but this time Louis yanked *my* sleeve. 'No. It's not what you think. Did no one explain to you about trail hunts?'

I stopped.

'It's still *just* legal to hunt with hounds in this country – thanks to my uncle – but you mustn't hunt a fox. So we use a trail. Someone goes ahead and through the woods to lay a track of scent.'

I tried to pull my sleeve away, but he held on, and his hard blue eyes stared at me imploringly. 'Greer. Ty *asked* to do it. I said we couldn't start without her, and it was true. She's the most important person here. She *wanted* to be part of the hunt, but as you'd imagine, she doesn't ride.'

As you'd imagine. That short sentence contained within it centuries of unquestioning privilege. *As you'd imagine.* Of course, in Louis's mind, Ty Morgan from a council estate on the Isle of Dogs would neither have had the means nor the opportunity to learn to ride. He let go of my sleeve and I looked at the others, who'd been listening, uncertain. The story could just about be true. But Ty didn't seem to be carrying or dragging anything. My understanding of trail hunting was that the hunt servants laid a trail of fox urine or dragged an aniseed bag through the undergrowth. Then I twigged. Ty wasn't carrying any scent because she *was* the scent. Henry Baskerville's missing shoe, Ty's missing trainer. All they'd needed was to show that to the hounds. I turned to Shafeen but suddenly Rollo was beside him, having moved to the front of the pack, golden horn at the ready.

He put a friendly hand on Shafeen's shoulder. 'The game's afoot, old chap. Hope you enjoy it.' The hand slapped the shoulder in approval. 'Ah – look at you! You're the image of your father! You feel the hunt in your *blood*, just like Hardy did.'

It was true that Shafeen's dark eyes were fixed on that figure running across the fields. But Rollo had misread his expression. It wasn't the hungry look of a predator. I knew Shafeen well enough to read what he was thinking. Whether or not Ty was a willing participant, the optics were really bad. One black girl on foot, running away from a lot of white folks on horseback. That intense look in his eyes was disgust. Shafeen shrugged the hand away and spoke right into Rollo's face. 'I will never, *ever* be a part of this.'

Rollo recoiled as if he had been hit. He dropped the hand, making no answer, and as he spurred his horse to move to the front of the pack I won't swear there weren't tears in his eyes. But I had no time to cry for Rollo. The three of us hung back and steered our horses into a little huddle.

'*Now* what do we do?' asked Nel.

'We go and get her,' said Shafeen shortly. 'They can find someone else to be their prey.'

I looked at the determined figure running easily towards the horizon. I know it sounds weird, but Ty didn't *look* scared. She wasn't glancing back fearfully over her shoulder, only forward. She looked as if she had a purpose. I had a sudden misgiving. I remembered what she had said. *I'm coming for them, Greer.*

I'm gonna let slip the dogs of war. 'What if this is part of a plan, and we ride in and ruin it? Isn't this that White Saviour thing we talked about?'

'I'm not white,' said Shafeen. And he dug his heels into his horse's belly and shot away over the fields.

A second later, playing catch-up, the horn sounded, sweet in the blood. The silent hounds started up a frantic baying and streaked after Ty and Shafeen. I felt a thrill of terror as the placid Sweetbriar carried me along with the rest.

We were off.

It was one of the most exciting and terrifying moments of my life. Even though I technically knew how to ride, there was nothing I could have done to stop Sweetbriar at that moment. I was right in the middle of this Charge of the Light Brigade and there was a cacophony of sound – the winter wind rushing past my ears, the jingle of the bits, the thunder of the hooves and the music of the horn shivering my ribs. Above it all, though, I could still hear the members of the hunt braying at each other, their faces puce with shock at what Shafeen had done.

'Dashed bad form, getting ahead of the Master like that!'

'Ought to be horsewhipped, arrogant young puppy.'

'Coloured feller – what d'ye expect?'

I spurred Sweetbriar on, hoping to leave the hate behind.

50

Throughout that winter morning, I had a crash course in hunting.

I learned when to hang back, and when to press forward. When to follow a line, when to check. I even began to interpret the call of the hounds – the keen, bloodthirsty baying of a trail found, and the whining complaint of a scent lost.

I barely got to see Nel and Shafeen, separated as we were by the field, and could communicate only in shaken heads and shrugs. But even from these vague mimes I could tell, with a sinking heart, that neither one of them had seen Ty. And of course it was pretty tricky to identify anyone, as we were all wearing basically the same thing. I thought again of *The Thomas Crown Affair* when all the decoys wear bowler hats and it's impossible to pick out the real Thomas Crown. Equally, I saw very little of the Medievals. Esme complimented me, with her trademark insincerity, on how I looked in my riding gear. Cookson once held a gate open for me and touched his hat ironically with his crop when I thanked him. But other than that, there was no real interaction until lunch, and of the one person I really wanted to see, there was no sign.

We all stopped for lunch at this beautiful little medieval pub on the Longcross grounds called the Trip to Jerusalem. It had lots of crazy beams and a sign with a crusader wearing the cross of Saint George – presumably this was the original baddie in this particular screenplay: Conrad de Warlencourt. We all dismounted and gathered in the pub courtyard. A legion of grooms appeared out of nowhere to rub down the horses and give them bran mash and water, while we all trooped inside for sandwiches and beer.

I sat with Shafeen and Nel, well away from the Medievals and the twins. I still liked Cass and Louis, but as they were all sitting together, we swerved that table completely.

It was too loud for much conversation, but when I did manage to say, 'I haven't seen Ty all morning, have you?' they both shook their heads. We ate our sandwiches, grim-faced. Plenty of people, either covertly or overtly, had something to say about Shafeen's 'ill-mannered' riding, so that didn't exactly improve his temper, but the mood among the rest of the Longcross hunt seemed pretty buoyant. Spirits were high, spirits were drunk. As far as I could tell, we'd just had what passed for a great morning's sport. They were all talking over each other and laughing, and getting louder and louder, to the point where it was actually a relief to get back outside into the cold afternoon.

But as the afternoon wore on the mood changed.

It was getting dark. Heads and tails down, hounds truffled in the undergrowth. A mean, mizzling rain began to fall and riders pushed cold hands into their riding coats, turned up collars against the wind and took out their silver flasks for a restorative chug of brandy. Nel, Shafeen and I took shelter in a little spinney of trees, enjoying the spectacle of the hunt disintegrating. Now our moods swapped over from what they'd been at lunch. We grew more cheerful, the rest of the hunt more despondent. 'D'you think Ty just screwed them over with a crazy trail? You know, just went round and round like Mr Messy until they didn't know which way was up?'

'I dunno,' said Nel. 'Good for her if she did though.'

'Well, whatever she did, I hope she's OK,' said Shafeen.

And then, as if summoned, a figure emerged from the undergrowth like Will Smith in *Aladdin*, and suddenly Ty was in front of us. Even the placid Sweetbriar flinched at the red figure and skittered on the mossy ground, and I had to really hang on to her reins.

'Jesus, Ty. Are you OK?' I wanted to lean down and hug her, but I probably would've fallen out of my saddle.

'Yes,' she said. 'I'm fine.'

To be fair, she looked fine. She was on foot in her red onesie and we were on horseback in posh hunting gear, but somehow she was the more powerful. 'Has it been all right? No one's hurt you?' asked Shafeen.

She flashed a grin. 'Not yet.'

'Why didn't you call?' asked Nel. 'You just . . . stopped communicating.'

'They took my phone,' Ty replied briefly.

'*What?*' we chorused.

'That is . . . I don't know for sure,' she backtracked. 'Cass saw me using it, and she seemed cool at the time. But the next day it was gone from my knicker drawer, and I haven't seen it since. My mum will skin me.' Suddenly she was like the old Ty.

'My dad will sort you out with a new phone,' said Nel comfortingly. 'But we did what you asked. We found out about Foxes.'

'Me too,' said Ty, serious again. 'I found out *all* about them. But listen – you guys have to let this play out.'

'What do you mean?' asked Nel.

'Hang back,' she said. 'Stay out of the way. Everything's chill.'

'*What's* chill?' I asked.

'No time now.'

'Can't we help?' Shafeen offered.

Ty seemed to think about this. 'If you want to help, tell them the hounds picked up a scent in Acre Wood. You got that?'

'Acre Wood,' I repeated.

'Gotta go,' she said, and began to recede into the trees.

'Ty,' I blurted.

She turned back for a moment. There were so many things I wanted to say. *Be careful. Stay alive. We're with you.* But instead I said, 'Your mum says hi.'

For a moment her face crumpled. Then that familiar look of stubborn resolve replaced the sadness, and she was gone.

PART 17
PRIZE

51

As we looked out of the spinney at the rain, a lone horseman rode into view.

The height, the banded boots of the Master of Foxhounds and the golden gleam of the horn at the saddle told us it was Rollo.

I had a niggling doubt. If we passed on that information for Ty, what exactly were we complicit in? What lurked in Acre Wood? I'd seen enough crime movies to know about being an accessory before the fact.

But Shafeen had no such qualms. He rode straight up to the earl. 'I'm sorry about before.'

Rollo turned in his saddle.

'You were right. You were right about everything. I see it now.'

Rollo looked genuinely touched and raised a friendly hand again, but this time, instead of patting Shafeen's shoulder, he cupped the younger man's cheek. It was a weirdly intimate gesture. 'Attaboy,' he said, a word I didn't understand at all, but it was clearly a compliment.

'And I think I'm getting the hang of it,' Shafeen went on. 'I think the hounds picked up a scent in Acre Wood.'

Rollo looked at Shafeen as fondly as a son. 'Good enough for me,' he said, and raised the horn.

The terrible song brought the hounds and riders running, and above the melee Rollo shouted, 'To Acre Wood!' We were carried along like cavalry – we could have been those ancient crusaders who charged across the mosaicked walls of the STAGS Club. I lost the others as Sweetbriar found herself shoulder to shoulder with Rollo's stallion. I remembered what the head groom had said about Sweetbriar and Harkaway being stablemates and resigned myself to being right in the thick of the action. Aware that it was absolutely forbidden to get ahead of the MFH, I reined Sweetbriar back a little, but I was right behind Rollo when we plunged into the twilight darkness of Acre Wood.

I was right behind him when the branches whipped at our faces as we followed the speeding hounds through the murk.

And I was right behind him when *it* happened.

We reached the centre of a clearing and Rollo reined back his horse and stopped. I hauled on Sweetbriar's reins and stopped her too, before we could cannon into the back of him. Rollo held up his hand. Everyone stopped. The hounds washed about his horse's legs like sea foam, seeking the next scent. There were about five different ways we could go from there, five pathways leading into the dark, and no one seemed to have a clue. Except Rollo. He was very still, listening, sniffing the air like Hannibal Lecter, a born hunter.

Then something extraordinary happened. A little figure trotted out of the trees. He was also wearing a red coat, his four paws black like little boots. His face was a pointy mask, his ears sharp as blades.

344

He was a fox.

I swear he stopped for a second to look at us from amber eyes – he regarded us, we regarded him. He was brazen, cocky and utterly unafraid, just like Fantastic Mr Fox. For that split second we were all as still as Rollo, even the hounds. Then Rollo spoke a single word. Not to us, not to the hounds, but to the fox.

'Reynard.'

At the sound of his name, the fox turned and ran.

The spell was broken. Rollo plunged after him, crashing through the undergrowth. Sweetbriar followed her stablemate closely. And we were once again in the darkness of the undergrowth. It was hard to see even your hand in front of your face, it's true. But I'll swear to my dying day that I saw what I saw.

Despite being in the thickest undergrowth, the path was true and straight and led downhill. Rollo was gathering speed when suddenly a figure rose up out of a hidden stream. It was dark, enormously tall and black-clad. *The Grand Stag*, said my rabbit's heart, but this was not he. There were no antlers, and no empty cowl, because this figure had a face underneath a black slouch hat. And even in the dim twilight I could see the face clear as day because it was a mask of glowing white, all except for the quizzical black eyebrows, the grinning red mouth, the curling moustaches and the neat goatee beard.

It was the face of Guy Fawkes.

At the sudden sight of the spectre, Harkaway spooked. He stumbled and checked, then reared in a flash of flying hooves and whiplash reins. Rollo fell hard, and the stallion stood for a moment on his haunches, statuesque.

345

Sweetbriar wheeled and backed away, and I fought just as I had done at Speaker's Corner, to calm my mount. Now, as then, Shafeen arrived to lay a firm hand on the reins, closely followed by Nel. By the time we'd slid to the ground to run to Rollo, there were already other huntsmen there. Sweetbriar pulled away and I let her go to nuzzle and comfort Harkaway, who was carrying one of his legs as if he couldn't put weight on it. His reins were trailing, and he was shaking and shaking his head as if bothered by a fly.

But the Earl of Longcross did not move. Ice cold, I jostled to see the red-clad figure stretched on the winter earth. *Two hooves on the ground, killed in battle.* Was he dead? He had a little crowd around him, and it was difficult to see through all the riding boots and crouching huntsmen, but after what seemed like a lifetime I did hear the fallen figure give an unmistakable groan. 'He's OK,' I said, with a warm rush of relief.

I ran to the stream and looked to the left and right. Night had fallen, but I thought I might see the flash of the white mask as the phantom made its escape.

Shafeen and Nel followed, questioning as they came.

'Greer, what the hell?'

'Who are we looking for?'

'Him,' I said, 'Guy Fawkes. Did you not see?'

Shafeen grabbed me by my shoulders and looked at both my eyes in turn, as if he was diagnosing concussion or something. 'Greer. Did you fall?'

'No!' I pulled away. 'I've had about enough of people thinking I'm crazy. I *saw* him.'

'You *saw Guy Fawkes*?'

346

'Yes,' I said. 'No. I mean, I saw the mask. A man, all in black, with a big black hat. And he was wearing a mask, one of those *V for Vendetta* ones that all the Fawkeses were wearing at Speaker's Corner.' I pointed. 'He jumped up out of the ditch to frighten Rollo's horse. The horse got spooked and reared, and that's how Rollo fell.'

Nel said, 'You're sure it was a man?' It was an odd question, but at least she seemed to believe in the idea of a figure.

I considered. 'Well – he seemed pretty tall. Who else would it be?'

'Well,' said Nel, 'think about it. Ty told us to bring him here. To Acre Wood.'

I could not think that of her. And if she'd done *that*, then the enormity of what *we'd* done swelled to scary proportions. We'd led Rollo into a trap. 'No,' I protested. 'No. He was tall. Really tall. He was as tall as . . .' I turned to Nel, wide-eyed.

'No,' said Nel.

'. . . as tall as the Abbot,' I finished.

'Well, it can't have been him,' she said decidedly.

'No, no, of course not,' I agreed uneasily. 'And besides, the figure didn't lead him here, Reynard did.'

'Reynard?'

'The fox. There was one here, in the covert. He led Rollo down the path. I know it sounds like mystical bullshit, but he led Rollo the right way. Or rather, the wrong way.'

While we talked there was a buzz of activity as the hunt gathered round Rollo like red ants. Princes and prime ministers knelt in the dirt to give him aid, all concerned for one of their own. I had a massive sense of déjà vu as the hunt servants took

347

the five-bar gate from beyond the ditch off its hinges and laid Rollo on it, just as we'd done with Shafeen after he'd been shot. Rollo was conscious, but his normal florid colour had drained away and he looked as pale as paper – as pale as the Guy Fawkes mask.

Six red coats carried the gate like pall bearers, and Caro had appeared from somewhere and walked alongside her husband, holding his limp hand. She was very bright and British and keeping her emotions in check, but she looked as pale as her husband, and the hunt was clearly over for the day. None of us had the appetite to ride, so we led our horses out of the covert and down the hillside towards the cruise-ship lights of Longcross Hall, sailing on the black sea of night.

One of the huntsmen led Harkaway home, and the stallion was still limping, carrying one leg.

'I hope he'll be all right too,' I said uneasily.

'He'll be shot,' said Shafeen shortly.

'No way,' I gasped.

'Yes way,' he countered brutally. 'He's no use for hunting now. You think they're going to send him to a farm in the countryside? There's no point keeping a horse you can't ride just to eat its head off and cost you vet bills.' He pulled the peak of his hat down against the rain, a flourish of finality. 'He's dogmeat, Greer. That's how you reward a hunter for years of loyal service.'

As we walked the horses back in the freezing rain, all I could think of was what a brutal world this was that I'd ridden into, for humans and animals alike.

PART 18
HOME

52

I knew from bitter experience that a minor injury wouldn't be enough to spoil a dinner at Longcross, especially not one as important as this.

Rollo was pronounced to be fine, with no more than a mild concussion. The countess made a little speech as we sat down to dine, saying that her husband was being treated by the family doctor, and that he'd insisted that we were all to enjoy the Hunt Ball. Everyone seemed to find this perfectly normal, and I could only assume that hunting injuries were commonplace and that nobody thought it was a big deal, just 'hard luck'.

The Great Hall was just as I remembered it – the tiger skin rug, the stags' heads above the candle light and the duelling pistols crossed on the wall; but it was also different. It was full of people this time and no longer just *ours*. Longcross was at its full-on *Gatsby* finest, with music and champagne, and the tinkling of glasses and laughter. This is what it must have been like in those halcyon days of old, every chair filled, every room occupied, stuffed with guests like us above stairs and servants like Bates below. Even the tiger-skin rug gaped in amazement at such opulence.

Louis, at the head of the table in Rollo's chair, was visibly enjoying himself. There was an empty chair on his left, which I thought must be for Ty, because as yet she was nowhere to be seen. All I wanted was for her to come through the doors, rocking her red dress, and show us all that she was OK, that she'd been a willing participant, that she was in one piece. I was determined to ask Louis, but there was something that had to be got out of the way first. 'How's your uncle?'

'A touch of concussion, as Aunt Caro said,' he replied.

I didn't really know how serious that was. 'I know, but will he be OK?'

'Of course. It often happens after a fall. No one ever died of mild concussion.'

I felt a rush of relief. However monstrous Rollo was, I didn't want him to, well, *die*. But I thought that was exactly what someone *did* want. Who had been behind that Guy Fawkes mask? Who had jumped out at Rollo's stallion and made it rear in that sickening way? Was it Henry, who had stored up years of enmity towards his father? What about Cass, who hated Rollo on behalf of a well-loved cousin? Or Louis, impatient for his title of Earl of Longcross? Or even Ty herself, who could have got ahead of the pack and donned the mask in the undergrowth? What was the 'plan' she'd hatched that we had to let play out?

Of course I could say nothing of this to Louis. 'So everybody is happy with the ball and everything going ahead? Even without your uncle?'

'Doesn't matter if he's here,' said Louis, slathering butter on a white roll. 'I'm here, aren't I?'

It was clear: Louis was more than happy to stand in as the host with the most. Fine. Now I could move on to my main concern. 'And at the risk of repeating myself, where is Ty?'

Louis sighed and smiled, but he didn't seem irritated. He was far too buoyant tonight for anything to burst the bubble of his happiness. 'Greer, you're like a broken record.' This was a typical Medieval metaphor – they'd always reference something archaic. 'Didn't we have the same conversation this morning? I told you you'd see Ty, and you did. She'll be down in a minute. She's just getting ready. Something about Afro hair. Apparently, it's much harder to manage than normal hair. Especially when it's rained. Or something.'

I bumped hard on the word 'normal', but at the same time, something about this dreadful sentence was reassuring. There was no way that Louis could have made up that excuse. It sounded like Ty, and furthermore it sounded like Ty buying time. What was she *really* doing up there? It could't be taking her this long to get ready, whatever she'd sold Louis about her hair. Was this all part of her mysterious plan? She'd asked for our help; she'd asked us to find out about Foxes. We'd done that, and then when we'd seen her in the wood she'd asked us to stay away. There was only one explanation. In the interim, while she'd been at Longcross without her phone, she'd got the help she needed.

From someone else.

Being with Louis reminded me of something else. Throughout the entire hunt, what with Ty and the fox and the sudden appearance of the Guy Fawkes figure, I'd achieved the impossible: I'd forgotten about Henry. Now Cass's words about her cousin's fate came back to me. *I think Louis'll find out tonight . . . Everybody will.* Was there going to be some sort of announcement? Might the empty chair be for Henry?

This idea was swiftly nixed by Cass herself sliding into the empty place. For once, she'd followed convention and was wearing a floor-length ballgown of white lace. With her elfin cropped hair she looked like a fairy – ethereal, almost transparent and very *Blithe Spirit*. She wreathed her arms about her twin like a vine and kissed Louis very tenderly on the edge of his jaw. She was more affectionate to him than ever, but something about the gesture made me uncomfortable. There was something weirdly valedictory about it. It was almost as if she was being super-nice because she knew this was his last act as king – that the pretender was about to be replaced by the rightful ruler. When Cass sat down I clocked that the seating was boy-girl-boy-girl, and although I'd got lucky on one side with Louis, the scales were tipped on the other side by Piers. Nel was on his other side with Shafeen beyond her, and opposite us, Charlotte and Esme flanked Cookson. *Fasten your seatbelt, Greer*, I told myself. *It's going to be a bumpy night.*

Never one to miss a chance to be superficial, Esme instantly began to talk about my appearance. 'Darling, you look lovely in the white. Goes great with the black bob.'

'Why *is* everyone in white anyway?' Numbed by the shock of Rollo's fall, I'd automatically put on the white satin sheath dress that had been left out on my bed, and clipped into my hair the pair of 1920s diamond hairslides. It was only now, looking around, I clicked that as well as all the men being in white tie, a lot of the women seemed to be in white too.

'Not everyone,' admonished Esme teasingly, 'just the ladies under twenty-one. It's a debutante thing.'

'A *what* thing?'

'Your "coming out" ball.'

Now I was confused. 'But I'm not even gay.'

Esme laughed her tinkling laugh. 'No, silly. Queen Charlotte held a ball in the eighteenth century to introduce the young unmarried women to society. They were all presented at court wearing white. It still happens. Have you never heard of Queen Charlotte's ball?'

'I've never even heard of Queen Charlotte.'

'I think Caro wanted to revive the tradition. Perfect opportunity, since there's to be dancing.'

My stomach did a little flip. It seemed to me this evening had massive potential for me to make a fool of myself. I'd never learned to dance, and the full extent of my knowledge came from watching *Strictly Ballroom*. How did you dance at a ball? I had a sudden and wholly unwanted Jane Austen fantasy about dancing with Henry.

'Don't worry,' said Esme, reading my expression. 'You'll be the belle of the ball.'

I pulled a face.

'Don't you like the white?'

'Feels a bit bridal.'

'Well, you never *know*, Greer,' sing-songed Charlotte, breaking into our conversation. 'Maybe *soon*.'

Although I was sitting near to Shafeen, no one looked at him archly or smiled at him in that nudge-nudge-wink-wink way. Suddenly I got the strongest feeling they weren't hinting about him. They were hinting about *Henry*. Did they, his closest schoolfriends, *know* that he was going to make a comeback tonight? Was I his chosen consort, from all those *Cinderella* maidens dressed in white? Was that why they were all being super-nice to me? Lara, sitting beyond some chinless guy on Charlotte's right, managed to look bored and sour at the same time. If they were talking about Henry, it was probably crossing her tiny mind that a little over a year ago she would have been on the receiving end of arch comments like this. I couldn't feel sorry for her. I couldn't feel sorry for any of them. I downed another wine.

Suddenly Shafeen was at my elbow, saying, 'Steady on,', but I was in no mood. I suddenly realised what a strain we'd been under, and that we'd been on the go since dawn that morning.

'Not now, sweetie,' I said. 'Mama's had a day.' I ceased to care about this table of deplorables and what they thought of me. It was time for some straight-talking. 'How's Oxford, Piers?' I asked.

He put his elbow heavily on the table and turned to look at me in an unfocused way. 'It's *exactly* the same as school.'

This gave me a chill. If I was going there next year, would I be in the crosshairs of these poisonous predators once again? Well, I wasn't having it. I wasn't going to be a victim. I was in a hunting mood. I was a fox in a hen coop, and it was time to ruffle some feathers. 'Does that mean you're carrying on your little reindeer games into further education?'

'Greer . . .' warned Shafeen. But I was on a roll. There was an element of relief in my drinking. Ty hadn't been hunted down, and all we had to do now was wait for her to come down, get through this evening and go. I waved my glass for a refill of my wine from a passing footman, and Shafeen had to return to his seat to make way for him. The footman poured for me, eyes down, but I wasn't having that. 'Thanks. What's your name, sorry?'

He raised his eyes an inch, surprised. 'Bell, miss.'

I took the wine and it sloshed over my hand a little. 'Not your last name, silly. I meant your *first* name.'

Then he looked me in the eyes. 'Joshua, miss. Josh.'

I raised the glass to him. 'Well, thank you very much, Josh.'

'You're welcome,' he murmured, taken aback. 'Is there anything else I can do for you, miss?'

'No,' I said, 'you've done quite enough.'

And he moved on along the chairs, hand behind his back, pouring the bottle until it was gone, no one even sparing him a glance.

Reluctantly, I turned back to Piers. Frankly, I'd rather talk to Josh than him. 'What are you even studying anyway?'

'Twentieth-century poetry.'

'Ah!' I raised my forefinger. 'Do you know that poem about Reynard the Fox?'

'Of course. John Masefield.'

I poked the forefinger into his shoulder in congratulation. 'Yes!' I watched him closely, but neither the mention of foxes, nor the name Reynard, seemed to set any suspicious bell ringing in his personal belfry. There was no doubt about it, Piers was hard work. I looked across to Shafeen longingly, wishing I was close enough to chat to him, and as I did so I saw Bates come to stand behind him, politely wait for a lull in conversation, and then bend to murmur in his ear. I was close enough to see Shafeen turn in his chair, his face a mask of surprise. He rose from his seat and walked the three places to me, crouching on his haunches. 'Rollo's asked to see me.'

Despite my tipsy fog, I was surprised too. 'Just you?'

'Yes. But will you come with me?'

'Of course.' I got up too, slightly unsteadily, as the wine rushed to my head. As we walked past all those Very Important People, those shining royals and polished politicians, Shafeen slipped his hand into mine. We walked like that into the great hall and up the stairs, following Bates's ruler-straight back.

53

The butler led us to a part of the house I'd never seen before, a wing guarded by knights in shining armour, visors closed for business – a part even more ancient, it seemed, than the rest of the house.

Bates opened the door into a dark room, all chocolate-brown oak panels, and a magnificent bed in the centre of the space hung with swags and swathes of old gold tapestry. In the middle of that bed, even a man of Rollo de Warlencourt's stature seemed very small. The ancient doctor – the Doctor Morand who had patched up Shafeen's shotgun wound the previous year – was attending the earl, white head bent over the bed. He gestured impatiently to Shafeen. 'Come in, my boy. There's not much time, I fear.'

Not much time. My brain, slow as slime, could not quite understand what this meant. Shafeen, suddenly very serious, walked forward to the bed like a man in a dream. I was not required in this peculiarly male moment, so I hung back. But even from the doorway I could see how Rollo looked. I don't know what I'd expected the effects of mild concussion to look like, but it wasn't *this*. The earl looked awful – somehow shrunken. His breathing was laboured and his face a sickly yellowy green. His skin seemed almost stretched across his cheeks and the fine bones of his nose. He fixed watery blue eyes on Shafeen as the younger man knelt beside the bed, almost as if he were praying. The earl reached out and clasped Shafeen's brown hand, his own pale knuckles knotted with the blue snakes of his veins.

'Hardy,' he croaked.

Shafeen said, softly but a little coldly, 'It's not Aadhish. It's Shafeen. His son.'

The doctor, straightening up, stood over them both, shaking his head. 'He's confused. I've seen this before, very near the end.'

Shafeen looked at the doctor for a long moment. Then he looked back to Rollo and did the sweetest thing. He squeezed the hand that held his. 'Yes,' he said. 'It's me, old friend. It's Hardy.'

'Hardy,' said Rollo, a smile stretching his pale blue lips. 'We had some gay old times, didn't we?'

Shafeen lifted the papery hand to his cheek so the earl could feel him smile. 'That we did.'

'Hardy. I've wanted to contact you for ever so long. I wanted to say I'm sorry. I'm sorry for what happened that Justitium weekend, in 1969. What we did to you.'

There was nothing Shafeen could say to this, so he said nothing.

'But I'm not sorry for what we did together,' gasped the earl breathlessly. 'Never that.' There was a silence. 'Hardy. Can you ever understand?'

'Of course I can,' said Shafeen. 'I do.'

The earl's face seemed to slacken with relief and release. The hand relaxed and fell back on the coverlet.

A figure loomed from the darkness behind me, and my heart leaped for one stupid moment – was it the man from the woods, the Guy Fawkes character come to claim his victim? But no – the one shape and colour I could see in the gloom was a white dog collar.

A priest.

The doctor clocked him. 'Stand back now, my boy,' he said to Shafeen. 'Let Father Wright do his work.'

Numb, I watched as the priest kissed his ceremonial sash and placed it round his neck, and then began, very methodically (how many of these had he done?) to arrange his oils and his candles and his silver vials and begin the process of an ending. As this holy man dabbed holy oil onto Rollo's forehead and chest, I didn't have to wonder what he was doing. I knew about this from *Brideshead Revisited*. *These are the last rites*, I thought, as the mumbled Latin prayers hit my ear. The priest was giving the last rites. This was how Catholics checked out.

There was no drama, no big end-of-life speech, no final cross sketched by the quaking hand over the failing heart. But when the ritual was over Rollo held out his hand to the doorway, looking past the priest and the doctor. They could no longer help him. He reached out to Shafeen. 'Kiss me, Hardy,' he said.

I looked at Shafeen, as he looked at Rollo. I could see him doing battle with himself. Suddenly that *Lion in Winter* thing that Rollo had said the very first time we'd met made sense to me.

When the fall's all that's left, it matters a great deal.

I stared at Shafeen until my vision blurred. *Do it.* I willed him. *Just do it.* Whatever Rollo had done, whatever kind of monster he was, give him this one last gift. Then Shafeen walked forward, bent and tenderly kissed the hectic cheek of the Earl of Longcross.

I'd never seen anyone die before, but I can tell you it is a moment of real clarity. There is absolutely no mistaking it – it is very binary. One moment the earl was there on the bed, the next moment he was gone.

If I had been drunk when I came into the room, I was now absolutely stone-cold sober.

We watched, numb with shock, as the priest finished his work – he snuffed out the candles with absolute finality. Then, as he knelt to pray with the body, the doctor ushered us out of the room. He closed the door behind him and there were just three of us in that passageway, but a million questions crowded in there with us. 'But ... but ...' I began, but I didn't know how to finish. *But he couldn't just check out like that. But he had a roomful of guests downstairs. But what about Henry? He never got to say goodbye.* Eventually my brain zoned in not on a question, but a statement – something I'd heard Louis say less than an hour ago, before the world had changed. 'But no one ever died of mild concussion.'

The doctor pushed his half-moon glasses up his nose and now *his* hand was shaking. He cleared his throat. 'I've been practising medicine for fifty years and I can tell you that one can never account for the vagaries of chance. Sadly, the concussion must have been the manifestation of some sort of head trauma. These things happen.'

'These things happen?' Shafeen found his voice. 'These things *happen?*' He moved closer to the doctor – he towered over him. His eyes were full of contempt. I remembered what he'd said on the day he'd been shot in the arm – that this Doctor Morand had been covering up the injuries that ensued from the Order of the Stag's death hunts for years. Shafeen got right in his face until the older man was backed up against the panelling.

'I've been practising medicine for exactly *no* years,' said Shafeen bitingly, 'but even *I* know that what I saw on that bed wasn't just concussion. How do you account for the jaundice of the skin? The high temperature but the cold extremities? The cyanosis of the lips?'

I was proud of Shafeen and scared of him in equal measure. How did he know this stuff? He was a *badass*. The doctor began to shake his head, the loose skin of his chins shivering like a turkey's wattle.

'I think you'd better start talking,' said Shafeen in a steely voice. 'Your protector has gone now, and as far as we are concerned, you did your very best to save him. But there is a different version of events: that you were incompetent. That you were unable to diagnose a secondary condition. That you let the Earl of Longcross *die.*'

The doctor looked from Shafeen to me, and back again.

'I happen to know Lord Fenton of the General Medical Council,' said Shafeen. He wasn't lying either – I remembered the bow-tied guy at the STAGS Club. 'Perhaps I should discuss the earl's cause of death with him?'

That did it. The doctor began to bluster. 'Well,' he said, 'without a post-mortem I couldn't possibly say with any certainty . . .'

'. . . but . . .' prompted Shafeen.

'. . . but if I was a betting man,' whispered the doctor, 'I'd say poison.'

The shock of that word, toxic and potent, percolated through my own veins. It didn't make any sense to me – I could barely process what had just been whispered in this ancient passageway. I could think only of what would happen next. 'What shall we do now?'

Sweating, Doctor Morand ran a finger inside his collar. 'Go back down,' he croaked, 'and act as if nothing is amiss. Don't say a word until I've had a chance to tell the countess privately.'

54

Shafeen looked at me and nodded, and like a couple of zombies, we drifted back down the stairs.

Outside the door of the great hall, Shafeen stopped.

'Are you OK?' I asked him. He looked far from OK.

He shook his head. 'I feel like I need an M on *my* thumb.'

I clutched my own brand. 'But . . . why?'

He started pacing. 'I led him to Acre Wood. *I* did. I *told* Rollo to go there. Then he was ambushed and had the accident. Greer –' he nodded upstairs to the room of death – 'did I do that?'

'No,' I said, very definitely. 'You heard Doctor Morand. He was poisoned.'

'But who would *do* that?'

I actually thought there were quite a few candidates, the same Usual Suspects I had in the frame for the Guy Fawkes figure.

I caught his hand. 'Let's not do this now. We've got to put on a show.'

We heard the clashing of cutlery and crystal and the rising laughter of the guests. It seemed impossible to walk back in there like nothing had happened. But it suddenly seemed very important that we should. I squeezed Shafeen's hand and plastered on a smile. Together we walked through the great doors and behind the lines of chairs, and no one even noticed us but Nel, who leaned back in her seat with a quizzical look. With the coded communication we'd perfected during the last extraordinary year, I shook my head a tiny amount. She rocked back into her place, watching us guardedly, but asked no questions.

Mechanically, I parried Piers's increasingly drunken conversation. 'Hear you've been in town,' he slurred. 'What d'ye get up to?'

I could have boasted about the STAGS Club, or the House of Lords, or even the London Oratory. But I didn't care any more for Piers's good opinion, so instead I said, 'We went to the Isle of Dogs.'

He barked with laughter. 'Ah, the *Îles des chiens*. The Canine Islands.'

'You been?' I asked.

'*God*, no,' he said, and I turned away from him. The food was gravel in my mouth, the wine vinegar. I couldn't look at Shafeen, couldn't look at the countess, as the minutes crawled by. I assumed Ty had come down by now, but I couldn't check. I couldn't look left or right. Where was Doctor Morand? What was he doing up there? Why was he not coming down to give the dreadful news to the countess? Was he informing an unseen Henry that he was now the Earl of Longcross and ensuring the succession? *The king is dead, long live the king.* I couldn't think about Henry or Ty or anybody else but Rollo.

What crimes he and Aadhish committed in 1969 that needed to be forgiven?

The snow fell politely outside as the guests inside got more and more raucous. The whole thing was so Agatha Christie's *The Mousetrap* it wasn't even funny. It was post-modern as hell. We were even snowed in inside a country house on Boxing Day. Actually, it was more like a giant game of Cluedo. We had three clues – the earl in the bedroom with the poison. But whodunnit?

This was awful. Shafeen and I knew and no one else in this room did, and to cap it all, the countess leaped to her feet and clapped her hands. Now I had to look at her, and her happiness was devastating. 'Bates,' she called, 'I think it's time for the Veuve Clicquot '84. We'll go ahead with the speeches and the toasts as planned, and of course drink to dear Rollo's health.' I swallowed miserably. How ironic to call for her husband's favourite champagne when he was already dead. How awful that I would actually get to taste it for the first time once there was nothing to celebrate. How dreadful that, while Rollo was lifeless in his bed upstairs, the faithful Bates was to be sent scuttling to the cellars for the legendary vintage his master would never taste again.

The cellars.

The champagne that didn't exist.

The hundreds of bottles swaddled in straw.

'If you were to shake it – disaster.'

The cellars of the Houses of Parliament.

Guy Fawkes and his lantern.

Remember, Remember . . .

I got to my feet. 'Get out,' I said.

Everyone was chatting and laughing – no one heard me. I shouted it. 'GET OUT!'

Now the people close to me started to hear. Dear Shafeen, dear Nel, the twins and the Medievals. Shafeen started to his feet and took hold of me. For the second time that day, I shook him off. I climbed up on the chair, and then onto the table. China cracked under my feet, glasses overturned, cutlery crashed. I shouted it again. 'GET OUT! EVERYBODY, GET OUT!'

Now there was a proper torrent of reaction – and above the hubbub I could hear, over and again, the same comment: 'The girl's drunk.'

I had been, but I wasn't any longer. 'No,' I yelled. 'I'm not drunk. We all have to get out *now*!'

A couple of footmen approached, Josh and another guy – white gloved hands reaching up to pull me down. There wasn't much time.

I took a deep breath and shouted as loudly as I could, projecting like an actor. 'In the name of Henry de Warlencourt and the Dark Order of the Grand Stag, I charge you all to leave this place at once!'

I don't know where that came from – maybe the ghost of Ben Jonson. And I didn't know whether it was the archaic form of words, or the fact that I'd invoked the name of their cult, but it certainly shut everyone up. In the brief silence I looked desperately at the countess. I met those blue eyes, so like Henry's, and knew at once what had convinced her. It was the name of her son.

She gave a single, regal nod and everybody moved as one. Everyone got up with a scrape of chairs and a flurry of napkins, flying and falling like doves. 'Out of the house,' I shouted above this new row. 'Into the driveway and just keep going.' Now I took Shafeen's proffered hand and jumped down. 'GO!'

Everyone flowed through the double doors into the great hall, then out of the front doors into the shock of the night air. In the doorway I bumped against Josh and I clutched his liveried arm. This couldn't just be an exodus of the affluent. 'Get everybody from downstairs out of the house immediately,' I said, emphasising every word. 'You got that?'

'Yes,' he said, and ran.

55

I wasn't heroic enough to wait for everyone else to go first; I jostled with the rest as we flooded out into the atrium.

There the doctor, finally, was coming down the great staircase and watched this exodus through bewildered eyes. 'Is anyone else upstairs?' I shouted.

'Just the earl,' he said, mystified.

It was too late for him. 'Get out!' I said.

There was pushing and shoving as the panic spread. As we emerged into the snowy night, I breathed a lungful of frigid air with relief. But I kept going. I was in the front now, leading everyone up the drive, marching ever forward, shrugging off questions from lords and ladies, politicians and princes. I kept going, and we were nearly at the frill of the forest before I looked back. When I stopped and turned, everyone else did likewise. I watched with infinite relief as all the footmen, kitchen maids, under-butlers and cooks hurried up the drive until the flow trickled, then stopped and there was no one left. I saw Doctor Morand physically holding Caro de Warlencourt back from returning to the house, talking and talking until she collapsed against him, convinced at last that there was no point going back for her husband. So that was everyone.

Everyone.

I found Nel and grabbed her wrist. 'Ty came down to dinner, right?'

She looked at me blankly.

'While we were upstairs, Ty came down, right?' My voice rose. 'She was at the dinner, right?'

She spread her manicured hands. 'I don't know. That is, I didn't see her. Look, Greer, what the hell are you –'

Then I ran.

I ran back down the drive, pushing through all the people running away, swimming against the stream, a trout in the tide. Shafeen and Nel were at my heels, but I was too fast for them. I had to get to the house, had to get back to Ty, before –

The force of the blast blew me back.

I threw an arm across my face against the incredible heat, then took it away to see tongues of fire licking through the windows, and an inferno taking hold of the roof.

I fell to my knees, tears streaming down my face. All I could think of was Missy Morgan. If her shining girl was in that conflagration, I might as well have lit the fuses myself. Shafeen's and Nel's arms enclosed me in a strong circle. The three of us clasped each other on the icy ground, our backs frozen, our fronts warmed by the fire, like on Bonfire Night.

'No,' I moaned. 'No, no, no, no, no,' over and over again. No one could survive that blaze.

And then, indistinct at first, then clearer and clearer, a silhouette formed in the heart of the flames like a phoenix.

The blur resolved into the shape of a figure carrying another figure. As they came closer I recognised the one being carried first, her Afro hair a dark halo. And, carrying Ty, his hair as golden as the fire, was Henry de Warlencourt.

We all rushed forward. Henry was breathing heavily, staggering with the strain, his face black with soot, his blue eyes shining out. Ty was conscious but coughing harshly. Shafeen took her from Henry's arms. 'We've got her,' he said. Then, 'You did great, Henry. You did great.' He looked, in fleeting disbelief, from Henry to me. I let out a half gasp, half sob. Ty was safe. And Shafeen had finally seen Henry.

But there was no time to lose. Shafeen, fully in medical mode, took Ty to the grass to lay her down and shouted to Nel to run and find Doctor Morand in the crowd. Henry, still gasping for breath, wordlessly took my hand and smiled. Face filthy with ash and soot, only his eyes were unchanged. Then, before anyone else could recognise him, he pulled his fingers from my grasp, turned and walked away in the direction of Acre Wood. My hand released, I found I could no longer stand. I sat back heavily on the cold ground, unable to speak or move. I sat and watched the fire and it was some moments before I realised I wasn't alone.

Tame as a lap dog, a fox sat by me.

He was watching too, with eyes of fire.

We were just a girl and a fox, sitting together as if it were the most natural thing in the world. And together we regarded what, in another story and another land, his kind had done, the fiery foxes among the Philistine corn.

And the ashes blew towards us with the salt wind of the sea.

EPILOGUE

EPILOGUE

56

I stayed in my room a lot those first weeks of Hilary Term.

The shock of the fire still burned in my mind, a flame that wouldn't be doused. According to the traumatised twins, the damage to Longcross Hall was considerable, so at the moment no one could live there, not even a ghost. As there had been no big Henry reveal on the night of the fire, Louis was, as far as he knew, the Earl of Longcross. As such he had thrown himself into a grand rebuilding and restoration programme of his ancestral home. The twins both treated me like a heroine; there had been no bodies found inside, except for their already deceased uncle, and the shell of the house had been saved. Only Bates, the faithful family butler, hadn't been seen since the fire. I thought of what Henry had said – that a faithful old family retainer would never betray the family. How wrong he'd been. Bates had waited until the countess had ordered the champagne to detonate the fuses in the cellars, certain in the knowledge that everyone would be seated for the speeches and toasts, and perhaps even for the Return of the King – Henry de Warlencourt. I couldn't avoid the sickening conclusion that, as Bates had been so close to the blast, he'd been as good as vaporised by the explosives. Had his ashes drifted on those thermals, high above the house he'd served for so long?

Even though my hand hadn't been the one to light the fuses, I felt like the villain of the piece. If only I had figured it out earlier. If only I had realised what Bates was up to with the champagne. If only I had realised that the big conspiracy that we'd been trying to uncover wasn't *by* the Order of the Stag, but *against* them. Perhaps, then, everyone could have been saved.

We talked, quite a lot, about the champagne that didn't exist. It was Nel who came up with the best theory, possibly because, when we'd first got to Cumberland Place, she'd felt very much like a spare part and was able to observe everything closely. One evening when we were all leaning on the Paulinus well, our old haunt, she cracked what Sherlock Holmes might have called 'The Champagne Problem'.

'How come Rollo asked Bates for the Veuve Clicquot '84,' I mused, 'when both of them knew it didn't exist? And how come Bates just obediently went to get it every time?'

'*My* question,' said Shafeen, 'would be, how did those non-existent champagne bottles turn up in the cellars of Longcross Hall, full of explosives.'

'I've been thinking about this,' said Nel. 'Do you remember, when we first got to Cumberland Place, every time Caro tried to talk about Henry being alive, her mother, Lady Whitehaven, rang her up? And then it turned out she wasn't on the phone at all – it was just a ruse to get Caro out of the room.'

I picked a frill of lichen off the well and flicked it from my fingernail. 'Yes . . .'

'Well, I began to notice,' Nel went on, 'that when Rollo sent Bates for the Veuve Clicquot '84, as soon as Bates was out of the room Rollo started to talk about some big family secret. Once he talked about Henry. Once he talked about the plan to block the fox-hunting bill. And once, Shafeen, he talked about your dad and Longcross in 1969. All things he wouldn't necessarily want a servant to hear.'

Shafeen frowned. 'But Bates would *know*. Bates would *know* the wine he was being sent to get didn't exist.'

Nel nodded. 'That was weird to me too. But try *this* on for size: what if it was some sort of agreed de Warlencourt code to clear the servants from the room? Bates accepts it, and obeys it, because he's a servant and has been faithful to the family for about a hundred years.'

'But he *wasn't* faithful to the family,' I said. 'Not in the end.'

'Well, that's exactly it.' She got all animated, pointing her finger in my face. 'When the time came for Bates to put his gunpowder plot into action, what better way to get explosives into a cellar than to disguise them as wine? Wine lives in a cellar anyway.'

I straightened up. 'That's exactly what the original gunpowder plotters did. Guy Fawkes pretended the barrels of gunpowder that he stored under Parliament were wine.'

'There you go,' said Nel. 'And what better name for this mythical wine than the one that had been used for years to keep the servants out of the room, to exclude the lower classes, to keep the kids away from the big boys' table? Calling the

377

explosive "Veuve Clicquot 1984" was pure social justice on a wine label. It *literally* said it on the tin.'

I looked down into the blackness of the well as I thought about this, another door into the dark, just as the cellar door had been at Longcross that day. 'But wasn't that risky? What if someone had walked past?'

'Someone did,' said Nel. 'Us. And we only happened to go past the cellar door because we came in the tradesmens' entrance. All the other hoity-toity guests went in the front door. They wouldn't *dream* of poking around in the cellars.' She shrugged. 'We *saw* Bates unloading the bottles. Greer, you even picked one up.' The thought made me shiver, knowing what I now knew. 'But we didn't know there was anything odd about them. Who would?'

'Rollo,' said Shafeen. 'If Rollo had seen, he would have known there was something afoot.'

'But Rollo wouldn't go to the cellars. He has servants for that.' Nel smoothed the facings of her Tudor coat, like she was a barrister, before delivering her closing argument. 'Rollo was strictly upstairs. Bates was downstairs. That's the point.'

Ty was off school for a bit – it was her turn to be in Alnwick Cottage Hospital as a precaution against smoke inhalation – but as soon as she was back, I tracked her down in Lightfoot.

We hugged for a long, long time, sat on her bed and talked about the fire. 'Where were you during the hunt dinner?' I asked. 'You weren't just doing your hair, were you? Not for all that time.'

She looked down, pleating the bedspread between her fingers.

'No,' she admitted. 'I was making a new acquaintance.' Then she looked up.

'Henry,' I said. It was a statement, not a question.

She nodded.

'So he was actually with you when the blast happened?'

'I guess. He came to find me in my room and we talked – for ages. Then there was a noise and a flash and I don't remember anything else except being carried out by him to you.' She bit her lip, as if it cost her to say what she had to say. 'He saved my life, for sure.'

There was much, much more to ask. I desperately wanted to know why Henry had sought her out, what they'd talked about. But there was one more urgent question. 'Ty,' I said, tracing the tiny flowers on her bedspread, 'what were you doing in the covert that day? Who told you to lead Rollo to Acre Wood?' A thought occurred to me. 'You know he's dead, I suppose?'

She didn't quite meet my eyes. 'Yes,' she whispered. She sounded wretched.

'*Please* tell me you didn't have anything to do with that.'

'Oh God, Greer, I don't *know*.' She was close to tears. 'He was only supposed to fall off his horse. You have to believe that. Not . . . not *this*.'

I thought again of my first conversation with Rollo at Cumberland place, about *The Lion in Winter* and the fall of a king. 'But the fall wasn't all there was,' I said. The fall hadn't killed Henry and it hadn't killed his father. 'Rollo was poisoned.'

Ty looked as if she'd won the lottery. 'He was?'

'According to the family doc.' I took her hand and spoke sternly. 'Ty. You'd better tell me everything. You said Rollo was only supposed to fall off his horse. But it got much bigger than that. The explosion at Longcross . . . that was . . . that was . . .' I searched for the right word. '*Terrorism*. It was attempted mass murder. Who planned that? Are you . . . are you working with them?'

The shutters came down again, and she pulled her hand away. 'I can't tell you.'

'*Can't?*'

'All right, I won't.' It sounded pretty final.

I said carefully, choosing my words, 'You won't tell *anyone*? Or especially me?'

'Especially you.' There was no hostility; Ty just sounded matter of fact.

'*Why* especially me?'

She said bluntly, 'Because I don't know which side you're on.' Now she looked at me very directly. 'Do *you* know?'

I got up from the bed and walked to the window, looking down into the White Quad. It was peopled by students in blood-red stockings huddled down into their black Tudor coats against the mean January wind. I said, very softly, 'He did save your life.'

'And took how many others?' She got up and pointedly opened her door for me. 'You can't run with the fox *and* hunt with the hounds, Greer.'

57

Of course I had to broach the subject of Henry with Shafeen too. I sought him out after I'd talked to Ty, and found him at the Paulinus well. He didn't turn around at my approach, so I folded my arms around him from behind and rested my cheek on his back.

'I feel like he's here,' he said. 'I feel like he's watching us.'

'Welcome to my world,' I mumbled into his shoulder. 'I've been feeling like that for the last year.'

Shafeen put his hands on mine, clasping them to his heart, but didn't turn. 'How the hell did he manage it?' he said bitterly. 'Why didn't he *die?*'

This should have been quite shocking, but I couldn't blame Shafeen. 'In the fire?'

'No. At the waterfall.'

I spoke into the cloth of his coat. 'In *The Final Problem* – the Sherlock Holmes story, I mean – Sherlock twists out of Moriarty's grasp at the last minute by using a Japanese wrestling move. Moriarty goes over the falls, but Sherlock saves himself.'

I felt, rather than heard, Shafeen breathe out a bitter laugh. 'I can't see Henry in the WWA.'

I squeezed him a bit tighter. We must have looked weird, clasped together like that over the well.

'And where is he now? He can't be at Longcross.'

'No.' Now I turned him around. 'But wherever he is, he's not here. Not at this school.' I put both my hands on his cheeks tenderly. 'He can't affect us.'

He held my hands at the wrists and gave me a piercing look. 'Can't he?'

58

I spent quite a lot of time with the police that term. Serious, sharp-eyed police from London. When the STAGS were attacked they clearly pulled in the very best, not the bumbling country plods they'd hired to cover up Henry's death. These guys were from the Counter-Terrorism Unit at Scotland Yard, and they meant business. Of course, as I'd been the one to evacuate the house, they'd immediately wanted to talk to me. And, by extension, Shafeen and Nel.

They didn't like, not one little bit, that we'd burned the Monteagle Letter in the library of Cumberland Place, leaving no evidence that it ever existed, and even to me that did sound massively dodgy. For a time it seemed like the eye of suspicion would fall on us. But I was always treated well, and eventually they let me go, and I wondered if that was the work of Henry – if I was being protected by the de Warlencourts, who now regarded me as their saviour. I told the police about Bates, and the champagne that wasn't champagne, but some nameless instinct prevented me from telling them anything about the figure in the Guy Fawkes mask who had ambushed Rollo, or the fact that I knew only one man who was that tall.

Abbot Ridley, in fact, had been positively angelic since we'd come back to school. He'd given us time off lessons, he'd kept our parents in the loop and he'd arranged extra coaching for the bits of the syllabus we'd missed while helping the cops with their enquiries. When the CTU finally drove away from the school in their unmarked cars for the last time, I watched them go from the gatehouse. The Abbot appeared at my shoulder and watched with me, his hands tucked into the sleeves of his habit in a curiously monkish posture. 'And so, they go,' he said. 'And now the real work begins.'

I turned to look up at him. 'Real work?'

'To forgive yourself.' He smiled down at me. 'You shouldn't blame yourself for what happened in Acre Wood.'

'I know,' I began, 'but –' Then I stopped. 'Acre Wood?' I said. 'I never mentioned Acre Wood.'

The charming smile faltered. 'The police –'

'No,' I said forcefully. 'I never told them either. I never said a word about Acre Wood.'

He was the picture of innocence as I looked up at him. In the winter light his handsome features could have been carved out of marble, his curls backlit by the low sun. He looked like some sort of Renaissance angel out of *A Room with a View*. But I wasn't buying the good-guy act this time. 'And don't tell me I'm mad, or crazy, or I've been under a lot of strain, because I've got to tell you, I'm pretty sick of hearing that.'

'I would never say that to you,' he said, seemingly with complete sincerity. 'Whatever you may think, I am on your side.'

'Prove it,' I said.

'How?'

Very clearly, so he could not mistake me or twist my words, I said: 'Show. Me. Your. *Thumb*.'

I had him. He was cornered, checked like a fox corralled by the hounds. The colour drained from his face, and his hands stayed clasped determinedly within his sleeves. His reply, when it came, was entirely unexpected. Mimicking my delivery, he said, 'Check. Your. Post. First.'

'*What?*'

'Greer,' he said in quite a different voice, 'we will come back to this, I promise.' He sounded more direct, more urgent than his usual amused and laidback self. 'But I think you should check your letters.' He turned on his heel and stalked away, and there was nothing for me to do but head to the sixth-form Common Room to check my mail.

59

I'd been watching the post like a hawk, praying for my acceptance letter to Oxford. If I didn't get in, I didn't know what I was going to do. I just wanted to get the hell away from STAGS, to be with Shafeen and Nel if they got in, in a world of sanity. I wondered if the Abbot knew something I didn't, that my Oxford letter had finally come, but what did that have to do with Acre Wood?

This being STAGS, the sixth-form Common Room had a whole wall of these little pigeonholes for post, with small brass letters of the alphabet screwed onto them. I looked in M for MacDonald and, sure enough, there was a stiff cream envelope with my name handwritten on the front. As I slid it out there was no Oxford postmark to be seen, no *University of Oxford* franking stamp. In fact, there was no stamp of any kind.

I turned the envelope over and saw a wax seal. Memory made my heart begin to thud. Not because I recalled that long-ago invitation slipped under the door of my room. But because I remembered a letter at Cumberland Place, a letter that was so dangerous it had to be burned.

For this wax was not the blood red of the STAGS stockings

and the Longcross dog rose. It was a more orangey, rusty red. And the imprint on the wax was not a pair of antlers, but a face.

A pointy animal face.

A face that belonged to a fox.

I broke the seal and this is what I read:

Greer,

We bear you no ill will, even though you foiled our own particular Gunpowder Plot. You should not blame yourself for not uncovering us sooner – you made a mistake, but you are in good company. That same mistake was first made by a king.

When James I heard about the first Gunpowder Plot he was actually out hunting. His response, when he heard his assassin's name was Fawkes, was, 'I have known a king to hunt a fox, but never a fox to hunt a king.' So you see, he got the name wrong too.

Ever since then there has been an underground movement – the sons and daughters of those thirteen gunpowder plotters – who have been fighting against the Establishment. We have multiple branches, and myriad names. But mostly we have assumed the title James I gave us when he mistook the name of our leader. You see, it seemed to encapsulate the careless, cavalier way those with power treat those without. Did James ever bother to learn Guy Fawkes's true name, even when he was hanged, drawn and quartered? Probably not. And because of this, that mistake became our name.

The FOXES.

<u>If they don't know who we are, Greer, they never see us coming.</u>

The Order of the Stag has been our most ancient foe. This time you saved their hides, but we feel, most strongly, that in your heart you might be more of a Fox than a Stag. We have pledged to bring down the corrupt Establishment, to fight inequity, to smash the patriarchy. The fox is our emblem, a sigil of the fightback, the hunted turning to bite the hunter, the uneatable pursuing the unspeakable. Like the Order of the Stag, we have a leader, an opposite number to their Grand Stag. And, just the same, that title is passed from generation to generation. It is a name you know well, and it is the one with which I will sign this letter.

Yours, in the hope that you will join our struggle,

Reynard

Historical Note

In the autumn of 1605, a group of young Catholic men gathered for a supper party in a private house on the Strand. They included Robert Catesby, Francis Tresham and Ben Jonson, playwright and convicted manslayer.

The topic of conversation could hardly have been more dangerous. They discussed a daring plot to blow up the House of Lords when James I would be attending the State Opening of Parliament, at one stroke assassinating the king and most of the ruling class of England.

In the following days the plot was put into action. Jonson's friend Guy Fawkes, a soldier he had fought alongside in the Netherlands, was recruited to help. Using the alias John Jonson, Fawkes rented a cellar beneath the House of Lords. He filled it with thirty-six barrels of gunpowder.

More and more conspirators were recruited, until there were thirteen plotters in all. But the number proved unlucky. On 26 October Lord Monteagle received a letter, thought to be from his cousin, the plotter Francis Tresham. Tresham warned his friend to stay away from the opening of Parliament. The letter contained the line *'they shall receive a terrible blow this parliament; and yet they shall not see who hurts them.'*

It was the king himself who interpreted the letter as an assassination attempt. His prime minister, Robert Cecil, ordered a search of Parliament.

On the night of 4 November 1605 Guy Fawkes was discovered in Parliament's cellars. He held a lantern with which he planned to light the fuses the very next day, 5 November.

Hearing the news of Fawkes's arrest, the plotters fled London. On 8 November they were traced to Holbeche House in Staffordshire. Catesby, the ringleader, was killed at once. Meanwhile Fawkes was imprisoned in the Tower of London, where he was tortured until he confessed, then put to death. The remaining plotters were tried and executed.

Only Ben Jonson was spared. He was arrested following the plot, but freed by Cecil on condition he use his Catholic networks to identify a priest who could implicate the plotters. Although Jonson protested that he'd done everything he could, no such priest was ever found.

Many historians now believe the Gunpowder Plot may have been a conspiracy by Cecil's government. Before it, King James was disposed to be tolerant of Catholicism, the religion of his mother – Mary, Queen of Scots – and his wife. After it, his attitude hardened and England was once again a firmly Protestant country.

There are still many questions to be answered about the Gunpowder Plot. How did the plotters get hold of so much gunpowder, when its supply was in the gift of the government? Why did it take ten days for Cecil to act on the Monteagle letter? And was Catesby killed so quickly in order to silence him?

We don't know all the facts, but a woodcut survives naming all of the plotters. One of the thirteen was Robert Catesby's loyal servant.

He was known only as Bates.

HISTORY OF S.T.A.G.S.

S.T.A.G.S. was founded in the seventh century by St Aidan the Great. The name Aidan means 'fire' in Gaelic, and he is considered to be a protector against fire. He was dubbed 'the Great' in order to distinguish him from the lesser saint St Aidan of Ferns. Our St Aidan was born in Ireland, and became a monk on the Scottish island of Iona. He travelled to Northumbria, where he was made Bishop of Lindisfarne. Realising the value of education, he founded a school in the hope that he would train the next generation of Christian leaders. The school began with just twelve boys as pupils, but it grew into a centre of education and a jewelhouse of scholarly knowledge.

Aidan was canonised upon the performance of a miracle; he saved a stag from the hunt by turning him invisible. That stag gave the school an emblem, and a name. Today, after a thousand years of exceptional scholarship, S.T.A.G.S. has educated a dozen British prime ministers and countless members of both houses of parliament. St Aidan's dream that he would train the future leaders of men has become a reality.

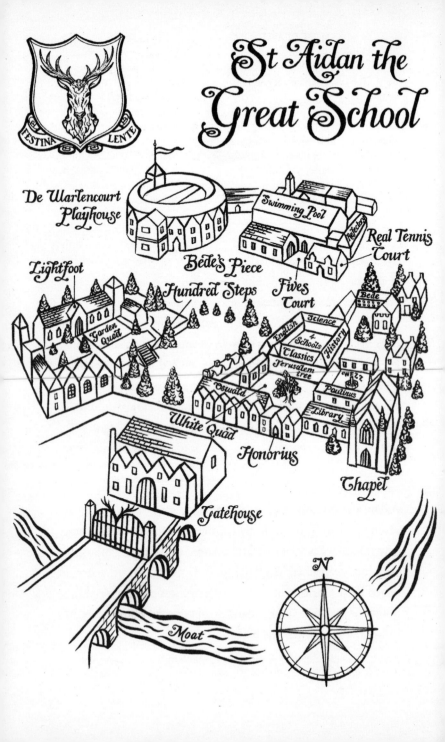

- **DE WARLENCOURT PLAYHOUSE** – built in 1969, the theatre is an exact replica of the sixteenth-century Swan Theatre which used to stand on London's bankside.

- **BEDE LIBRARY** (incorporating the Scriptorium) – named after the Venerable Bede, the library has several notable architectural features, including the medieval Scriptorium, a remnant of the original monastery school, and the Tudor Reading Room.

- **GATEHOUSE** – the gatehouse forms the entrance to the school, reached by crossing the medieval moat. In the days of the monastery school, the drawbridge was raised at night to keep marauding Scots away from the treasures of the chapel.

- **BEDE'S PIECE** – STAGS boasts extensive playing fields, named for a piece of common land enclosed by the school during the eighteenth century.

- **CHAPEL** – Founded in 683, the chapel is the oldest surviving building of the first monastery school. The stained-glass window of Aidan and the stag is original.

- **REFECTORY** – This long building with vaulted ceilings was rebuilt at the time of the Civil War after a fire. The wooden benches and tables on which the students dine are the original ones from the monastery, on which the monks ate their breakfast of bread and beer.

- **ENGLISH SCHOOLS** – In the reign of Edward VI, New Quad –a quadrangle of exquisite Tudor buildings – was built at STAGS to represent the four pillars of learning. The first of the schools (always referred to in the plural) is the English Schools, and the original sign still remains carved above the door.

- **HISTORY SCHOOLS** – The second side of the quad, the History Schools houses the original copy of Bede's work.

- **CLASSICS SCHOOLS** – The third side of the quad, the Classics Schools still fulfills its function of teaching Latin, the language of law and learning.

- **SCIENCE LABS** – Originally the Theology Schools, the fourth side of the quad, despite its Tudor appearance and theological sign carved in stone, now houses STAGS' extensive science laboratories.

- **THE HUNDRED STEPS** – this ancient stone stairway connects the upper and lower schools. Legend has it that in 1348 Edmund de Warlencourt rode up the hundred steps on his horse for a wager.

- **POOL** – The STAGS swimming pool is Olympic-sized and fully compliant with the regulations of the Fédération Internationale de Natation. It is 164 feet long, 82 feet wide and 6 feet deep, with eight swimming lanes marked with rope and buoys.

- **FIVES AND REAL TENNIS COURTS** – Both courts are fully enclosed, and constructed of their original timbers. The Real Tennis court is fashioned after Charles II's court at Hampton Court Palace. The Fives court is designed to replicate one of the exterior bays of the chapel, where the game was first played after Mass.

HOUSES AT S.T.A.G.S.

HONORIUS

Honorius was Archbishop of Canterbury in the seventh century. His is the oldest and grandest house at STAGS. The White Quad, dating from the tweltfh century, features at its centre the Jerusalem Tree, a cedar tree grown from a seed brought home from the Crusades by Conrad de Warlencourt.

Honorius house colours: a white stag's head on a ground of red and gold with a cedar tree as a charge.

BEDE

The Venerable Bede was an English Benedictine monk who wrote The Ecclesiastical History of the English People, a draft of which survives in the Scriptorium at STAGS. Bede house incorporates the extensive playing fields known as Bede's Piece.

Bede house colours: a white stag's head on a ground of red and blue, with a book as a charge.

OSWALD

Oswald was king of Northumbria from 634, uniting the kingdoms of Bernicia and Deira to become the most powerful ruler in Britain. Oswald did much to promote the spread of Christianity in the north, and fittingly the school chapel can be found in his house.

Oswald house colours: a white stag's head on a ground of red and green with a crown as a charge.

PAULINUS

Paulinus was a Roman missionary and the first Bishop of York. The Paulinus Well, built during the bishop's mission to Northumbria in the seventh century, stands in the middle of Paulinus quad. The waters at its depths were said, upon drinking, to turn a sinful man to God.

Paulinus house colours: a white stag's head on a ground of red and purple with a well as a charge.

LIGHTFOOT

Lightfoot is the girls' house at STAGS, and is the newest of all the houses, built originally as a dwelling for masters in 1550. It is a handsome Tudor building with its own Garden Quad, and it was first named Aidan's House. The name was changed when Bishop Joseph Lightfoot of Durham successfully lobbied for the admission of girls in 1880. Since then, Lightfoot House has borne his name.

Lightfoot house colours: a white stag's head on a ground of red and silver, with a bishop's mitre as a charge.

⚜ UNIFORM POLICY ⚜

By the first day of Michaelmas Term, all students must be equipped with the following uniform

- Black Tudor coat
- Scarlet stockings (unless you are a Medieval, in which case you may wear knee-high stockings of a design of your choosing)
- Narrow brown deer-leather belt
- Plain white wing-collar shirt
- White clerical tie
- Black knee breeches
- Black deer-leather lace-up shoes
- Regulation black PE kit with STAGS crest

Uniform may be purchased from our suppliers: Keytes of Berwick-upon-Tweed.

The STAGS uniform must be strictly observed year round. A scarf in the colours of one's house may be worn during Michaelmas and Hilary Terms.

GLOSSARY

JUSTITIUM – a short holiday that falls roughly in the middle of each term, when students are permitted to return home if they wish

MEDIEVALS – the prefects, usually between three and six in number, chosen from among the final-year students at STAGS

PROBITIONES – final examinations at STAGS, set in the final year

FESTINA LENTE – the STAGS school motto: 'Make Haste Slowly'

MEDIEVAL – anything traditional or historical, in line with the highly prized values of the school

SAVAGE – anything modern or technological, considered not in keeping with the ethos of STAGS

Acknowledgements

First and last, my apologies to Daphne du Maurier for bastardising the first and last lines of *Rebecca* to bookend this novel. It came from a place of love.

I'm indebted as always to my friend and agent – Fragent™ – Teresa Chris for her constant support.

Thank you as ever to the triple threat of Emma Matthewson, Holly Kyte and Talya Baker for editing, copy-editing and proofreading *F.O.X.E.S.* so forensically.

Thank you to Jane Harris and all the team at Hot Key Books for their hard work and support for the STAGS series.

The amazing artwork in the endpages of this book is by Sally Taylor.

In Medieval terms I'm indebted to one book in particular – *Ben Jonson, Volpone and the Gunpowder Plot* by Richard Dutton (Cambridge University Press, 2012). One of my favourite childhood books, *Flambards* by K. M. Peyton, provided the names Fowler and Sweetbriar and opened my eyes to the tragic fate of injured hunters. I was hugely inspired by John Masefield's epic poem *Reynard the Fox*. Chunks of part two of the poem are reproduced here. The whole thing is worth a read.

And now for the Savage: I reference a couple of online resources in the book, notably Eduardo Goncalves's article 'Don't be Fooled by Boxing Day Trail Hunts' in the *Independent* online (26 December 2017), and the *Prospect* online article entitled 'Gunpowder, Treason and Jonson' by Rosalind Miles (20 November 2005). I researched trail hunting on the Fox Hunting Evidence UK and League Against Cruel Sports websites. My synopses of *The Hound of the Baskervilles* and *Volpone* came from every kid's favourite revision site, Sparknotes.

Thank you to my oldest friend, Janette Ballard, for taking me on a tour of the Houses of Parliament.

The *V for Vendetta* mask, based on Guy Fawkes's face, comes from the DC comic of the same name, by Alan Moore and David Lloyd. It has become the symbol of the Anonymous movement and is to be found wherever there is protest.

Thank you to the 41 in Westminster, which provided the model for the STAGS Club – in terms of interior design only, I hasten to add!

The guidebook that you get when you buy a ticket to Westminster Abbey is very informative, and I used some of the information in it in this book.

Thank you to the Headley family for their advice on Jamaican names and culture.

L. Cornelissen & Son near the British Museum really is a jewel of an art shop. I recommend a visit.

Thank you to wine specialist Freddie Morley Fletcher for letting me know that 1984 wasn't a vintage year, and for sending me a picture of the stairs at Veuve Clicquot's cellar.

The Trip to Jerusalem, the pub on the Longcross estate,

is inspired by the pub of the same name cut into the rocks beneath Nottingham Castle. One of the oldest inns in the world, and one of my favourites. Incidentally, it's where I had the idea for this book.

Thank you to Ross Nye Stables in Hyde Park for taking me horse riding on Rotten Row.

The film *The Lion in Winter* (1968, directed by Anthony Harvey) is referenced throughout – definitely worth a watch if you are at all into power and kingship.

Thank you to my family. To my husband Sacha for dreaming up some of the evil things that could lurk inside the STAGS club. To my son Conrad for finding Ben Jonson's (pretty well hidden) gravestone among the pavings of Westminster Abbey. And to my daughter Ruby for saving me from reading the entire Catholic mass in Latin looking for the word 'orare', by telling me about searchable text.

Lastly – and I think you'll be seeing a lot of these kinds of acknowledgements in books published in 2020 – I'd like to thank the NHS. I finished a book during lockdown. They saved lives.

M. A. Bennett

M. A. Bennett is half Venetian and was born in Manchester, England, and raised in the Yorkshire Dales. She is a history graduate of Oxford University and the University of Venice, where she specialised in the study of Shakespeare's plays as a historical source. After university she studied art and has since worked as an illustrator, an actress and a film reviewer. She also designed tour visuals for rock bands, including U2 and the Rolling Stones. She was married on the Grand Canal in Venice and lives in north London with her husband, son and daughter. Her first YA novel, *S.T.A.G.S.*, was published in 2017, shortlisted for the YA BOOK PRIZE 2018 and won the Great Reads 'Most Read' 2018 Senior Award. *D.O.G.S.*, the second in the world of STAGS, followed in 2019.

@MABennettAuthor
@mabennettauthor

Thank you for choosing a Hot Key book.

If you want to know more about our authors and what we publish, you can find us online.

You can start at our website

www.hotkeybooks.com

And you can also find us on:

We hope to see you soon!